The Unfinished Symphony
of You and Me

The Unfinished Symphony of You and Me is Lucy Robinson's third book and follows on from her highly successful novels *The Greatest Love Story of All Time* and *A Passionate Love Affair with a Total Stranger*. Prior to writing Lucy earned her crust in theatre production and then factual television, working on documentaries for all of the UK's major broadcasters. Her writing career began when she started a dating blog for *Marie Claire* about her fairl pathetic attempts at Internet dating.

L was brought up in Gloucestershire surrounded by various stupid animals. She studied at Birmingham University and lived in London for many years before disappearing off to South America to write her first two novels. This is the first novel she has written in a sensible manner (i.e. at home).

cy lives in Bristol with her partner, The Man. She likes dogs cheese and horses and seals and cake and baths, and she daily about funny things that have made her smile today.

www.lucy-robinson.co.uk
@lucy_robinson

The Unfinished Symphony of You and Me

LUCY ROBINSON

PENGUIN BOOKS

PENGUIN BOOKS

Published by the Penguin Group
Penguin Books Ltd, 80 Strand, London WC2R ORL, England
Penguin Group (USA) Inc., 375 Hudson Street, New York, New York 10014, USA
Penguin Group (Canada), 90 Eglinton Avenue East, Suite 700, Toronto, Ontario, Canada M4P 2Y3
(a division of Pearson Penguin Canada Inc.)
Penguin Ireland, 25 St Stephen's Green, Dublin 2, Ireland (a division of Penguin Books Ltd)
Penguin Group (Australia), 707 Collins Street, Melbourne, Victoria 3008, Australia
(a division of Pearson Australia Group Pty Ltd)
Penguin Books India Pvt Ltd, 11 Community Centre, Panchsheel Park, New Delhi – 110 017, India
Penguin Group (NZ), 67 Apollo Drive, Rosedale, Auckland 0632, New Zealand
(a division of Pearson New Zealand Ltd)
Penguin Books (South Africa) (Pty) Ltd, Block D, Rosebank Office Park,
181 Jan Smuts Avenue, Parktown North, Gauteng 2193, South Africa

Penguin Books Ltd, Registered Offices: 80 Strand, London WC2R ORL, England

www.penguin.com

First published 2014
001

Extract from *Look Down* from the musical *LES MISÉRABLES*
By Alain Boublil and Claude-Michel Schönberg
Music by Claude-Michel Schönberg
Lyrics by Alain Boublil, Jean-Marc Natel and Herbert Kretzmer
Publisher: Alain Boublil Music Limited/Editions Musicales Alain Boublil
Copyright © 1980, 1984, 1985, 1986, 1987, 1988, 1990, 1991, 1992, 1993, 1994 and 2012
Lyrics printed with permission

Extract from *Empty Chairs at Empty Tables* from the musical *LES MISÉRABLES*
By Alain Boublil and Claude-Michel Schönberg
Music by Claude-Michel Schönberg
Lyrics by Herbert Kretzmer and Alain Boublil
Publisher: Alain Boublil Music Limited
Copyright © 1986, 1987, 1988, 1990, 1991, 1992, 1993, 1994 and 2012
Lyrics printed with permission

The moral right of the author has been asserted

This is a work of fiction. Names, characters, places and incidents are either the product
of the author's imagination or are used fictitiously, and any resemblance to actual persons,
living or dead, or to actual events or locales is entirely coincidental.

Set in 12.5/14.75pt Garamond MT Std
Typeset by Jouve (UK), Milton Keynes
Printed in Great Britain by Clays Ltd, St Ives plc

PAPERBACK ISBN: 978-1-405-91158-0

www.greenpenguin.co.uk

MIX
Paper from
responsible sources
FSC
www.fsc.org   FSC™ C018179

Penguin Books is committed to a sustainable
future for our business, our readers and our planet.
This book is made from Forest Stewardship
Council™ certified paper.

This one is for you, Grandpa.
Thank you for the music.

Overture

I was pretty horrified by my reflection in the mirror. I looked like a shrivelled grey boggle. 'Arggh,' I said helplessly, at my reflection.

'Arggh,' said the alien in the mirror.

I had spent most of the day in the wardrobe with my old teddy bear. His name was Carrot. We'd hidden in there because tomorrow my life was going to change significantly and I was terrified.

I wasn't normally a victim of intense fear. By and large my life had been quite free of drama and I'd gone to some effort to keep it that way. But on the rare occasions when I faced danger beyond my control I would crawl into my wardrobe, shut the door and emerge only when I felt safe again.

I wasn't looking for Narnia in there. In fact, I'd have been furious if some jolly man with a furry bottom and cloven hoofs had turned up. I was there for the solitude, the silence and the safety. And Carrot.

Normally, those four solid wooden walls did the trick. I'd stew in there, hot and helpless, until eventually I managed to boil myself down to some sort of equilibrium. Steadier and saner, I would crawl out again, ready to face the world.

That had not happened today. I had stewed for hours on end, hot fear singeing my face and burning painfully down my back, but calm hadn't come. I'd eventually had to drag myself out, half mad, half shaking. *Not even my wardrobe can help me*, I thought hysterically, staring at my boggly reflection. *This is an emergency!*

It was an emergency. Tomorrow I was starting a postgraduate diploma in opera at the Royal College of Music, alongside ten of the world's most talented young singers. Even though I was not a performer of any kind. Let alone an opera singer, with a wardrobe full of satin gowns and a family who owned a large country estate in Gloucestershire with butlers and horses. I was a quiet girl from a council estate in the Midlands, who hated attention. Did you hear me? *I was not an opera singer.*

I stood still as my insides, like some amateur microbrewery, contracted and pressed against each other. 'Arggh,' I whispered again. It was a helpless, mewling sort of sound.

I stared palely in the direction of the kitchen and wondered if food would help. Food normally helped. Maybe a little gentle bingeing?

Slowly, woodenly, I shuffled out of my bedroom and over to the fridge, rolling up my sleeves.

But Fate was against me. As I served up my Wiltshire pork belly fifty minutes later, making a pathetic attempt at a jolly whistle, an unexpected visitor – a man – was making his way towards my front door. And this man had nothing to do with tomorrow and the singing: this man would change my life *today*.

Sunday night was M&S Meal Deal Night; something I normally relished. According to Barry from Barry Island, it was inevitable that a peasant like me was so fond of meal deals. The combination of maximum food at minimum price was designed for 'my sort'.

Barry never hesitated to share his views on my eating habits. Or indeed anything, really, and the reason I allowed him to insult me with such impunity was his Welsh accent. I so deeply loved it, was so completely entranced by everything he said, that I had somehow lost the instinct to defend myself.

'Sally, you're a greedy pig,' he'd tell me matter-of-factly. 'You look nice now but you're headin' towards chronic obesity, Chicken.' He'd smile sadly, then return to his grilled goldfish or whatever stupid morsel was on his plate. I would return to my half-price-but-full-fat lasagne, muttering amiably that he was a Welsh devil and deserved to get hugely fat when he retired from ballet.

As was customary for Meal Deal Night, Barry had declined to eat his half of the spread so I was sitting alone at the table surrounded by food. It looked splendid: pork belly, rosemary potatoes and some funny-sounding little thing called Berrymisu for dessert.

Yet the sight of it did nothing for me. I felt sicker than ever.

Barry was trying out a new dance belt in his bedroom. He had a lot of trouble with dance belts, for the same reason that I had trouble with G-strings. Neither of us liked anything synthetic wedged up our private parts.

'Barry?' I called pointlessly, in the direction of his bedroom door, through which Shakira was pumping. Perhaps if he came and sat with me I'd be able to stomach at least one mouthful.

I had never known fear like this. Even after the catastrophic things that had happened in New York last year I had still been *myself*, Sally Howlett. Calm, short of stature, wide of bottom. Reliable, measured, articulate. Now I was a wobbly ball of highly explosive gas.

'Barry?' I tried again. The flat was shaking slightly, which meant that he was performing flamboyant Amazonian dance movements in front of his mirror to 'Hips Don't Lie'. He went wild for Shakira and was often caught shaking a billowing Latino mane that he didn't possess.

'BARREEEEEEEE!'

Barry was not coming. I needed to do something, fast.

The iPad that my (very rich) friend Bea had impulse-bought for me last autumn – along with a Fendi handbag and a rare Robert Piguet perfume, all designed to cheer me up after the New York trip of doom – was on the work surface. I grabbed it and started hammering out an email, my useless fingers landing on all of the wrong keys. The big ugly diamanté ring on my right hand, which I hadn't quite brought myself to remove since getting back from New York, made my typing still worse.

fOina, please come home. I need you here funnyface, I;m fecking TERRIFIED ARGHHH! I really muiss you, Freckle. Please come back soon. I so hate you not being here. Tomorrow is all your fault anyway. You and your 'seize the day' nonsense! I love you, please come back.xxxxxxxzzx

I pressed send and then reread the email, imagining my cousin Fiona reading it. When Fiona wasn't being manic, she had such a beautiful smile; the sort of smile that would

4

be described in the opening pages of an epic Russian novel from the nineteenth century.

I missed Fiona terribly. We'd grown up as sisters, not cousins. Played horses together, written love letters to boys together, compared our first pubes. When I moved from Stourbridge to London, Fiona had been my house-mate for seven (mostly) lovely years. But after last year's drama she'd refused to leave New York and had yet to change her mind even though I had begged her repeat-edly to come home. (Barry, less optimistic about the chances of her returning, had moved into her room about nine months ago. I'd swapped my pale, freckly, dif-ficult cousin for a pale, freckly rude little shit from Barry Island. Although, for all his appalling comments, I loved him madly.)

Momentarily, I allowed a Fiona-pain to glow some-where in my chest, then pinched it down, returning my attention to the inbox in case she happened to be online. And reply instantly.

She didn't.

In the absence of her or Barry, I toyed with the idea of calling Bea for support. Bea was down in Glyndebourne, having finally left the Royal Opera House after ten years at the helm of the makeup and wigs department. Now she was attaching curly beards and prosthetic noses to opera singers in a dappled Sussex country estate and was evidently very busy: we'd spoken for all of ten minutes since their season opened five months ago in May.

I called her now, just in case. She didn't answer.

I even pondered the idea of calling home, but felt agi-tated and angry just thinking about my parents. Mum and

5

Dad were stunned and clearly appalled that I was starting this course; they'd doubtless encourage me to pull out if they detected uncertainty. 'Do you really think you belong in that world?' Mum had asked. 'With *those* sorts of people? All posh and snobby?'

Of course I didn't.

But I still resented her asking.

Someone knocked on the front door.

I looked round at my empty kitchen, taken by surprise. Someone must have got into my apartment building and up to my front door – which, these days, was quite a feat since a forgotten bunch of forgotten Occupy London people had helped themselves to an empty flat on the fifth floor, and Mustafa the security man had taken up residence.

I jumped up from the table, forgetting that I was wearing pyjamas with pigs on them, and threw open the front door with my best smile in case it was God, there to help.

The man standing at the door, with a strange sort of a smile on his face, did not look like God. But he was definitely familiar. So familiar, in fact, that I wondered if he was famous. He was certainly attractive enough to be famous. Impossibly handsome and stylish; the sort that had a large house in Santa Barbara and did photo shoots at sundown on his private beach.

An absolute show-stopper of a man, I marvelled, in my momentary trance, *although not really my sort of thing*. He had long shiny hair and a blindingly smart shirt worn with crisp jeans and pointy brogues. Some luxury musky aftershave floating off his pampered, tanned skin and a big fat Rolex. I half smiled, baffled. What was a man like this doing on my doorstep? And why did he look so familiar? Had I once fitted a costume on him or something?

It was only a few seconds later, when he said, 'Hey,' in a half-Devon, half-American accent, and I found myself thinking that it was a huge mistake for him to grow his hair long, and wondered why he'd changed his perfume, that I realized he was not a celebrity, or a singer from the Royal Opera House, but someone I knew very well.

He was also someone I'd never wanted to see again. Whom I'd worked so hard to strike from memory that he had all but ceased to exist.

The room started to bleach white and I closed my eyes. When I opened them again he was still standing there.

'Hey,' he repeated sheepishly. It felt like half a lifetime since I'd heard his voice. That accent. The oddest accent in history. 'I guess this is a bit of a surprise, right?'

I tried to reply but nothing happened. I looked down at my pig pyjamas and didn't even care. The floor wobbled miles below me.

'Sally?' he said gently. 'Are you OK?' He watched me, patently anxious. For a few strange, flabby seconds I watched him back, still incredulous. Only his face was that of the man I'd once known. The rest of him was unrecognizable. Smart, crackly, groomed. An alien landscape.

'Oh, man, Sally, I'm sorry. I shouldn't have just *come*. But I didn't know how else to . . . to . . . Hang on.' He started rooting around in his pockets.

It was as if I had one foot jammed on the accelerator and the other flat on the brake.

He pulled a little piece of yellow paper from his jeans pocket and his hands shook slightly as he tried to unfold

7

it. I noticed he had a smart, starchy man-bag I'd not seen before. Then I recognized the Post-it note in his hand.

'I wondered if this was still valid,' he said quietly, holding it out. *Varlud*. Nobody else on earth had an accent like his. A cross-bred silly joke of an accent. Once accompanied by fluffy hair and forgetfulness. Once so dear to me.

I didn't look at the Post-it because I knew what it said. 'Go away, please,' I heard myself whisper. 'Please can you go away and not come back.'

He smiled sympathetically. How *dare* he look at me like that? As if I were a tantruming child?

'Go, please,' I repeated more clearly. I started to close the door as anger compacted and heaved upwards in me. How could he? How could he just march in, after he had . . . after he . . . ?

After a brief consideration, he shrugged. 'OK. I'll go for now. But, Sal, I *can't* leave you alone. You see –'

'GO!' I shrieked. (I shrieked? I had never shrieked in my life!) 'GET OUT OF MY HOUSE! DON'T YOU DARE BOTHER ME AGAIN! EVER!' I was charged. Super-charged. Maybe even dangerous. Although probably not.

The man pushed the door back open with one of his expensive shoes. The air between us flexed and rumbled angrily, like sheet metal.

'Now, listen up,' he began, apparently not having heard me. 'Sal, if you'll let me explain . . .'

Then something happened that I found very surprising. I, Sally Howlett, avoider of *anything* that resembled confrontation, spun round and grabbed my Marks &

8

Spencer pork belly from the table. And then I spun back round, like a shot-putter, and lobbed it at the man standing at my front door. Straight at his face. I missed him, of course – I'd always been poor at hand/eye coordination – and it whistled past his ear, hitting the wall outside where it slid to the floor leaving a greasy track mark. It was accompanied by a little scream, which had apparently come from me.

The man looked round at the cooked meat on the hallway carpet, then back at me. There was a long, weighted silence.

'I hate you,' I whispered. And I did. Violently. A great pit of fury and sadness burned in my chest. 'I don't ever want to hear from you again.'

I slammed the front door in his face.

I stood there until I heard him move away, then I turned back to the table.

'No way,' breathed Barry from Barry Island, in his amazing Welsh accent.

He was standing at his bedroom door, naked apart from the flesh-coloured thong. His frighteningly pale skin and freckles seemed almost Day-Glo under the kitchen light. He ran his hands through his fine strawberry-blond hair and left them on the side of his face in a dramatic, end-of-world fashion. 'Was that who I think it was?' he whispered. 'Dressed as a poncy get?'

I nodded, and started crying.

Barry's eyes widened. 'Oh . . . my . . . *God*,' he said, in awed tones. He looked at me and I looked back at him. Neither of us had the faintest idea what to do.

The Woman Who Sang in the Wardrobe

An Opera in Five Acts

ACT ONE

Scene One

Stourbridge, West Midlands, 1990–2004

It all began on an April day in 1990. I was playing horses in the kitchen with Fiona, my cousin, who had recently moved in with us because she didn't have any parents of her own. We were in the final round of a tense show-jumping competition when I heard an unusual sound coming out of the radio.

One of the DJs on Beacon FM was playing Cio-Cio-San's famous aria from *Madam Butterfly*, 'Un bel di vedremo' ('One Fine Day'). Opera was not the norm on Beacon FM; as I recall, it was part of a very unfunny DJ joke. But the sheer spine-tingling tragedy of the tune took me by surprise. I looked over at Fiona who, at seven, had already endured more tragedy than most people would in a lifetime, and promptly burst into tears.

The show-jumping was paused while I cried and hugged my little cousin, who was embarrassed by my actions and told me that I was being something called a lesbian.

When the aria ended, I stared, awed, at the radio. What had that been?

It was my first exposure to opera. I liked it.

But the second time I heard opera, later that year in July, I *loved* it. I loved it so much that my insides started to do funny things. I stopped eating the choc-ice that I had in my chubby little hand. It was ten fifteen p.m. and I shouldn't have been awake, let alone eating choc-ices, but Mum and Dad were at a bingo dinner and had left Karen Castle babysitting Dennis, Fiona and me. Karen Castle was the closest thing to liberal and artsy that my parents would allow in their house.

I had been asleep about an hour when she arrived in my room, holding my big brother Dennis by the hand, and told me that we had to go downstairs and watch a very important thing on the telly. It was the 1990 World Cup and the famous Three Tenors concert was being beamed in live from Rome.

'Forget Live Aid,' Karen Castle whispered fiercely. 'This is one of the most important moments in music history. It's going to bring opera to the masses. It's *huge*.'

'Don't want to,' Dennis mumbled sleepily, but I remembered exactly what opera was and flew down the stairs like a precision missile in pink pyjamas.

Pavarotti, Domingo and Carreras changed my life that night. I found their Andrew Lloyd Webber megamix a bit so-so, but when they started the serious stuff, I was listening. And when they brought that ancient stadium thundering down with 'Nessun dorma', I knew that nothing could ever be the same again.

Fiona had been completely unmoved. Dennis had fallen asleep.

I raided my piggy bank and bought a tape called *Opera*

Favourites. Everything on it became my favourite. I tingled with pleasure listening to it and after a while – singing as quietly as I could – began to join in. While my school friends rapped along with MC Hammer I kept it real with Joan Sutherland and Marilyn Horne, who sang words I couldn't understand to tunes that I really could.

If there was anything odder than a seven-year-old girl developing an opera-singing habit, it was a seven-year-old developing a top-secret opera habit. I couldn't quite put my finger on why but I felt instinctively that I could never, and *should* never, sing in front of anyone else. So I sang in my wardrobe where nobody could hear me.

And I never really questioned this because extreme privacy was a core value in the Howlett family. Mum and Dad, in spite of living on a council estate where private issues were mostly discussed in murderous screams, shared a strangely fearful, Victorian attitude towards privacy. They spent their lives muttering about how our neighbours had no shame, living their lives on show like that, and tried with all their quiet might to be completely invisible.

Which was quite a problem for them, because the circumstances under which Fiona had come to live with us recently had been reported not just in the local papers but the nationals.

Woman's body found in Midlands Canal

Where's the daddy? Nationwide search mounted for touring actor: who will claim this little girl?

No father for Fiona: Canal orphan taken in by dead woman's sister

We were a family 'beset by tragedy', the papers had said. They showed pictures of Mum at her sister's funeral and gave them captions like 'Frozen with grief, Brenda Howlett with her little niece Fiona'. At school Fiona and I overheard a special assembly (from which we had been banned) where the head told everyone that our family had been torn apart by a dreadful catastrophe and must be treated with the greatest sensitivity and respect.

I wondered if everyone had confused us with a different family. There was no grieving in our house. No sense of catastrophe. When Mum was told that her sister had been found floating in a lonely section of the canal, she thanked the officers for their time and went to bed for a week. Then she got up, put on a black nylon dress for the funeral and never spoke about it again.

Dad had busied himself making Fiona a bedroom while a half-hearted search for Fiona's dad had taken place, and Fiona had just watched TV all day and all night. Dennis and I hadn't said anything about it because nobody else was saying anything about it.

That was just the way we did things in our family.

The press, hoping for a big circus of grief and hysteria, didn't like it. They stayed on our doorstep way longer than necessary. 'Tell us how you're all coping,' they wheedled, through the letter box.

'We don't air our dirty laundry in public,' Mum reminded us all. There was a frightening edge to her voice. 'Mandy has gone and we don't talk about her, in or out of this house. Understood?'

So, by the time all the fuss had died down, the press had straggled off our estate and Fiona had been installed in the converted cupboard under the stairs, just like Harry Potter, Mum and Dad's hatred of being visible had become pathological. 'Seen and not heard' was no longer enough. From now on, the Howletts did not wish even to be seen.

Years later, a man with intense blue eyes and an unironed T-shirt would hold my hand in a jazz bar in Harlem and remind me that grief made us behave in very strange ways.

But back to 1990. Summer. IRA car bombs and scorching weather, bright green ice pops and scabby knees. Little Sally and little Fiona living together for the first time on a small council estate in Stourbridge; the Howlett family learning to breathe again after weeks of press hounding.

My wardrobe singing had become the highlight of my day. Singing made me feel tingly and alive: feeling the breath rush in through my mouth and expand deep into my belly, and hearing it coming back out in a proper tune – in the right key, and in the right time, and with a richness that amazed me – was better than cheese and pickle cobs or oven chips or Wotsits. It was better even than Arctic Roll.

Singing insulated me from the hollowness of my family and the tragedy we weren't meant to discuss. It stopped me worrying obsessively about Fiona, who couldn't possibly be happy in our house. It lifted me high above everything my little mind worried about and suspended me above my life, as if I was in a hot-air balloon on a summer evening.

But top-secret opera habits are seldom simple.

Fiona was my best friend but she was also very

annoying and, somehow, she managed to overhear me one night. The next day she teased me noisily at school, saying that I sounded like a posh old fat woman, and would only stop when I agreed to dump Eddie Spencer on her behalf, then punch him on the arm and tell him he smelt of bad poos. I did it and Fi, mercifully, stopped teasing me.

Next came the problem of taking opera to the masses. Even though I didn't want anyone to know that I sang, I did feel quite strongly that the world – or at the very least the town of Stourbridge – needed to know about opera. I began by playing my *Opera Favourites* tape to my first boyfriend, Jim Babcock, who looked bored and farted and said that my music was rubbish. Then at Saturday-morning roller-skating I asked the DJ if he could stop playing 'Ghostbusters' and try some Puccini. He announced my request to the leisure centre, the crowd revolted and everyone, including Fiona, told me I was a massive wazzock.

Fiona bought me a blue Slush Puppy from the café afterwards to say sorry, but my lesson had been learned. Opera and Stourbridge would not be friends.

Unfortunately, Mrs Badger – a failed concert pianist and the deputy head of my primary school – had other ideas. She had overheard Fiona teasing me and pulled me to one side during lunch hour. She was armed with a big smile and a very persuasive tone. Somehow, she talked me into singing a short solo in the Christmas concert, even though the concert was usually for the top-year juniors. But Fiona, who was already an outstanding little ballet dancer, was going to do a solo too, and Mrs Badger promised me chocolate and I gave in because I found it almost impossible to say no to anyone.

'You'll be wonderful,' Mrs Badger assured me. 'Think how proud your mum'll be!' I wasn't convinced but Mrs Badger's eyes were flashing emotionally. She told me that it would be one of the most memorable nights of my young life so far.

Mrs Badger was not wrong.

By the day of the concert I was ill with nerves. Jim Babcock had hated my opera music. The leisure centre had hated my opera music. And Mum and Dad would . . . I didn't know what they'd do, but I knew they would be really upset and possibly angry that I was singing a solo when we were still meant to be in lockdown.

But an innocent, sweet, stubborn little part of me maintained that if opera singing could make me feel so happy, maybe it would cheer up Mum and Dad. Maybe they wouldn't be so embarrassed and awkward if they could hear how lovely it was.

To calm the nerves I had to eat everything in my lunch box, and then everything in Fi's lunch box. (Fi, aged eight, was already on her first diet.) Nonetheless, by the time I stepped on stage I was shaking visibly and my breath was short and shuddering.

In a hazy sea of faces I caught sight of Mum and Dad, who had obviously just realized what was going to happen. Mum's eyes were bursting out of her head. With pride or embarrassment I'd never know, although pride was unlikely. All I knew was that as Mrs Badger started playing the introduction to 'L'ho perduta' I felt a stunning certainty that nothing was going to come out of my mouth.

Nothing came out of my mouth. I stood, frozen, a little

girl with a scab on her chin and a badly fitting pinafore dress, completely mute.

Mrs Badger was having none of it, and started the intro again so that I could collect myself. Once again I caught sight of my parents, who seemed like they were in cardiac arrest. Mum's face, white and frozen, looked like it did the day the police came round and told her that the woman found in the Wolverhampton canal was her sister Mandy.

Then I felt warm liquid run down the inside of my left leg. I stood right there on stage, in front of all the other parents (*and* Jim Babcock, who I knew was going to dump me), and felt the warmth sliding down towards my feet, pooling in a fat oval shape on the floor. I stopped thinking, maybe even breathing, and stood there until Fiona ran on from the wings and dragged me off.

When we got home, Mum marched upstairs where she ran a bath. She filled it with Matey bubbles and rubber ducks, even though it had been years since I'd liked rubber ducks and they were all mouldy and black on the bottom. While it was filling she took me into my bedroom and said, in a scary voice, 'Where is it?' It wasn't a question, it was a command.

I didn't even bother to ask what 'it' was. I simply reached into my wardrobe for my *Opera Favourites* cassette and handed it to her, along with the *Opera* magazine I'd bought a few weeks ago so that I could stare solemnly at the pictures of big-boobed singers.

Mum looked at the cassette and magazine as if I had presented her with a steaming pile of dog shit, and took them downstairs. 'Sally,' she called sharply. I followed. Mum threw both in the kitchen bin, then scraped the remains of Dennis's ketchupy fish fingers on top of them. For good measure she added a pile of orange mush, the remains of Fi's. Fi's favourite thing at the moment was to mash up her dinner and not actually eat any of it. I could see Maria Callas's face with blobs of deep-fried breadcrumbs sliding slowly down it.

'No more singing,' Mum stated.

My lip wobbled. In spite of what had happened tonight, I knew I loved singing. It was the best feeling I'd ever known.

'You can't do that!' Fiona butted in. Fiona was the only person in the house who ever dared take on Mum. 'She's really good at it!'

Mum didn't even look at her.

'*No more singing,*' she repeated. 'If I catch you at it again there'll be serious trouble. It's for your own good, Sally.' Mum never really raised her voice, just hissed in varying shades of angry snake. 'We don't need no more trouble with . . .' Mum paused. 'With *performing arts,*' she concluded shakily. 'Now go upstairs and get yourself clean, Sally.'

That was that.

But that wasn't that, not really. I carried on singing because I couldn't not. Now I did it *only* in my wardrobe and *only* when there was no one else in the house. 'Nobody,' I promised myself, 'will ever hear me sing again.'

On the outside Sally Howlett resumed being normal, dependable and solid. There would have been no point in trying to be alternative and unreliable even if I'd wanted to be: Fiona provided enough drama to keep the entire primary school (indeed, at times what seemed like the whole world) entertained. It sent Mum and Dad crazy and Fiona was punished again and again, although seldom with any effect. Fiona set fire to things. She tormented people. She showed her flat chest to the boys during Thursday-afternoon hymn practice, then flashed at the headmaster when he tried to tell her off. She cheated at netball and she stole from the canteen. Frequently she implicated me in her crimes but she was seldom believed.

And I didn't really mind, because she whacked anyone who caused me trouble and wrote stories about me being a brave and beautiful princess and made up pop songs about us being together for ever. She climbed into my bed every night and hugged me and told me she loved me. And I told her I loved her back because I did; more than Dennis, more than Mum and Dad.

'You shouldn't spend all your time with Fiona,' Mum often said. 'Don't put all your eggs in one basket, Sally. Find some other friends.'

I ignored her. Fiona was my best friend in the whole world.

Fiona Lane, that naughty, tragic little girl whose father ran off with the theatre, whose mother had gone barmy and drowned herself in the Wolverhampton canal. And Sally Howlett, her chunky, reliable cousin, who never caused any trouble, ever. I did what I was told and kept people happy. I solved problems, never created them, and at all times I was calm and cheerful. As a girl, as a teenager, as an adult, I was one and the same.

On the day that the man arrived at my front door and had pork belly thrown at him, I was thirty years old yet I looked pretty much the same as I had aged seven when I heard my first aria. Dumpy, short and wide of bottom.

Unnaturally thick blonde hair (once described by a hair-dresser as 'coarser than a shire horse's tail') and what I thought to be an unremarkable kind of face.

Wherever I went, whatever age I was, people said things to me like 'You're a rock,' or 'What a calm influence you have on this place, Sally!'

Sometimes I wondered what they'd think if they knew that I sang opera in my wardrobe, and that as the years passed I had continued to listen to it on my Walkman, then my Discman, then my iPod. I found VHS, then DVD, then internet masterclasses of famous singers tutoring eager pupils and used those recordings to teach myself.

There was no denying that my voice was good, how-ever alien self-praise might have been to me. But I could also tell that I had missed some vital stages in my training by going straight in at the top with professional master-classes. Largely because a lot of the things my video tutors said sounded completely mental. 'Hold that stentando all the way to the end!' they shouted. I imagined what a stentando might be and pictured an iron-age weapon.

'More diaphragmatic attack!' they'd yell, or 'You're being misled by those accents, this is NOT SFOR-ZANDO!' (A Russian bread?)

But nothing, not even my inability to understand most of what my VHS tutors said, or the fear of what people would think if they ever found out, detracted from the creamy dollops of pleasure I felt at hearing an operatic sound coming from my own mouth. 'L'ho perduta ... Blum blum bluuum blum ... ackie saaa duh duuuh duh duh ...' I sang, quietly alight with pride. (I had yet to learn Italian.)

Fiona, aged eleven, was packed off to the Royal Ballet School to honour the request her mother had made before dying, leaving the house suffocatingly quiet. Although I was glad she'd escaped my seemingly emotionless parents, her absence made my life seem beige and pointless, and Mum made it very difficult for us to see each other in the holidays. She encouraged me instead to play with Lisa from next door. But I hated Lisa. She was patronizing and evil and all she ever wanted to do was follow my brother Dennis around.

Singing took the edge off all of that. Nothing on earth felt quite so comforting as that first breath, the feeling of muscles contracting, the feeling of my vocal cords coming together, seemingly without any help from my brain, and producing a sound that was fairly reminiscent of my *Opera Favourites*.

So I became the little girl who sang in the wardrobe. I sang in that wardrobe every day, and when I moved to London fourteen years later I made Dad drive it down the M6 in Pete-from-next-door's Transit. And nobody ever knew.

ACT TWO

Scene One

London, United Kingdom, 2004–11

'Our parents are shocking,' Fiona told me, one evening shortly after I'd moved to London.

We were sitting on the floor of our newly rented flat in the crap bit of Southwark. It featured a Juliet balcony overlooking an illegal rubbish dump where foxes mated, it smelt of Stilton and there was a mushroom growing in the bathroom. It was a disgusting flat and we were very happy. Not least because we had discovered that Mr Pickles, who ran the tired little café underneath us, was also from Stourbridge.

Fiona and I, now twenty-one, seemed still to be the best of friends in spite of our ten-year separation. I was ecstatic. There hadn't been a day when I hadn't missed the mad little stick insect, or wondered if things would be the same once we were both grown-ups and could live together again.

We were eating out of takeaway Mr Pickles boxes. As usual I was wearing cheap jeans which showed my bum crack, although it would be the last time I dressed like that.

'I said, our parents are shocking,' Fiona repeated, when I didn't respond. 'Like, *CHRONICALLY SHIT.*'

Fiona did this often. She couldn't stand it when things were calm so she'd poke and prod at those around her until someone exploded.

'Oh, they're not too bad,' I replied, even though I completely agreed with her. 'I mean, look what they're putting up with.'

Fiona snorted. 'What? *Letting* us live together, pursuing our dreams? As if that wasn't our *right*?'

Fi certainly had a point. Mum's reaction to our new jobs had been, at best, lukewarm.

Fi had just been made a soloist with the Royal Ballet after being part of the *corps de ballet* for three years. I had recently finished my degree in costume design so she had been pimping my CV around the wardrobe department at the Royal Opera House, although neither of us expected anything to come of it. But three weeks ago I'd been called in for an interview and had been offered a dresser's job. AT THE ROYAL OPERA HOUSE! I had been so grateful and delighted that I had burst out into the piazza in Covent Garden and screamed, then whooped all the way back to Stourbridge, where Mum took one look at me and hissed, 'Pat! Someone in London's spiked her with them magic mushrooms and Ecstasy tablets! Pat! *Pat!* What'll we do?'

My job was only a bottom-rung-of-the-ladder affair but it would eventually lead me to my dream, which was to be a proper, senior costume person in the world of opera. A supervisor, maybe even a designer. A job that kept me out of the limelight but surrounded by my beloved opera? It was a miracle!

And I'd really believed that a career involving textiles and clothes-making would thrill my parents. Aged eighteen they had met at Hall's, a clothing factory on the Hagley road, and had worked there ever since: Mum had taught me how to load a bobbin even before she showed me how to use the kettle. One of the few times I'd seen pride in her face was when I won a regional dressmaking competition in Dudley aged sixteen.

But my shiny new career hadn't thrilled them. There had not been even a fraction of the pride there had been when Dennis (who had, of course, married Lisa from next door) started a self-storage company called Crate-World in Harrow.

In fact, Mum had been really quite aghast. 'The Royal Opera House?' she said anxiously, as if I'd just announced that I was off to work at an exotic massage spa. 'But there'll be all sorts of people there! Show-offs. Snobs. *Homos.*'

Dad, who rarely took any notice of what anyone was saying, looked up over his glasses. 'Really?' he asked. 'Gays?'

Mum nodded, her face siren red with alarm. Dad puffed harder on his pipe. 'Well then . . .' Even he looked concerned, which was quite a big deal because Dad didn't do emotions. He cleared his throat. 'It sounds like a good job, our Sal, but will you enjoy it? All of those singers? I mean, we're proud and all, but –'

'But we're not sure this job is *you*,' Mum interrupted.

I felt my eyes smart. What did they even know about

me? Mum avoided talking about anything that wasn't a logistical arrangement and Dad avoided talking about anything full stop. *You don't know me*, I thought angrily, saying nothing. *You don't know anything about me.*

'And it could be dangerous for you, working in the same place as Fiona,' Mum added, suddenly shifty. 'What if she causes trouble and it rubs off bad on you? You should keep your distance.'

I should have known. Should have known that anything to do with theatre would be too much for them. Too noisy. Too jazz-bandsy. Too like Aunty Mandy and all the trouble she'd caused, running away from home to have a fling with an actor, then having to return to Stourbridge single, pregnant and disgraced.

'I guess they were a *little* bit unenthusiastic,' I conceded sadly to Fiona. 'About all of this.' I gestured grandly towards the rubbish dump out of the window, as if it were a premium view of the Thames from a penthouse.

'A little bit unenthusiastic?' Fiona replied indignantly. She put her carton of bolognese back in its plastic bag to signal that she had now stopped eating. I ignored her. Fiona rarely ate more than five mouthfuls of her dinner. She could always be relied on to drink, however, and before continuing she took a long gulp of cheap wine direct from the bottle.

'Sally, our mother – *your* mother, to be precise – is a bitch.'

'Oh, Fiona, come on . . .'

'No! Stop making excuses for her! She should be proud of you! Proud of *us*!' Her eyes were flashing.

'She is, underneath it all.'

'Is she bollocks! She's ashamed! She's embarrassed! She's cross that we're both working in a *theatre*, even though it's not a bloody theatre, it's a world-famous opera house, just because of what my mum did. Why can't she let it go?'

'Um, because she lost her sister in a really awful way and she decided to blame it all on –'

'On what?' Fiona snarled. 'The performing arts? She can't cocking well hold the performing arts responsible for what happened! My mum was a mentalist! She shagged an actor who didn't care about her! Whatever! It happens all the time! Why are we being made to feel guilty because we've happened to work in a vaguely similar industry? *Jesus!*' She glugged at the wine with accomplished venom.

I glanced round the room as if to seek help, but found only the reflection of my half-exposed bum in the mirror; paper-white and bashful.

'Your mum,' Fiona continued, her voice now wobbling like a drunk ballerina, 'is about as warm and loving as a dishcloth. And she's made you feel shit, yet again, for taking a job that isn't in a bloody textiles factory. Even though nobody in England works in a textiles factory any more. Why do you keep on defending her?'

'She just doesn't understand my job . . .' I began lamely, then petered out. Everything Fiona had just said was true. When I thought about my own childhood, I felt quite resentful. But when I thought about Fi's, I felt the twisting ropes of rage. I needed to change the subject.

'I bet she hates you living with me,' Fiona said quietly.

'Of course not! Look, Freckle, you're right. They're shit, properly shit, so let's just agree on that and move on.'

'Humph,' she said darkly.

I swallowed a mouthful of bolognese without chewing and burned my mouth. Damn Fiona. She was so good at winding me up.

'Seriously, let's not talk about them.' I sounded laid-back, even though that wasn't how I felt. 'We can do what we want, Freckle, with or without Mum's blessing. We're adults now.'

Fiona took another swig of the wine and I watched her deciding whether or not to push it a little further. She decided not to. 'S'pose so . . . But I'm not so sure about this "adult" thing, Sally.' She grinned eventually. 'This morning when I walked into your room you were telling Carrot that he was a big handsome boy.'

'He is!'

'You're a twonk.' She sighed. 'But, teddy bears aside, we *are* adults, and there's no reason why working in the theatre is going to turn us into mentalists like my mum. SO THERE.' She stuck her fork into my spag bol and twirled it round. (It didn't count if she ate extra food from someone else's plate.)

Clinking our forks against the bottle of wine, we made a pact. From now on, we would be proper grown-ups.

We got really drunk and choreographed a contemporary ballet in our empty sitting room, then got a bus into Soho where we staggered around looking for somewhere cool and grown-up to dance. Somehow we got sidetracked and ended up buying vibrators and going for tea and cake at three thirty a.m. It was one of those blissful nights when Fiona fell asleep before she got drunk enough to start causing trouble.

I was happy.

Scene Two

The next day was my first at the opera house. I smelt like methylated spirits. I was collected from the stage door by my new colleague Faye, who wore écru slacks; she smelt of organic oat bran and west London. Immediately, I regretted my cheap outfit.

Following Faye through the endless corridors, I wondered when my first tea break would be. My head was doughy and my brain full of dense fog. I desperately needed a lie-down and a high-fat snack. *Balls*. Why had I gone out drinking the night before my first day here? Did I have to do *everything* Fiona suggested? I was a moron of desperate severity.

But then I was rescued by the most wonderful sound, a tannoy announcement made by a woman with a silky voice: 'Mr Allen and Miss Jepson, this is your five-minute call. That's your five-minute call, Mr Allen and Miss Jepson.'

It wasn't the names or the announcement that excited me: it was the sound of music in the background. The announcer must be practically on stage herself, within metres of what I immediately identified as *Così fan tutte*.

31

'*Così fan tutte!*' I exclaimed at Faye and her écrus.

She looked pleased. 'Yes, well done!'

An extraordinary sensation of relief flooded me, rolling away the filthy waves of hangover. Finally. *Finally* I was somewhere where it was impressive to know about opera. *I need never hide it again*, I thought dazedly. *This is amazing!*

A man was walking towards us in a suit and I presumed he was some sort of executive until he started making zooming noises with his voice.

'ZzzeeeeeeeEEEEEeeee,' he zoomed, suddenly breaking off and making a speedboat sound through his lips. He was wearing heavy makeup.

I realized it was Thomas Allen and nearly passed out. Thomas Allen was dead famous. So famous that I owned a DVD masterclass with him. I goggled at him and he smiled back in a very pleasant manner. 'Hello,' he said, breaking off from his speedboat noises.

I stared like a moron for a few more seconds, then remembered that people liked me because I was as cool as a cucumber. In fact, that had been one of the major pieces of feedback from my successful interview.

I smiled, and said calmly, 'Oh, hi, Thomas.'

He nodded and walked on, still smiling pleasantly.

I grinned. I might be as drunk as a stoat and smelly as a ferret but I was going to love this job. And I was really going to nail it.

And, as it turned out, I did. Unfortunately on that first day my vibrator went off in my bag (I had forgotten to remove it because I was still drunk) and it rattled so loudly that one of my colleagues asked Security to open the locker. And the next day my inexperienced dressing was responsible for a bass's trousers falling slowly to his feet during a duet – but, minor mishaps aside, I took it on quickly. I kitted myself out in soft, tasteful fabrics that smelt of Cornish crops and felt like peach skin (and then didn't have enough money to eat anything other than cheap bread for the first month, but that was fine).

I became Sally Howlett the Rock. I knew what I was doing when it came to clothes and costumes. Things involving fabrics and scissors and measurements. Boxes of buttons, safety pins, hooks and eyes, spools of thread and ribbon and piping. Notions, those bits were called. I'd wander through the stores, piled high with boxes of scraps and swatches of material, and I'd wish desperately that Mum and Dad would one day agree to come and visit because they would bloody *love* this place.

As a dresser I had what was called a plot for each opera performance: an important list of instructions that told me whose costume to change and when. The plots at first sounded mental – '*Take Marchesa Act III dress to SR quick change area; ***ORANGE BRA!!***, strike Café des Amis stuff*' – but I learned quickly how to decipher them.

Once again I became popular because of my unflappable nature and ability to problem-solve. I got on with everyone I met, massaged the egos of singers whose egos needed massaging and settled into a routine of unthreatening friendship with the rest. To my surprise, many of them were very normal. And even the grandiose ones who referred to 'The Voice' in the third person seemed to enjoy my Black Country accent and matter-of-fact world view. They liked that I had a bum as big as theirs, and that

I'd managed to call a singer named Regina Wheatley 'Vagina Weekly'.

There was a delightful baritone called Brian Hurst, whom I particularly loved. He was from Huddersfield so his accent was as out of place as mine. We ate chips from Rock & Soul in Covent Garden. Sometimes pies. He was heaven. He was quite a star, and sang in opera houses across the world, but he drank dandelion and burdock and never tantrumed, and often I'd find him smiling at me as I sprinted past with a bum patch for a singer who was tantruming because someone had just dared spray hairspray near The Voice.

'You're a good influence on us loonies,' he told me.

And there was the music. All day, every day, through the tannoy, on the stage, in the dressing rooms, in the rehearsal rooms. Scales, arpeggios, arias, recitatives. Big, booming choruses that made me want to punch the air and bellow through a theatrical beard. For the first time in my life, I felt I was at home.

The wardrobe staff, who had originally seemed so alien to me, with their cool casual trousers and elegant crops, must have appreciated my hard work because they offered me a wardrobe assistant's job after only nine months.

The first day I hung up my coat amid the hanging rails and steamers I felt a thrill that was rivalled only by mastering a difficult aria in my own wardrobe.

After two years in that job I got a further promotion and after another year I'd saved enough money to contribute a small deposit towards a tiny new-build flat by the canal in the southern reaches of Islington. On my twenty-sixth birthday I opened the door to my dream hidey-hole: extremely clean, orderly and carefully designed. Clever storage space. A car park with a gate. A pristine white bathroom and gentle, humming stillness.

It was heaven after the cramped, paper-thin-walled house of my childhood, decorated with an impossible combination of austerity and tack. Or the squalid flats that Fiona and I had rented since moving in together.

Fi, who had not saved so much as a penny in the last four years, moved her chaos to my little second bedroom and paid me a pathetic rent. Mum grumbled sporadically about me needing to separate myself from her: wasn't it enough that we worked together?

I ignored her and carried on being Fiona's unofficial mother. It suited everyone perfectly and we had a lot of fun.

Scene Three

Not long after starting at the opera house, I made two important friends.

The first was Barry from Barry Island, a principal dancer with biceps like tiny rocks and the best Welsh accent I had ever heard. I didn't work with him – I was opera, not ballet – but he was impossible to miss. One morning as I sat with a *pain au chocolat* in the canteen, gazing over Covent Garden market, I was joined by a very pale, very beautiful man with piercing sea-coloured eyes and a tub of grilled chicken.

'Don't,' he said, as I looked sympathetically at his breakfast. 'I can't eat no pastries.' He opened the tub with affected sadness, then grinned evilly at me. 'If I did I'd end up with one of these' – he gestured at my belly, which was poking through my dress – 'and they'd sack me. Not being funny or nothin'.'

I told him that I was cool about being chubby if it meant I could eat delicious freshly cooked pastries whenever I wanted.

His face crumpled with desire. 'Freshly cooked?' he

said hoarsely, staring at my *pain au chocolat*. Without warning he grabbed it and took a large bite. 'Aaah,' he moaned. 'Now that's what I'm talking about.'

I burst out laughing. 'My cousin does that,' I said, 'all the time. Do you know her? Fiona Lane?'

The man grinned and revealed perfectly white teeth. 'Oh, yeah, Fiona. She's a right little one, I'll tell you that for nothing.'

God, his accent. It killed me. I loved it. I stared adoringly at him and told him it was the best accent I'd ever heard. 'Well, thank you, Chicken,' he said. 'Do you mind if I call you Chicken? It seems right, as I sit here on this lovely morning eating chicken.' I nodded my assent (and became Chicken for ever more).

'Great. Well, I'm Barry and I come from Barry Island in the great country of Wales, and I have to tell you that I'm in agony.' He opened up the plastic tub and put a small, sad morsel into his mouth.

'Why?'

He lowered his voice to a brave whisper: 'It's my dance belt, Chicken.'

I looked blankly at him. 'Dance belt?'

'The dance belt,' he told me, in tones of deep Welsh tragedy, 'is a terrible thing I have to wear every day and hate more than I can tell you. It's a G-string and it covers my tiny penis with a great big mound of wadding. It spreads it all out into a . . . a soft bulge. Like a horse's ball bag, you know.'

I shuddered.

Barry looked grateful. 'Thank you for understanding,

37

Chicken,' he said emotionally. 'Thank you. You don't know how lucky you are, being able to wear all those . . . those *bedsheets* around yourself.'

I fiddled with my voluminous linen skirt and felt like a bit of a tool. I knew I fitted in with the wardrobe lot now but I still wasn't convinced that this look was very me.

The next day I bumped into Barry in the canteen, this time with Fiona, and we somehow arranged to go dog racing in Walthamstow the following Saturday. At the stadium Barry started playing Madonna on his phone and nearly got us into a punch-up. Fiona made the very uncharacteristic move of ordering chicken in a basket but then passed out drunk in it. And I managed to give my number to a minor-league gangster from Essex.

Drunk as lords, we ended up back at my flat and the next day I forced both ballet dancers to have a proper fry-up. As we ate our sausages and bacon we listened to the messages that my randy suitor had left on my answerphone at three a.m. – a romantic little line about how he wanted to drink peach Bellinis off my 'bangers' – and laughed until we cried. And that was that.

The other firm friend I made was Bea. Bea was Italian and extremely rich. It was never clear to me why she was working, really, but she was incredibly good at her job. Beatriz Maria Stefanini was a supervisor in the makeup and wigs department and she was just about as fabulous as it was possible to be without being a handbag.

She was – in every sense – the toughest person I'd ever met. I had always seen myself as quietly strong but in truth that was only because the people in my life tended to be weak or mad. But Bea was something else. She was a force. An opera in herself.

We became friends when she caught me standing in the wings, rooted to the spot, as I watched Brian the baritone bowling around the stage in *The Magic Flute* with a moustache somehow attached to the crotch of his cream trousers. It was the funniest and most dreadful merkin in history, and it was my fault.

'Excellent,' Bea remarked crisply, watching Brian. 'I have been wondering where that moustache had gone. Did you pin it to his crotch on purpose?'

I was aghast. 'Of course not! I don't know how it got there. But I do know that this is a disaster.'

Bea let off a sharp bark of laughter. An assistant stage manager waved at her to be quiet and she ignored him. 'What's your name?' she asked.

'Sally,' I replied. 'Sally the merkin girl. Perhaps you should offer me a job in the wigs department.'

Bea laughed again and clapped a strong, scented arm around my shoulders. 'Welcome to the world of the stage,' she said. 'This happens all the time. And when it does, it is priceless. Come up to the wigs room after the show. You need a drink.'

I walked in an hour later and gasped. It was up in the eaves of the opera house and had a stunning view across the West End and right down to the far reaches of south London. The Crystal Palace radio mast blinked at me as I wandered through a bewildering sea of wig and makeup paraphernalia. Kirby-grips, prosthetic disfigurements, hairdryers, glues, brushes. Half-completed beards, makeup charts, magnifying glasses, scissors and hairspray. A treasure chest of disguises.

'Sit,' Bea said, opening a mini fridge under one of the tables. I looked round and eventually sat on a stool, rubbing my hands together. They were always cold. 'Oh, put your hands in an oven,' she said breezily, gesturing at a little room full of metal stationery cupboards.

I frowned. 'Oven?'

'*Sì*. Those are wig ovens. We set the wigs in there overnight. Useful at this time of year,' she added, pulling what looked like an incredibly expensive cashmere shawl around herself. She showed me an oven full of wigs on head blocks and then propped open the doors of another, which was empty. She pulled up two chairs next to it and handed me an impressive vodka and tonic, which even contained ice and lime wedges. We sat with our backs to the warm oven and looked out over London.

'Sally the merkin girl,' she said, chinking my glass. '*Eccellente*.'

I chuckled. 'They'll probably sack me.'

Bea snorted. 'Darling, they'll probably promote you.'

'Hear hear!' said a man's voice. Brian Hurst, the lovely dad-like baritone, had just arrived in the wigs room with the errant moustache in his hand. 'This is yours, I believe,' he said pleasantly, handing the moustache to Bea. 'Great work, Sally,' he added.

'You two both have very strange accents,' Bea announced.

Brian laughed. 'Ghetto kids, Sally and I. We keep it real.' He smiled, then left.

Bea looked delighted. 'Oh, *favoloso*!' she exclaimed. 'A ghetto child! Where are you from?'

'Um, Stourbridge?'

She looked blank. Of course. Why would a rich Italian woman know where Stourbridge was?

'It's in the Midlands, near-ish to Birmingham,' I explained. 'Southernmost tip of the Black Country?'

Bea nodded vaguely. 'Your accent is precious, darling.' She smiled. 'I like you.'

And with that I was taken on.

We saw each other almost every day for years. Right up until that fateful night in New York after which she disappeared to Glyndebourne and Fi refused to come home.

Scene Four

June, 2011

'But . . . but you're a BALLET DANCER!' I exploded. Fiona glared guiltily at me and then at the line of cocaine that was racked up neatly in front of her. It was so large that it had a nasty, grainy shadow under the bare light bulbs round the mirror.

I was twenty-eight. I'd been working at the Royal Opera House for seven years and had become deputy wardrobe mistress; the second act of my own personal opera was coming to an end. I could sense Act Three on its way. Acts One and Two had been very gentle but this new era felt different. Smelt different. It was everywhere: a heady current that pulled me along and refused to say where it would deposit me.

That morning, Bea had summoned me upstairs to the wig-washing room and announced that she'd secured me a job on the Royal Ballet's summer tour. '*The Rite of Spring*, six weeks touring the east coast of America,' she purred. 'Starting in New York at the Metropolitan Opera House.'

I gaped at her. 'But . . . I don't work on ballet,' I mumbled. 'I'm opera . . .'

Bea snorted, tossing her mane. 'So was I, darling, but it's time for a change. I'm flexible. So are you.'

I looked at her doubtfully. I was a creature of routine. I wasn't sure I knew how to costume those lithe, muscled little creatures in the ballet department. And, more to the point, my job in the summer was to oversee the inventory and repair of several hundred operatic costumes at our store in Cardiff. I'd done this every summer for years and quite enjoyed the holiday romance I always had there with a friend of Barry's who owned a coffee shop. He was genuinely called Jesus, in spite of being white and Welsh.

But Jesus was not part of Bea's plan for me that summer. She had sorted everything out, in the way that only Bea could. After seven hot summers in the wardrobe stores, my boss, Tiff, had agreed that I deserved a break and had borrowed someone to stand in for me. And the deputy wardrobe mistress from the ballet department, who should have been going to America, was about to give birth to triplets.

I was in.

'Barry will be dancing in the tour, as will Fiona,' Bea concluded, applying a creamy red lipstick called FURY! in the mirror. 'The four of us will take America by storm. I know people in every city we will visit. We will drink cocktails and eat lobster every night. It will be . . . how do you say? . . . *monumental*.' She blotted her lips. 'Yes. Monumental.'

If Bea said it was going to be monumental, it would be monumental.

Although the thought of being on tour with Fiona made my nerves prickle. Fiona had found out recently that she had been passed over once again as a first soloist, leaving her at the same rank she had held for the last seven years. She had decided that it was because she was too fat and last week had stopped drinking alcohol 'to get *THIN*'. From what I could tell she had also pretty much stopped eating.

How will you cope with her abroad? a small voice asked me.

I ignored it. I was going to NEW YORK. We'd muddle through; we always did.

'Now, I've ordered you some proper luggage,' Bea told me. 'You will not tour with your nylon suitcase, Sally. We do this in style, *sì*?'

'I . . . *Sì!* Thank you,' I gasped. 'Oh, my God!' Bea kissed me on the cheek and dismissed me, as was her custom.

I bowled down the corridor to the lift, imagining myself eating pastrami sandwiches on an iron fire escape and maybe bumping into Carrie Bradshaw. There was a spiralling joy in my chest, an opening up of possibility.

A lone soprano was singing a jolly little bit from *I puritani* in the corridor and I felt so giddy with excitement I joined in under my breath. '"*Son vergin vezzosa*"!' we sang. '"*Ah sì! Son vergin vezzosa in vesta di sposa*"! "Oh, yes! I'm a charming virgin in a wedding dress"!' I giggled all the way back to the wardrobe department.

And then, a few hours later, I found myself standing in a dressing room with my cousin and a line of a class-A drug. Two cherry-red spots pricked her cheeks and her mood was deadly. Fi had always been completely insane around food and quite dangerous around drink but this . . . This was new.

It was an hour before tonight's performance of *La Bohème* and I'd just walked into the children's dressing room looking for a missing pair of derby boots. Bracing myself for a tussle with eight mental stage-school kids, I'd been somewhat surprised to find that they'd been moved to a different room, and that there, in their place, was Fiona with a pile of white powder. I was dumbfounded.

'And this is the CHILDREN'S DRESSING ROOM!' I continued in a panicked hiss.

'Oh, babes, stop being silly.' Fiona, who was regaining her composure, dismissed me as if I'd caught her cheating at bridge. Without warning, she leaned down and snorted up half of the line. Her lovely freckled face looked pinched and nasty as she inhaled; it strangled my heart.

'Stop, Freckle!' I whispered desperately.

'Sssh!' she said, with a little laugh. A laugh that someone had scooped the insides out of. 'It's just coke! Coke isn't serious, babe.' She sniffed the last few bits of powder up into her nostril. 'Everyone does it,' she added conversationally. 'You're probably the only person I know who doesn't.'

I baulked, uncertain. Really?

Fiona started tidying up the other half of the line ready for action, a delicate blush spreading over her bony shoulders. As a result of her recent diet she was gaunter than ever. From behind she looked like a child: skinny, underdeveloped, soft downy hair on the nape of her neck like gossamer threads.

I couldn't stand it. 'Freckle . . .' I whimpered, tugging

on her ponytail like I'd done since we were tiny. '*Please* stop.'

She took the rest of the line. 'You should live a little, Sally,' she said lightly, 'before you start judging everyone else.' She licked her finger and ran it round the dressing-table, then rubbed the remaining powder into her gums. 'Your twenties are for pushing boundaries, *enjoying* yourself.' She turned round, now smiling brightly, although the smile was cruel. An accusation that *I* had comprehensively failed at being a twenty-something. 'I'm just doing what *everyone else* does, silly Sally!'

Really? Was she?

I wasn't sure. None of the other dancers were like Fiona. They seemed to have lots of fun but they also looked after themselves with such incredible care, wrapping their legs up until they went onstage and hanging out only in the heated parts of the building so they never got cold. They even *walked* in a special way. They ate tubs of chicken and had special massages and stretched all the time. Surely, when they went to such lengths to look after their bodies, they wouldn't be taking drugs.

Fiona was forever freezing cold and stomping around. She drank a lot, she was noisy and sometimes she didn't even bother to warm up properly. She was a beautiful dancer but I couldn't help wondering if she'd failed to get promoted because she looked such a mess.

No! I didn't believe her! There was no way the others were taking drugs. Fiona was on her own. I felt my hands tremble as if my blood were fizzing.

'Look, I can take or leave this stuff,' she told me, head cocked to one side. 'Coke isn't serious. If I was on crack or scag or something, fair enough, but, Sally, this is just a bit of fun! No side-effects, no hangovers.'

'But it's still a drug,' I whispered.

Fiona did that hollow laugh again and pulled her big dancer's holdall over her shoulder. 'You're not dead yet, Sally. You and your middle-aged outfits could still have a good time. I'm off out. Laters, babes.' Any warmth in her farewell was as synthetic as a Primark sock.

I watched the door close behind her and uneasy silence opened up around me. *You're not dead yet.* I stared at the mirror. Did she think I looked middle-aged? Did other people think I looked middle-aged? But I'd just said yes to New York! I'd . . .

A ball of salt water wobbled uncertainly down my face and I realized I was crying.

In truth, I probably had failed on the wild front. Since moving to London seven years ago I had mostly just explored the gastropub scene; I'd travelled a bit but only really to European cities that had opera houses. I had not tried drugs, I had not dabbled in lesbianism or gone to a forest rave, and I'd had a succession of pleasant short-term boyfriends, who had been distinctly mild, not wild. And I dressed like I did because, well, it helped me feel I belonged. Was that failure? Was *I* a failure?

No! I countered desperately. *Fiona isn't allowed to write me off like that!* Taking big deep breaths, I made myself stop crying and patted my face dry. I got a wet wipe out of my wardrobe belt and cleaned the surface in case of residual cocaine.

I am not boring, I am not boring, I am not boring!

In the corridor, terrified someone might somehow

know, I bumped into Brian. As if sensing I was unhinged, he touched my shoulder and smiled kindly before walking on. He disappeared round the corner, softly singing something from *La Traviata*.

As I watched his very normal, very reassuring back retreat down the corridor, I finally began to come back to myself. *I'm fine*, I told myself, breathing deeply. *Fi was just lashing out because I caught her red-handed. And if she says coke isn't serious, then she must be right.*

After all, what did I know about drugs? Everything would be OK.

That night Fiona apologized profusely, telling me she had just been 'dicking around' and that she wouldn't take coke ever again if it was going to upset me. 'I can take or leave that stuff,' she reiterated. 'But I can't take or leave you, Sal.' The next morning, as a sign of her contrition, she even went all the way down to Southwark to get my favourite breakfast from our long-lost Mr Pickles.

'You're not dull at all, Sal. You're my idol. You and I are going to have DA BEST TIME in New York! BFFs, right?'

I smiled and got going with my egg muffin. I cared too much about Fiona to stay angry. And, apart from anything else, I wanted what she was saying to be true.

ACT THREE

Scene One

June 2011, London

The day we flew to New York was the day I discovered that Barry was pathologically afraid of flying.

'Not comin', Chicken,' he told me briskly, when I eventually tracked him down in a far corner of Terminal Four. He was sitting on a luggage trolley, green of face, rocking back and forth, with his hands round his knobbly little knees. 'Changed my mind.' He gave me an authoritative nod to reassure me that this had been decided by someone who knew what they were talking about.

I smiled. 'Nonsense. We're going to tour *The Rite of Spring* round America. For six weeks! You've never been more excited in your life!'

Barry scrunched his face at me, just like Bea did at people who owned fake-leather handbags. 'Please go away, Sally.' He sounded darker.

'No.' Barry's tantrums were rare; they were also child's play next to Fiona's. I sat down beside him. 'I didn't know you were afraid of flying, Barry, but –'

'Well, I am, and that's all I've got to say on the matter so I'm just gonna pop off home now, Chicken, OK? Bye.'

He sprang up and staggered a few steps. Almost as quickly he sat down again on the floor, putting his head between his knees.

'I'm dyin', Chicken,' he muttered. 'Dizzy. Quick, let me take refuge in your linens.'

'You're not dying, you're just scared. Listen, Bazzer, I've got amazing news. Delta have upgraded you and the other dancers to business class!'

Barry looked at me desperately. 'I'm not flyin',' he protested.

'You are. I'll look after you till we get on the plane and Fi can look after you in business class. You can get drunk and sleep all the way there on your FLAT BED!'

Barry's face went greener. '*Sleep?*' he hissed, as if I were completely insane. '*Sleep?* Chicken, I need to be awake every second of the way! Vigilance! I'm not usin' no bed!'

I stood up, pulling him with me. 'Come on,' I said firmly.

'*You* have my bed,' he said. 'We'll swap, Chicken. I'll take your economy seat. No bloody danger of me fallin' asleep back there.'

I argued, but he was having none of it. So when I boarded Delta 3, my first ever transatlantic flight, I turned left. Just like they did in books. There was champagne in my hand before I could whisper, 'Noo Yoik!' and the world's jolliest man, named Henk, forced blinis on me and told me I was going to get a FULL-SIZE DUVET LATER ON. And a PILLOW. 'Can I get you a cocktail, darling?' he asked. I nodded dumbly and wondered how a woman with a fat bum and a Midlands accent had pulled off something like this.

After a five-course banquet I sat back clutching my stomach, blissfully happy. There had even been cheese after the pavlova. And unlimited wine! Champagne! 'Shall we make up our FLAT BEDS, babe?' I asked Fi, who was sulking in the seat next to me. The other dancers – whom Fi had gone somewhat cold on since she had missed out on promotion – had chatted animatedly over dinner but then gone to sleep, and Fi's usual partner in hard drinking, Bea, had upgraded herself to first without even telling us.

Barry, whom we'd visited in economy, was fast asleep in spite of his earlier promise to stay AWAKE and VIGILANT for the duration of the flight. Now Fi had that dangerous look in her eye. The one that said: *Play with me NOW. Or I'll go and find something else to do. And you won't like it.* 'One more drink,' she wheedled. (She had forgotten she'd given up drinking as soon as we'd arrived at the airport.) 'There's a bar upstairs in first and Henk said we could go up if it was just the two of us . . . Come on, Sal. When are two pikeys like you and me ever going to fly business again?'

I yawned in the hope that this would get me off the hook. It didn't.

'Just a nightcap,' she pleaded. 'How are we going to get off to sleep otherwise? Listen how noisy those engines are!'

Fi always had a reason for a drink. If she was ill, it was a hot toddy; if she was nervous, a brandy. If she couldn't sleep, a cheeky nightcap. And there was frequently a requirement for a 'winding-down' wine or a little celebratory vodka. It had always made sense but as the years had passed I'd finally begun to notice that neither I nor anyone else I knew – except, perhaps, Bea – had such a regular and pressing need for medicinal alcohol.

I sighed, knowing I'd cave in. I so very, very often wanted to say no to Fiona yet I so very, very rarely did. Partly because I loved her and was desperate to maintain what fragile happiness she had, but mostly because I would do anything to avoid an explosive tantrum.

We went upstairs and sat at the Skybar where an atmosphere of sleek naughtiness prevailed. This was obviously the province of those who didn't *need* their flat beds because they were going to see this bitch through with bourbon. There was a power-suited woman, hammering out something on a tablet, and a couple of overweight men in chinos, arguing about someone called Jamie. And a man, a very arresting man, with tight jeans and brooding dark eyes, nursing a Scotch. As we walked in he took us both in. I experienced the usual disappointment as his eyes skimmed over me and slid away, finding Fiona and her tiny little legs poking out of an Acne skirt. He raised an eyebrow at her and then – *what? Seriously?* – his glass. Oh, my God. I was an extra in the Ferrero Rocher advert.

I followed Fiona over to the bar, somewhat reluctantly, and we sat down with the man. The crackle of electricity as Fiona drew near him at least reassured me that my services would not be required for long. 'Hey, girls,' he said comfortably, as if he were used to summoning women with an eyebrow. 'What are we drinking?'

I thought this was a bit unnecessary, given that it was a free bar. 'Diet Coke,' I responded stoutly. Fiona grimaced, embarrassed by me, and murmured something about cognac.

'Raúl,' he said, staring at Fiona in a sexy sort of a way. 'Raúl Martinez.'

'Off of the Branchlines,' Fiona said excitedly. Then she dropped her voice an octave. 'Cool.'

Raúl looked pleased. 'The very same,' he said, forgetting to be smooth. 'I didn't think English girls liked our music!'

And that was that. The gauntlet was thrown squarely on the carpeted floor of the onboard bar. Fi, chemically unable to resist a challenge of *any sort*, took it and ran.

'Actually,' she began, 'I used to be in a band. Our music wasn't that dissimilar to what you guys play . . .'

She had been in a band. A diabolical band called Summer of Love that bore no resemblance whatsoever to anything that the Branchlines had written. The calibre of their lyrics could easily be inferred from their signature song:

> Tell me I'm terrific
> Tell me I'm no pranny
> Tell me that you'd let me put my
> KNOB RIGHT UP YOUR FANNY.

When one of the dinner ladies had overheard this, my parents had been called in and our house was like a ghastly war zone for days afterwards.

I broke off from my dark reverie, realizing that Fiona and Raúl were looking at me expectantly. Fiona was already sipping coyly while Raúl held a Scotch in the flat of his hand in a way that said, 'Hi, I own a Scottish distillery.'

I looked back at them.

'You sing,' Raúl prompted me. Fiona blushed ever so slightly behind her cognac.

'What?'

'Oh, don't be shy.' He laughed easily but I couldn't. I knew instinctively that something was very rotten here. 'Fiona was just saying that you sing opera,' he clarified.

I felt sick. How did she know? Had she heard me? *When?* Oh, God, oh, God. Opera had been my secret for twenty-one years now. Or had it? *Oh, God!*

'Oh, I don't,' I said vaguely. Panic wound itself tightly round my stomach. 'Not really. Just a little bit when I'm in the bath or whatever . . .'

'She sings in her wardrobe for some reason,' Fi said, smiling. 'And you know what, Raúl, she's really bloody good! You should get her in as a backing singer or something!'

'So you don't have lessons or perform?' Raúl asked, signalling to the waiter for another brandy. Fiona had finished the first already.

'Jesus, no!' I trilled, getting up off my stool. *Fiona knew. She had heard me. All these years.* 'No, I just mess around. I'm not a *proper* singer . . .'

I was close to tears.

'She is,' Fiona insisted. 'And she does nothing about it. I mean, *I*'m meant to be a good dancer and I'm trying my best to make it, even though my bosses are doing their best to hold me back, but Sally, she's not even trying!' It was a crummy, self-pitying dig, which Fiona instantly tried to soften by smiling encouragingly at me.

'Well, don't you waste your raw talent.' Raúl sounded like an *X Factor* judge. 'My best friend wasted his opera-singing talent and, man, I think he's a dick.'

'I'll have to be a dick, then.' I laughed hollowly. 'Ha-ha! Night!'

I slunk off to my flat bed and felt tears of panic build in my eyes. Why was she doing this to me? Why bring it up now if she'd known all along? And who else had she told?

It didn't occur to me to wonder why it mattered so much. It just did.

My singing is my business, I thought shakily. *Mine and mine alone. Fiona can bloody well move out if she's going to start causing trouble.*

Singing was the best thing I had. And it was private.

Scene Two

I took a sleeping tablet but I was horribly awake and still pumping adrenalin two hours later. The drowsiness the pill caused simply made my sleeplessness more offensive.

Fi knew I sang, and the worst of it was that she wasn't the only one. Someone else knew. I had a letter in my handbag to prove it. Between them, Fi and this other stupid, interfering person could make sure that everyone in my carefully protected world knew that I was the girl who sang in her wardrobe.

I tried to steer myself back to sense. Surely it didn't matter that much.

But it did. It mattered more than anything else.

The worst of it was that it was *my fault* that the other person – Brian the baritone – knew about my singing. My stupid, clumsy, self-indulgent fault.

I had gone to work at seven thirty yesterday morning to make sure I got everything finished before leaving for America. It had been a beautiful day and the air was milky when I got off the 38 bus at Holborn. Walking along Drury Lane I felt as if I'd been suspended in a pleasant sepia bubble. Things moved calmly, gently; even the vans disgorging coffee beans, wooden boxes of lettuce, stacks of croissants seemed to belong to another time when people moved slowly and worried less.

As I often did when I got to work super-early, I headed for the empty auditorium. Even now – after all these years – it gave me a greater high than any drug I could imagine.

The front-of-house door shut softly behind me and the red, velvety silence reached around and hugged me. I exhaled happily, looking up at tier after tier of boxes, exquisite little treasure chests of gold, red velvet and marble. The candle lamps were dimmed and the beautiful gold roof arched up away from me, like a great shell, staggeringly high above the stalls.

I sat in a seat and closed my eyes, breathing gently, imagining this same air tonight: warm and swollen with hundreds of voices, thick with the smells of old-fashioned powder and the sharper, sexier perfumes of the young. I imagined the orchestra tuning up in their pit, all long, low blasts and high-pitched squeaks, like a ship's dockyard. The stage managers buzzing around with their headsets and tiny Maglites; the makeup team pinning wigs and powdering faces, my wardrobe colleagues sliding things off hangers with the quiet, unfussy efficiency on which we prided ourselves.

And finally I allowed myself to imagine the singers waiting behind the safety curtain. Dressed in a hundred different colours; warmed up and ready; simultaneously relieved and frustrated not to be in the spotlight tonight. Somewhere among them would be the two stars, still nervous after all these years, breathing, stretching, humming. Ready.

'Keith!' someone yelled offstage. 'They're craning the *La Bohème* set out of the workshop. Move your fat arse.'

Smiling, I slipped out of the auditorium and took the lift up to Wardrobe, thinking about *La Bohème*. This coming autumn, once I was back from New York, we had a cast change and I was overseeing the costumes for the incoming singers.

It would be an honour: *La Bohème* was my favourite opera of all time. A love story that managed to be both beautiful and devastating, unfolding against a musical score that (to me at least) had no equal.

Mimi and Rodolfo's duet in the first act, in spite of being one of the most famous and overplayed in the world, was utterly perfect. As Barry had once pointed out, 'It's bollockin' mental, the idea of two people meeting in a sitting room and declarin' their undyin'. Unnatural, Chicken. Unnatural.' But the melody of that duet somehow made it believable. Made it totally acceptable for two people to meet and say, *Oh, hello, I'm Mimi, I'm Rodolfo, oh, your hands are cold, sit down, you pretty little thing, and tell me about your life . . . Oh! What the hell is this? I'm in love with you! I will love you for ever! And you'll love me for ever! Awesome!*

When you heard the music, it just made sense. Listening to that duet was the best way to use six minutes that I knew.

As I'd progressed through my twenties my ability to sing it had improved and, as I'd gone about my work in the workshop yesterday morning, I had found myself humming it.

Normally I didn't let myself so much as whisper opera when at work. It would have been mortifying if someone had heard me and concluded that I was some frustrated out-of-work singer.

But nobody was due in for hours; it couldn't have been a safer time.

I started to sing softly, pleased by the sound of my voice. It filled a small part of the room and did so rather well. '"You love me?"' I sang, raising the volume another notch. I imagined the sensation of falling in love as deeply and totally as Rodolfo and Mimi.

'"I will be yours for ever,"' I sang, allowing my voice to curl outwards.

'"For ever!"' Slightly powerless now, I felt myself build momentum. I was aware that I should stop singing – or at least take it down a few decibels – but I couldn't.

'"I will never leave you!"' It rushed out of me and filled the entire room. I stopped singing, shocked. Sound waves snapped and fizzled around me.

I sounded like a proper singer.

'Oh,' I said to the empty room.

'*Sally?*' It was Brian the baritone, appearing suddenly through the door like a very unwelcome genie from a lamp. He was 'popping in' sometime this week to be measured for his *La Bohème* costume next September. I'd been really looking forward to seeing him. Until now.

'Was that you?' He looked stunned.

'No.'

Brian's brow furrowed. 'Oh, I heard someone . . .' His eyes scanned around for someone to pin the blame on but came back to me. 'No, it was you,' he insisted. He peered at me over his half-moon glasses. 'You were singing Mimi. And it sounded ruddy amazing.'

I wasn't much of a blushing type because I never got myself into a situation where blushing would be necessary. But blush I did, so intensely that I must have looked like I'd been at the crazy tomato festival that Fi went to every year in Spain. *This is why you never sing outside your wardrobe*, I thought furiously. *Too many interfering –*

Brian interrupted my rising anger. 'I cannot tell you how good you sounded,' he said quietly. 'Are you a singer? Have you been wasting away all of these years, Sally?' He was looking at me far too intensely for my liking.

I squirmed, wishing I could vaporize. Horrible memories of Mum's panicked face during the school concert hung in the air around us. I shook my head.

Brian smiled. 'There's nothing to be ashamed of,' he said. 'Quite the opposite, in fact. Carry on! I'd love to hear you!'

I muttered something about having come in early to order a load of knickers and disappeared into the laundry room, adding that Tiff would take care of his costume measurements. Brian must have known that I couldn't order many pairs of knickers in a room full of washing-machines but, thankfully, he left it.

My heart was racing for a long time after the incident, but by lunchtime I'd managed to get a lid on it. It was OK. I was going to New York tomorrow, he'd be away all summer, and by the time we saw each other in September he'd have forgotten about it.

Only he hadn't. When I left at the end of the day to go home and pack, Ivan from stage door handed me a letter. From stupid, horrible, interfering Brian. Whom I had stopped loving until further notice.

It had burned a hole in my bag for the next twenty-four hours and had somehow managed to get on the plane with me:

I'm retiring [he'd said]. *The wife's had it with me running off round the world every five minutes. I'm in the middle of interviews for a contract teaching singing at the Royal College of Music starting at Easter 2012. They have an internationally renowned opera school there. If you were even a fraction as good as I thought you were, you have to audition, Sally. Don't bury your light under a bushel. YOU WILL REGRET IT!*

The plane jolted as we passed through a tiny patch of turbulence but, unlike my mind, it quickly straightened out and resumed its calm, low growl through the black silky sky.

It went without saying that I would never audition for an opera school. But if Brian was going to start hassling me – Fiona, too, for all I knew – I could be in deep water.

I'll leave, I thought angrily. *I'll leave that job before I allow people to start gossiping about me.*

Finally, at about three a.m., I closed the door on my head. *You have a choice here, Sally*, I told myself. Drowsiness rolled over me, gently repeating like a wave. *You can wallow in the fear of something that's not yet happened, or you can go and enjoy America. What's it to be?*

I was asleep within minutes, only to be woken by the lovely Henk bringing me perfectly scrambled eggs with smoked salmon and toast. When we started banking into New York an hour later, and Barry forgot that he was afraid of flying, galloping into Business to scream excitedly at me and Fiona, Henk somehow found him a seat to land in and Fiona told me she was a dick and would never mention my singing again cos she knew I was 'weird and private', like my folks, and then I saw those buildings thrusting elegantly into the sky, reigniting memories burned into me by a thousand films, and I finally gave up and burst into tears. Happy tears.

I couldn't believe it. New York. City of dreams! The most exciting thing I'd ever done. The beginning of my Act III; the greatest adventure of my life.

ACT FOUR

Scene One

Monday, 10 September 2012, fifteen months later, London

From: Sally Howlett [mailto howler_78@gmail.com)
To: Fiona Lane [mailto fionatheballetlegend@hotmail.com)
Sent: Monday, 10 September 2012, 07.03.55 GMT

Fi – ARGHHHH! IT'S TODAY! It's today it's today it's today!

You are in a world of trouble, Fiona bloody Lane. This terrible
horrible scary opera course at this terrible horrible scary music
college is *all your fault*. I didn't sleep last night. I just lay there
going mental and thrashed around and had diarrhoea (NB not
in my bed) and pulled big clumps of my hair out and ate a
multipack of Wotsits and maybe had a couple of tots of minging
dark rum cos that's all me and Barry have in the house. The main
point being that I hate you. Arggh!

I think it's very rude of you not to come back to London
to help me through my first week in this diabolical place.
EVERYONE IS GOING TO BE POSH AND AWFUL AND THEY
ARE GOING TO THROW ME OUT BECAUSE I WON'T BE
GOOD ENOUGH AND THEN I WILL BLOW MY HEAD OFF
IN AN OVEN AND IT'LL ALL BE YOUR FAULT.

Right. Breakfast is out of the question and if I have coffee I will FLY THROUGH THE FECKING ROOF so I'm just going to, oh, I don't know, sit here for another hour and STEW MY FAT ARSE OFF.

How's New York? Lovely and autumnal? Hmm, I'm sure it is. Damn you, you selfish bugger.

And love you. Lots.

Please come back soon. If only for a quick visit. A day, even! We all miss you. Xxx

Scene Two

The same day

The air was brisk but warm when I got off the tube at South Kensington. After a wet summer the trees were confused and their leaves had already begun to curl inwards and make for the ground. They skittered along the pavements, playful dancers in a cityscape of discordant traffic and relentless human momentum. For a few seconds I allowed myself to remember the turning leaves in Central Park, breathtaking in their autumnal technicolour. But I shut down the memory almost as soon as it had started. Stirring up thoughts of New York was not helpful on a day like today.

As I walked up the side of the Natural History Museum, its windows ablaze with a sudden burst of sun, a coach from none other than Stourbridge disgorged a bunch of feral children. I thought how much all of this would have pleased me, were the circumstances different. The leaves, the sparkly new puddles, the noisy children from my hometown.

Not today. 'Ah wunt to see the dinosaurs noe!' one of them shouted, and I couldn't even smile.

They inhabited another world. Their greatest fear probably centred around the potential ratio of horrible fruit to delicious trans-fats in their Natural History Lunchpacks.

'Hullow. Are you from London?' one of them said to me. He offered a manly wink and a toothless grin and waited for my response with surprising confidence for a child of no more than seven.

'Hullow,' I said to him. I tried to sound jolly. 'I'm from Stourbridge too, actually.'

'She's a liar,' he reported confidently to his friends. 'Probably a slag too.'

I carried on, capable of neither amusement nor outrage. It was as if I was being propelled a few inches above the pavement; the momentum of my body coming from somewhere else. But this was not a blissful floaty sensation: it was one of pure, out-of-body terror.

A girl dressed as a giant coffee cup handed me a free flapjack and I tore it open gratefully, only to find myself unable to eat.

God, this really *was* an emergency. I lived to eat. Yet I hadn't done so in more than twenty-four hours. Last night's pork belly would never have made it into my tummy even if my unwelcome visitor hadn't turned up. And this morning's cereal had gone hard in its bowl. Now a flapjack. A slice of happiness! Not only was I incapable of eating it but, oh, Christ, I'd dropped it. *It had simply fallen out of my hands.*

No food, especially food containing syrup, fell out of

my hands. I looked round for a stray dog, but stray dogs, I realized, were probably few and far between in SW7.

Stately, ostentatious red-brick buildings rose high above me. People walked purposefully and with aggression. A man shouted into his mobile about how it was time to fucking well do something about Marta. And I couldn't eat. I felt insane. I twiddled my completely OTT ring around my finger and considered throwing up in a dustbin.

Fiona had been singularly unhelpful when we'd spoken last night. No matter how I'd pleaded with her she'd just reminded me, five times, ten times, a thousand times, that I'd promised her I'd go to opera school. I'd given her my word. 'Seize the day, remember?' she'd said. 'You promised me in New York, Sal!'

'Seize the day,' I'd repeated hollowly.

And now here I was, my heart in my mouth, a chasm of terror cleaving down my middle.

There were signs everywhere for the Royal College of Music, the Royal Albert Hall, the Skempton Building, the Science Library. I ignored all of them and stared fixedly at the map on my phone, perhaps in the hope that it would direct me to a different Royal College of Music. Ideally the one situated in my wardrobe in Bevan Street, Islington. Although I didn't particularly want to go home either. I was terrified that last night's visitor might come back. And if that happened I didn't know what I'd –

'STOP IT,' I snapped at myself. Today was bad enough as it was; I had no mental space for him. I just had to trust that he'd taken note of the high-speed pork belly and would not come back. Ever. The *scumbag*. The bullshit-peddling, weak, spineless *scumbag*.

'WILL YOU JUST *STOP IT*!' I told myself, louder. I meant it this time. The college was drawing closer and I needed to start pretending to be calm. *Seize the day. Seize the day. Seize the day.*

And there, resplendent opposite the Albert Hall, it was. The Royal College of Music. A terrifyingly grand, turreted red-brick Gothic affair with a Union flag flying above its fussy glass portico. Grand steps leading up to heavy ornate doors through which I had not been bred to pass.

This building had been designed with great people in mind. 'For more than 125 years our students have gone on to international stardom,' the brochure had said. I swallowed. I didn't want *any* stardom, let alone that of the international variety. Any more than I wanted to study at a place that was so posh it needed a French name. For this, I had been told by a worryingly trendy undergrad who was helping at the auditions, was a *conservatoire*. I hadn't looked up the word but I knew that its definition would have something to do with *exceptional and talented* people who did not speak with Black Country accents. In fact, it was probably designed for people who hadn't even *heard* of the Black Country.

I felt fat as I cowered at the foot of the steps, painfully aware of the stone I'd put on since New York. Although I was by no means enormous, I felt grossly unsuitable for something that called itself a *conservatoire*. Barry had done nothing to assuage this fear. 'Maybe I'll blend in,' I'd gabbled earlier. 'Opera singers have always been on the chunky side.'

'But not *your* kind of chunky,' he'd countered,

squidging my stomach fondly. 'They're aristocrats and stuff. They eat goose fat and fine imported meats. You mark my words, Chicken, those opera singers don't buy four-packs of steak and kidney pie.'

Sodding Barry. Sometimes I found myself thinking that living with Fiona had actually been easier. She had been madder than a mushroom but she'd at least pretended I wasn't fat.

I glanced furtively along Prince Consort Road, which was surprisingly quiet. There was a madman hobbling around vaguely at the far end of the street but there were certainly no music students in view. I could, if I did it now, still run. Tell them I'd been attacked and my vocal cords stolen, and explain that I hadn't yet touched the scholarship money and could pay both of my scholarships back without delay. (How had I got *two*? It made things so much worse. I was accountable not just to the Associated Board of Something but also to some bloke called Lord Peter Ingle, who probably wore a cape and a monocle.)

The hobbling man had decided to hobble in my direction now.

And I knew it was time to go.

I turned and ran, away from the hobbling man, back towards the tube and freedom. Engaged in an activity that actually made sense, my body responded with uncharacteristic enthusiasm.

As my muscles pumped, my head cleared. Of course I couldn't do it. Of course I couldn't go and study for a performance diploma in opera or whatever the stupid course was called. It didn't matter a monkey's bollock that I could sing: *I was not a performer*. Standing in front of panel after panel of poshos for my auditions – including bloody Brian from the opera house – had been the hardest thing I'd done in my entire life: I'd had diarrhoea constantly and had been anguished ever since. I'd been fighting with Barry, whom I never fought with, I'd been fighting with my brother Dennis and his wife Lisa, whom I always fought with, and I'd even been trying to pick long-distance fights with Fiona, an activity made all the more infuriating by her uncharacteristic refusal to engage.

It was settled. I would pay back the scholarships, I'd apologize to Brian and the other folk at the college, I'd beg the opera house for my job back and I'd return to a life in which I felt very comfortable and perfectly happy. Fiona and her seizing of days would have to lump it.

'MUHHH!'

'Paaaaah!'

Two bodies colliding hard.

Obviously it was Brian. Of all the people who might have been turning off Exhibition Road. And obviously, being Brian, he looked extremely jolly, rather than extremely furious.

'Oh dear!' he exclaimed, as if I had just dropped a pencil, rather than galloped into his chest, like a charging rhino. 'Forgotten something?'

'Only my mind,' I muttered. 'Brian, I'm very sorry, but there's been a mistake. This is not for me, it's –'

'No,' he said lightly, and without the faintest hint of surprise. 'You don't get away that easily, Sally. Do you have any idea what the competition is like for places here? More than thirty people were turned down for your place alone.'

I wondered if he was serious. How was that an argument?

He was serious, by the look of things. 'Well, then, you'll have twenty-nine brilliant singers to choose from,' I told him, picking up my bag.

'No. *You* are the brilliant singer we picked,' Brian said firmly, taking me by the elbow and turning me back towards the college. He started walking; I didn't. So he pulled my elbow until it came with me behind it.

'You'll be OK, kid,' he said, more gently, and I heard his soft Huddersfield accent. 'Just come and register, OK? Get to know the place. You won't have to sing today.'

'I won't?' A slender ray of hope.

'Nope, no singing,' he confirmed. We were nearing the entrance again and I noticed that the hobbling man was walking directly towards us. 'Jan!' Brian cried merrily. 'My fine fellow! You made it!'

Jan was a short, angry-looking man with hair swept forward from the crown of his head into a dramatic curtain around his face. He looked like something from my VHS recording of *La Bohème* actually; one of the smelly art students in Café Momus during Act Two. He was wearing a long torn coat and what looked suspiciously like nineteenth-century trousers. His collar was cravated (no! No no no!) and a grubby handkerchief poked out of his front pocket alongside a fat old Nokia. Oh, and he was wearing only one shoe. In fact, as he bounced forward to shake Brian's hand, I realized that he wasn't hobbling. He was simply wearing one shoe and so was completely unbalanced.

For real? my head thought. 'For real?' my mouth said,

before I knew what was happening. Fortunately my rudeness was lost in Brian's effusive greeting.

'Welcome!' he enthused. 'Welcome to the Royal College! To London! To England! Excellent work getting here, Jan!'

'Thank you, thank you,' said Jan, in a strong Eastern European accent. 'It take me many days. Now I am here! I am student!'

'And so you are!' Brian cried. They shook hands again. Jan's face still looked furious, even though he was clearly very happy. I learned quickly that his 'furious' look covered a wide range of emotions.

I stood like a fat moron on the edges of Brian and Jan's greeting ceremony and wondered if I could sneak off.

Brian was having none of it. 'Sally Howlett, meet your classmate Jan Borsos,' he said, stepping back to allow us to shake hands.

I decided on the spot that I liked him. Jan Borsos was even more out of place than I was, standing lopsidedly outside that vast, Hogwarts-like building. I held my hand out to him but he rejected it, choosing instead to bow deeply towards his shoeless foot.

'Mrs Sally,' he said respectfully. 'Jan Borsos. I am from Pzjhkjhkjbjbjkbhjb in Hungary.'

'Hi, er, Mr Borsos,' I replied, with what I hoped was the right amount of respect. 'Call me Sally. I'm . . . I'm, er, from Stourbridge. In the West Midlands. Where did you say you were from?'

Brian ushered us through the door, the cunning bastard, while Jan repeated himself. 'I am from Pusztaszabolcs,' he said very slowly, 'south of Budapest. I studied at the

Budapest Opera School until the age of sixteen when I married with beautiful Russian *répétiteur*. I was young and stupid and I pause my studies for love, but we divorced ourselves one years later and I did study opera at the St Petersburg Conservatory. I wrote letter to the great master László Polgár and he said, "Yes, Jan, I will teach you in Switzerland, you come to me soon." I did study him for two years before he was dying.'

Jan stopped talking and his face clouded with sadness. I stared at him in amazement. I hadn't been expecting a life story but I was impressed by it: it sounded like an opera in itself. 'Wow,' I said brightly. 'So what have you been doing since then?'

'It was a small two years ago,' Jan whispered. 'László did die and then I travelled to Budapest to grief. I sing for two years in church for no money but I knew I must continue my study. So I come here to London. I hope not to fall in love with any more beautiful *répétiteur*. For me they are dangerous. Today is my twenty-three birthday.'

Before I had time to wonder what a *répétiteur* was, or to panic about being on a course with a twenty-three-year-old, I realized I was now standing in the reception area of the Royal College of Music. Auditions had been so terrifying that I'd barely looked beyond my own feet last time. Now I gulped, scanning around me with fresh eyes, while Brian loped off to talk to a tall, beautiful woman in a leather jacket.

Two kids, who seemed no more than fifteen, were strolling past with big cello cases strapped to their backs. They both wore cool duffel coats, short skirts with thick tights and hi-top trainers. They were carrying lattes. I

73

didn't understand. In these lofty environs, with busts of Mozart on the walls and glass cases containing priceless old manuscripts, would the musicians not have pointed beards and cassocks? 'Did you know that Adrian's been banging Chen all summer?' one reported to the other.

'Fuck off!' was the reply.

I nodded respectfully. No cassocks here, then.

On either side of an old wooden staircase were doors to the college's famous concert hall. I thought about what this hall meant and tried not to throw up. I'd been told that we would be 'lucky' enough to get to perform concerts and take masterclasses in this 'unparalleled' performance venue throughout the course. Catching a glimpse of a high ceiling and a long, large balcony, I thought that performing in there would be among the most unlucky experiences I could possibly imagine.

'Wow,' Jan Borsos said, peering in the same direction. 'I cannot believe we are here! It is miracle! We have much luck!'

'Yusss,' I croaked.

'Sally, Jan,' Brian called merrily. 'Come and meet Violet Elphinstone. Another coursemate. How fantastic that you all arrived at the same time!'

I tried to give him a look that warned of impending homicide if he didn't tone down all of this unnecessary jollity but my face was frozen. Which was probably a good thing because he was no longer a colleague but a tutor. *My tutor*. Oh, God.

Violet Elphinstone's face was also frozen, although hers was frozen into a smile she almost certainly didn't mean. She was probably five foot ten but a pair of caramel-coloured ankle boots took her to well over six feet. There was nothing stooped or awkward about her. She just looked like she got a lot of sex with film stars. She had one of those shiny graduated bobs that never greases over and *her face was perfect*. As in, mathematically, golden-ratio-proportioned, da Vinci-certified perfect.

'Hi, nice to meet you both,' she said, meaning, 'What the fuck are these two moronic freaks doing on MY OPERA COURSE?'

I shuffled over, feeling intensely fat and linen-covered, and shook her hand. 'Likewise,' I said. 'I'm Sally.'

'Um, yes, Brian just introduced you,' she pointed out sweetly, then giggled, putting an insincere hand on my arm so that I couldn't take offence.

For a few awkward moments we tried to find something to say to each other. I came in first with 'Amazing boot!'

Violet Elphinstone started to reply, a standard 'Thanks, they're Gina, I like yours, where are they from –'

But I interrupted her, booming, in my broadest Midlands accent, 'BOOTS.'

'What?'

'Sorry. Boots. I said nice *boot* but I meant nice *boots* . . . Oh, sorry, Office,' I added, remembering she had asked me where mine were from. 'Five years ago, I think . . .' I stared down at my soft brown boots, worn and grooved like walnuts, and felt embarrassed. I should have bought better shoes. And I should have just shut the hell up.

'Oh, I *love* a bit of Office sometimes,' Violet said conspiratorially. 'BARGAINOUS! But don't you find you have to dress down a bit when you're wearing cheap

75

footwear? Erm, like, *balancing act*, right?' She fiddled with her Chloé satchel, pointedly ignoring my unstructured grey dress. Which was not made of silk or expensive Japanese crêpe. 'Oooh, and I love your ring too,' she whispered, bursting with insincerity. Nobody, not even me, loved my ring. 'Nothing like a big statement piece!'

I was used to this sort of passive-aggressive behaviour. A few of the younger and more wanky opera singers at work had used it; it was an outward display of egalitarianism – *I'm still your friend, even though people pay £350 a night to watch me sing and you're just a twat with a sewing-machine* – but the subtext was always clear. *We are not equal. We never will be.*

I need to go shopping, I thought glumly. Everyone around me, especially this shimmering column of a woman, was cool and youthful. No nice middle-class bohemian fash-ion, like I was used to at work. Just lots of . . . trendiness. *But it's a bloody music college!* my mind wailed. *Shouldn't every-one here be a posh geek?*

Fortunately, Jan Borsos stepped in. 'Violet Elphin-stone, good day,' he said grandly, stooping into another deep bow. 'Please you forgive me for my shoe. I did lose one in France on my pilgrimage to London. It is a pleas-ure to meet with you today.'

I watched Violet decide what to do about this strange man flourishing theatrically at her feet. I waited for her lip to curl, but it didn't. Instead, she began to smile. 'What a *fab* greeting,' she said. 'Like, wow, *Jan Borsos*, what a name!' Jan kissed her hand and she giggled, pulling the Chloé bag up her arm so it wouldn't thump him in the face.

'I don't think I'm going to like her very much,' said a

girl who'd appeared at my elbow. She had a messy brown ponytail and perky pink lipstick, and was clutching a big home-made folder saying, 'OPERA SCHOOL YEAR 1'. She glared at Violet, who was prancing around Jan Borsos. 'Thoughts?' she asked. Then: 'Oh, Jesus, she's not your sister, is she?'

I was appalled. 'What do you think?'

The girl chuckled. 'It didn't seem likely.'

'Correct. But for the record, no, I don't think I'm going to like Violet very much.' I paused, looking fearfully at the throng of students moving around me. 'Although I'm not sure I'm going to like *anyone* very much. No offence or anything.'

The girl sniggered. 'You're right up my street, then,' she told me. 'Helen. Helen Quinn. I'm not just nervous, I'm fucking terrified. I haven't eaten in three days and I'm thinking about running away.'

I nearly cried with relief. 'Oh, Holy Mother of God,' I whispered. 'Thank you, Helen Quinn, for your honesty. You might just have saved me.'

Helen grinned and wandered off towards the opera school.

Brian, I noticed, was watching the whole pitiful scene like a proud dad. Right at that moment I hated him. I hated everyone, really. Brian for hearing me sing in the first place and Fiona for blackmailing me into auditioning. I hated the Royal College of Music for taking me on with cries of 'What a wonderful story! Wasting away in the wardrobe department!' and other such balls. And I supremely DETESTED everyone I worked with for being so lovely and encouraging about it, once word got out that I could sing and was trying to get into opera school.

'This is just *so* exciting!' they'd all yelled.

Bunch of tossers, I thought fiercely. I'd like to punch them all, one by one.

Please, please stop it, I begged myself.

It felt sad that I was so mental these days. Since New York, the landscape of my life had changed dramatically and nothing was certain any more, especially my feelings. I missed being controlled and predictable. I missed the pleasant sense of calm I'd had when I woke up in the mornings, the knowledge that even if Fiona went bonkers or I lost a costume everything would be OK. These days I seemed to spend all of my time firefighting feelings. It was exhausting and distressing. I didn't *want* to start college in this way.

Although, really, I didn't want to start college at all.

Scene Three

Later the same day

From: Sally Howlett [mailto howler_78@gmail.com)
To: Fiona Lane [mailto fionatheballetlegend@hotmail.com)
Sent: Monday, 10 September 2012, 22.59.55 GMT

Fiona Freckle. Hello darling. Now, I know I say this all the time but I miss you. More than ever. Is there any chance of you coming back to London? *Please?*

Bah. I hadn't cried today but now I'm bawling. I don't even know what's wrong with me. I suppose it's still New York. Grief, anger, that sort of stuff. Having J turn up at my house last night didn't help matters. Or maybe I'm just mental because of this stupid course. I HATED it, Fi. It was triple crap and I felt like such a big fat biffer.

We didn't have to sing, which was a blessing because I would have actually shat myself, right there in front of everyone. I was mute for most of the day so everyone probably thinks I'm arrogant. I got lost *every* time I went anywhere; it's a rabbit warren. And then I did a really noisy nervous poo in the toilet next door to this amazingly beautiful woman called Violet who is

79

going to be the star of the course and she and I will never be friends because she looks INCREDIBLE and I'm fatter than ever AND SHE HEARD ME POO.

There was a welcome talk in the theatre. It was awful. The man was saying, 'You only get to be a student here once, so don't waste the opportunity,' and other scary things. I mean, he was very nice, and he was obviously really excited for us, but I just . . .

Ah, it's pointless. People are there because they're going to be the best in the world. Fi, I don't *want* to be the best in the world. I don't want to 'make the most' of my time there because I don't want to be there at all. And then I feel even worse because everyone else is exploding out of their skin with pride at having got in.

Urgh.

My coursemates are a funny bunch. I expected them to be like the boarding-school kids we used to thrash at netball – what was that school called? Well, I thought they'd all be like that. WRONG. This Violet bird is super-posh and there's a few other proper aristos – Hector someone, who has this distinguished fifty-year-old's bouffant, in bright orange (he's actually thirty), a mega-rich Malaysian guy who went to Eton, and a couple of girls who look exactly the same and keep saying things like 'No *waaaay*.' But everyone else seemed quite normal. There's even one who's poorer than me. He's from Hungary and he's mental. Only twenty-three but he's a right little power rocket of a man. He's already married a repetitor (I think I've spelt this wrong. Basically, a pianist who accompanies people while they sing) AND got divorced and trained with some operatic legend. As I said, by the age of twenty-three. WTF?!

But get this – this bit is the absolute best – he WALKED ACROSS EUROPE to get to the college. From Hungary to Calais and then across to London! He had to walk because he lost most of his money in his divorce and then blew the remainder coming over for the auditions in February. I AM NOT JOKING! He even lost a fecking shoe in France! AND CARRIED ON WALKING! It's bonkers, Fi. You'd love it here.

Actually, writing all of this, I sort of hate it a little bit less. Maybe.

Anyway this Jan seems to want to be my friend, which is nice because everyone's fallen madly in love with him already, and there's also a really nice girl called Helen whose dad's a doctor; she stole a prescription off him and got herself some beta-blockers so she wouldn't die of fear in the first week! I like that. I might ask her for some myself – she seemed pretty chilled on them.

What's weird, though, is that everyone except me and Jan seemed to know each other, or know each other's singing teacher, or have done some stupid workshop together last year. It's like a knitting circle, Fi. Everyone knows everyone else's business. Don't like it.

Anyway. Back in on Wednesday when we watch a master-class with Julian Jefferson from America. He's well famous in the States and they've got him in to 'inspire' us although I can't see that happening for me. Wednesday's also my first singing lesson but I refuse to talk about that. Or think about it.

I am going to want to kill myself. Urgh. But I'm seizing the day. Wearily.

LOVE YOU but also HATE YOU Freckle,

Me

Xxxxxx

Scene Four

Two days later

When I arrived at college on Wednesday – my first full day – I was somehow lured into the building by the sound of bells from the Queen's Tower. I had been standing under the glass portico, considering another sprint back to the tube, when the most ethereally lovely chiming began and I somehow lost my mind. They weren't just crappy old 'It's now ten o'clock! Ho ho ho!' bells, they were pure music: rich, fat peals which made me think of *Brideshead Revisited* and transported me to Oxford University on a warm summer's evening in the 1920s. I became a willowy student wearing a boater and drinking port while the Christ Church bells chimed hazily in the distance.

By the time I remembered that I was a fat-bummed student wearing expensive new clothes that I wasn't sure I liked, standing outside a college on a snippy, rain-spitty sort of a day in central London, I'd somehow fooled myself into walking through the front door and had already navigated my way to the opera school.

I was cross with myself for having been lured in by a

load of stupid bells. I texted as much to my new friend Helen, she of the beta-blockers.

Glad you came back. Meet me in the dressing room, she replied.

I found my way down to the dressing room, which would apparently become my second home while at college. It was a fairly unprepossessing room: large, subterranean and rectangular with a long hanging rail for costumes and a lot of mirrors. But my fellow opera-school students had made it really quite jolly with photographs and good-luck cards, and the bulbs round the mirrors were sufficiently reminiscent of my safe world at the opera house to calm me a little. Dressing-tables ran around the walls; I'd been given one at the back by the fire exit.

Helen was not there yet. Nobody was there. I breathed in the smell of dressing room – surprisingly familiar – and felt my heart slow down a notch. If I could stay here, stay hidden in this womb-like –

'SALLY!' It was Violet Elphinstone. She was wearing extremely tight shiny jeans and a loose-fitting top with expensive leather sleeves. She was also wearing glasses, which made her look ready for action. Ready for work. Ready for sex.

You'll spot the stars of the school straight away, one of the opera singers at work had warned me. *They know they're the best. If you're lucky, they'll be nice. If not . . . Good luck.*

Violet Elphinstone knew very well that she was the star of the school. It would be impossible for a woman that attractive to be bad at anything.

'Hullow,' I heard myself say. During challenging times my Stourbridge accent was at its strongest.

Violet's face cracked open in a big film-star smile.

'Oooh, just love your accent,' she said chummily. 'It's *fab*. Where are you from again?'

I started to reply but was cut short by a heavy pounding on the fire door next to me. I stared at it uncertainly. A drug addict? A murderer? My panicked, fractured brain believed anything was possible.

'Open it, lovely,' Violet prompted, sitting down. 'It'll be one of the girls.' Violet had already been at the college for two years on the master's course and she knew how everything worked. On Monday she had laughed at me for sitting at a table in a corner of the canteen when, apparently, as a singer I must *never* sit *anywhere* other than the Singers' Table.

I duly opened the fire door and was immediately assaulted by loud screams and the thundering of boots. 'BABY!'

'VIOLET!'

'EEEEEEEK!'

'OH, MY GOD, I MISSED YOU!'

There was a sizeable scrum of hugging, squealing women with Violet at its centre, screeching merrily. I stood at the periphery, bewildered.

The scrum continued; it started jumping up and down. Helen arrived through the main door. 'Hi, ladies,' she said calmly.

It wouldn't have occurred to me to interrupt them. She must have been on the beta-blockers already.

The scrum began to fall apart. 'Hello!' one of the girls said warmly, dusting herself down and walking over to shake Helen's hand. 'I'm Ismene ... Are you Sally Howlett?'

'Hiya,' Helen said, shaking Ismene's hand. 'No, I'm Helen Quinn. That's Sally Howlett.' She pointed at me.

Ismene swung round. 'Oooh,' she said, eyes wide with excitement. 'Sally! I've been really excited about meeting you!'

I was surprised. Clearly Helen was, too, but her beta-blockered Calm Face registered amusement, not offence.

'Thanks, Ismene. Um, I've been excited about meeting you too?' I tried. I wasn't sure what was going on here.

Ismene laughed me off. 'Don't be silly. You're the big story,' she told me conspiratorially. 'Our big news. Apparently you're absolutely *AMAZING* and you've never had a lesson in your life! Is that true?'

Helen started to snigger. I decided I liked Helen quite a lot.

'Oh, that. Yes, it's true,' I said. 'Not one single lesson I'm afraid.' Helen had warned me on Monday that my training would be the first thing everyone would ask me about. *Where did you train, who with, what have you got coming up?*

But Ismene loved my response, for some reason. As did the other girls in the gaggle. 'OH, MY GOD!' gasped one. 'You're like ALFIE!' They told me about a now world-famous tenor who had arrived at the college with no training whatsoever, just several years' experience as a car mechanic and an incredible voice. Now he flew first class all over the world, performing in concerts for extraordinarily large fees, and had women throwing roses at him from the stalls.

I found the story of Alfie to be in no way reassuring.

'Alfie and I are *not* the same,' I stated, rather forcefully. It was embarrassing to identify myself as an imposter at the college but I knew that it was important to fool nobody. 'He might have an outstanding voice but I don't. Honestly. I'm mediocre and rusty and untrained.'

'How *fantastic* that they let you in without any training at all,' Violet said. She had detached herself slightly from the rest of the group and was watching me with a smile that I didn't like. 'Good on them for taking such a huge gamble!'

She said it with excessive enthusiasm but I detected precious little sincerity. She knew I was a fat-arsed pretender. She knew I didn't belong there.

But she was good. Oh, she was good. She was far too clever to try to freeze me out: instead she was going to *friend* me out.

'They must have loved you, Sally!' one of the other girls chipped in. 'I heard they were unanimous about you! How fantastic!'

I realized that, once detached from Violet, these girls were actually rather nice. Unlike her they all looked genuinely thrilled to meet me, and they wasted no time in telling me the story of my auditions, overlapping excitedly.

'Turned up to audition for the master's course in February . . .'

'. . . halfway through her second aria they stopped her . . .'

'. . . couldn't believe it! Apparently Hugo was speechless! Can you imagine Hugo speechless? How cool is that?'

'. . . told her to leave immediately and come back to audition for the opera school diploma instead . . .'

'. . . gave her a standing ovation . . .'

'. . . begged her to take the place! On the DIPLOMA!

86

Even Nicole didn't get a place on the diploma! They said the competition was the stiffest ever . . .'

'. . . and yet she . . .'

'. . . isn't it *amazing*?'

'. . . and now you're here!'

They stood, beaming at me, waiting for me to deny it.

I couldn't. It was all true. After weeks of intense inner battles once I'd returned from New York – full-scale warfare at times – I'd realized I had no option but to apply for the stupid course at the Royal College of Music. I had made a solemn promise to Fiona that I would, and even though it filled every cell of my body with terror – no, every last *atom* – I knew there was no alternative.

Brian, who started his job there soon after, was overjoyed. 'They'll snap you up,' he'd told me, offering unlimited coaching for the auditions. I declined. It would be an absolute waste of time: I wouldn't be able to breathe in a one-to-one lesson, let alone sing. My only hope was just to turn up with my favourite wardrobe arias, hoping I didn't have a seizure and die.

I'd been confused by the bewildering array of courses on offer but Brian had told me I'd be best off auditioning for the master's: I'd learn the basics there and it would feel far safer and easier than the college's professional diploma at the opera school.

But it had all gone wrong. I'd been auditioned by three (admittedly pleasant) singing teachers, only to be stopped, told that I sounded 'sublime' and ordered to come back in a month for the opera school auditions instead. 'But I'm not . . . *ready*,' I whispered, remembering what Brian had said.

'You're ready,' said Hugo, the head of the opera school. 'Mark my words. I don't know about you, ladies, but I feel this is a special moment.'

The 'ladies' had agreed. As had Fiona when I'd called her in New York. 'SPESHUL!' she'd yelled excitably, in a bad American accent. 'VERY COCKING SPESHUL, Sally! You have to go back!'

I'd come back four weeks later and had had to audition for a panel of different people, including Brian.

It had been painful beyond any description. My entire face was shaking so badly that they'd had to give me special exercises to halt the shaking. After three arias, during which I'd all but blacked out, I was given a round of applause and told that I had been sensational.

They were wrong. All of them. Probably desperate for another Alfie story, I thought. I would make a great PR stunt. I had a broad Midlands drawl and a total void where there should have been years of school concerts, weekend workshops and minor opera festivals. I had never studied foreign languages so at best I had the vague gist of the words I was singing. I didn't know those silly Italian musical terms either. I was a joke.

Which meant that, if the college had a secret admissions target for unknown-losers-come-good, I must be perfect. It probably also explained my two hefty scholarships, which covered all of my fees and a big chunk of my living expenses too.

'Of course you got two scholarships, you wonderful clever girl,' Fi had said, when I spoke to her. 'Sally, this is meant to be!'

I didn't agree.

'Honestly, I'm not a great singer. I think they were all mad,' I said to the girls in the dressing room. They laughed, told me not to be so modest and dispersed, pulling up chairs at their dressing-tables.

Helen, Violet and I were still standing. 'Fair play to you, Sally,' Helen said laconically. 'You've got balls. I mean, you told me you had no experience but I didn't realize you meant . . . well, *nothing*.'

Violet was smiling brightly. 'You're a brave little saus-age,' she said firmly.

Sausage?

'I mean, I'd be terrified in your shoes! So much to learn, so little time . . .' She shuddered in an affected show of respect for my bravery. 'By the way, Sally, are you going to put yourself forward for the TV audition?' she asked.

There was a new notice on the opera school board recruiting female sopranos. They needed a solo recording of the famous bit from *Prince Igor* for some TV advert – a 'fantastic opportunity' allegedly.

'No!' I laughed. I was determined to laugh when I was around Violet Elphinstone. It would be my armour. 'No, I have a part-time job. I'll be doing that for extra pennies.'

Violet raised an inquisitive eyebrow. 'I'm a deputy wardrobe mistress,' I said proudly. Just saying the words made me feel safer. 'Well, I'll be doing wardrobe assisting for now, because I can only do part-time hours . . . But, yeah, I work at the Royal Opera House. I've been there several years.'

'Oooh, so you were trying to get in through the back door?' she said conspiratorially. 'You sly bugger!'

I stiffened.

'I don't think so,' Helen said calmly. 'Didn't you just hear her story? She was dragged here kicking and screaming by the sound of it.' She gave a definitive nod, as if to say the subject was now closed, then pulled up her chair, patting the dressing-table delightedly. 'Yesss,' she whispered to herself, already oblivious to Violet. 'I'm here! At last!'

I definitely liked Helen. She was stout and cool and wore a battered leather jacket that, unlike Violet's, didn't look like it had cost two thousand pounds.

Violet laughed tinnily, not willing to be dismissed. 'Well, you must really love your wardrobe job. Literally *everyone* else here subsidizes their studies by doing singing gigs. But *good on you* for wanting to do something different.'

I looked at her warily. Really?

'You know, concerts, soirées, festivals, recordings . . . I suppose some of the less talented ones teach singing,' she added vaguely, to distinguish herself from them.

I wasn't just a fish out of water, I was a fish trying to live on Mars. It was hopeless.

I took a deep breath and sat down at my own dressing-table, trying to remember what I was doing.

Ah, procrastinating, that was it. My first singing lesson was in a few hours – directly after this stupid masterclass we all had to watch – and I'd come down here to try to get some beta-blockers.

'Any chance of some drugs?' I whispered to Helen, who was loading her locker with musical scores and libretti.

'Not a chance on earth,' she said spiritedly. 'You're obviously an operatic legend. As a lesser mortal I need them, Sally. I've only got enough to get me through the first couple of days. Hands off.'

'Arggh,' I said sadly. In desperation I tried to latch on to the conversation that Ismene and the others were having, rather than listen to my mad head. They were gossiping, it seemed, about a poo scandal.

'Oh, do tell,' I said timidly. 'I like a good poo scandal.'

Delighted, Ismene explained that there was a mystery pooer at large. 'We have our own bathroom,' she said, gesturing towards another door. 'It's our own private one, just for us girls in this dressing room. And someone has taken it upon themselves to leave a massive log there every morning. They're not even flushing it! It's DISGUSTING!'

The girls were giggling and tutting crossly.

And then Violet said – and I would probably remember this for the rest of my life – 'Oh, now, I think I know who that might be . . .' She gave a coy little laugh and looked at me. I waited, excited, hoping that this might be her attempt to draw me into the circle of friends.

And then she didn't say anything, but kept on smiling at me, and I realized that she was accusing me of being the mystery pooer. Because of that business on Monday when I'd done a terrified noisy one in the toilets upstairs while she was in the cubicle next to me.

She started to giggle. 'Anything you want to share, hon?'

Scene Five

As we filed into the Britten Theatre soon after, to watch the masterclass, I was still burning with shame. I was not the mystery pooer, of course, but the more strenuously I'd denied it, the redder I'd gone and the harder Violet had laughed. She had actually given me a show-hug and told me my secret was safe with the girls.

I was beaten already, and it wasn't yet lunchtime.

Hugo Dalton came onstage to offer us an enthusiastic welcome. 'And without further ado,' he said, 'it gives me great pleasure to introduce to you someone very special indeed. As I'm sure most of you will know, Julian Jefferson – one of the most exciting lyric tenors to emerge in the last ten years – graduated from our opera school back in 1997. We're incredibly excited to have him joining us as a vocal coach for this academic year and are thrilled that he's agreed to take our first masterclass of the term. For this man really is a master. Ladies and gentlemen, Julian Jefferson!'

What's the point in bringing a world-famous tenor here? I thought, clapping listlessly. I knew vaguely of Julian Jefferson, of course, although I'd never seen him in anything.

I don't want to watch a bloody international success. I want to watch someone who's as terrified of singing as I am.

I watched the back of Julian Jefferson heading for the stage and, sighing, committed to listening and learning. What else could I do? I got out a notebook and pen and took a proper look at him as he took his place downstage centre.

And my vision tunnelled slowly. The sound of the room compressed until there was just a soft ringing in my ears.

It was Julian. *My* Julian. With the same bizarre long-shiny-hair-and-ultra-smart-clothing combo that he'd worn when he turned up at my house on Sunday night.

He stood there on the stage, smiling and nodding at the raucous applause and cheers and, once again, time stood still.

Shock and confusion made my head soupy. He wasn't called Julian Jefferson. He was called Julian Bell! And he wasn't a *singer*! He lived in New York and worked on a stupid trendy newspaper called the *Brooklyn Beaver*!

And he had been my boyfriend. I had loved him so much I'd hardly been able to breathe with it.

My thoughts came slowly, like heavy waves with distorted sound. What did they mean, world-famous tenor? I tried to pull off the ring on my finger but it was stuck. Everything was stuck.

The applause continued.

Like a drunk trying to string a sentence together, I tried to search for any clues from New York.

At first, nothing came. Our relationship had ended a year ago when I'd fled the city and the ensuing pain had

93

been so black that vast sections of my New York memory bank had been deleted, like corrupted computer files.

But then a few smudged scenes curled up like smoke: Raúl telling me, at the first-class bar on the Delta flight, about his opera-singing friend who'd 'wasted his talents'.

And then Julian and I, a heap of limbs on his bed one summer morning. The sound of a neighbour singing drifting in on the warm breeze, and Julian saying – what? Something about singing being a favourite hobby of his?

No, I thought angrily. *None of these was enough! This isn't real! He isn't an opera singer! He just ISN'T!* The Julian I'd fallen in love with had been the scruffiest, sleepiest, most forgetful, bumbly, shambly man on earth. He'd worn dog-hair-covered jumpers and constantly missed editorial deadlines and lost his mobile phone every five minutes. He always had bad overgrown hair because he never remembered to get it cut; moreover he had *fluffy* hair because he never remembered to use hair gloop and he was no more likely to own smart suits than – than, well, *me*. He was lovably useless! A scruffball! A big handsome bear!

Not this. Never this.

But as Smart, Snappy-suit Julian smiled and bowed to the continuing applause, I was punched in the stomach by another memory. The evening we'd met, and that spontaneous song, and how good Julian had sounded.

Oh, God, oh, God. I gulped for air. Julian Bell was not Julian Bell at all. He was a famous tenor called Julian Jefferson, and I'd never had even the faintest idea.

How? How had I not recognized him? I scrabbled dementedly for an explanation. Of course I was aware of Julian

Jefferson; everyone was. But had I ever seen him perform live? Actually, no. Had I seen him on telly? Maybe. I couldn't remember. But even if I had, he'd have been wearing a full wig and beard and God only knew what else. AND HE WOULD HAVE BEEN CALLED JULIAN JEFFERSON.

I gripped the armrests on either side of my seat, fearing a blackout. Two faces, moonlike and hissing, turned towards me.

After a febrile pause I realized they were whispering to me. It was Helen and Jan, my two new friends. I couldn't hear them. I found myself staring vacantly at the stage as Julian raised his hands to bring an end to the clapping. He was nervous. And being able to see that – to read him so effortlessly, after all this time – was frightening. Nobody else in this room would spot it – the slightly flatter smile, the hand jammed in a pocket, the slight twitch of an eye – but I had once loved Julian Bell so very much that I knew every movement in his physical repertoire.

Yet I now hated him so completely that I felt bile in my throat just looking at him. He'd destroyed me. Destroyed my family. Blacked out every patch of colour that had begun to flourish in my life.

'ARE YOU OK?' Jan hissed. He was gripping my hand and staring at me with a filmic intensity that begged for shafts of moonlight and a howling wolf. 'DO YOU NEED MEDICAL ASSISTANCE?' His face looked as furious as ever.

His features swam slowly into focus. I didn't know why, but I smiled and shook my head, mumbling something about a dodgy cheese sandwich. What else could I do?

Then I turned to Helen, who was watching me with some alarm, and whispered, grinning frighteningly, 'You see that man on stage? Julian? I used to go out with him. Can I have some beta-blockers now, please?'

Helen gaped. 'Piss OFF! Are you for real?! *Julian crapping JEFFERSON?*'

'I'm for real.' I smiled, teetering on the brink of something dreadful. 'Can I have some drugs?'

Helen said no, but offered me a Chewit. 'I'm sorry, I just don't believe you, Sally. The whole *world* wanted to sleep with Julian Jefferson. You're delirious.'

Then Julian opened his mouth, thanked the room and introduced himself, even though there was apparently no need. '. . . And as some of you may know I recently had to take a long break from singing. So it gives me great pleasure to be starting here as a coach, not least because . . .' His voice sliced me into limp shreds. I couldn't focus on more than a few sentences.

'WHAT IS HAPPENING?' Jan Borsos hissed. 'WILL YOU BE DYING IN THIS MOMENT?'

'My singer today is a rising star of the opera school,' Julian was gushing. 'And I'm really thrilled to be working with her. Ladies and gents, Violet Elphinstone.'

Of course he kissed her cheek, then withdrew behind the piano, smiling encouragingly as she told us what piece she had chosen to work on today.

I hadn't known he played the piano.

Violet loosened her shoulders in a very unnecessary and self-conscious way, smiling confidently at Julian. But his eyes were scouring the auditorium. They found and locked on mine and time stood still.

After a pause as tiny as it was catastrophic, Julian smiled and shrugged apologetically – a tiny gesture, visible only to me – as if to say, '*This* was what I was trying to tell you . . .' I felt silver darts impinge on my vision and the tunnelling became acute.

Then Helen whispered, 'Holy mother of shite, you're telling the truth! He just smiled at you!'

I gave up and fainted in my chair.

ACT THREE

Scene Three

June 2011, a little over a year earlier, New York

New York was like a blow to the head.

Sirens, dry heat, neck-craning wonder. DON'T WALK in red, the 6 Train in green, taxis in yellow. A mesmerizing cross-stream of feet and wheels; subway trains rumbling below, planes whining above. Delivery boys darting through the crowds with their brown-paper bags and steaming cartons. The steam vents, the beeping, the echoing sirens. At every corner a new, breathtaking view sliding into focus; another scene stolen straight from a film set.

Nobody wasted time sitting still. Men sipped sexy energy drinks and conducted phone conferences while they traversed the streets; women drew up sugar-free vats of Frappuccino through straws and typed furiously on their BlackBerrys. The city wore sunglasses, wispy dresses, sweaty suits. It was boiling hot or crisply air-conditioned. It was fired, wired, smartly attired.

Every day I emerged from our hotel into the electric glow of Times Square and quaked in wonder as if I was seeing it for the first time. How could a city like this have risen from marshy wasteland? How was such an outrageous tessellation of humanity possible on a daily basis? And how was it that so many people wished me a great day and seemed actually to *mean* it?

'You're *certainly* welcome!' they trilled, when I thanked them for being so nice. No amount of suspicious staring on my part persuaded them to drop the smiles.

'They actually *care*,' I breathed to Bea. 'They actually care if I'm having a good day!'

'Of course they do not.' She laughed. 'They do the smiling and the cordiality as easily as you English do the angry and the awkward. But they do not mean it.'

'They bloody well do,' Barry interrupted. 'THEY ARE THE NICEST PEOPLE ON EARTH AND I SWEAR THAT BY MY HAT.'

He was not wearing a hat but he looked very ferocious, so nobody questioned him.

If I was in awe of New York I was literally dumbfounded by the Lincoln Center, home to the Metropolitan Opera House and now the Royal Ballet for the next two weeks. The wardrobe department alone was bigger than my parents' council estate but ten times more welcoming. I felt comfortable the moment I walked in there.

The wardrobe staff were mad and friendly and they owned two cheeky little rats that had been part of a previous production. They treated me and the other Royal Opera House wardrobe girls like old friends; they took us out for cocktails in Chelsea, to gay piano bars in Greenwich, to secret restaurants in the East Village. Bea received an equally warm welcome from the Met's wigs people, and the dancers were given carpeted dressing rooms with chaises longues. *Everyone* was happy. Especially the audiences, who gave standing ovations for *The Rite of Spring*.

I loved those first two weeks. They were like starting my life again. Being born aged twenty-eight into a noisy, intoxicating, beautiful world where things just didn't seem to matter so much. One morning I actually caught myself skipping like some oversized lamb along the 'sidewalk'. It was not typical Sally Howlett behaviour and I couldn't have given a flying arse.

I discovered early on that Fiona was seeing someone. She claimed to be very happy but the whole thing made me nervous.

'Oh, it's that guy from the plane,' she said off-handedly. It was coming towards the end of our first week in New York, and Barry, Fiona and I had just had dinner at Café Select in SoHo. Fi, having picked at her delicious potato *rösti*, had just airily announced that she was off to see a man about a shag.

'Raúl, remember? At the on-board bar? We exchanged numbers. He's really interesting, actually. He lives in *Brooklyn*.' She waited for us to express admiration, even though none of us had ever been to Brooklyn.

'Shut up, you knobber,' Barry interjected calmly. 'Fiona, I'm from Barry Island. And she's from Stourbridge. Why, I ask you, would we know *anythin'* about Brooklyn? Do you know what I'm sayin' here, babe?'

Barry had always been good at plucking Fiona out of whatever lofty fantasy she was floating on and depositing her rudely back in the present.

'Ah, shut up yourself,' she replied warmly. 'Well,

Brooklyn,' she mused, taking a chug of her Manhattan. (We'd been unable to resist.) 'Well, it's . . . it's cool and interesting and alternative.'

Barry snorted. We both knew that someone else had put these words into Fiona's mouth. 'Lots of . . . um, vintage shops and cultural initiatives,' she continued. Barry was now openly laughing. 'Raúl went halves with a friend on a derelict warehouse, about fifteen years ago, and he lives on the top floor and rents the rest out for a fortune. I think some of his tenants are artists. Oh, shut *up*, Barry.' She fiddled with her hair self-consciously.

'Sorry, girl,' Barry said, clearly not meaning it. Fiona patted his hand, forgiving him without a moment's hesitation. Like me, she let Barry get away with basically anything. 'You're just jealous that you stayed in economy class and didn't get to pull fit blokes at the bar like me.'

Barry started to say something about Fiona hitting on dark times if she thought that snogging a twat on a plane was something to be jealous of, but I interrupted. She could only be pushed so far. 'Well, as long as you're happy,' I said firmly.

She looked grateful. 'Thanks, Sally.'

Then something tricky started to take shape in her face. 'Um,' she began. 'Sally, I want to talk to you about something. I . . .'

I blanched. Please, no trouble. I was enjoying myself so much . . .

'Actually, Bazzer, can you give us some privacy?' she asked, after a meaty pause.

Barry laughed out loud and said lots of things like 'What next?' and 'Priceless.' He kissed us both on the cheek and said it was time for bed. 'See you tomorrow, you weird family of weird people from a weird part of England.'

'Night, you Welsh wazzock,' I replied.

Fiona smiled faintly and composed herself. 'I've been wanting for a few weeks to say sorry to you,' she began carefully. 'For . . . well . . . for being a nightmare. I know I've been even worse in the last year. I'm sorry, Sally, I really am.'

I was too surprised to speak, so I finished my Manhattan and signalled to the waitress for another. Fiona usually apologized quickly for her indiscretions but had never, in her whole life, acknowledged how difficult she was to live with.

This would be a good time to get honest. To tell her that I *was* tired of the way she behaved; that I was fed up of having to be responsible for her. And that actually, yes, she *had* been more difficult than ever. The drinking had worsened and it had been a dreadful shock to find her with a bloody silver straw up her nose.

But she knew. 'I know,' she said quietly, before I was able to say a word. 'I really do know. I see what I do to you and I detest myself for it. I'm just a bit mental, you see. Ha, ha. You know. Abandonment issues. Tragic orphan stuff.'

We both smiled tiredly; I was on the edge of tears. My heart ached for Fiona, all the loss and loneliness in her life, yet I knew I was approaching the end of my capabilities as her carer. I couldn't do it any more. I needed to focus on *me* and my life. New York had infused me with an energy and bravery I hadn't known I had; I wanted to invest in that little spark. I wanted to nurture and grow it.

Not run round after Fiona, her unpaid bills and neurotic outbursts.

'I'm not sure I want to be your mum any more,' I heard myself say. My voice was full of nervous splinters but it held. 'I worry about you so much I feel sick at times.'

There was a long silence. She looked upset but I didn't crumble. I had a duty to myself that I'd been neglecting for a long time.

'I just want to be your friend. Your cousin,' I told her.

She nodded, processing this. 'God,' she muttered. 'I really am awful.'

A further silence.

'You do know that it's all because I hate myself?' she asked.

I winced painfully. I didn't want to hear this, largely because I couldn't bear it.

'Difficult, arrogant people,' she continued, 'like me, they always hate themselves. Deep down.'

'You shouldn't hate yourself,' I muttered. She looked so lost and tiny. 'You really have nothing to hate. Look at you, Freckle. You're beautiful. You're funny. Clever. And you're a mesmerizing, glorious ballet dancer. Aunty Mandy would have been so proud to see you on this stage. She . . .' I ran out of words. The sadness and injustice of Fiona's circumstances were as raw now as they had been twenty-one years ago.

Aunty Mandy *would* have burst with pride seeing her daughter dancing at the Metropolitan Opera House. She'd have been yodelling in her seat at the curtain call. Unlike Mum, who would have refused to come to New York in the first place.

Tears stood in Fi's eyes and she nodded, perhaps seeing the same image of her mother cheering and whooping. Seeing her cry set me off and for a few minutes we sat in silence, tears coursing down our two very different faces. But while our grief might have been painted in different colours, it came from the same place. Now, as ever, we were more like twins than cousins.

Our drinks arrived.

Fi pushed her cocktail away. 'I'm stopping drinking for good,' she said, wiping at the lacy patterns of mascara on her cheeks. 'I'm getting it all under control now. That's what I wanted to tell you. Since meeting Raúl I've realized I don't need booze or diets and I certainly don't need drugs. I'm ready to be a grown-up!'

And, as usual, I believed her. Raúl had cured everything. Of course he had.

Scene Four

New York, Boston, Philadelphia, Washington

Our two weeks in Manhattan were the happiest of my life. When we travelled north to Boston I tried to write in my diary but just drew a massive, goon-like smiley face. Then I drew a big knob on it because I knew I was being a big knob and I couldn't have cared less.

After Boston we headed south to Philadelphia and finally Washington. The taxi journeys from the airport into each city were identical, regardless of where we were. Huge green metal plates suspended above the highways announced turnpikes and beltways and Interstates with giant, iconic American trucks thundering underneath them. For no obvious reason, I loved even the road signs.

And for even less obvious reasons I loved and couldn't stop photographing those illuminated signs that thrust up into the darkening sky – Denny's, Wendy's, IHOP, Duane Reade – announcing our arrival in every single city.

I also found American hotels very comforting. There was always someone wanting to help you, always more food than anyone could eat, always a laundered towel and a blackout blind and a huge wardrobe in which to sing. I felt strangely calmed by the sterile chatter of infomercials on the hotel TVs, and the hum of aircon frequently sent me to sleep even when I was wired after a mad performance. It was such a scintillating time, brimming with excitement and newness, yet it was marked by anonymous, silent bedrooms. Another American paradox of which I was very fond.

Fiona was a different woman. I couldn't tell if it was the excitement of the tour or the gradual unfolding of her relationship with Raúl but, to my astonishment, she remained true to her word. Each day she got up, warmed up properly, like the others, arrived in time for rehearsals and performances and occasionally even ate proper meals. She seemed quite genuinely to have stopped drinking, which was a miracle on an unprecedented scale. In a tiny fish restaurant in the North End in Boston, Bea, Barry, Fiona and I shared our childhood dreams, and Fiona said, simply, 'I just wanted to be like Sally,' and everyone had a bit of a cry until Bea ordered another carafe of blood-red wine and told us all to shut up.

I didn't stop worrying about her, of course. I'd never stop worrying about her. I felt uncomfortable that she spent so much time on the phone with Raúl, and her intense chattiness, even early in the morning, was plain weird. I was used to her being hung-over and sullen. One night she and Bea went out dancing and didn't get back until five a.m. Even though Fiona was still full of energy when she returned I could tell from her breath that she hadn't been drinking. I had no idea how she'd managed it but I wasn't about to start interfering.

She was still late and chaotic, at times, and every now and then would become horribly irritable only to disappear off on her own for a while and come back happy. Barry and I decided she had taken up meditation.

Barry had a fling in Philadelphia with a civil engineer called Richard, who was extremely nice and funny and whom I strongly wanted Barry to marry. Barry was more practical. 'Chicken, I didn't come here to find me no husband,' he said sternly. 'I came here to express myself using the medium of dance. Richard and I had a beautiful time and now it's over. I'm not gonna lie, he was a fine specimen of a man, but we live on different shores, Chicken. Different shores.'

I had no romance whatsoever.

I found men and relationships very complicated. Deep down I suspected that I was scared of the whole thing, that if I were to embark on anything serious it would generate feelings larger than Sally Howlett could handle. So I typically went for men with whom I had (a) fun and (b) absolutely no connection. Sure, we had to get on, but I'd never had even a whiff of that other-worldly thing that Fiona claimed to be developing with Raúl.

That sort of connection would be available only with a man I felt to be truly sublime, and the men I felt to be truly sublime were way out of my league. I knew I was nice enough, but I wasn't special. I'd never be special.

So nothing happened on our tour. I concentrated on work and exploring the east coast and enjoying Fiona's new, improved, drink-free behaviour. I put Brian's letter and the whole singing thing out of my mind and felt safe and happy.

A few months later, once Julian had exploded

into – and then out of – my life, and I had gone back to England with the wreckage hanging stone-like around my neck, I would look at my photos of those sunny weeks and wonder what had happened to that carefree girl.

The ballet tour drew to a close in August, and as it did, I became aware of an odd sensation every time I thought about New York. There was something a bit broken and crunchy in my chest when I remembered my fortnight there; something that needed attention.

The sensation became a feeling, and the feeling became a thought: I had unfinished business in New York.

What? Maybe it was just that I needed to eat some more of that amazing French toast in the Noho Star; maybe not. What *was* clear was that the pull of New York was muscling up every day. *Don't go back home. You were happy in New York. Stay. Stay longer. It's important. Really important.*

So when the Metropolitan Opera's wardrobe mistress emailed me out of the blue asking if I'd be interested in a four-week sickness cover job on their new production of *Turandot*, I just said yes. Even though I had no visa and would have to do it as an unpaid intern. Even though I had no idea where to live. Even though Mum was stoutly silent when I told her on the phone.

Three days later, in mid-August, I waved goodbye to the Royal Ballet at Washington Dulles International Airport and took the train back up to New York.

On my first morning before work I went to SoHo for a bagel and sat in the sun, watching kids shooting hoops in Thomson Street playground. And I knew, with absolute certainty, that I was in the right place. New York had brought me back for some reason and I was listening.

Scene Five

New York

I settled in quickly to my job at the Met. Being there the second time round did nothing to lessen the fantastical scale of the place. It was, simply, awe-inspiring. Even down in the bowels of the building, far below the stage, where unseen machines hummed and men did technical things in workshops that I couldn't have hoped to under-stand, I found it ridiculously exciting. When I wasn't on duty I would stand quietly in the corner of a subterranean rehearsal room or sit in the auditorium during a set changeover, watching with wonder as upwards of two hundred people hammered, screwed and unscrewed, lifted, shouted, abseiled, adjusted; a factory of humanity assembling the next stage set in bafflingly few hours.

Turandot was an epic production, and although my role was minor, I was working at full steam. Tiredness didn't register. I was high on New York. 'YEAH!' I shouted at myself in the mirror each morning, and I wasn't even being ironic.

The very best thing about my return to the city was that

my friends had come too. All three had been so jealous of my month-long extension that they'd found ways of doing the same. Fiona and Barry weren't needed in rehearsals for a little while and Bea had decided to take another month off because she was Bea and nobody messed with her.

On Fiona's absolute insistence, we rented a vast warehouse conversion in Raúl's building on the north edge of McCarren Park, Brooklyn, somewhere between Williamsburg and Greenpoint. 'Cool people live in that area,' she told us, without any irony. We grimaced. 'And Raúl owns the building. He's renting the apartment to us for almost nothing.' We stopped grimacing.

Barry and I didn't much care where we lived as long as it was affordable, which Manhattan was not. Bea, of course, was disgusted at the idea of living in Brooklyn but came round quickly when, on visiting it, she bumped into an ex-conquest in the entrance lobby. He had recently moved over from Chelsea. 'He is worth millions.' She sniffed. 'If Brooklyn is good enough for him, it is good enough for Beatriz Maria Stefanini.'

The apartment was sensational. The 'central space' (as Fiona called it) was big enough for her and Barry to perform complex ballets and there still be enough room for me to have a nice cup of tea on the massive horseshoe-shaped sofa in the centre of the floor. Plus space for Bea to hold wine tastings with her old shag from upstairs and Raúl to prance around singing old Branchlines hits. Which was what, on more than one occasion, we were all to be found doing. We had privately agreed that it would be wise to have Raúl nearby: his Fi-calming properties were too useful to be overlooked.

We were on the ground floor so our views were of a jungly courtyard. Bea's ex-shag (who had quickly become her current shag) was two floors above us and his view was a lot more exciting; from there you could see quite a bit of Manhattan. But the very best view was from Raúl's apartment, which was on the fifth floor. From there, Fiona told us, you could see for miles in each direction along the East River and across to the most iconic buildings in New York.

It was indeed a cool area, in a slightly twatty sort of way. The men just loved to team their big bushy beards with tiny little ironic ponytails and tight, knee-length shorts. I found them hilarious and appalling. So did Barry. Bea probably couldn't even see them, they were so far under her radar, but Fiona thought they were all extremely trendy and aspirational.

'Raúl's just so cool!' she gushed one day. 'I'm learning so much about fashion and stuff, he's really changing my perspective!'

'Fiona,' Barry interrupted loudly, 'you sound like a twat. Pull yourself together, girl. You're from Stourbridge.'

Fiona giggled. 'Actually, I was going to go vintage shopping. You know there's loads of it round here? Raúl said he might take me to some warehouses out past Bushwick where they have LOADS more stuff. I mean, I don't want to wear smelly old eighties stuff but who's to say I wouldn't find a rare Vivienne Westwood? It could be AMAZING, don't you –'

Barry interrupted: 'Fiona, will you slow down? And maybe lower the volume of your voice? We're only over here.'

'Agreed, my darling,' Bea said sweetly, from her table. A Brazilian man had come in to massage her. 'Relax.'

'Oh, my God, guys, I was just saying . . . Chill out, yeah?'

'I think that's what we were advising *you* to do, my cupcake,' Barry replied. 'Seriously, let go of this vintage shit already, know what I mean?'

Fiona shrugged haughtily as if we were all dicks, then jumped up and started marking out some ballet on the floor while texting someone and fiddling with her hair. It was odd to see her up and active all the time, not slumped around being moody.

I carried on with my work, keeping an eye on her. It was Saturday and I had the afternoon off, but to save time next week I'd brought home a beautiful Oriental gown that needed some work.

'So, guys,' Fiona burst out, breaking the silence, 'on the subject of being a bit of a tosser . . .'

She took a deep, self-conscious breath. Barry put down his crossword eagerly.

'Raúl wants us all to come out tonight, to this bar in the East Village. It's, um, a poetry slam,' she added bravely.

'I'm sorry,' Bea murmured, to the Brazilian masseur. 'Please excuse me.' She got up, naked, and walked over to where Fiona was sitting, hands on hips.

'Fiona, my darling, did you just invite us to a poetry slam?'

Barry hopped up and handed Bea her Chanel robe. She wasn't very good at wearing clothes and often needed reminding. 'Put it away, babe, right?' he whispered. Then he, too, turned to Fiona and crossed his arms. 'Are you for real, my friend?' he asked her. 'Or did you just make an error? I think you made an error.'

Unable to help myself, I was giggling. Only a few weeks before, Fiona would have been furious, but today's Fiona glanced at me, then started giggling hysterically.

'Oh dear, I know, I know! But Raúl's got together with his oldest school friends tonight, cos one of them's got the anniversary of his wife's death, and they're like *artists* and *philosophers* and stuff and they really want to go to this poetry café . . . Raúl doesn't want to go either but he loves them. And I love him. And if you love me, you'll come . . . *Please?*'

'Oh, my days,' Barry muttered dazedly, taking off his glasses and polishing them on his T-shirt. 'Oh, my days.'

But I'd already forgotten about the poetry café. 'Freckle, did you just say that you *love* him?' I put my sewing to one side.

Fiona blushed. 'Maybe.' She grinned.

There was a pause. All eyes were on her.

Bea put her hands on her hips, forcing open her poorly tied robe.

'PUT YOUR MUFF AWAY,' Barry shouted ferociously. 'Sorry about her,' he mouthed to the Brazilian masseur, who shrugged. He was a lot more interested in Barry than in Bea's manicured muff.

'Well?' Bea said, tying up her robe. 'Is this true? You love this strange bohemian man? With his widowed friends and poetry? Hmm?'

Fiona fiddled embarrassedly with the button of her shorts. 'Yes,' she whispered, with a nervous giggle. 'I reckon so. I think it's really serious. Like, I've *never* felt this way before, we just *get* each other, he's so amazing, he really is one in a million, so lovely and gorgeous, and he's mad about me too . . . I . . . ARGGH!'

'Champagne,' roared the Brazilian masseur, marching over to our gigantic fridge. He had been massaging Bea for a week now; he knew how she rolled. Sure enough, three bottles of Dom Pérignon were chilling inside.

'*Preziosa!*' Bea cried expansively. 'I am happy for you! Of course we will come to your poetry café then! *Santé!*'

Barry looked a bit put out. 'Now hang on a minute,' he began. 'I mean, I'm happy for her an' all that but, seriously, did you not hear what the girl said? She wants us to go to a poetry slam! Do any of you actually know what a poetry slam *is*?'

'Do *you*, pumpkin?' Bea asked him, popping the champagne cork.

'Well, not strictly, but –'

'Then be quiet,' Bea said graciously. 'We go to the poetry café. We listen to some poems. We give the couple a blessing. And I tell Raúl that if he upsets our little girl I will make mincemeat with his penis.'

Fiona laughed nervously. 'He's very lovely,' she pleaded. 'I really don't think that you'll –'

'Ignore her.' I got up to give her a hug. 'We won't let her anywhere near his penis. I'm really happy for you, Freckle!'

And I was.

Fiona, who should have been tired because she'd been up all night, exploded into a mad dance, chattering at Barry, who was squarely ignoring her. After a while Bea joined in and I watched them curiously, wondering what I needed to do to get that much energy into me on a sleepy Saturday afternoon.

Because I had a bit of a hangover and had been mostly useless all day, I stayed behind after they'd gone to the East Village so I could finish off my Oriental gown. It was gone eight now and darkness brushed our jungly court-yard with soft fingers. The nights were getting shorter and cooler, after a sweltering summer, and I found myself looking for a cardigan for the first time in weeks.

As I sewed, I pondered Fiona's news. Certainly, Raúl seemed like a nice chap. He was a bit too concerned with cool things but, really, he could have been a hell of a lot worse. Earlier that day I'd been waiting for Barry in Bagel-smith when a man in hi-tops, eighties satin running shorts and a string vest had walked in. He'd been wearing a sun visor and flying goggles and was definitely not on his way to a fancy-dress party. (I knew that because Barry had asked him.) Raúl was not even a tenth as bad. In fact, if I hadn't looked him up on the internet I'd never have believed he was in a band. He seemed to spend most of his time playing Angry Birds on his phone or taking Fi on lovely dates. The Ferrero Rocher behaviour on the plane must have been nerves.

And he definitely liked her. A lot. He called her all the time and even when they (occasionally) decided to 'have a night apart' he inevitably cracked and came down to our apartment. He held her hand in public and called her Freckle, which I liked. He also seemed to buy her a lot of things, and she was letting him, which was unlike her. Fiona was crap with money but infuriatingly proud.

And best of all was the effect that Raúl seemed to be having on Fiona's drinking. I hadn't seen her so much as sip a beer and she mostly seemed to have a lot more energy. And far greater interest in talking to us. She still flew off the handle but forgot about it more quickly. Generally, she was a lot better to be around.

I stabbed my thumb with a needle and swore into the darkness. How had it become almost pitch black without my noticing? I reached over and switched on one of the industrial steel Anglepoises that were dotted round the apartment. Nothing happened. I got up and switched on the main light. Nothing happened.

'Oh,' I said, to a dark room. 'We have a power cut. A power *outage*,' I added, in my very bad American accent.

I considered abandoning my Oriental gown and going out to find the others, but remembered I was wearing a nightie and a cardigan and had not yet washed my hair. A poetry café, I reflected, was quite likely to contain people with similar issues, but my unwashed hair had the added disadvantage of smelling of smoke and beer after an alfresco pizza-binge at Roberta's in Bushwick last night.

I set about trying to find a torch in the 'utility' cupboard but found nothing.

Oi! Where are you? Come come come! NOWWWWW! XX, Fi texted me. Dammit. I wanted to be there for her tonight.

I fumbled my way out to the corridor to see if the *power outage* was everywhere. It was. Although there was light on the top floor where Raúl lived. Flickering light. It looked like someone had left a candle outside his door.

Artists. *Weirdos*. Why on earth did they need to leave a candle lit in the hallway when they'd gone out drinking and poeming?

I ran up the stairs to borrow it for a few minutes.

It was in a long glass tube and actually looked rather lovely on the big industrial landing, casting soft shadows from the banisters on to chipped, whitewashed brickwork. Whoever had left it out had circled it with stones. *Those artists aren't all so bad*, I conceded generously, nicking the glass tube. Then I paused. Here was I, mocking artists, while simultaneously stealing their candle?

I should at least *check* that no one was still there.

'Um, hello?' I called, knocking gingerly at the door. Knowing my luck, the mad artist who was dealing with the anniversary of his wife's death would be inside, chanting woefully and doing naked interpretative movement on the subject of loss.

'Hello?' called a man's voice.

I froze. 'Oh, sorry,' I replied. 'I was just stealing your –'

The door opened.

'– candle,' I finished guiltily, holding it out in front of me. I started to babble: 'I mean, I wasn't *stealing* it, I was borrowing it because my hair smells and I'm trying to go and meet the others in the café, and – Hang on, why aren't you with them?'

The man at the door was almost certainly an artist. There were no fisherman's pants or bandannas or anything, but his T-shirt was on inside out and back to front and his flies were undone. Plus his hair was only just the right side of monster. In spite of all those things he was very nice-looking.

'Um, what?' he said, after a pause. '*What* was all of that you just said?'

He had the strangest accent I'd ever heard. He was also amused.

I put the candle back on the floor. My face and neck were scalding with embarrassment.

I straightened up and faced him. *Always own up when you've done something wrong*, Mum used to say. *Don't you wait one minute longer, Sally! Do you understand?*

I cleared my throat. 'What I said was, I was borrowing your candle and I apologize.' I paused. 'Except I wasn't borrowing it, I was stealing it, really, because knocking on the door was an afterthought.'

The man leaned against the doorframe, trying not to smile. 'Go on,' he said.

I gulped. 'So, I'm very sorry about that. I'm not a thief. I've never stolen anything in my life. Except my brother Dennis's He-Man, and I only stole that because it needed mending and Dennis wouldn't let it go . . .' I trailed off as the man raised an eyebrow. What in the name of God was I saying?

He put his hands into his pockets, waiting for me to continue. *He's trying not to laugh at me*, I thought miserably.

'Then I explained that the reason I needed a candle was that I wanted to wash and change because, well, I need to.'

'Is that exactly what you said? I thought there was something about smelly hair.'

Something inside me began to die. 'Oh. Um, yes. I said I have smelly hair. And then I asked why you weren't at the café with the others.' I hung my head. 'It wasn't my best greeting. I'm sorry. I'll leave you alone now. Apologies for everything.'

For a minute, the man said nothing. Then he started to shake. And then it exploded out of him, a great tidal wave of laughter. He laughed and laughed, eventually bending double. 'Please,' he howled, 'please don't go! Come in! Come in this minute! I want to talk to you some more!'

Where was he from? He sounded as if his mother was an upper-class Manhattanite and his father was a shaggy old pony from Devon. Actually, that fitted the bill lookswise, too.

'Oh, no, I won't come in, I've already bothered you enough . . .' I shifted from one foot to the other.

The man began to recover, although he was still getting giggly shockwaves. 'OK. But what are you going to do about your smelly hair? You're still going out, aren't you?'

I was keenly aware of not wanting him to know about my smelly hair. He watched me, all the time trying to do up the strap of his watch, which was partly held together with gaffer tape.

'I wish I hadn't said about the smelly hair,' I blurted. 'I don't normally have smelly hair . . . We were sitting outside last night and everyone was smoking, that's why.'

'It was the most charming opening line I've ever heard.'

'I've got better ones.'

'Really? Tell me some. I can't imagine a better opener than "I'm stealing your candle, my hair smells, and WHY AREN'T YOU OUT WITH EVERYONE ELSE?"'

'If you heard me the first time, why did you make me repeat it?' I asked.

I had a dim awareness that this was called banter. It was not something I knew well but it was actually quite fun. And now the initial embarrassment had worn off I didn't feel at all scared, like I normally did with gorgeous men.

Hmm. Yes. Gorgeous. He was *really* gorgeous. Even more so than I'd thought ten seconds ago, in spite of the hair (which, I noticed, was not just mad but also very fluffy). I should probably leave soon. Handsome men were not my area of expertise.

'I asked you to repeat it because it was quite brilliant,' he said. 'Oh, crap.' His watch fell to the floor.

'Would you like a hand?' I asked. 'You're not having much luck with that.' I was keen to distract attention from myself. The man held his wrist out. It was a nice wrist. A warm, smooth wrist. I did up the watch and realized I had to go: I was beginning to fancy him. 'Sorry about everything and goodbye,' I said firmly. 'I'll maybe see you at the poetry café.'

The man's brow was furrowed. He folded his arms across his chest, ignoring my farewell. 'I'm sorry.' He tried not to smile but failed. 'I'm sorry . . . But where the fuck are you *from*? Your accent is crazy!'

'Pot and kettle! You sound like one of those American chat-show hostesses mated with a shaggy old farmhand and gave birth to you!'

At this the man folded himself in half again and roared. I tried not to join in but it was hopeless. My accent *was* ridiculous. And his was even worse. We both roared, him with his fluffy hair, me with my smelly hair, a candle flickering between us. I had no idea what was going on but I felt radiantly, bubblingly good.

Eventually, we recovered and he asked me where I was from. 'Oh. Stourbridge in England. It's in the Black Country-ish, southernmost corner, sort of near Birmingham but –'

'I know where Stourbridge is,' he said.

'Wow! Nobody knows where Stourbridge is. Especially not Americans!'

'I grew up in Devon,' he said, to my great surprise. 'My mom's American and I spent years here in Brooklyn. But my dad's a . . . what did you say? A shaggy old farmhand? He has a farm in the Teign valley. Where I grew up. That's why I sound so crazy.'

'Oh! Well, I was only joking about your accent . . . But it was a good guess . . .' I really did have to leave now. The man and I shared unusual accents but probably nothing else.

'Julian,' he said, shoving out his hand as I turned to go.

I took it. 'Julian what? I'm Sally.' I held his hand for a fraction of a second longer than necessary, looking him in the eye. What was wrong with me? I was as bold as a badger tonight!

He paused before answering. I wasn't entirely surprised: he absolutely looked like the sort who'd forget his surname. 'Um, Julian Bell,' he replied eventually. 'Do you want to come in? Please come in.'

I squinted at him through the gloom, wondering if he was one of those types who looked normal but was in fact preparing to bundle me into a sink and pickle me in vinegar.

'Sure,' I heard myself say. I moved past him and strode inside, wondering what on earth I was up to. My body had done this without any prior consultation with my brain.

The room was full of candles. The man, Julian Bell, shut the door behind me.

ACT FOUR

Scene Six

London, September 2012

From: Sally Howlett [mailto howler_78@gmail.com)
To: Fiona Lane [mailto fionatheballetlegend@hotmail.com)
Sent: Wednesday, 12 September 2012, 20.06.30 GMT

Fi, I found out today that Julian is my vocal coach at college.

I can't do this, darling. I'm so sorry.

I've tried, because I love you, but I can't go back there to study. It's not my world, I hate being there and, most of all, I can't cope with seeing Julian every day. He ruined my life, Fi. If anyone understands that, it's you.

I'm going to talk to Brian tomorrow and explain that I can't carry on.

I love you so much and I'm so sorry.

Sally XXXXXX

Scene Seven

The next day, London

Brian looked at me over his glasses. In spite of my over-whelming shame and sadness I still felt a great warmth for this man: a renowned opera singer who wore the same crappy three-pound reading glasses as my parents. On an old shoelace round his neck.

He didn't say anything for a little while. I stared out of the open window to the Royal Albert Hall and felt the warm, heavy air moving sluggishly around me. We were having a minor September heatwave, which made my decision to leave college all the more difficult. *Grey skies and a cold, dank building would have made it easy*, I thought darkly. I could forgive myself for leaving this place if it was sensually depressing.

It was not. I could hear someone practising one of the Bach cello suites nearby and the sound was so beautiful I could have wept. The trees outside were rustling gently and sunlight slid slowly through their leaves.

I was bitterly disappointed in myself, standing there in

Room 304: a room in which so many brilliant and dedicated singers had fought to train.

But I didn't belong there. I didn't deserve this daily view of the Royal Albert Hall and I wasn't worthy of a moment of Brian's tutelage. I was not special or brave enough to be there. More importantly still, I couldn't breathe. Not with Julian Bell in the building. Or Julian bloody *Jefferson*.

After the workshop yesterday I'd fled, crying, and had holed myself up in the wardrobe with Carrot until Barry came back. I'd called Fiona but she'd sounded so distant I could barely hear her, which made it all the worse.

For once Barry had been utterly serious and for a good half-hour he'd sat in the wardrobe with me in grim and respectful silence. 'Fucking Julian. The fucker, the fucker,' he repeated quietly. 'Fucker. He doesn't deserve a job. Let alone one in a place like that.'

Later he'd ordered me a pizza (he even, quite valiantly, ate a slice of it) and together we had sat down to google Julian.

Julian Jefferson is a renowned American tenor, Wikipedia began. Julian – the smart, weird version – smiled out of the page in black and white, dappled sunlight on his face and soft-focus brickwork in the background. He was wearing a crisp, perfectly pressed white shirt (no sign of his faded, holey T-shirts) and his hair was in the same minging, smarmy long wavy style that I'd seen at my door and then at college. He looked confident and talented and masterful. Like his name should be Horatio. Clearly, he was still Julian, yet he was a million miles away from the man I'd once loved so madly.

Barry stared at the photo for a while, muttered something about him looking like a twat who ran hedge funds, then burst out laughing.

Distracted almost to insanity, I just watched him.

'I'm sorry, Chicken,' he cried. 'But what the flamin' hell is he playin' at? Julian's as fit as bugger, so why'd he want to ruin it all by gettin' himself up like a long-haired Michael Ball? That *hair*! Oh, my days . . .' Met by my anguished silence, he eventually stopped laughing and resumed looking sombre.

Who are you, even? I thought sadly, staring at the screen. Watching Julian teaching Violet Elphinstone yesterday had been like I imagined a bad acid trip to feel. Hearing all of those Italian terms and opera in-jokes – and watching him genuinely improve Violet's aria in a mere *hour* – was both awful and surreal. Nothing I'd previously heard him say, nothing I'd seen him do, had given even the faintest suggestion that he was . . . this person. Julian Jefferson, the world-famous tenor with a substantial entry on Wikipedia. Someone who owned a Rolex and smart leather shoes.

Julian Jefferson YouTube, Barry typed.

I wanted to stop him because I knew I shouldn't listen to Julian singing, but my voice stuck in my throat. I sat there, mute, watching several hundred Julian Jefferson videos load. Sighing, Barry plugged his speakers into my iPad, and we braced ourselves.

Julian's voice travelled into my heart like an intravenous drug. It was *incredible*. As it began to spill out of the speakers, rich and warm and oddly familiar, I felt myself tense, shiver and give in. Helpless, I went to a place I'd not

128

been to for more than a year, allowing that intense, perfect love to build up again.

It was as chemical, as visceral, now as it had been then.

The music continued. Barry and I were spellbound.

'Um, Chicken,' Barry muttered, after a minute or so. 'Have you got a wide on? Because I think I've got a chub.'

I was speechless. Julian's voice was otherworldly.

'Motherfucker,' Barry remarked, stopping the video. 'He could at least be awful at singin', hey, Chicken?' He put his arm round my shoulders and squeezed hard.

'He's *phenomenal*,' I breathed.

Barry pulled away from me and looked me straight in the eye. 'Chicken,' he said quietly. 'Chicken, promise me you won't go fallin' in love with him again. *Promise me*. He's bad news, know what I'm sayin'?'

Reluctantly – for this sensation of old remembered love was so pleasurable I wanted it to go on for ever – I shut down that portal in my head and drove myself back to Barry and to the facts.

Because the facts were simple: Julian had destroyed everything. Not just for me but for *everyone*. Our lives had changed irrevocably because of him, and for that reason it was essential that I leave college.

As suddenly as I'd been invaded by love, I was heavy with anger. *His name wasn't even Julian Bell.* What other lies had he told me? And what other lies was he telling the college? Did they know they'd employed a criminal?

'Oh, Sally,' Brian said, taking off his glasses and polishing them absently with the corner of his shirt. He stared down at the piano keyboard, thinking hard. Then his steely grey eyes met mine again. There was a kind smile somewhere in them. 'I just can't accept this. I'm sorry, Sally, but you're too good to lose.'

'I'm sorry too,' I said mulishly. I'd gone over this several times that morning; anticipated his responses and rehearsed my own counter-arguments. 'I really am, Brian. But the simple fact of the matter is that I don't want to be an opera singer.'

It might not have been the sole reason for my departure but it was true enough. Watching my coursemates over the last few days, I'd felt none of their determination or self-belief. None of their sense of destiny. They wanted to be opera singers and would move mountains to make that happen. I did not and would not.

Brian looked thoughtful. 'The problem is, you *are* an opera singer.'

'I'm not.'

'No, really, you are. If I'm sure of anything, young lady, it's that. Every single person who auditioned you reported that you had the purest, rawest talent they ever remember having heard. You can't waste it.'

I shifted on to my other foot. I knew my script. 'That's really nice of you to say, but I'm happy to waste it. Sorry.' I picked up my bag off the floor. 'I'll contact my scholarship people today. Organize paying them back. Brian, I can't spend my life doing something I hate, especially at other people's expense. They're shelling out thousands for me! And think of all the other people who want to study here. Give them a chance.'

Brian slammed his fist on the piano keyboard. An angry, discordant sound filled the room and my heart quickened. I had never seen him lose his temper. Even when he was being angry onstage I always felt it to be of the Paddington Bear variety.

'No,' he said forcefully. 'I said this to you on Monday. It was *you* we chose. Don't you feel any sort of responsibility to yourself, Sally? What about your parents? What would they say about you wasting an opportunity like this? This is the *Royal College of Music*! It's a once-in-a-lifetime opportunity!'

A deep sadness entered me. 'My family don't want me here either,' I replied. 'Trust me, they'll be delighted.'

'*Why?*' Brian was truly angry. 'Why in God's name would they want you to leave?'

I felt my defences slam down. I didn't need to stay here and have someone try to unpick my family. God knew I'd tried hard enough to do that myself. 'Because they want me to do a proper job,' I said simply. 'They think this is ridiculous. Making a spectacle of myself.'

Brian looked astonished. 'I don't believe you.'

'Well, believe me. I'm going, Brian. I am truly sorry.'

Brian sighed long and hard and I put my satchel on my shoulder. He looked out of the window, as if for inspiration. A large crowd of people were standing outside the Albert Hall, staring up and photographing. Their tour guide pointed and babbled.

'Just have one lesson before you go,' he said, turning back to me. 'Let's just do one lesson. You and me. It'll be safe, nobody will hear you. Because that's the problem, isn't it? You don't like singing in front of other people.'

I squirmed.

'Sally, it was obvious from the word go,' Brian said

gently. 'The only time I've ever heard you sing without fear was last year before you went to America. I caught you singing in the wardrobe department at seven a.m. when you thought everyone was hours away, and it was beautiful. But as soon as you had people watching you, you fell to pieces.'

I said nothing. I was too afraid of crying, which would not fit with the dignified departure I'd planned.

Brian looked thoughtful. 'What is this fear?' he asked. 'Do you think it's something we could work on?'

I shook my head.

'Lots of people get stage fright,' he continued. 'There are things you can do. Exercises, techniques, therapy . . . Some people even use medication. But they deal with their stage fright *because they're worth it*. And so are you, Sally.'

How could I tell him? How could I possibly explain why it was so important to me that nobody ever heard me sing? I barely understood it myself. But it had been with me since I was tiny and it was as instinctive as breathing. 'I don't want to *perform*,' I said wearily. 'I could maybe cope if I could just stand there and sing but you've got to . . . *act*. Do all of those stupid facial expressions and emotions. I can't do that stuff.' I remembered a phrase I'd heard at the Royal Opera House. 'I'm more of the park and bark school,' I added.

Brian smiled. 'Ha-ha! The park and bark school. Yes, we have to act nowadays. But, Sally, that makes the singing easier. Better. It makes the performance more thrilling!'

'I DON'T WANT TO BE THRILLING!'

My voice hung in the air for a few charged seconds,

then dispersed into small ripples of anger. Was that me? Had I just roared at Brian?

I had. He folded his arms over his chest, perhaps to defend himself. 'Well, now.' He chuckled. 'Finally. There is life in there. It's been like talking to a catatonic toad, Sally. You rehearsed everything you've said to me so far.'

I shook my head tiredly. 'Look. I'll do a singing lesson with you, if you want. And then you can really wallow in the tragedy of losing me. Or, more likely, you'll find you're making a lucky escape. But I'm not staying. Today is my last day.'

Brian looked absolutely delighted. 'You will? My dear, you have my *word* that it's safe to sing with me.'

I shrugged. I was exhausted already and it was only ten fifteen in the morning.

Brian shuffled some papers around. 'I've got a student now, and then I'll need a cup of tea . . . But if you came at eleven fifteen I could do a session then. Will you come back? In an hour?'

I had no energy for a fight. 'Yes. Fine. See you then.'

I turned to go but Brian had jumped up and shot between me and the door. 'Please. Whatever your head tells you, just come back. Promise me.'

'I promise.' My voice was hollow, but my promise wasn't. I liked Brian. I owed him that much.

Scene Eight

I went to the canteen and sat in the corner, ignoring my opera-school fellows at the Singers' Table. They all looked so normal, sitting there munching croissants in those stupid *bucket chairs*; so relaxed. Jan Borsos had the two posh girls, Sophie and Summer, in fits of laughter while Violet and Ismene giggled away with their gang. Hector, the one with the ginger bouffant, was trying to work his chinos-and-blazer magic on Helen, who was laughing in his face in that very pleasant manner she had. He seemed unaware.

They were all trendy and nice and young and talented. I felt stupid and clunky in the 'trendy' outfit I'd bought to fit in. And ashamed that I'd bought a special outfit at all, especially given that I wasn't planning to stay. What was wrong with me? Why was I always on the outside of everything, trying to fit in? Never belonging. Never quite at home.

Separate. Different. Weird. My gut twisted savagely, self-pity like an ocean swell.

'You'll get into the swing of things soon,' said the assistant at the till. 'They're not as bad as they look.' She was a kindly-looking woman of around sixty, whose accent was very familiar.

'They're lovely, actually,' I admitted. 'It's me that's the problem.'

'Aha!' Her face lit up at the sound of my voice. 'Black Country?'

'Just about. Stourbridge. Not sure I belong somewhere like the Royal College of Music.'

'Walsall,' she said proudly. 'And I *do* belong at the RCM. So do you, bab. You'll see.'

I smiled, not knowing what to say, and took my bacon sandwich to the corner.

Helen came over almost immediately. 'I see,' she mused. 'So . . . everyone's sitting over there and you're choosing to sit in the corner. Really?'

I liked Helen. For someone who had resorted to medication to overcome her first-week nerves she was also rather ballsy, in an understated sort of way. Plus she was now offering me a Rolo, which made her doubly brilliant. No one bought Rolos any more.

'Thanks,' I said grudgingly. 'I'll take two, if you don't mind.'

'Be my guest. Rolos are magic with a bit of bacon.'

I smiled.

'Are you OK?' she said. 'I don't want to act all chummy when we've only just met but . . . Well, you don't seem to be having a good time of it.'

I struggled to know what to say.

'And I'm not a lesbian either,' she said sternly. 'I just like you.'

I felt a tiny glow somewhere in my stomach that had

nothing to do with the Rolos. 'I like you too,' I said shyly. 'And now I feel like I'm ten years old and should ask you to be my best friend for ever.'

'Actually, that'd be great,' she said, sitting on the arm of my chair. 'I dumped my best friend recently. It would be *so* convenient if I could just slot you in there.'

In spite of myself, I laughed. 'Why? Your best friend, I mean.'

Helen's best friend, it transpired, had been sending flirty text messages to Helen's fiancé, Phil. Things like *I hope Helen knows how lucky she is. Don't tell her I said that* and *Can't wait to see you at the altar. You're going to look well bloody handsome. xxxxxx*

'Wow,' I said, marginally more cheerful. 'Hasn't she missed the point? Flirty banter with a man who's MAR-RYING SOMEONE ELSE?'

Helen laughed too, although not without sadness. 'Phil was so scared he eventually just gave me his phone and shouted, "Help." It's not the first time she's cracked on to someone I love. I had to ditch her.'

'Must've been horrible,' I said sympathetically. 'Losing your best friend is as bad as losing a lover, I think.'

Helen nodded reflectively. 'Mm. So, you too?'

I thought of Fiona, so far away, and felt sad. 'Me too.'

'Oh, go on. I've shown you mine. Show me yours.'

I took a deep breath. I didn't like talking about me and Fi because whenever I did the huge gap between us, and all of the mess in between, began to feel real. So I kept it vague. 'My cousin,' I replied eventually. 'Practically my sister. We're still best friends but she's buggered off to New York and won't come back. We can only chat every few days now.' The bottomless sadness started to tug and sting.

'Which is why,' I continued brightly, pinching another Rolo and perking up a little, 'I think this is an excellent project. Let's be best friends. We should have a ceremony.'

Helen nodded. 'Excellent. I'll dig out some My Little Ponys and we can paint them with nail varnish. Or whatever you do with a BFF. Go and buy tampons together. Shoplift them, probably.'

I sniggered.

She picked up my plate and stood up. 'Come on. Get your arse over to the table. Singers have inhabited it for several decades, they say. We can't let the side down!'

I looked at them all, so bright and cheerful. I felt heavy and pathetic. I couldn't even rouse the strength to tell her I was leaving.

'Come *on*,' she insisted, walking off. 'If we don't socialize with other people we'll get too intense and have a massive fight and then I'll have to find *another* bestie. Frankly, Sally, I can't be arsed.'

I laughed out loud. 'You're funny,' I told her.

'STOP TRYING TO CRACK ON TO ME.' She grabbed my arm and marched me off to the table. 'Lesbian!'

We sat down between Hector-the-ginger-bouffant and a guy I'd not yet spoken to – I thought I'd heard someone refer to him as Noon. I'd disregarded this information, presuming it an error. 'Hi there,' he said cheerfully. He had a ponytail and a biker jacket. 'I'm Noon. We've not yet met . . .'

'Sally,' I said. I didn't understand. Why was his name

Noon? Why would anyone's name be Noon? I looked round the table at smiling faces, half-drunk lattes and discarded KitKat wrappers. I thought about how at the Royal Opera House none of the singers had gone anywhere near dairy products – problematic for the vocal cords, apparently – and I marvelled at how relaxed my fellows were. It confounded me. Why were they not breaking into terrified sweats and running to the toilets with a Code Brown at the thought of the day ahead?

Helen, I noticed, was on her second packet of Rolos. 'Butt out,' she muttered, noticing my attention. 'I've run out of beta-blockers.'

I forced myself to talk to Hector and Noon for a while and, in spite of relating to nothing they said, I relaxed slightly.

But not for long. At around eleven I became aware of something having changed in the room and before I even looked around I knew it was Julian and his stupid long, shiny hair. He was getting a cup of tea. Just for a minute, I forgot everything and started to giggle. He looked so completely ridiculous; so not Julian. He was wearing *cords* and a *smart shirt* and a *blazer*. I italicized those items mentally, still baffled and more than a little amused. What was he on?

You don't know who Julian actually is, I reminded myself. The sniggering stopped, which was lucky because Helen was watching me keenly.

Julian paid for his tea and some biscuits, then scanned the room. Looking for me?

Looking for me. He caught my eye, just before I snatched it away, and smiled, waving a snack packet of Jammie Dodgers in my direction. A million feelings, none of them comfortable, exploded across my abdomen like shooting stars, and I found myself staring at my lap, willing him not to come over. Jammie Dodgers. That was a cruel trick.

'Hello,' he said, arriving at our table.

'Hi!'

'Hello!'

'Oh, HI THERE, Julian!'

Everyone, I realized, was overexcited about seeing him. Summer, the posh girl, actually pinched Sophie, the other posh girl, and Hector's face lit up like a summer's morn. 'So good to meet you,' he muttered, jumping up and pumping Julian's hand. 'I'm *such* a fan of your work. And that masterclass yesterday . . .' His hands circled wildly in the air and he trailed off, apparently dumbstruck.

'You didn't notice that I called Rossini Italian?' Julian grinned. 'Or that when I demonstrated that little bit on the piano I played like an animal with cloven hoofs?'

Everyone roared with laughter and told him not to be silly. I wondered how I'd ever found his silly accent appealing. It was horrible. Stupid. And why had I always found him so funny? Why did everyone else seem to think he was funny?

'It was fantastic, Jules,' Violet gushed.

I scowled. *Jules?*

'Meh,' Julian said modestly. He opened the packet of Jammie Dodgers and offered them around. Everyone giggled about his choice of biscuit except me. I knew what he was up to. Trying to remind me of the past. Make me smile. Bastard.

'You are totally magnificent. I have much honour to meet you,' Jan Borsos said. His customary furious expression was even more furious than normal, but it was full of warmth.

'Hey, man! You must be Jan Borsos! I heard you walked here. Good work, dude!'

Jan all but died on the spot, his furious face a-thunder with awe, pleasure and disbelief. 'Dude,' he muttered in wonder. 'I am dude.'

Faced with the loveliness of Julian's smile – a loveliness I now knew to be completely untrustworthy – Violet couldn't resist coming back for more. 'It was SO fab working with you.' She beamed. 'And I'm surprised I've never met you before, actually. I was on that workshop last summer at the Chicago Opera. How odd that –'

I tuned her out. I tuned them all out, all of them with their pointed mentions of people they'd trained with whom Julian might know, or performances they'd seen him in that had blown them away. Had I been a screamer I'd have screamed loudly, told them they had no idea. That he was a dangerous liar. A criminal.

Julian, all modest rebuttals and witty one-liners, stood in their midst like some sort of flowing-haired biscuit-toting saviour among the hopeless and starving. 'Aw, thanks, man . . . No, not at all . . . Oh, come on, mate, I wasn't *that* good . . .' My skin crawled with loathing. 'Man' one minute, 'mate' the next. *Shut up, shut up, shut up. Go back to New York. Or Devon. Or Siberia. Just go.*

Helen was watching me, one eyebrow raised. *Tell me*, her face said. I shook my head in reply. Where would I start? *How* could I start? She nodded respectfully, as if to say, 'Whenever you're ready,' and I felt gratitude for that decent, steadfast girl.

Eventually, Julian stopped accepting pleasantries and made an announcement. 'So, ladies, I just came over to find out who's going to audition for the advert. Did all of you see the poster?'

Lots of affirmative nods.

'Definitely auditioning,' Violet said. Summer, Sophie, Ismene and even Helen came soon after.

'Great,' Julian said warmly. 'Get practising. I want you to sing the shit out of that aria! We don't want some pikey from Guildhall or the RAM getting it, right?'

Everyone giggled, except me. ('Pikey!' 'Isn't he hilarious?' 'OMG, I can't believe he said that, hahaharrr!')

Julian looked in my direction. *Don't. Don't you dare speak to me.*

'Sally?' he said. He sounded a little less sure of himself. 'How about you?'

Eyes swivelled towards me. Violet smiled brightly, her face transmitting various messages, such as 'You're not ready to audition' and 'Why does he know your name?' and 'I really do *not like you.*' At that moment I didn't care about Violet or what she thought of me. Only Julian and I were in the room now. Julian and his lies and masks.

'Pikeys?' I heard myself blurt mulishly. 'Really?'

Julian folded his arms across his chest, but I knew him well enough to know that it was a sign of discomfort rather than confidence. 'I was joking, clearly,' he said quietly. 'If the very talented students of those venerable institutions are pikeys then I share the same status as a sickly fly living on one of my dad's cowpats.'

('Cowpats?!' 'HAHAHA!' 'Oooh, Julian, does your

141

father have cows? Out on a big American ranch or something? Cool!')

Stop it, I thought furiously. *Don't you dare make intimate jokes with me.*

Julian was watching me. 'Well? Are you going to audition?'

'I don't think I'll have time,' I muttered. 'I have a part-time job.'

Violet nodded, pleased.

There was a momentary silence as the other girls waited for him to try to change my mind. But he was out of ideas. He just stared nervously at me, a tiny pulse beating above his eye. He was wearing some extremely expensive scent I'd never smelt before and his shirt was ironed to within an inch of its life. It was all bollocks.

It was a great relief when he nodded politely, allowed Jan to hi-five him and mooched off to join Brian, who had just arrived and was making himself some tea. As he went I noticed a little patch of his hair that had escaped the gel and sat, fluffy as a poodle, around his ear. It was the final straw. I felt my eyes sting and had to dig my fingernails into my palms so hard the skin broke. *Don't. Don't you dare*, I ordered myself.

'Isn't it nice that he's learned everyone's names?' Violet said. She looked expectantly at me, wanting me to tell her how Julian had known mine.

'Isn't it just,' I agreed wearily.

Brian and Julian were deep in conversation over by the hot drinks machine, which was making me even more uncomfortable. I didn't want my lovely Brian to be infected by Julian.

As if reading my mind, Julian paused, mid-conversation, and looked at me; Brian, too.

I bristled. They'd better not be talking about me.

Julian said something to Brian, who nodded thoughtfully, then patted Julian's arm and wandered out with his cup of tea, humming to himself. Julian went off to read in a corner.

I spent the remaining minutes before my first and last singing lesson in conversation with Noon and Ismene, and I didn't hear a word they said. It was a relief to think that I wouldn't have to talk to these people again. They were lovely, nothing like I'd expected, but they were part of a world that I simply wasn't ready for.

I stood up to go to my lesson, saying nothing. I couldn't explain it to these people when they'd waited their whole lives to train here.

But as I left the canteen, someone stepped in my way. Someone my body knew to be Julian, even before my eyes confirmed it.

'Hey,' he said quietly. 'Are you OK?'

I blinked at him, keeping my eyes away from the fluffy hair by his ear. 'Am I OK? What do you think?'

Julian was too handsome for his own good. Even now, as he stood in front of me, patently uncomfortable, he was like a long-haired, sleepy-eyed angel. How was it that someone so bad could look so good?

'I was just talking to Brian about your fear of singing,' he began.

I gasped. 'You *what*?'

'No, I was trying to help, I was –'

I swung past him and out into the corridor, my vision blurred by tears of shame and anger. How could he? How could he just steamroller his way into my life like that, as if he were my friendly neighbourhood singing teacher?

I lurched along the windowed corridor towards the music rooms. I would go and tell Brian that I couldn't do a lesson. It had been a stupid idea, a waste of time.

'Sally!' It was Helen. I could hear her walking fast behind me, trying to catch up. I quickened my pace.

'*Sally!*' It was Julian. He was after me too. I broke into a run, sobs packing tightly in my chest.

'Sally.' He stopped me in my tracks with just one hand and swung round in front of me. 'Please,' he said. And then, 'Oh, God, oh, Sal, please don't cry. I –'

'Don't you dare call me Sal! Get off me!' I sobbed, furious. I had to get away from him. I turned round, seeing Helen standing a few feet off, watching us uncertainly.

Sorry, she mouthed, backing off. I tried to stop her but Julian had me still.

'Please,' he said quietly. 'Sally, we really have to talk. We can't go on like this. We have to work together. I'm down as your vocal coach. I'll be teaching you at least once a week.'

I was crying the tears of the hopeless and cornered. 'I'm not staying,' I told him, weeping down into the floor. 'I'm quitting. Remember seize the day? Well, you've ruined it.'

'No,' Julian whispered. 'You can't leave. We have to find a way through this, Sally. For Fiona –'

'WHAT?' I gasped. 'How dare you drag Fiona into this? How dare you even say her *name*? You are a man of no shame, Julian. Who even are you? Who the fuck is Julian Jefferson? Was *anything* you told me in New York the truth?'

Julian sighed and ran his fingers through his stupid hair. 'Everything I told you was the truth,' he said. 'Julian Bell is my name. I was the editor of the *Brooklyn Beaver*. And I did love you. I loved you so much I'd have swum the Atlantic Ocean for you. I was going to tell you about the singing, the stage name, the . . . well, everything, but then everything went wrong and I –'

'EVERYTHING WENT WRONG BECAUSE OF YOU!' I cried. 'You ruined my life! You ruined Fiona's life! And all the while you were pretending to be someone else!'

Julian stared at me, hopeless. I could still read him just by being near him: he was absolutely devastated.

My anger dissipated. It was pointless. Everything was pointless.

'Leave me alone,' I repeated tiredly. 'Just leave me alone, Julian whatever-your-surname-is. I don't want to be part of any in-jokes. The biscuits. The chat about your dad's farm. I want to be just another student.'

He was silent.

'Julian? Did you hear me? I asked you to leave me alone. Do you understand? You've done enough damage. I can't take any more now. I can't.'

Julian let his hands swing uselessly against his leg. 'Fine,' he said flatly. 'I'll respect your wishes.'

I took a deep breath, pulled what was left of me together and walked past him, round the corner towards the staircase.

'Sally?' He was still standing behind me. I stopped walking.

'I – I'll leave you alone. But I just wanted to pass on my mom's best wishes. She was so unbelievably happy you took this course . . .'

I walked on, squaring my shoulders against his words. Another punch to the face. I'd loved Julian's mum. She'd written to me twice in the past year but I hadn't been able to face anything from her. The letters had been returned, unopened, and I was no more ready to hear from her now than I had been then.

I heard Julian's strange leather shoes click off, defeated. *LA, LA LA LA LAAAA*, I sang in my head, terrified even of my own thoughts.

I floated in an uneasy, dreamlike state. Students moved past me; a tiny wisp of a guy with a huge double bass and a stool struggled by. He seemed no more substantial than a shadow.

'Sally,' said a man's voice. I looked up, squinting at the face that was coming into focus in front of me. It was Jan Borsos. He was grinning, in his peculiarly furious way.

'I wish to take you out for dinner,' he said.

I stared vaguely at him, not really sure what he'd said.

'You come for dinner with me?' he pushed. 'Tomorrow? Yes? Yes! We are in an agreement!' And off he strode, a little king of a man.

Just as I drew level with Room 304, he called my name again from down the corridor.

'Sally! I take you for dinner! But you have to pay! I do not have my scholarship for one more week!'

Scene Nine

'Well done,' Brian said quietly, as I entered the room.

'What?' I blinked at him. I was still miles away, my head back in New York.

'Well done for coming back,' he said, giving me a chair. 'That took guts.'

I closed my eyes and took a few deep breaths. I didn't want to upset Brian by being mad. He was such a lovely egg of a man, and if I had any strength left in me, I would give him the nicest farewell speech anyone had ever heard.

He sat quietly, letting me compose myself.

Eventually I looked up, pushed my shire horse's tail out of my face and smiled. 'I'm not staying,' I said eventually. 'I'm so sorry, Brian, but I don't want to do even a lesson. It's not just about the fear, there's other things too. I –'

'OK,' Brian said softly. 'God knows this breaks my heart, Sally. But if you don't want to stay, you don't want to stay. I can't make you.'

During the silence that followed we turned to look out of the window. The sun had shifted and was now pouring fatly through the windows. Outside the day was gaining momentum. A bird sang, out of view, and a car stereo blasted out McFly.

It was time to go. 'Thanks,' I said to Brian, standing up. 'For everything.'

He shrugged, smiling at me over his glasses. 'Stay in touch,' he said. 'And take good care of yourself, Sally.'

I nodded, not trusting myself to speak without crying, and turned to go.

Then I stopped.

There was a big wardrobe in the corner. A big wardrobe that hadn't been there when I'd left an hour ago.

Brian came over and stood next to me, hands in pockets. 'That was for you.' He sighed. 'It was Julian Jefferson's idea. He said you like singing in wardrobes.'

I looked at him, amazed. Brian smiled. 'I asked the stage manager from the Britten Theatre to run it up for us and I thought – ah, well. Never mind.'

I tried to thank him but couldn't speak. I just sort of honked sadly.

Then, without warning, Brian marched into the wardrobe and shut the door.

He started singing Papageno and Pamina's duet from *The Magic Flute*. For a moment I remained frozen but then – in spite of the mad hurricane in my head – I started to laugh. I laughed at the absurdity of my singing teacher chirping away to himself inside a wardrobe (he was singing the woman's part in a bad falsetto) and I laughed at the memory of him mincing around with a moustache on his crotch during the same duet in the Royal Opera House's production of *The Magic Flute* all those years ago. I laughed because everything about my life, at that moment, was so tragic as to be really quite funny. Who cared?

Before I knew it, I'd put my bag on the floor, opened the door and hopped into the wardrobe with him, just in time to take over Pamina's part.

Through the chink of light coming in I could see Brian grinning from ear to ear. We rattled along to the end of the duet and I didn't even think about what I was doing. At the end, Brian slid out of the wardrobe, leaving the door slightly ajar, and took a seat at the piano, muttering, 'Fantastic! Fantastic! Let's begin!'

The pain and the panic had slid sideways, somehow, giving me space to breathe for a little while. Sure, I'd leave college today. But the feeling that was pounding through me right now was too big to squash down. Fatherly support and a wardrobe to sing in? This was all I'd ever wanted!

'You're warmed up, I presume?' Brian called.

'Um, no?'

'Really? OK, well, then, I suppose let's start with some ascending Es.' He played a chord on the piano.

I did nothing.

'Sally? Can you hear the piano in there?'

'Yes.'

'Great! Let's start off with some ascending Es.' He played the chord again, making it into a little introduction. But when the bit came where I could tell that I should start, I still hadn't the foggiest idea what I was meant to be doing.

'Um . . .' Brian got up and crossed to the wardrobe. 'Sally, do you *know* how to warm up your voice?' He looked a bit nervous.

I smiled at him through the chink. I was safe in that wardrobe: I could tell him anything. 'Nope.'

'Oh, God.'

'Never had a singing lesson in my life! You know that!'

There was a silence.

'Right,' Brian said carefully. 'So you've *never* warmed up before singing?'

'Correct,' I said from the wardrobe. 'Or, at least, not in a formal way.'

'Good Lord,' he said, momentarily stunned. 'I mean, I suppose I knew but . . . How on earth did you audition so well if you hadn't warmed up? I'm at a loss, Sally.'

I poked the door open a little wider. 'See? It would have been a nightmare having me at college! A singer who doesn't even know how to warm up!'

'Now stop it,' Brian said. 'We can teach you to warm up. We can teach you music theory, Italian, German, whatever. Good heavens above, if you can't learn those things here you can't learn them anywhere.'

'But I'm leaving,' I reminded him. 'Although I don't mind doing one lesson. In the wardrobe. In fact, I'd like to!' I was impatient to get going. I wanted to open up my lungs and SING. Here in the wardrobe I was safe, and when I was safe I loved to sing more than any other activity. Even eating. '*LalalaLAlalala!*' I sang under my breath.

Brian yelled excitedly that what I had just sung was an arpeggio and so began our warm-up. Brian led me through all sorts of strange sounds, teaching me how to open up my soft palate – it was sort of like imagining someone had shoved a big hot potato into the roof of my mouth – and almost passed out with excitement when I sang an effortless top C sharp.

'Is a top C sharp good, then?' I called from the wardrobe. God, this lesson felt fantastic! I was zinging!

Brian stopped playing. 'WHAT?' He put his head into his hands.

I watched him through the crack, confused. 'Brian?'

'Oh, my God,' he murmured. 'You can't read music, can you?'

'Of course not!' I said cheerfully.

Brian started to laugh. 'Christ on a bike.' He sighed. 'But . . . how did you get through the auditions? We test your musicianship during the master's auditions!'

'They stopped me halfway through and told me I was so good I had to come back and audition for the opera school instead,' I reminded him. 'I only got halfway through my second aria.'

Brian laughed even harder.

I started to laugh too. 'Told you,' I called. 'It would have been *well* crap for you trying to be my singing teacher.'

We started off by working on 'L'ho perduta', which was one of the simplest arias in the soprano's repertoire and something I'd been singing since I was eight. It was also the aria that I'd tried to sing at primary school, somehow managing instead to wet myself onstage and receive a lifetime ban from singing, courtesy of Mum.

I'd had little enthusiasm for it since then. But the joy of singing it again, somewhere I couldn't be seen, where Mum and Dad's suffocating anxiety couldn't reach me, was monumental. It was like someone had turned on a brilliant white light in my chest.

Brian picked it apart with me, laughing despairingly when he realized that I hadn't a word of Italian, and therefore only knew the gist of what Barbarina was singing. He translated it for me word by word. Barbarina was singing the aria because she had lost a very important pin, on which quite a lot depended, and she was feeling a bit scared. She sang a whole aria to express this.

'Opera's ridiculous,' I shouted from inside the wardrobe. 'They take about eight pages of music to express one emotion. Over and over again.'

Brian chuckled. 'That's the aria for you. But it's the music, no? Doesn't that bring it all to life?'

'Yeah,' I agreed, sighing. I couldn't deny it. Opera *was* ridiculous, in so many ways, but it was also the best thing in the world. If I possessed the pumping strength that opera gave me on a day-to-day basis, I'd be able to get through anything. *Anything!*

Rather stupidly, I said this to Brian.

'Exactly,' he roared, throwing open the wardrobe door.

I blinked at him. 'Go away.'

'I'm your singing teacher. You don't get to tell me to go away.'

'You're not my singing teacher. I'm about to leave the course. You're my friend.' *And practically my dad*, I wanted to add.

'Oh, Sally, you infuriating . . . *moron*,' Brian exploded.

I raised an eyebrow. 'Steady on, Brian . . .'

He started laughing. 'Look at you! Look how confident you are right now. Can you imagine saying, "Steady on, Brian," half an hour ago? And listen to what you just said! You could get through anything if you felt like you did when you sang opera. THAT'S THE POINT!'

'Oh, no,' I said, pulling the door shut. 'Don't think you're going to trick me into coming back. I'm OK here, in a wardrobe with the door shut. I couldn't get out there and sing in the real world.'

Brian put his hands into his pockets, shaking his head.

'I can see you shaking your head,' I called.

Brian chuckled. 'Oh, Sally. Just try it. Just try a month. Think about how you feel, right here and now, in the wardrobe, singing. You feel fantastic. You're alive. Tell me you don't want more of that.'

A complex battle was playing out inside me. Part of me shut down, discounting any possibility of staying on. Staying would mean exposure, daily terror and probably deep humiliation. Not to mention Julian and his stupid posh suits and weird hair. But staying here would also mean freedom, happiness and daily exhilaration. The feeling I had right now was like nothing else I knew. It was powerfully, viscerally liberating. Maybe he was right. Maybe I could actually get through it if I had singing as my medicine.

But how could singing be the cure when it was the problem?

I went round and round in circles, sitting in the wardrobe. Brian stood there, hands in pockets, waiting quietly for my response. And when I spoke, he looked like he might actually cry.

Because I'd said yes. Yes, I would give it a go. For a month.

*

'Chicken, that is amazing,' Barry enthused later on. 'You bangin' little beaver!'

I looked up from my bangers and mash. 'Um, beaver?'

Barry frowned. 'Fair enough,' he conceded. 'That was not my best use of imagery. But you know beavers, they're fearless little buggers, industrious an' stuff . . . They gnaw down trees and build big complex homes an' the like . . .' He trailed off and stuck his leg out to the side, as he often did when he had become aware that what he was saying was a bit strange.

'I think beaver is an excellent word,' I told him, shovelling in another delicious mountain of buttery mash. I would need a lot of comfort food over the next four weeks. 'But if you don't mind I'd rather stick with Chicken. Beaver reminds me of . . . of . . .'

'Of the *Brooklyn Beaver*,' Barry finished, his face going pale. 'Oh, Chicken, I'm sorry. As if you don't have enough cause to be thinking of that arse-twat Julian.'

He sat down next to me and sawed off a slice of my sausage. 'Are you OK?' he asked. 'This ain't an easy time.'

I shrugged. 'I'm just trying to keep my promise to Fi,' I said quietly. 'But, yeah, it's hard. The wardrobe was Julian's idea. I can't *stand* him trying to win me over with random acts of kindness. It's just so . . . shameless. AND he brought up his mum earlier.'

'Oooh, he's a bloody devil,' Barry agreed angrily. 'But he can't go buyin' his way out of what he did by bein' all nice. Too bloody late, Chicken.'

There was a depressed silence. 'Anyway. I'm seizing the day, Bazzer. Just like I promised I would. I'm going to stay at college for a month.'

Barry licked his lips. 'And have you, um, told Fiona?'

I concentrated on my dinner, noticing how Barry's tone had gone a bit too casual for my liking. 'Yep,' I replied briefly. 'I told her earlier.'

'And?'

'And she was really pleased.'

I could feel Barry nodding uneasily. I wished he wasn't so weird about me talking to Fiona. Yes, she had put us through all manner of shit in the last year. But what did he want me to do? Abandon her? Just dump her in New York and never talk to her again?

'So, I'm going for dinner with a guy on my course,' I said brightly.

'GET AWAY. Who? Where? When?'

'His name's Jan Borsos. He's the mad Hungarian one I told you about. Who was divorced by the age of eighteen and walked across Europe to get here.'

Barry stared at me incredulously. 'But, Chicken, didn't you say he's about fifteen?'

'Ah, well, there is that. He's twenty-three. Quite barmy, too, as it goes. There's something oddly handsome about him, though . . .'

Barry roared with laughter. 'Oh, my days, Chicken. You've lost it.'

ACT THREE

Scene Six

An apartment in Brooklyn, September 2011

I stood in the apartment of candles and realized I had no idea what to do next. The banter at the front door had stopped and in its place was a noisy silence. Who even was this Julian Bell?

The answer was that he was a complete stranger, a man with whom I was suddenly, shockingly, alone.

Julian was leaning against the wall – half confident, half curious – watching my face as he straightened out his T-shirt. He seemed unaware of the fact that it was back to front and inside out.

'So, um, sorry again for trying to steal your candle,' I said.

'Don't you worry, Sally.'

I grinned, hearing him saying my name. His accent was absolutely amazing. I told him so.

He looked sceptical. 'Sally, I think you just told a lie. You think my accent is completely stupid. You've done almost nothing to hide that fact.'

'Maybe. Mine's no better, though!'

Julian smiled. 'You're damn right it's no better. Can I fix you a drink?'

'Yes,' I said decisively. 'I'd like a bourbon.'

'Really?'

'No.'

'I didn't think so.' He crossed over to a kitchen area. 'What *would* you like?'

I grinned. 'I'd actually like some white wine, please.'

At this he laughed out loud. 'I say things like that.' He chuckled. '"I want a bourbon" when actually I just want a nice cup of tea.' He paused, smiling at me. 'You're funny.'

The idea of him finding me funny was strangely appealing. I watched him as he got a bottle of wine out of the fridge, somewhat confused by what was happening. Here in my skin was a confident girl who just marched into the flats of handsome strangers and asked for bourbon, then wine, and didn't care if she looked stupid. Who was she?

'Is this Raúl's wine?' I asked. It smelt zesty and crisp, and the glass was already misting. As Julian handed it to me I had an inexplicable urge to cancel everything and just stand in the vast kitchen space drinking cold, heady wine with the man in front of me, who was pouring a glass for himself with a concentration I found endearing. He was nice and broad across the shoulders, I noticed. I liked a man whose shoulders were broader than my backside.

Careful, Sally.

'It's Raúl's wine,' he confirmed, replacing the bottle in the fridge. 'I come here and steal his wine often. He has excellent taste, I have none. And my apartment, unlike this one, is a shithole. Are you any good at wine?'

158

'Yeah, not too bad . . .' I began. Then: 'No, actually. That was another lie.'

'You don't look like a wine connoisseur to me.'

'Why not?'

'Because people who know about wine tend to be very commanding and boomy,' he said speculatively. 'You're kind of uncertain and a bit mad. You also look quite scared. I don't want to kill you, you know.'

'Good. Although how do you know I don't want to kill *you*?'

'I don't,' he conceded. 'But I wouldn't rate your chances. I have guns of steel.' He flexed a biceps to show nothing of the sort, which made me giggle.

I took a sip of the delicious, perfectly chilled wine and noted that Julian Bell was smiling all over, even though his face had gone poker-straight.

'Why are you trying not to smile?' I asked him.

'I'm not!'

'Yes, you are.'

He started to laugh. 'I guess it was the same as you asking for a bourbon. I wanted to cultivate mystique. I've always liked the idea of being a silent, inscrutable man. You know. Strong, dark.'

'Oh. That's not going so well, I'm afraid.'

We looked each other straight in the eye.

He frowned, as if sizing me up.

'You're doing it again!' I heard myself squeak. I sounded more flirty than I'd have liked. 'Why are you looking at me like that?'

'I don't know,' he said slowly. 'I don't know why. You're

just . . . Hang on.' He turned and walked out of Raúl's kitchen and disappeared round the corner.

I pretended not to follow him with my eyes, and tried to ignore the fact that something borderline wild was going off in my stomach. It felt very early for Julian Bell to make any sort of judgement about me. At the same time, it felt very exciting.

'AHA!' I heard him shout from an unseen room. He really was quite bonkers.

He came back waving glasses in one hand. 'I'm pretty blind without these.' He chuckled. 'I wanted to get a better look at you before I said anything more. Can I look at you? Properly?'

'That depends what you mean. I'm not taking my clothes off.' I blushed immediately. I had never said anything like that before.

Julian agreed. 'No. That would be strange. I'd just like to look at you fully clothed, please. May I?'

'Um . . .'

'Excellent.' He put the glasses on and he looked especially handsome. Clever, too. Thoughtful. Classic . . . *Shut up*, I told myself.

Julian looked me up and down briefly but was mostly concentrating on my face. 'My glasses are broken and they fall off all the time,' he told me, 'so I never wear them. I'm always being told off for it. By my mom, my roommate, my friends, co-workers.' He folded his arms and I tried not to look at the inside-out seams of his T-shirt. 'But this is why I need to be better at wearing my glasses,' he announced. 'You! You're . . .' He cocked his head to one side, thinking.

'Smelly?' I tried, unused to intensity.

160

'Hmm . . . Nope.'

I sipped my wine, waiting for him to find the right adjective.

He carried on smiling at me. 'Cool.'

'What?'

'I said, you're cool!'

'Oh.' I did a big Italian tomato of a blush again. 'Thank you. But you've just met me. You have no idea if I'm cool.'

'OK, pretty. I don't need to know you to say that.'

I gaped at him.

'No, strike that. Stunning. I think you're a little bit stunning!'

There was a beat.

And then the magic that had been flitting lightly around us dispersed. I was in the flat with a cheesy pervert, the mad widowed one probably. A tiny shiver ran down my spine. Was I even safe?

'Oh, for fuck's sake!' He grinned, shaking his head. 'You British! So uptight! Is it so bad to tell a cute girl that she's cute?'

'Don't you "you British" me!' I replied. 'There's nothing uptight about finding it odd that a man you've just met is employing strong adjectives on the subject of your appearance. And you said *stunning*, not cute.'

He was laughing now. Openly. And before I could stop myself, I was laughing too. How ridiculous I sounded. Uptight indeed, getting angry with a man who'd just said something so nice to me. A man who was so patently *not* a mad, cheesy pervert.

'But you're British too!' I protested. 'No Englishman says things like that!'

He shrugged, picking up his wine glass. 'I guess I picked up the best of both worlds. That's why I can say things like "You're stunning" and not prolapse with the effort of it.'

There it was again! *Stunning*! A scrunch in my stomach. Then I remembered that I was not even a little bit stunning and wondered why he was telling porkies.

'Oh, stop it,' he ordered, as if he could read my mind. 'It doesn't matter what you're wearing or how you think your hair smells. You were just there, stealing my candle, babbling away and pretending to like bourbon. A girl like you marching around in her nightshirt, generally being a bit of a dick and able to laugh about it, is fantastic. *Stunning*. So there.'

'Well, then, thanks,' I said. For a second, I even started to believe him.

'I call cows beautiful, if that helps me sound less cheesy,' he added. 'And dogs. Especially dogs. My roommate's dog, Pam, is fat and stupid but she is still the most beautiful dog on earth.' He chuckled, probably imagining Fat Stupid Pam.

'It's good to be associated with a fat, stupid dog.'

Julian, laughing, took off his glasses and looked gorgeous. Then he put them back on and looked gorgeous. Then he took them off and put them back on and eventually smacked himself on the side of his head, disrupting a cloud of mad hair. 'Come through and check out Raúl's view,' he offered. 'Before I make any more of a cock of myself.'

The view, which opened out as if in slow motion, was fantastic. Not perfect: there was a good mile of industrial

162

mess between us and the river, and someone had plonked a large group of new luxury flats in the way, but it was still like nothing I'd seen before. The East River was dark and slick while Manhattan was vast and twinkling.

'Jesus,' I breathed. 'No wonder Fiona likes Raúl so much.'

Julian smiled. 'What's your family name?' he asked.

'Howlett.'

'Hi, Sally Howlett.' He offered me his hand, which I shook warmly, delighted by the incongruity of it all. *He tells me I'm stunning and then shakes my hand? This man is potty! I like him!*

'Well, I'm Julian Bell. Me and Raúl are friends from school. He turned into a rock star and I turned into a small-scale journalist. He lives in a warehouse overlooking Manhattan, I share a crappy apartment with a fat dog and her mad owner.'

'That's a good self-summary,' I said. 'What about me? Well . . . my cousin Fiona, whom you've probably met, has turned into a renowned ballerina. Whereas I'm just a crappy old wardrobe mistress. She's –' I stopped. 'Actually, scrap that. I'm not "just" a wardrobe mistress. I'm proud of my job.'

Julian nodded approvingly. 'Oh, good.'

'In fact, I love it,' I said, buoyed by his encouragement. I never really talked about my enthusiasm for my work, even though it had made me so happy and kept me so safe. 'I'm working at the Met on *Turandot* and, seriously, Julian Bell, I'm *loving* it . . . The Met's wardrobe department is off the scale!'

'How so?'

'Um . . . Hard to explain to someone who doesn't know anything about the industry. You don't know opera, do you?'

Julian smiled in a vague way. 'Oh, a little bit . . . Not much. Tell it me like I'm a total novice.'

'It's just . . . well, amazing. The dye room alone is bigger than my whole flat in London, and they've got twenty-three thousand costumes and the people are *so* talented. It's like, even if you need someone whose speciality is crooked witches' hats with secret panels that bats can fly out of, you'll find them. I love it! I feel happy just thinking about it!'

Julian was chuckling. '"Crooked witches' hats",' he repeated, in a dreadful Black Country impression. 'Crooked witches' hats, oh, man, you're great.'

'Stop laughing at me!'

'No way. I like you, Sally Howlett.'

What did he mean, he liked me? I still hadn't fully got the hang of Americanisms. Did this mean what it meant in English? As in, I esteem you? I'd like to snog you at some point?

'What does it mean when an American says, "I like you"?' I heard myself ask. *What was I on?*

Julian continued to laugh at me. His whole face creased up and his glasses slid down his nose. I enjoyed the sound of his laughter very much. It was rich and bear-like and it made me feel like I was the funniest person on earth.

I blushed faintly red.

'"I like you" means I like you,' he said. 'It means, I think you're cute, and you don't say the things that other girls say, and I'm liking us hanging out.'

'Same,' I said shyly.

Julian, who'd been standing a few feet away, drifted over so he was standing closer to me. 'Good,' he said, staring out at Manhattan. I tingled with confusion and anticipation. This was weird! This was right. It was mad! It was lovely.

I did like him. He smelt nice too. A bit like a Jo Malone candle Bea had bought me last Christmas.

'You smell like my candle,' I said. Then I winced. 'Oh. The whole flat is full of candles.'

Julian just smiled at me. His hair, I noted with pleasure, had got slightly out of control during our chat. It was sprouting all over the place, fluffy bits sticking up.

Energy sparked almost visibly between his body and mine and I kept on staring at his hair to stop myself exploding.

'Oh, shit,' he said suddenly, clapping his hands up to his head. 'It's fluffy, isn't it?'

I peered at his hair politely as if noticing it for the first time. 'Oh. Not really,' I lied.

'Liar!' he shouted. He pulled his T-shirt up over his face and head. Then: '*Bollocks and bollocks!*' He lurched off sideways like a big, disorderly ghost. 'Goddamn stupid arse-twat fluffy hair. Arggh!'

He crashed into Raúl's sofa and reeled off towards the kitchen. His glasses fell out of the bottom of his T-shirt.

'Where are you trying to go?' I asked. 'Do you need some help?'

'Shut up,' he said, pointing in what he thought was my direction. It wasn't. 'Don't you laugh at me, Sally Howlett. You have no idea the battles I have with this hair, it's – ARGGH.'

By now I was shaking with laughter. Julian's T-shirt was still pulled up over his head as he stumbled around, but the offending fluffy hair was sticking out of the neck-hole, like a naughty puppy. 'Everyone gets fluffy hair once in a while,' I tried.

'I'VE BEEN GETTING FLUFFY HAIR SINCE I WAS BORN,' Julian yelled. He let out some sort of a war-cry, crashed into the dining table, fell sideways into a massive pouffe, pulled his head out of the T-shirt and sprinted through one of the doors.

I sat on the floor and wept with laughter.

As I finally pulled myself together, Julian returned and sat down beside me, hair tamed and smelling slightly of coconuts. 'I don't ever want to talk about that again,' he announced soberly.

I nodded. 'Understood.'

He looked sideways at me. I looked sideways at him, then back out of the window because I didn't know what to do with myself.

Manhattan twinkled away. The candles twinkled away. The connection between us twinkled away. It was thrilling.

'Do you think I'm a dick?' he asked.

'Definitely. Do you think *I*'m a dick?'

'One of the worst.'

'I can't be worse than you,' I said. 'For starters, your T-shirt is still back to front and inside out. Second, your accent is the maddest on earth. And, third, you are stand-ing in an apartment of *candles* overlooking Manhattan. It's like a scene from a weird porn film. What's wrong with you?'

Then I stopped and almost gasped. What was wrong with him? He was the widowed one! My insides turned over. He had probably been sitting amid the candles, talking to his dead wife.

A terrible, selfish disappointment gripped me. I liked Julian Bell. I was sitting close to him in a candlelit room and if I could have fast-forwarded the tape by a couple of hours I knew I would want to kiss him. I'd never felt that about anyone I'd just met.

But there was no place for me in the life of a grieving man.

I tried to backtrack twenty minutes to a time when Julian Bell was not in my life, but I couldn't. Already he'd claimed a seat at my table.

'What the hell is going on in there?' Julian was watching me intently. 'You look like you've gone into psychosis.'

I couldn't stop myself. 'Are you the widowed one?' I blurted.

If the question bothered him, it didn't show. 'Yep.'

I hated myself. Big, insensitive fool.

But, to my surprise, he was smiling again. 'You think I was sitting here communing with the dead, don't you?' He laughed.

'Perhaps.'

'Ha-ha! I was finishing my editorial for my magazine. We've got a power outage and my laptop's running out of juice. That's why I'm not with the others. Yet.'

'Oh.' I didn't believe him and continued to hate myself. Had I not had sufficient training with bereavement? *We carry on as if nothing's happened*, Mum hissed. *No fuss of any sort.*

'Well, Sally, I *was* widowed, and it was more than five years ago. I always meet up with the boys on the anniversary, because my mom expects me to have a breakdown and so do my friends, so they get together and fix it so that I'm not on my own. They think I don't know what they're doing. If I'm honest, I just do it for their sakes. I'm fine.'

I wanted desperately to believe him. 'It's true.' He shrugged. 'Of course I feel sad. Devastated, at times. Of course I wish she hadn't had to die. But it's not the biggest thing in my life any more.'

There was a long silence. 'That's pretty cool, actually,' he reflected, pleased. 'Go, me!' He took off his glasses and cleaned them on the corner of my cardigan.

'I'm really sorry,' I said eventually. 'It's absolutely none of my business and you shouldn't have to explain it to me. I'm just a weirdo who turned up at your front door. I should go. I'm sorry.'

'OK,' he said. 'Or you could stop having this little drama and we could have some more wine and hang out.' His eyes were mischievous. 'What's it to be?'

Finally, gloriously, I relaxed.

'Wine,' I said definitively. I sat down on a big hessian pouffe in the window and smiled. 'Let's get mildly drunk!'

He bounded off to the kitchen. 'Although, if you prefer,' he called, 'I can sit here wailing out love songs into the sea of candles.'

When he came back with the wine bottle, he was pointing at me. 'Lift up your index finger,' he instructed. I did so. Julian pushed the tip of his index finger against mine as if pressing a button.

'Reset,' he explained. 'Awkward widower-talk over. Start again.'

I liked it. 'We're reset,' I confirmed.

He topped up our glasses and sat down next to me again. The upper windows were still open and a freshening breeze prickled delicately at my shoulders.

We talked to the end of our glasses and agreed, reluctantly, that we should go and join the others in the poetry café. I didn't want this to end. I could tell Julian Bell didn't want it to end. But the need to be there for Fiona had become immutable.

'I'll go and change quickly,' I told him. 'Thank you for the wine!'

Julian stood up too. He was close to me. 'Thank Raúl,' he said. 'I stole it.' We both grinned.

Then he just stepped forward and, in a really matter-of-fact way, kissed me on the lips. I let him, because I wanted him to kiss me on the lips. He moved back, watching my face, and I wished he'd stayed for more.

'I don't normally behave like this,' he said. His voice was quieter. 'Was that too much?'

'No. I enjoyed it.' An irrepressible smile was erupting out of me.

He was blowing out candles as I left to go and change.

Scene Seven

The venue for the poetry slam was on an unprepossessing street on the edge of the East Village. 'This is Alphabet City,' Julian announced. 'There's quite a lot of assholes in this part of town, people who like to call themselves activists and creatives but who really just like themselves a bit too much.'

'Sounds like Williamsburg.'

He sniggered. 'Right.'

'Actually, I'm quite an activist,' I told him. 'I like protests and movements and things.'

'No, you're not,' Julian said firmly.

'What?' I tried to sound outraged.

'You're about as much of an activist as Pam the dog, Sally.'

'Who says?'

'You gave yourself away as soon as you opened your mouth.' He giggled and I giggled too. I couldn't stop myself. Everything about this man, from his fluffy hair to his odd brown trainers, was funny. 'You said, "I'm quite an activist." Nobody is "quite" an activist, you mad little hamster!' He giggled even harder. I giggled even harder. I liked being called a mad little hamster.

We were approaching the entrance to the poetry-slam venue, an unobtrusive glass porch leading into what looked like a dismal little building. It was called the Nuyorican Poets' Café. I braced myself.

'And you can stop that right now,' he said, even though I hadn't said anything. 'It's a really special place. Me and Raúl used to come here as students.'

'Right you are,' I said bravely.

Julian burst out laughing again. 'Oh, *look* at you! Ha-haaa! The hat. The outfit. And your little face, looking so appalled that I go to poetry slams. The whole thing is just . . . awesome. I like you.'

On the L train, while he was telling me about the magazine he owned and edited – a properly funny-sounding weekly called the *Brooklyn Beaver* – he'd caught me covertly sniffing my still-dirty hair. So when we'd got off at First Avenue he'd bought me a beanie from a little corner store. 'To stop the hair-sniffing,' he explained. I was touched and had put it on without hesitation, even though the All-Saints dress I had shoved on before we left was not its ideal partner.

Julian Bell was still laughing. 'Sally Howlett, you look like a proper Alphabet City beat-poet grassroots-activist patchouli-loving student,' he said. 'And I like it.'

I had no idea what most of this meant but I embraced it. 'Lead me to the creativity,' I ordered.

The poets' café was not so much a café but a proper little performance venue, with a stage, a large wooden floor and a balcony. A small bar ran along the wall from the entrance and – to my great surprise – the place was overflowing. Fiona, Raúl, Barry, Bea, Bea's Brazilian masseur and a few other men I identified as Raúl and Julian's friends were sitting halfway back, bottles of wine and beer already littering their table. Julian and I had obviously entered during some sort of hiatus but the crowd was already settling down for the next poet. Fiona looked flushed and excitable. 'This is actually really good!' she whispered. And then: 'WHO THE HELL IS THAT?'

I shrugged, and chose not to explain that he was the widowed bloke who, in the last hour, I'd met, kissed and slightly fallen for. Even Fi, with her wild imagination, would have struggled with that.

Raúl and the other boys sniggered in Julian's direction. 'Fast work, bro,' Raúl said, with an impressed nod.

I didn't mind. I sat down, marvelling at how normal it felt to be at a poetry slam with a widowed journalist, a rock star and an assortment of other crazies. Although, I realized, scanning the venue, they actually weren't crazies. They all looked quite normal. Even Bea didn't look out of place, although in fairness she had declined to wear her customary spike heels.

The next poet took to the microphone.

He was a slight, nervous-looking man who called himself 'Elf, from the Bronx', and he was dwarfed by his oversized suit. I felt my skin crawl with vicarious embarrassment, knowing that a man so uncomfortable in his own skin was quite unlikely to have poetry inside him.

How wrong I was.

I'd never heard performance poetry before – I hadn't wanted to – but I wanted that man to talk into the microphone all night. His poem was called 'Double Life' and it was all about the way he edited himself so that nobody could see who he really was. It was brutal and yet there was not so much as a whiff of self-pity. In fact, he was often so funny that Barry fell under the table laughing, although this was something Barry quite enjoyed doing.

When Elf finished I made myself hoarse cheering. He'd just told my story.

The night wore on and eventually ended, but Raúl was good friends with the owner of the café and got us locked in. I couldn't help but laugh at the sight of Beatriz Maria Stefanini taking part in a lock-in after a poetry slam, but she was in her element.

I took a mental snapshot of the place, knowing that whatever happened next between me and Julian Bell – even if it was nothing – I wanted to remember tonight for ever.

Heavy drinking ensued. Julian was next to me all night and I stopped thinking he was great and started thinking he was stupendous. He was generous with drinks, warm towards me, kind to his friends and consistently amusing: he called Fiona a wazzock – which nobody else would have attempted – and he and Raúl had us all in stitches with their banter. And yet he said to me, as I came back from the bar with a round of drinks, 'You crack me up, Sally Howlett. Why are you walking sideways to hide your bottom? It's magnificent!'

I blushed and demurred. 'You are extremely funny,' he informed me. 'Especially when you're not trying to be.'

He was definitely laughing at me, but I was definitely laughing at him. His hair escaped the products he'd shoved on hurriedly before we'd left, and started to fluff as the night got later and the mood wilder. He caught me looking at it, howled loudly and stole my new beanie.

'SO,' Fiona broke in, 'what do you think of our Sally? GORGEOUS, isn't she?' Fiona was very noisy tonight. And . . . weird. Something about her unsettled me. She spent quite a lot of time talking right in Raúl's face, then Julian's face, then my face, and kept starting pointless debates about things she lost interest in two seconds later. She was also, I noticed, with a twinge of fear, being difficult with Raúl. Clingy, then rude, then mad.

Julian began to compose a reply when Fiona interrupted, '*Everyone* loves Sally! Sally's the real star at our work, not me. She's like a sister to me, Julian, so if you mess with Sally, you mess with me —'

'Oi,' I cut in. 'Shut it.'

Fiona was so surprised she did. 'OK!' she squeaked, bounding off to tell Barry the news that I'd just told her to shut it.

'Is she normally like that?' Julian asked, looking curiously across at her.

I was torn between maternal defensiveness and the strong urge I felt to tell him the truth about everything. 'Yes and no,' I said slowly. 'She's difficult. But there's something particularly weird tonight . . .'

'I think she's high,' Julian said.

I went pale. 'No!'

He continued to watch her. 'Does she have a problem?'

'No! I mean . . . Well, I did catch her doing some coke in June, but she said she could take or leave it. She said she'd stopped.'

Julian nodded. 'Hmm.'

'I believe her, though. She stopped drinking too. She said she'd sorted herself out.'

'They always say that.'

'They?'

'Drug users.'

My stomach knotted. 'She's not a cokehead. She told me she'd given up. Completely. And she stopped drinking too. And she's been great! Much more reliable and . . . and she's FINE!'

Julian slid a hand over mine. 'Hey,' he said. 'Don't worry. I could be wrong.'

I stared at him, clutches of panic in my abdomen. 'Um, how come you know so much about drug users, Julian?'

He grinned. 'Fancy a line?'

'What?'

Then he laughed. 'I'm JOKING!'

Seeing me waver, he squeezed my hand. 'I was one hundred per cent joking,' he said quietly. 'I am not a cokehead. And I'm sure your cousin isn't either. I don't know what I'm on about.'

I nodded. 'OK . . .'

'I'm having a lovely night,' he said simply. His eyes were so close to mine. 'This is all pretty mad, isn't it?'

Everything faded to quiet. Fiona, the fear, the constant worry. I took a deep breath. 'Mad but good.'

Very briefly, before Raúl and the others had time to notice, Julian kissed me lightly on the lips. 'I like you even more than I did when I said it earlier.' He got up to go to the bar, the label of his still inside-out T-shirt flapping around under that mad hair.

*

Much later – by which time I had probably at least a couple of bottles of wine in me and was mumbling things like 'I NEEDA GO HOME BUT I'M TOO DRUNKA MOOOOVE' – someone started playing the piano. Bea, yes, that was who. Bea had a baby grand in her five-bedroom flat in Marylebone and knocking out Haydn sonatas was just another part of her repertoire.

'I still don't unnerstand why she works,' I confided in Julian. 'I mean, she's, like, thaaaaaaat rich. She could buy Barack Obama's house . . .'

Julian raised an eyebrow. 'The White House? Wow.'

'And DONALTRUM'S HOUSE! DONALTUMP'S HOUSE! I mean TRUMP'S HOUSE. No! I don't mean TRUMP, I mean DONALD –'

'Oh, my God, seriously, stop talking.' Julian was wetting himself. 'You told me you were a good drinker!'

'I lied,' I confirmed happily. 'I'm terrible. TRUMP! TRUMPY DONALT —'

We were interrupted. One of the other boys staying in Raúl's flat – an artist the shape and size of a large tank – came over and pretty much picked Julian up. 'Come and sing,' he instructed.

'Oh, dude, no . . .' Julian protested. 'I don't want to, I'm talking to my fine lady here, she's –'

'Come and sing,' the guy repeated. 'Jorge asked for you. He's been serving us beers way past his home time,' he added. Jorge was the owner and apparently a friend of this group of bohemian nutters.

'OK, OK! Let go of me, you douche.' Julian went off to the piano.

Bea looked up from the keyboard and shrieked

delightedly. 'They tell me you are a great singer,' she purred. 'Come and sit next to Beatriz . . .'

As soon as he was gone, Fiona closed in on me. 'What the *fuck*?' she hissed. 'Did you two have *sex* or something? You're like electricity!'

I did a double-take. Sometime during the evening, Fiona had started drinking. I hadn't noticed: perhaps because I was hammered, perhaps because I was so used to the sight of her with a smudged wine glass slopping around in her hand. But she was drunk. Her eyes were yellowy and unfocused and she was right up in my face. I could smell the booze on her breath. Maybe something else. Sharp, chemical.

Let it go, I told myself. I was drunk too. Bollocksed. Everyone was allowed a night off the wagon once in a while, weren't they?

I tried to smile what I thought to be a secretive, enigmatic sort of smile, but it turned into a moronic leer. 'Julian's *lovely*,' was all I could manage. '*Luvverly*.'

'Well, one of us should be happy,' Fiona replied. 'I mean, I'm never going to be promoted at work and I'm getting all fat and I'll probably fuck up with Raúl, but you might as well be happy. Go for it, I say.'

I sighed despairingly, and started to compose a reply, but Fiona giggled naughtily. 'I'm *joking*!' she said, punching my arm.

But then I stopped hearing her voice. Suddenly, the room was slowing down and there was a sound that filled me with the purest, not-drink-related joy. Bea was playing the duet in *La Bohème* where Rodolfo and Mimi first meet in his freezing garret in the Latin Quarter, where they fall in love on the spot. The tune poured into me and the hairs on the back of my neck, drunk and disorderly as they were, stood up. Oh, God, it broke my heart, this music. It killed me. It was *beautiful*.

Fiona had stopped talking to me and was staring dreamily at the piano. Someone had started singing Rodolfo's part very well. *Julian Bell*, I realized, had started singing Rodolfo's part. He clearly wasn't a proper singer or anything, but he was singing it very nicely indeed. Softly, perfectly pitched, and with an impressive sensitivity for someone who had drunk a good few buckets of wine.

Bea threw in Mimi's lines in her crow's shriek, which made everyone laugh.

'This is, like, a fraction of what he can do,' the tank man told us proudly. I didn't believe him, because if Julian could sing any better than that he'd have been a singer. But I felt myself taking in Tank Man's infectious pride. *You're amazing*, I thought dazedly, watching Julian sing. *Really amazing*. Briefly I remembered having thought only a few weeks ago that amazing men were way out of my league, never interested in someone like me.

'This is your favourite, this duet, isn't it?' Fi whispered.

I nodded, and even though Bea was screeching horribly through Mimi's part, I had tears in my eyes. I felt so happy, watching the brilliant man who kept kissing me, surrounded by people I loved, that to hear my most precious, favourite piece of music in candlelight was almost too much.

Fiona put an arm round my shoulders and kissed the side of my face. 'I love you so much, Sal,' she whispered, sweaty and close. 'I don't know what I'd do without you. You're my world.'

I allowed the tears – some happy, some despairing – to fall.

Julian and Bea carried on but as the higher, louder notes approached, Bea stopped playing. 'I cannot do this!' she shrieked. 'Someone sing Mimi, please!'

And without hesitation, without *thinking* about it, I just got up, walked over to the piano where I stood in front of Julian, looked him in the eye and started singing.

After it was over I became aware of a lot of noise. It was Bea, shrieking again. She wasn't singing this time, she was screaming at me. 'You sing? You SING? *DIO MIO*, SALLY, MY DARLING, THAT WAS BEAUTI-FUL!' Fi was jumping all over me and all of the others were clapping and whistling. I looked around wild-eyed. I'd sung?

Finally, I looked at Julian, who was staring at me like I was on fire. He shook his head and whispered something. In spite of the racket I heard it clearly: 'Shit. You were *incredible*. What was that about?'

And I knew I should care, that this was my cue to fade and disappear and die, that I should pretend it hadn't happened and fudge over it as if it were some silly mistake, but I couldn't and didn't.

As if we were the only people in the room, Julian leaned over and took my hand. 'Well, you certainly kept that one up your sleeve. You dark horse, Sally Howlett. Let's go. I'm fed up of sharing you. Can I have you to myself now?'

Scene Eight

It is a fact universally acknowledged that no sane person can really fall in love in one night. At best, it is an obsession. A compelling feeling that *this* person, *this one*, out of all the millions of others, is the answer to all of your problems. At worst, it is misplaced horn.

I must just be in lust, I told myself drunkenly. *Simple old lust. And loneliness.*

Julian was saying goodbye to the owner, Jorge, at the door. Jorge had the air of a man who seriously worshipped Julian. As we wobbled off down the street, he called after us, 'Take good care of my friend Jules! This guy saved my ass, not to mention this café!'

'What did he mean?' I asked.

Julian put the beanie back on my head, in case I got cold, and pinched my nose. 'Ah, nothing. He just means I spend a lot of money in there. We go back a long way. Such a lovely, lovely man, Jorge.'

You're a lovely, lovely man, I thought. *A really lovely man.* I'd been brought up in a house where kind words were seldom spoken about other people. Julian was different. He was generous.

'Now,' he said, refusing to move off, 'tell me right now about that voice of yours.' His eyes sparkled with curiosity and amusement. 'You just sang the *shit* out of Mimi! I'm not sure I believe you're just a wardrobe mistress.'

Panic slashed my insides briefly but I managed to pull myself together. 'I am honestly a wardrobe mistress,' I told him.

'But you must have had singing lessons. Years of them. Wardrobe mistress or not . . .'

'I've never had a singing lesson in my life,' I said truthfully.

Julian folded his arms across his chest, smiling. 'Why are you lying, Beanie Girl?' he asked. 'It's not possible to sing like that without training.'

I folded my arms across my own chest. 'And how do you know that? You weren't so bad yourself.'

There was a minor face-off, which I ended by glancing upwards at his hair.

'What?' he said, hands flying to his head. 'Is it fluffy again? ARGGH.'

I grinned. 'No. And I'm not a singer. Not now, not ever.'

Julian watched me for a minute, then chuckled. 'Ah, you make me laugh. You just make me laugh, a lot. Come on, mad little hamster.'

He walked me to Avenue B where he hailed us a cab. He looked like a scruffy film star and he held my hand as if it were the most natural thing in the world. It was ridiculous and completely normal all in one.

Neither of us said anything as we sped over Williamsburg Bridge. The previous inhabitants of the taxi had left the windows wide open and I let the air, now cool and fresh, fly through my still-dirty hair. As we hit Brooklyn and turned north, I looked sideways at Julian. His eyes were closed but I could tell he wasn't asleep. He smiled. 'Stop staring at my fluffy hair.'

'I wasn't!'

He just smiled sleepily and pinched my leg.

I looked out of my window at the still-busy streets. Williamsburg was alive and kicking. Trendies – *hipsters*, I had to start calling them – were standing smoking outside the Union Pool and two girls in vintage shoes were trying to navigate the flyover slip-roads with great bravery.

'You sing like an angel,' he said, after a pause. I could feel him looking at me. Most strangely, it didn't feel threatening, the attention. He'd just complimented a part of me that nobody ever saw and I was fine with it.

'You sang nicely yourself. How do you know the words to that duet?' I asked idly. I was still turned away from him, watching the edges of Williamsburg flash past my window.

'Oh, I learned it once. I liked it.'

'It's utterly, utterly beautiful, isn't it?' I said happily. I didn't feel even the slightest bit twattish.

As we levelled 10th Street, Julian leaned forward and tapped on the cab driver's window. 'Can you make a left and leave us at 11th and Wythe?' The man didn't acknowledge him but duly turned left.

'Where are we going?'

Julian ignored me; he just smiled.

'Will there be toasted cheese sandwiches? I want a toasted cheese sandwich.' I sounded comically drunk and resolved to keep my mouth shut.

But Julian roared with laughter. 'I would *love* a cheese toastie,' he said. 'And a cup of proper English tea. I'll see what I can do.'

A couple of minutes later we pulled up outside a brick building with huge red-lit letters, saying 'Hotel', up its side. I was puzzled but not particularly alarmed. Julian Bell didn't seem to be the sort who'd just check us into a hotel for a night of hot love. I hoped not, anyway. This thing was far too magical to end up ruined by a fumbly-rump.

He tried to pay the driver but I insisted: he'd been buying me drinks all night and if my parents had taught me anything it was that I must not let anyone else spend too much money on me. (*Why?* I wondered momentarily. *Am I not worth spending money on?*)

A little fissure of sadness began to make its way through the fabric of tonight but I stopped it in its tracks. I wasn't having it. Tonight had made me feel good about myself. My parents did not.

'Thanks for the cab, little lady.' Julian beamed, beckoning me over to the lift, which a fashionably dressed porter had called. Then: 'Oh . . . *SHIT*!'

He went to run out of the hotel but stopped by the door. 'My cell,' he said. 'I left my stupid cell in the stupid taxi . . . Ah, balls.'

The porter shook Julian's hand warmly. 'Dude, you lose your phone every month. It's great to see you, buddy.'

They laughed. 'But I'd had this one five months!' Julian complained, running his hand exasperatedly through his hair. It settled down into something reasonably respectable.

The porter grinned. 'You're learning, my friend.'

Julian shrugged helplessly. 'Meh. Now, how's your wife?' he asked. 'Is she doing OK?'

The porter smiled. 'She's going great. Better every day. I'll tell her I saw you.'

'Send her my love. She's a trouper, that one!'

The porter nodded proudly. 'She is. Now, go get a drink,' he said, waving us through. 'And thanks for asking, man.'

We got into the lift and I poked him. 'Um, excuse me. Why does everyone love you so much?'

'Because I'm phenomenal,' he said, scratching the side of his face. 'Even though I'm always late and I lose everything.'

I smiled. 'Well, I'm highly organized. It's quite boring. Your way's probably better.'

'Hmm. I was highly organized for a while, back in the day.' He yawned, screwing his eyes shut, and I thought that he looked like a sleepy bear cub. 'Sorry, I'm not bored, I'm tired. Aren't you?'

'No.' I wasn't tired. The light bulb he'd turned on in me earlier had become twenty. More were pinging on every minute.

'Good. Because I'd hate you to miss out on this.'

'What? Are you taking me to the matrimonial suite for rumpy-pumpy? Because if you are, you can –'

Julian snorted with laughter. 'Rumpy-pumpy?' he repeated incredulously. 'Did you actually just say that?'

'Absolutely. Get over it.'

'Roompay-poompay,' he repeated, in a surprisingly good Brummie accent.

The lift stopped and, to my disappointment, we walked

out into what looked like a poncy cocktail bar. No tea and toasties here.

'Oh, we're closed,' the girl behind the bar began. She was cashing up. Then her face lit up. '*Jules!* Hi, baby!'

She bounded round to greet him and I marvelled. How was the owner of a small and – according to him – pretty crap local magazine called the *Brooklyn Beaver* so well known in these parts? Clearly I was not the only person round here who thought that Julian Bell was a little bit amazing. The girl hung off him as if Brad Pitt had just walked into her bar and only really let him go when he introduced her to me.

'Oooh!' she said, staring at me. And that was it. She waved us past. 'I'll bring you a tray, Jules.'

'Thanks, Tasha. You're the best.'

And then I saw it.

The view. The heart-stopping view of Manhattan that made me actually gasp. I'd been so busy perving at Julian that I'd somehow failed to notice that we were in a glass-walled bar with a view of New York that put to shame any other I'd ever seen. It was *breathtaking*.

Julian, laughing at my awed paralysis, pushed me gently towards a door that led to an outside patio. 'It's pretty good, isn't it?' was all he said.

We stood at the edge and stared at New York. A thousand thousand lights twinkled across the river at me, each one a portal into a life, a story, a soul. I stood and stared, and felt Julian's smile burning into me somewhere off to the left, and couldn't deny it. Something special wasn't just *happening* to me, it had *happened*.

'This is the best view ever,' I breathed. Julian came and

stood next to me, sliding his hand under my hair to hold the back of my neck. His hand was warm.

'It is,' he agreed. 'But sometimes I stand here and think, *I miss the Teign valley. I miss Dartmoor. I miss scrubby grass and spiky gorse bushes and cow shit.* Sometimes I wonder why I'm standing here in this expensive bar when I could be sitting under a tree in the rain, all the sheep staring at me with their mad little faces, and nothing but the sound of rain dripping off the leaves. Perhaps the distant noise of Dad crashing around on his tractor. I dunno.'

I saw it. Julian sitting under a tree in the rain, somewhere rugged and beautiful. 'It sounds lovely. But I . . . I don't feel the same about my council estate. If I'm honest.'

Julian laughed. 'I love that you just say that. You just chat about coming from a council estate.'

'Why wouldn't I? Do you think I should pretend to be posher or something?'

'Jesus, no! But other girls would. That's why I feel . . . That's why, I, um, seem to like you so much.'

I believed him. We smiled at each other.

'Bugger. What have you done to me?' Julian asked. He stared out at Manhattan and stroked my neck. I tried to crane round for a snog but as I did the girl from the bar came out with a tray. 'Two cheese toasties and a pot of tea,' she announced, in a bad approximation of an English accent. 'Oh, and I managed to salvage some of those repellent oblong cookies from last time you were here. And the awful jam ones. Yuk.'

Julian's hand dropped from my neck. 'Custard creams and Jammie Dodgers?' he said hoarsely. 'You got me custard creams and Jammie Dodgers?'

She grinned and put the tray down on the table nearest to us, a beautiful, delicious, trans-fatty square of Britishness. 'You English.' She sighed. 'You're so cute.'

As she sashayed off back into the closed bar I smelt melted cheese and toast and watched, laughing, as Julian scrambled at high speed to pour the tea and dunk a custard cream. 'Oh, my God,' he muttered happily. 'This is the best night of my life.'

He whipped out his glasses to look at me, to check that I was as happy as he was, and grinned slowly, beautifully, when he saw I was completely ecstatic.

Then his glasses fell off his nose and, even though it felt impossible – ludicrous, even – I knew I was in love.

Later, I lay alone in my bed, tingling with excitement. I imagined Julian asleep three floors above me, surrounded by candles and his oldest, dearest friends, and felt like my chest would burst. I'd lived so cautiously for so long, hidden so much of myself, just like tonight's poet with his double life. But maybe it was time for a change.

Anything felt possible. I hugged my duvet and smiled and smiled until eventually I slipped into a deep, exhausted and blissful sleep.

ACT FOUR

Scene Ten

September 2012, the Royal College of Music

My second week at opera school began with a piece of good news and a piece of bad.

The good news was that I was given a chorus part in the November production, *Manon*, meaning I wouldn't have to sing a single word on my own.

Violet Elphinstone got the lead role. 'Oh, it was such a fluke,' she confided happily in me. 'I did a *dreadful* audition – they probably got me mixed up with you! After all, you're the one everyone's talking about.'

'I don't think they are,' I said anxiously, twiddling my horrid ring. I hoped not. My non-part in the November production would hopefully put paid to all the nonsense about me being special and different, and shine the spotlight on those who deserved it.

'Come off it, you're the star attraction,' Violet said, with a resentful smile. 'You're *so* going to get the main part next term. Once they've loosened you up!'

'Um, what?'

'Julian's my vocal coach,' she said casually. 'He said you

were scared of singing but that you could sing in a wardrobe or something. I was like, er, no, that can't be right!'

Rage came and went. Julian was out of order, discussing me with anyone. Especially Violet. But I wouldn't let him get to me. 'I do quite like singing in wardrobes.' I smiled. 'Yeah.'

Violet's eyes widened, in a patronizing way. 'Wow! You're so funny! My crazy little friend! Still love that ring of yours, by the way, it's like, whoa!'

It was strange, talking to Violet. She was so obviously stunning and so obviously talented, and it was so painfully evident that every man in the college wanted to have amazing sex with her (or any sort of sex, probably) that it seemed odd she was so determined to squash me.

I was not a threat to her. I was getting on with everyone but had only really connected with Jan and Helen – who were self-confessed marginal figures – so it wasn't as if Violet's popularity was threatened. Quite the opposite. I created barely a social ripple while everyone hung off her like fleas from a show dog.

And looks-wise, I was dog poo next to her gleaming pedigree fur. *Whatever* your taste in women, you'd fancy Violet Elphinstone.

And, to top it off, I was having singing lessons in a wardrobe because I couldn't face singing in front of anyone.

Quite simply, I was not and never would be on the same page as her. Why did she care so much?

The bad news was that Brian persuaded me to audition for the TV advert with a taped recording rather than a live audition, and I got the job. He had made up some nonsense to the advertising executives about me being busy with high-profile private gigs and convinced them I was so good they'd be mad not to hear me. Somehow they agreed. I was dispatched to a different type of wardrobe – a recording studio – and Brian hid below the sound desk so that I wouldn't feel watched. Every now and then his hand reached up and turned a knob; otherwise I was alone in the padded cell. Which was bearable.

And they bloody well gave me the job. I was appalled. But Fiona, whom I called immediately, was over the moon and put me right back on track. So I said yes to the ad. I was seizing the day for Fi.

'It'll be fine.' Brian smiled benignly. We were standing in a corridor, next to a display case full of funny old trumpets and horns. I had crammed myself into the corner and was probably wild-eyed with terror at the thought of recording an audio track for an advert. 'You'll be in a studio,' he said. 'Like the one you and I recorded in.'

'But nobody's going to hide under the sound desk to fiddle with knobs!' I took a deep breath, realizing that I sounded both mad and ungrateful. 'Sorry, Brian. Ignore me. I *do* want to do it. I do want to get through these nerves.'

I felt him smile. 'Good,' he said quietly. 'We might even get out of that wardrobe soon, eh?'

'Hmm.'

Brian cocked his head to one side. 'I had a request from Julian Jefferson,' he said. 'He's meant to be your vocal coach, as you know, but he asked if I could take over his classes with you. Meaning you'd only be singing with me, for now. He felt that would be much better for you, given that you're so nervous still.'

My initial relief was overshadowed almost immediately by prickly suspicion. What was Julian up to?

Brian was still watching me curiously. 'Julian seems to be very good at knowing what will help you sing,' he said. 'Are you a friend of his?'

I blushed. 'Definitely not.'

Brian's eyebrow shot up and I cursed myself.

'Julian *Jefferson* is not someone I knew before coming to college,' I said truthfully. 'He's a total stranger.'

Brian nodded. 'Well, the man is even more gifted than I thought. I completely agree with him that it's best if you stay with me for now. I'll have the office modify your schedule accordingly.'

Thank God. Me, Brian and a wardrobe might just be OK.

'Anyway,' Brian said, 'here's the information pack from the TV people. Everything you need to know is in there. Have a read, tell me what it's all about and then we can prepare together, OK? And I'll come with you to the recording.'

I wandered down to the dressing room, which was mercifully empty, and opened the envelope.

And my heart stopped.

What?

I read the first sentence again. No, there was no mistaking it. I stared at myself in the mirror, watching shame stain my face. I couldn't do this! What would Mum and Dad say? They'd die! I had to –

'Hello?'

Someone male had popped his head round the door

without asking. That was not cool. Even less cool was that it was Julian.

I was actually so shocked by what I'd just read that I didn't run in the opposite direction, or ask him to leave, or stare in wonder at his weird long, shiny hair and smart attire. I just gaped at him.

'All right,' he said, in that crazy Devon-Manhattan accent. He closed the door behind him and pulled a packet of Frazzles out of his annoying posh satchel. 'That's a nice face you've got on. Look what I got! Our favourite crisps!'

I turned away angrily.

'I just wanted to say congrats. On the advert,' he added, when I didn't reply.

He must surely be mocking me. Nobody in their right mind would congratulate me for getting a gig like that.

'Um, go, you!' he added uncomfortably.

'Don't take the piss out of me,' I said coldly. He was beyond belief.

'I wasn't! Sal, it's –'

'And STOP CALLING ME SAL.'

Julian put the Frazzles down on the side and sighed. 'OK. Sally it is, then. I understand. But whatever I'm calling you, I just wanted to say well done. A brilliant start to your career.'

The door burst open and Violet, Ismene, Sophie and Summer came in, Violet holding forth on how horribly embarrassing some recent experience had been and how she was 'so glad I turned them down!' Then her mouth formed a little 'Oh' as she saw me, and a bigger, happier 'OH!' as she saw Julian.

'Hi, guys!' she said casually. She shrugged off a little cashmere wrap so that her shoulders were bare, save for the straps of her yoga vest. Violet had just had movement class.

'Hello, Violet,' Julian said neutrally. Violet shook out her hair and pretended to massage her delicate collar bones. Julian raised his eyebrow a fraction, a tiny ironic movement designed only for me.

Not today. He could forget it if he thought I was going to join his club.

Suddenly Violet had moved across the floor and had gathered me up in a hug. 'Congratulations!' she said. 'I heard about the ad! You are *soooooo* brave!'

I felt part of me die.

'I did seriously consider it when they offered it to me . . . But I couldn't quite make myself do it. You're made of tougher stuff,' she added kindly, pulling up her own chair and shooting a conspiratorial look at Julian in her mirror.

'I'm not brave or tough,' I said dully. 'I didn't know what the ad's for because I didn't read the information properly.' Of course I hadn't read the bloody job description. It had been all I could do to get myself into the recording studio with Brian.

Julian was watching me. His face wasn't moving but I could see his amusement as clear as day. 'You didn't know?' he asked. 'What the advert was?'

'No,' I said briefly.

'What is it?' Helen had arrived in the room too. She hadn't auditioned, telling me she wasn't ready for that kind of stuff yet. 'Would rather stick my head in a blacksmith's stove,' she'd said cheerfully. *After* I'd gone and recorded my audition.

Violet giggled. 'Sally's going to be advertising something very special,' she said. 'Bless her!'

Helen looked at me, realized I was unlikely to reply, so turned to Julian.

He coloured slightly. 'It's an ad for, um, a sanitary napkin brand,' he said. And then he smirked.

Helen's gaze swivelled back towards me. 'You're advertising sanitary towels?'

I was frozen. I couldn't answer. Especially with Julian there, trying to look all sympathetic when in reality he was having serious trouble preventing himself bellowing with laughter. I couldn't tell him to get lost while the others were there so I stood up and slid out of the fire escape, mumbling about needing a packet of crisps.

I started crying as soon as the door banged behind me. Why had I been so confoundedly *stupid*? What on earth had possessed me to go for a singing job I knew nothing about? What had possessed me to go for a singing job of any sort, come to think of it? And to know that Violet had turned it down . . . I decided to head for the canteen for a packet of emergency Frazzles. I had no idea what to do.

A tissue was forced into my face.

'Cry,' Jan Borsos ordered. 'Cry, cry, cry.' Then he looked a bit confused. 'The imperative conjugation is *cry* or *crying*?'

'Can I answer that another time?' I sobbed.

'No. You are crying now. I must know the answer, please.'

195

'"Crying" is the present continuous tense.' I sniffed wearily. 'Like, *I am crying*. But "Cry!" is the imperative. The command. For example, "*Cry! Cry right now!*" But generally people don't command each other to cry.' The tears had already stopped falling and I was smiling weakly at the absurdity of the conversation.

'This is good information,' Jan muttered, scribbling something in a notebook. 'I did knew this but I think it is strange that you English do not have a conjugation separate for the imperative tense.'

I smiled briefly. Jan was ridiculous.

You used to think Julian was ridiculous, my head reminded me.

Perhaps out of desperation to avoid any thoughts of Julian, I found myself telling Jan Borsos everything. About how I was so terrified of singing that I was taking lessons in a wardrobe, about the recorded audition, and about discovering from Violet that I was going to be advertising menstrual products.

I kept the Julian story to myself for now. Jan Borsos was taking me out for dinner, albeit at my expense, and even though it was not and never could be a date I thought it best not to offend him.

Jan listened to me, scowling kindly. 'I think this situation is very funny,' he said. 'And I think you will find it funny also, when you are stopping the embarrassment about the sanatorium towels.'

And with the same speed that I'd stopped crying, I started laughing. Jan Borsos, I was coming to realize, was very good at snapping me out of spiralling negativity. The fact of the matter was that I was going to be paid three thousand pounds to advertise sanitary towels. Nobody would see my face: I just had to record an aria I loved in a wardrobe-like environment and then I'd be done. Really, it was me who was having the last laugh. I wiped my eyes and smiled. 'Thank you, Jan Borsos,' I said gratefully, drying my eyes. We started walking up towards the canteen. 'I'd lost my sense of humour there.'

'I am seeing this. Tell me, Sally, why are you so afraid of singing?'

I shrugged. 'Not sure. Bad childhood experience? I tried to sing at a school concert and got stage fright and . . . well, it went a bit wrong.'

'But why? Why were you having the stage fright?'

I paused. 'I honestly don't know,' I said thoughtfully. 'But if I work it out, Jan Borsos, I'll be sure to tell you.'

Jan Borsos offered me his elbow. I had to bend down slightly to link my arm through it. 'I am liking you call me Jan Borsos,' he said. 'Jan is not enough. Jan gives me the feeling that I am a short man. Jan Borsos gives me the feeling that I am a big man from Hungary with the voice of a large bear.'

I laughed and laughed. I was looking forward to our dinner very much.

Scene Eleven

Ten minutes after the start of my first movement class I was hauled out to meet Lord Peter Ingle, the very kind – and presumably very rich – man who was paying one of my scholarships. Although I would have liked more time to prepare to meet a lord I was certainly glad to have got out of movement class. There had been a lot of explanatory stuff about how we needed to learn to 'embrace the physicality' of whatever character we were playing, while 'supporting our breath', all of which had sounded a bit too drama school to me.

And on top of all of these issues I was deeply hungover after my dinner with Jan Borsos.

The class had started better than I'd expected because today we were just doing aerobics, a proper cheesy nineties workout. Initially I'd been quite pleased, especially given that it might reduce my massive arse. But then I'd discovered that the space in which we were working out was fully viewable from a mezzanine corridor that ran along two sides of the room. Helen, doing ungainly squats next to me, had suddenly hissed that I shouldn't look up at the balcony if I knew what was good for me. Obviously, I looked, mid-squat – as if I were settling in for a good long poo – and there above me was Julian. He walked along the corridor quickly, his eyes straight ahead, but I knew what he looked like when he was trying not to explode with laughter. He must have seen me.

'I told you not to look, you fool,' Helen said, shaking her head. She handed me a KitKat finger and we both got told off for eating chocolate during workout.

My upbraiding was interrupted by one of the administrators, Sandra, who fished me out to meet Lord Peter Ingle. 'Without him you wouldn't be here,' she reminded me. 'He's been so generous!'

I was given no time to change, let alone prepare. He was literally outside the door. He, too, had probably seen me poo-squatting.

'Sally Howlett,' said Lord Peter Ingle, tall and confident in those strange mustard-coloured cords that only the aristocracy wear. (Why? Why did they do that? What was it about money and status, conferred on you at birth, that meant you were predisposed to mustard or ruby slacks?) He smiled very warmly and I shook his hand, wincing at the sweatiness of my palms. Sandra from the office showed us into the empty Britten Theatre and we drifted down to the stage making small talk. A brief spasm of fear gripped me: he surely wouldn't expect me to sing something for him, would he?

I calmed down. He would not. He gestured to the first row of purple chairs in the auditorium and we sat down. I noticed that he had monumentally big ears. 'I came in to talk through some *stuff*,' he said – I nodded knowingly – 'and thought, what the hell, I'd see if you were around for a quick hello.'

'Hello,' I offered quickly.

'Hello,' he replied.

I cleared my throat. 'Thank you so very much for the scholarship, Lord Ingle. I cannot tell you how much it means to me – studying here is my absolute dream.'

Lord Ingle narrowed his eyes. 'Ha! Bollocks.'

'I'm sorry?'

'Bollocks, Sally. I know you don't want to be here.' He roared with laughter.

I started gabbling. 'Oh, but I do, it's a once-in-a-lifetime –'

Lord Ingle held a hand up. 'Bollocks,' he repeated. Then he laughed again. His ears jiggled. He was like the BFG. 'Brian's an old friend of mine,' he said. 'It was he who persuaded me to offer a scholarship to this place. I came to see him here in his graduation show, what, forty years ago? Christ, we're old bastards . . .' He drifted momentarily into a happy reverie and I realized I should probably contradict him.

'Not old!' I blustered.

Lord Ingle said, 'Bollocks,' again, and I decided it was best if I didn't talk for a while.

'Brian and I were roommates at Oxford,' he explained. 'I loved him from the start. Such a breath of fresh air at that bloody place.' He crossed his legs and leaned back in his chair, smiling. 'Brian knocked a lot of shit out of me. I'd been to Eton, obviously' (*obviously!* I loved it) 'and he'd been to some God-awful secondary modern and yet he taught me more about life in that year than I'd learned in the previous eighteen.'

I smiled. Brian really was a very special man. To have come from where he had and now be a renowned baritone, so brilliant that he'd been able to retire from performance when he fancied and take up a job at one of the world's best *conservatoires*, well, it was pretty cool.

'Anyway, I lost a few hundred thousand last year investing in some bad stocks, and when I told Brian, he just said, "Peter, stop throwing your money around and put it into a good cause, man!" So I did. You're my first scholar!' he exclaimed, beaming.

'Great,' I said woodenly.

'I hear you're of Brian's sort of upbringing,' he said, with the unperturbed confidence of those at the very top of the food chain. 'Which is cracking. Places like this should be all about talent, not money.'

I relaxed a little.

Lord Ingle smiled warmly. 'I do find it rather splendid that you'd rather gouge your own eyeballs out than be here.'

I blushed guiltily.

'Brian told me all about you,' he went on. 'He told me you kept trying to leave and that he eventually had to throw you into a wardrobe.'

'Brian's been very understanding,' I mumbled. I didn't think that Lord Peter Ingle was trying to embarrass me, but he was doing a fairly reasonable job.

'I'm sure he has. Excellent fellow.' He drummed his fingers on the seat, then looked at me. 'But, Sally, I do rather hope that you might be able to get out of the wardrobe and start singing to actual people. Soon.'

I shuddered. Apparently scholarship students often had to 'thank' their benefactors by singing at dinners or private concerts: I would rather pay back every penny of Lord Ingle's scholarship than do that. The very thought of all those privileged eyes trained on me, the smell of roasted game and tawny port from their tables . . . Urgh. No. Never.

'Fortunately,' Lord Ingle continued, as if reading my mind, 'I don't want you to come and sing at my Christmas ball. Or at my summer shooting party. Ha, I'm not even joking. I really do those things. Awful, eh?'

I raised a sort-of smile.

'No, Sally, I think my assignment for you will be a little more to your liking. I want to give something back to the community.'

'Uh-huh,' I said nervously. 'Tell me more, Lord Ingle.'

'PETER!' he cried, appalled. 'Lord Ingle? My God!'

'Peter,' I mumbled. The man was like an elephant. Although a charming one with big flappy ears that you'd want to stroke. I didn't dislike him in the slightest.

'What I didn't mention is that I also live in the south-ernmost reaches of the Black Country,' he said. 'We've got a lovely estate hidden in the middle of some God-awful hellholes. Miles and miles of beautiful parkland and then, boom, there's another monstrous factory or a shitty town. My ancestors sold out to the industrial revolution and lost thousands of acres in the process. Terrible error.'

I smiled inwardly. That sounded like my neck of the woods, all right. 'Anyway, we were saved from an arson attack a few years ago by some local chap who noticed a gang of hoodies climbing over one of the estate walls. He was just an ordinary bloke on his way back from a shift at Hall's – the clothing factory where I believe your parents worked?' I nodded, impressed. 'And he took them on. All of them. The bleeding little scrotes gave him a beating but he got the police to us just in time.'

'Wow,' I said, genuinely surprised. It sure as hell wouldn't have been Dad who'd rescued Peter's estate. Dad wouldn't even take on his own wife.

'Anyway. We realized we'd been living there all these years, my family and I, and had never taken any notice of the locals. Decided we wanted to give something back to the people, you know?'

I didn't know but I nodded politely. I strongly suspected that my 'people' were about to be patronized.

'We opened our house to the public a few years ago, so everyone can have a good nose around, but apart from the National Trust anoraks, nobody ever comes. The locals avoid us like the plague. We've held fêtes, concerts, all sorts, but they just aren't interested.'

'Are you surprised?' I heard myself snort.

There was a short silence.

'Sorry,' I said lamely. 'I didn't mean to be rude. It's just – well – I can't see my parents ever wanting to go to a, um, a fête.'

Peter slapped his leg. 'Of bloody course they don't! Why the bloody hell would anyone on a council estate want to visit some toff's country estate for a cup of over-priced tea served in a room full of gilt-framed photos of my ancestors? Dear Christ!'

I laughed.

'It was my wife's idea,' he said regretfully. 'She knows even less about real life than I do. But I had a chat with Brian about it, just in passing, and he came up with a cracking little plan.'

I waited.

'What Brian and I want to do is to start some outreach work. In schools.'

Outreach? I wasn't even sure what that meant.

'I had a chat with a few head teachers recently,' he said. 'They were telling me that they have almost no provision for the arts. They're badly stretched trying to provide the very basics so they seldom find themselves with money for decent creative extra-curriculars. I wanted to send you in, you and my other scholar, to do some singing with them. You can tell me what you think best – put on a musical, an opera, a concert? Give them lessons? Something like that?'

I was lost. Peter had obviously assumed that, as a working-class girl now studying at a big posh college, I held the creative solution to social deprivation. 'Er . . .'

He watched me keenly, but then his face fell. 'Ah, you haven't any idea either,' he said sadly. 'Well, please at least think about it, Sally. I spoke to the headmaster from your old secondary school, and he was really very keen, you know. He remembered you.'

I softened, thinking fondly of my mild-mannered head. 'Oh, well, I'm sure I can think of something,' I heard myself saying. 'A workshop, maybe?'

And that was that.

Almost. Just before Peter left, pumping my still-sweaty

hand enthusiastically, inviting me for tea at his country house, I remembered something. 'By the way, you said you had two students on scholarships here,' I said. We were now standing in the foyer. Outside it was fresh and sharp as a needle after a night of thunderstorms.

'Yes, yes! I have two of you. Must arrange to meet the other one – he sounds like a fine little chap.'

'Who is he?' I asked, a sinking feeling in my gut.

Peter scratched his head, trying to remember the name, and then his face cleared. 'Jan!' he exclaimed. 'Jan Borsos! Do you know him? Will you be happy to work with him? A great young talent, by all accounts.'

I nodded feebly. 'I know Jan,' I said, with as straight a face as I could muster. 'We'll be great together. See you soon, Peter!'

I was sunk.

The problem wasn't that Jan would be hideously incongruous at a school like Stourbridge Grange, or that he would steal the show with his passion for performance being ten times greater than mine. It was that Jan and I had had our dinner last night and, even though he was seven years younger than me, a good three inches shorter and madder than a box of Hungarian frogs, I had spent most of that morning having sex with him.

Scene Twelve

The night before

It had started well. My intentions involved only friendship.

I hadn't even been sure I should go for dinner, in case he saw it as a date, but Fiona had insisted. 'Meet him,' she said. 'It's time you knew how beautiful you are to men. Those lovely big soft eyes of yours, all that thick, luxuriant hair. You're way funnier than you realize and you're so bloody modest. The perfect package, Sally Howlett! Go and have some fun.'

Fiona had become quite a cheerleader for my self-esteem since she'd gone to New York.

Jan, whose college halls were in Shepherd's Bush, had chosen the Havelock, a nearby pub that I'd been to a few times. It was a nice place and, more importantly, it did yummy food. It was also close to absolutely nothing else so there was no danger of me getting drunk and agreeing to 'go on somewhere' for a late drink. I would have dinner, learn some more about my new friend, then take the magic overground train back to Islington where I would have a good long night's sleep and prepare for my movement class the next morning.

Jan had no classes in the afternoon so was already there when I arrived, sitting at a small table by the bread servery. He had changed. He was wearing a suit and tie. No, he was – Oh, God, Jan was sitting in a relaxed gastropub wearing a full tuxedo. With a *bow tie*!

I stopped in the doorway, panicking, then pinched myself and walked over to his table. Why shouldn't he wear a tux to his local? He was Jan Borsos. A human anomaly. And, really, I would get nowhere in life if I expected everyone to hide from attention as dementedly as I did.

He actually looked incredibly dashing, sitting there amid a sea of trendy rolled trousers and low-key media cashmeres. He also looked ridiculous, of course, but I rather admired him. 'I am wanting to wear something smart,' he said simply. 'This is all I have.' Which was fair enough. The man had walked across Europe for his place at the Royal College of Music.

I sat down opposite him, taking in the busy clatter and chatter of a pub doing brisk business, and inhaled smells of roasting goat's cheese, cooking lamb and fresh bread. Jan had already bought me a large glass of red wine, which was exactly what I'd wanted, and as I chinked his glass, I realized that I was ready to enjoy the evening. God only knew I needed to. The torture of having to see Julian every day was brutal. And for that evil *scumbag* to have stood there congratulating me for getting a gig on a 'sanitary napkin' advert ... It was an insult of agonizing proportions. I deserved a good night out.

After my first glass of wine I grasped that I was trying to persuade myself to fancy Jan Borsos. This was, first, because he had made it clear that he liked me: 'You are the variety of woman I want to marry with,' he announced casually, as my steak *frites* arrived. Second, it was because he was very funny. During a pleasant gossip about our coursemates he had written Violet off as 'a vagina with legs. She wants the attention only. She is an embarrassing to herself.'

And third, I had begun to think, with the classic egalitarianism of the drunk, that height and age did not matter a jot. Jan Borsos had a very wild, romantic sort of face, and even though he always looked furious I knew now that he was never furious. Or negative in any way. He'd had a tough old life for his mere twenty-three years and yet he was a through-and-through trouper. A pocket rocket. A mad, sweet, funny man, whose use of the English language was divine.

After my second glass of wine I stopped trying to persuade myself to fancy Jan Borsos because it was becoming increasingly probable that I actually did.

We had been talking for a while about our families. His were all dead, save for an angry aunt who lived in a town of many syllables somewhere in rural Hungary. He had been telling me about his father, who had died in the same car crash that killed his mother: 'He was a man of great rudity.'

'Rudeness?'

'Yes. Rudeness.' Jan broke off to scribble this in his little notebook. 'When people were saying hello to him in the streets, he was saying, "Fuck off." It was very effective. Everybody was not saying hello to him eventually.'

'Why did he tell everyone to fuck off?'

'Because he liked animals more better than he was liking people.' Jan Borsos shrugged. 'He had a pig. He liked his pig. He liked his wife.'

I roared with laughter. 'I don't believe you! He did not own a pig! You said you were from a town, not a farm!'

'My father owned a pig,' he said. 'You are thinking he was a peasantry. He was not a peasantry. He had plenty of money. But he liked pigs.'

'It's *peasant*, not *peasantry*,' I said. 'Peasantry is the collective noun. Either way, I didn't assume he was a peasant. Trust me, Jan, I'm assuming nothing about you. You defy expectation. I just thought . . . Well, it's funny. A man who hates people but loves his pig.'

Jan laughed, his face still in its customary furiousness. 'YES! That is my father. He hates people, he loves his pig.' His face fell. 'Him and my mother. They tell me I can do anything. "Anything you want to do, Jan, you can achieving it," they told me. I miss them.'

I paused. I simply could not imagine parents who said things to me like 'You can do *anything*!' And that felt shocking and sad. 'I'm so sorry you lost your parents,' I said eventually. 'I sort of know how you feel.'

'But you say your parents are alive?'

'They are alive. But we don't have much of a relationship. They didn't sing to me and encourage me like yours. Nor did they own a pig.' I tried to smile, imagining Dad, pipe in mouth, staring with mild concern at a pig.

'Why?' Jan shoved a forkful of pork loin in my direction. 'Sorry,' he said to it. 'I also like pigs but you taste good.'

I took it – Jan had been feeding me spontaneously throughout the meal, not in a romantic way but in a comical I-must-feed-this-woman sort of a way – although suddenly I had lost any sensation of taste. The rich, warm meat already felt like cardboard in my mouth.

This is why I avoid thinking about my family, I thought angrily.

One of the many painful fallouts from New York was the disintegration of any forgiveness or loyalty I'd felt towards my parents. Mum was a cold, horrible woman, who seemed not to care about me at all, and Dad was just a weak coward. Their seeming lack of interest in what had happened in New York and all the subsequent loss and agony I'd endured had been the final straw.

'Ah, we had some trouble last year,' I said vaguely. I liked Jan Borsos, and I was touched by the honesty of many of the things he'd told me tonight. But to open the can of worms marked 'Howlett Family' – particularly over dinner – would be pretty inappropriate.

I tried to explain without actually explaining. 'There was a bit of a disaster on a work trip to New York, lots of things happened . . . The family got split up somewhat and it's all been really difficult since. I mean it's *OK*, but . . .'

But what? It wasn't OK. I had never expected love or warmth from my family but their conspicuous absence since I'd returned was more painful than I could possibly have imagined.

Jan Borsos, sensing that this was too dark for me to go into, leaned over and touched the side of my face, smiling gently in a way that told me everything would be OK. It was the gesture of a man twice his age, but it touched me.

'I am sorry too,' he said. 'I miss my parents every day but I did always know that they loved me. They were telling me all the time, "We love you, Jan, we are proud of you, Jan, we hail you, Jan."'

I smiled sadly. 'We hail you, Jan.' *I*'d hail Jan Borsos. I'd be proud of him if he were my son.

'We will talk of other subjects,' he announced, after a respectful silence. 'Such as your singing. Sally, why do you hate to sing for people?'

'My singing. Ah. Well, that's another matter,' I bluffed. 'Um, any chance we could change the subject a third time?'

'No,' Jan Borsos replied. 'The subject of your singing is nationally important.'

I burst out laughing. 'What?'

'Ah.' Jan consulted his notebook, flipping back a few pages. Then his eyes lit up. 'I think your singing is a matter of national importance,' he read triumphantly. 'This is a good phrase, no?'

'It's a very good phrase. Who taught it you?'

'Helen.'

Helen had a very good turn of phrase. The text message she'd sent me en route to my date had read: *You and Jan = the impossible couple I've waited my whole life to see. If you mate, I will die happy.*

'I like Helen.' I smiled.

Jan agreed. 'She is the funny woman. She also does not like to sing for people. I think you are both very strange. You both sing beautifully.'

'Oh, you've heard Helen sing?' Then something dawned on me. 'Hang on, you've heard *me* sing?'

Jan looked delighted. 'Ha-ha! Yes! Ha-ha!'

Panic. 'What? How?'

'A voice like yours can fill a stadium,' he said. 'You do not think that the wardrobe stops us listening to you?'

I put down my knife and fork, horrified. The same old anxiety – so familiar it was like the arrival of an old friend – bowled in rapidly and took me over. Suddenly I was seven years old once more, cowering in the bath after shaming myself onstage.

'Who's been listening to me?' I stammered.

Jan looked perplexed. 'Everybody,' he said. 'We stand outside Room 304 and listen whenever you are singing in the wardrobe with Brian. The sound is glorious. Julian Jefferson is listening every time. He has the closed eyes while you sing.'

'*Fuck*,' I muttered. I didn't like swearing but 'fuck' barely covered this. Why couldn't everyone just leave me alone? Why couldn't Julian just *LET ME BE*? He had no right to hang around being all misty-eyed. It was too bloody late to start caring about me *after* ruining my life.

'I want you to stop listening to me,' I said weakly.

Jan shook his head. 'No. You have the most beautiful, powerful voice that any of us are ever hearing,' he said. 'How could we leave you alone? It would be against the law. I would have to telephone Interpol.'

I tried to relax. Perhaps – just perhaps – it was OK for me to sing if people really believed me to be that good.

'Either singing is or it is not,' Jan Borsos said. It was an unexpected and rather impressive aphorism for a man with such erratic English. 'What do you choose?'

Jan Borsos was right. Singing was or it was not. I had

been told by some of the very finest singers that I was excellent. Was it possible that I might actually *try* it?

After all, what else was I going to do? Just leave college again when my four weeks came to an end?

Jan Borsos broke into my thoughts. 'I will answer for you,' he said squarely. 'Singing *IS*. It is, for you, Sally. I do not want to have to collect my pistol and shoot you because of this.'

'Singing *is*.' I held out my right hand to shake on it, realizing that I would just have to keep working on my fear. Singing was right for me. The end.

Jan opted to kiss my hand rather than shake it. He pulled my arm towards him and kissed it all the way up to my elbow, which I found surprisingly enjoyable. The pub swayed and shimmered around me. I was drunk and surprisingly happy.

My resolve not to go for an after-dinner drink was forgotten. Jan Borsos took me to a converted public toilet underneath Shepherd's Bush Green where a hip-hop and rap night was in full swing. Hazy on Rioja and high on life, I danced with that madman – who turned out to be a really rather splendid mover, even within the confines of his tux – and when he stood on a step and kissed me with a Wagnerian passion it felt like the obvious thing to do: I put my arms round his little barrel of a chest and kissed him back. He was young and handsome. He had married a *répétiteur*. He had got divorced. He had studied with László Polgár in Switzerland or somewhere. He had walked Europe. He was a *legend*.

Scene Thirteen

The next morning I woke up with Jan Borsos in his bed-room in halls. It was all nineties peach and muted mushroom, blond wood and frosted lightshades. His bed was narrow but his duvet magnificent. Heavy, warm and covered with a typically odd floral print.

I was deeply hungover and covered with a sticky film of sweat. I smelt bad. This was something I instinctively knew but, thankfully, the tiny room was full of the smell of frying bacon, so my foulness was masked.

Hang on. The tiny room was filled with the smell of bacon?

Yes. The tiny room was filled with the smell of frying bacon. Being Jan Borsos, he had rigged up a tiny camping stove in the corner of the room. He was standing at it in Y-fronts cooking bacon, singing softly to *Aida* which was coming out of a record player. Of course Jan Borsos had carried a record player across Europe. Every single thing about Jan Borsos felt like it was from the sort of film you'd never believe.

I tried and failed to remember what had happened last night. I had a vague notion of jumping on the MC's mic at one point, mumbling something about diggity-doggity, and a potential snogging/grinding incident on a street corner. But coming back to his room? Having sex? Nothing.

For clarification I gave myself a quick body-frisk under the duvet. I hadn't had sex with Jan Borsos! There was fabric covering my lady parts! I stole a glance back over at Jan in his Y-fronts. He looked exciting and mad and really quite handsome.

As he flipped over the bacon, a pile of hair fell into his face. '*La fatal pietra sovra me si chiuse*,' he sang softly, and the richness of his voice made me shiver. Beyond him the morning sky was filthy brown and tempestuous. Jan notched up his voice a little more and I felt a rush of strange sensations. Another man had once won me over with his voice, far away in a poets' café in Alphabet City. But the other man, it had turned out, was not to be trusted. Here in Jan Borsos's nineties bedroom I felt I was as safe as I possibly could be.

'Hello,' I croaked.

'Sally.' He smiled. 'I cook bacon.'

'I know. It smells amazing.' It did. I shifted up a bit, conscious that I was still only wearing a vest and pants. 'Um, Jan, about last night.'

I waited for him to say that it was silly and we should forget about it. But he said nothing of the sort. Instead he hopped over the short distance to the bed and jumped in beside me, snapping his bacon tongs like castanets. He kissed me without any trace of shyness or morning-after reserve. The tongs continued to snap away to some Cuban rhythm that bore no relation to the melodic Verdi on the record player.

When I realized that I was far more interested in kissing Jan Borsos than I was in eating bacon, I grinned. I was glad we hadn't had any sex yet. I was rather looking forward to it. We'd go on a date maybe early next week. And then another, and *then* we'd do it. Barry had always told me it was imperative I never slept with anyone until at least the third date. '*IMPERATIVE, CHICKEN*,' I imagined him saying threateningly.

Suddenly Jan Borsos had put his hand inside my pants and *IMPERATIVE, CHICKEN* was forgotten. What was he ... Oh my ... 'OH!' Nerve-endings crackled between my legs. I wondered vaguely what he had done with the bacon tongs and then forgot to wonder.

'Oh, my goodness,' I heard myself say. Had I been more conscious of anything other than Jan's hands I'd probably have started laughing. Me lying there, all sweaty and smelly, bleating, 'Oh, my goodness!' while Jan fumbled with my pants underneath a frilly duvet in Shepherd's Bush. But this was no time for laughter.

Three seconds later, it was. Without warning, Jan leaned over and turned up the volume of the record player. The melody of the final duet blasted out, as Aida and Radamès prepared to die, and waves of pain and passion crested thunderously. Outside the sky exploded and a great boom of early-morning thunder rent the air. I started laughing. Jan's face retained its customary glare but I knew he was laughing too. We were going to have operatic thundery sex. There was no doubt about it.

With another impressive movement, Jan Borsos swished the duvet off me, although it was so thick and heavy that it got stuck around my knees and he had to wriggle down to kick it off properly. He staggered up to a standing position above me, amid the lightning and the Verdi, to which he was singing sporadically. I lay underneath him, giggling and twitching, hoping for more fumbling very soon.

'"*Morir! Si pura e bella,*"' he sang. And then, in a variation on the traditional magician's trick that I would probably remember for the rest of my life, Jan Borsos whipped out a condom from behind his left ear, which he then managed to drop down the side of the bed.

Another thunderclap tore through the sky, shaking the building, as he tried to pull the bed away from the wall to get at the condom. He failed. Anxious that it was because I was too heavy, I leaped out, then jumped under the duvet on the floor, suddenly shy, just as he wrenched the bed out from the wall.

It hit me on the forehead and I yelped. Jan Borsos yelped. He kissed my head, while reaching out behind me to rescue the errant condom. Clearly he couldn't reach it because he leaned so hard on me that we both fell sideways into his lacy floral duvet.

I started laughing. Jan Borsos, furious-faced, followed suit.

'Let's start again,' I said. I reached for my handbag and took my lucky condom out of my wallet, discreetly checking its best-before date. It had been a while. Jan Borsos heaved the bed back into place, pulled the duvet back on, then laid me on top of it, like a delicate princess. He was surprisingly strong for such a little man.

'*Cariad,*' he murmured, slightly to my surprise. Barry sometimes used that word. It meant 'sweetheart' in Welsh.

Jan stroked my legs reverently, as if their excessive width and dimpled texture was the most marvellous thing he had ever seen.

'*Cariad*,' he repeated, moving as if to sweep off my knickers casually with his stroking hand. Unfortunately, his watch caught on the cheap lace and we found ourselves stuck together. It took a lot of scrabbling and eventually a pair of scissors to unhook him. Any passion and spontaneity that still remained – and it was dubious as to whether there was any now – was finally destroyed when I raised my hips in that ungainly vertical pelvic thrust that allows knickers to be removed, just as Jan nipped down to remove them with his teeth. I hit him on the nose with my pubic bone. So hard that he gasped.

After another embarrassing hiatus, we got into a position and state of nudity that was actually conducive to sex. And just as I began to forget about the last abominable ten minutes, the bacon pan in the corner, which had been left unattended all this time, finally caught fire and the smoke alarm went off.

It was quite a surprise when, after a mortifying twenty minutes standing in a street off the Goldhawk Road, we went back inside and managed to have excellent, randy sexy sex with not a cock-up in sight. Except, of course, for Jan's.

ACT THREE

Scene Nine

September 2011, Brooklyn, New York

The day after I met Julian Bell I woke up and smiled right down to my toes.

I had met a man so amazing that my toes were smiling! And, rather than feel alarmed by the intensity of what had happened last night, I felt good. In fact, I felt so good that, for the first time in my life, I forgot to eat breakfast. I just ran around the living-room bit of our warehouse apartment squeaking, 'Raaah!' and 'Feeeck!' and 'Eeeee!' and when Barry wandered in and found me doing these very uncharacteristic things he laughed so much that he had to sit on the floor. Then he got up and joined me, and we raaahed and eeeeed for quite a long time. 'SEXY MAN FRIEND FOR SALLY,' Barry hissed, from time to time, performing a series of *grands jetés* across the floor in his pants. 'SEXY TIMES!'

Today was Fiona's twenty-ninth birthday, and Bea and I had planned a surprise party to which we'd invited all of the people we'd met since being in New York. I had ordered a massive cake from one of the stalls at the

Smorgasburg, a big food market for the trendies of Williamsburg. Barry had put together a 'streetdance interpretation of Fiona Lane' that he assured me would amuse rather than enrage (there was a fine line with Fiona when it came to laughing at herself). And, of course, there was also the small matter of a world-famous band playing. Raúl and his bandmates from the Branchlines had just finished recording an album and had promised to sing everything from their much-loved *Non-Sonic* album of 2007 and nothing from their subsequent recordings, which had been written for trendier mortals than us.

When I'd said goodbye to Julian last night, he'd said, 'If I hadn't lost my cell, like the total douche that I am, I'd be messaging you all day, saying what a great time I had. So I want you to pretend you're getting those messages all day long, OK?'

I was doing just that, this morning, and I felt insane with excitement. I was happy! Everyone was happy!

Or so I thought.

Fiona, since giving up drinking, had got a lot better at mornings. But today, when I surfaced at ten, there had been no sign. For a moment I was mildly surprised: the narrative that had played out in my head was that while I had been doing hard romance on the Wythe Hotel balcony last night, Fiona and the others would have come home and gone to bed.

I'd forgotten she'd started drinking again. *I really hope she didn't overdo it*, I thought nervously.

When Fiona and Raúl emerged from her bedroom at midday, all rat hair and vodka fumes, my heart sank. 'Murgh,' she said, when I bade her happy birthday. She didn't look in my direction. Instead she made for the fridge and drank some orange juice straight from the bottle. Then she stopped, looked at the nutritional information and put the carton away again. 'Fucking America,' she muttered.

'Eh?'

'They put sugar in fucking everything. Even in *juice*.'

'Oh, Freckle, you have to have *something* in your belly . . .'

With a brittle expression on her face that I didn't like, Fiona took a martyred and huffy glass of water from the tap and slunk over to Raúl, who was skulking around near the door, readying to leave.

This was the Fiona I was used to. Hungover and looking at calories. Seeds of worry began to sprout.

'Fucking OW,' she mewed at Raúl, pointing at her head, as he opened the door. I could tell she wanted him to stay longer, and knew that she would gladly cancel our birthday lunch if he did. But instead he kissed her politely goodbye, telling her to have a good day, and left.

They'd had a fight. It was obvious. Raúl, normally open and expansive, was folded tightly into himself and hadn't even said goodbye to me.

After Fiona shut the door behind him she stood in front of the mirror and checked her arms, legs and stomach, pinching at imaginary fat and pulling her flat belly in so tightly that her ribs sawed at her skin. Her face had the furious look that I recognized as 'My body is not as it should be.' She slunk off to her bedroom, radiating anger. Shortly after that her door opened and my heart sank even further. She was all hectic and sniffy and pinched, and she was wearing her running gear. With her hair pulled back in a severe ponytail she ran out of the door, ready to pound McCarren Park and work off all of the extra fat she didn't possess.

I didn't like it at all.

Not too long after she returned, though, the New Fiona was back. She'd showered, eaten something and was dressed in a pair of expensive trousers and a lovely vest. She had makeup on and was full of energy; she even came over to me for a birthday hug. I forced myself to write off her earlier performance as a one-off hangover.

As planned, we went for a low-key birthday lunch at the Smorgasburg. In keeping with tradition, it was just the four of us: Fi, Barry, Bea and myself.

And it was perfect. The air was hot but not humid; it smelt of cooking onions and seafood. Locals filled their bags with chutneys and artisan coffees, and a naughty dog ran around eating stray pieces of chorizo. We had juicy lobster brioche rolls with sauce dripping down our chins and, to my delight, Fiona ate most of hers. She laughed, gossiped and hopped around as if this morning had been but an aberration, although she did disappear quite a few times. And was perhaps a little on the irritable side when people bashed into her with their bags. And she had forgotten her wallet so we had to buy everything for her, which we would have done anyway, but she made it into quite a big drama. But it was mostly OK. Mostly.

Later, Fiona and I split off and wandered through East River State Park, down to the water. We sat on a driftwood log in the sun, covered our hopelessly white arms and legs with sun lotion and drank Brooklyn beer out of bottles wedged into the brown river sand.

'Hasn't it all been great? Aren't we having a great time? Isn't it a nice day?' Fiona chattered, gazing over at Manhattan. A large and impertinent-looking seagull sat on a 'Danger' sign staring rudely in our direction. Clouds moved lazily overhead through a bright blue sky that seemed almost to have been painted on to the ceiling of America. 'Like, the best? I'm happy. Really happy. Like, HAPPY.' She sniffed, wiping her nose on her trousers.

'Borrow this, you minger,' I said fondly, handing her a tissue. 'Have you got a cold?'

She frowned. 'Um, Sally, I'm not a *minger*. I've just got a cold.' Then: 'Sorry, that was unnecessary! I'm having a lovely day, Sal, a LOVELY day. All thanks to you. And a lovely time in New York!'

I looked back at the river. 'It has been amazing,' I agreed. 'I really don't want it to end.'

Fiona closed her eyes and leaned into my shoulder, playing an imaginary song on my arm with her fingers. 'Bah bah *bah*, *bah*,' she whispered. It sounded a bit like a rave.

'Are we OK?' she asked suddenly. The seagull barked at us. 'I didn't annoy you too much last night? Or this morning? I was just having a few drinks because, you know, it was a big night. And I'm just having this beer because it's my birthday. Just one, OK? Then I'll stop again. I don't want you worrying about me.'

I was worried, but I told her I wasn't. 'Are you and Raúl all right?' I asked tentatively.

'Yep. Of course. I was being a dick. I created a fight with him. But I sorted it out.'

'So everything's fine?'

'Everything's fine. Why?' She sprang up, searching my face. 'Did he tell you it wasn't? Has he been talking to you?'

'No. He hasn't said anything. It's fine, Freckle. Chill.'

'I am chilled!' She dug her beer into the sand. 'I'm FINE. Why are you coming over all earth-mother on me? I'm just having a nice beer in the sun on my birthday. I mean, it's not like . . . Actually I need to go to the loo, I'll be back in a minute . . .'

The seagull stared contemptuously at me for a few more seconds, then took off, shouting noisily as he swept out over the little wooden jetty that was rotting away in the water.

I felt odd. Splintered. Part of me was all curly golden swirls of excitement. I was going to see Julian later and he was *amazing*! Gorgeous, absent-minded, funny, kind. He seemed to really like me and we hadn't even known each other twenty-four hours! And, irrespective of gorgeous Julian Bell, I was *happy*. I was enjoying my life, finally. I was taking risks and I was in mad, pulsating, beautiful New York where I could eat lobster rolls in the sun.

Yet another part of me was steely, tensed. Waiting for the storm. I was back in the watchtower again, scanning the landscape of Fiona for signs of trouble.

I didn't want to be there. I thought I'd resigned.

By nine p.m., our apartment was full. Bea's Brazilian masseur had exceeded expectations and arrived with a set of decks and trendy but very danceable-to music, and people were indeed dancing. At only nine o'clock! Our party ruled! The sun had long gone but the air was still warm and all of our windows were thrown open.

All I could think of was Julian. Gorgeous, nicely scented, warm, smiley, funny Julian Bell. He had marched over, taken me in his arms and kissed me in front of everyone when he arrived. 'I've been thinking about you all day,' he announced. 'Did you get my telepathic SMSs? Oh, I like you. Have you been thinking about me all day too?' he asked, without any embarrassment whatsoever. That naughty, lovely smile was followed by a giggle and another big kiss. And a long hug. He was supremely beautiful, in spite of his creased shirt that didn't know if it was tucked in or pulled out.

I was batty about him. I didn't care that everyone was watching us. I was proud. And had I had any doubts that I'd fallen in love with him in two seconds flat, they were dispelled when I saw him sitting in the courtyard soon after, talking to the frog that lived there. 'I had one just like you when I was ten,' I heard him say, in that mad Devonshire-Brooklyn accent. 'His name was Fun Frog. He lived with Big Frog and Mad Frog and Falsetto Frog.'

Eventually, Bea detached me from his side so that she could cross-question me about last night. We stood in the jungly courtyard, which Julian had vacated, and glass after glass of champagne went warm in my hand as I talked excitedly and forgot to drink.

In the kitchen Barry had set up a cocktail dispensary. 'You can't have *anythin'* until you've tried one of my Blue Fionas,' I could hear him shouting. Bea smiled and left, saying she needed to go and see a man about a dog. I wandered happily into the kitchen to try a Blue Fiona.

Speaking of which, where was she? Pretty much everyone invited to the party was there, apart from Fiona. She'd gone up to Raúl's earlier to get something and I hadn't seen her since.

'Fi's not still in your apartment, is she?' I asked Raúl, offering him a plate of Parma ham and cheese things that we'd bought at the Smorgasburg. Something flashed across his face that I didn't like. 'Oh, actually, yeah, I think she might be,' he said, with unconvincing casualness. 'I think Julian's up there too.'

'Oh.' I was surprised. I scanned around and found that he was indeed absent. 'Is she . . . Are they coming back down soon?'

'Sure. Hey, what time do you want us to play?'

He was trying to change the subject. I decided not to push him any further. If Fiona was being impossible, Raúl probably hadn't the faintest idea what to do. So far he'd only known the nice, sweet, bubbly Fiona so the dark and difficult version must have been quite a shock. *I* still found it hard and I'd had nearly thirty years' practice.

I hoped Julian was faring OK. It was very good of him to keep her company or listen to her ranting. Or whatever was going on.

'How's about you play at elevenish?' I said to Raúl, slipping back into the crowd, then out of the door.

Raúl's front door was ajar and I knew Fiona was up there before I so much as walked into the room. I could feel the nasty, brittle energy that came off her when she was in one of her moods. Something clawed at my stomach. Why was this happening again? She'd told me! She'd said she didn't want to be difficult any more!

She doesn't always have a choice, said a voice in my head. There was a darkness in Fiona that was sometimes bigger

226

than her; bigger than all of us. Sensing that darkness, respecting its immense power, I always forgave her.

But as I arrived in Raúl's flat I felt that forgiveness might be beyond me.

Fiona was sitting on the floor by the coffee table, bony shoulders swaying rhythmically to Irene Cara, whose voice was pounding out of Raúl's sound system. In other circumstances I'd have enjoyed this impromptu disco, but at that moment she was racking up a line of cocaine and Julian was sitting next to her, chatting away as if she was baking a cake.

I stared at their two backs, devastated. They were facing out over New York together; Fiona was saying something low and fast to Julian and he was smiling, watching her tidy up the line. To their right was a MacBook with a picture of Fiona on it, mid-arabesque. *The new Royal Ballet website*, I thought blankly. *Yes, they said it would go live around now.*

Just as Fiona bent down to inhale the line, Julian held out his hand – to take a line himself, perhaps? – and said something. She listened, then smiled before inhaling deeply, hoovering up stray powder with her finger. She passed her rolled-up banknote along the table to him.

I'd seen enough. The opening bars of Odyssey's 'Native New Yorker' spilled happily out of Raúl's speakers, clashing with the pounding bass I could hear coming up the stairwell behind me. A film of thick sadness settled over me. Fi was not any better. She was taking drugs at a counter-party for two while her own party, which I'd so carefully planned, went on downstairs. And Julian Bell, who had been giving me butterflies all day, appeared to be at it with her. I couldn't stand it.

You should have known, a voice in my head said. *Of course it was never going to be a fairytale. You idiot. You fool. You silly, fat —*

I ran off down the stairs, slamming the door behind me. As I tore down I could see someone looking over the banisters from above, then heard Julian's voice calling my name, but I carried on running. I ran past our front door, out of which drifted happy laughter and cool music, then into the street.

I ran down Bedford Avenue through McCarren Park, breaking into a furious march and then a furious amble as I got more out of breath. I was dimly aware of bars and eateries crammed with hipsters as I got closer to the centre of Williamsburg, and decided it was too bloody happy there. Idiotic trendies were dancing to some silly musician off to my right and a pair of girls howled with laughter beside a Mexican food cart. Why had I run here, of all places? Without stopping to think, I marched straight down into the subway and jumped on the L train, which had just arrived at the platform. I sank into a hard plastic seat, jammed the heels of my hands into my eyes and cried.

When I reached the end of the line twenty minutes later, I got up and stood, breathing hard, on the platform. I didn't know where to go or what to do. It was intolerably hot now that I was off the train, and my hair stuck to my face. My dress, which I'd bought especially, was lank with sweat.

'Where next?' someone asked me. Probably some drunk. I ignored him. I stood and tried to breathe, to recalibrate my life back from hopeful to crap.

The man tried to touch my arm but before he had a

228

chance I stormed off towards the stairs to the interchange for the A train.

'Sally, please.'

The man took my arm again. It was Julian.

We stared at each other for a few seconds and, in spite of what had just happened, I felt last night's magic spark up.

'Why?' I said simply. I couldn't stand it. Julian Bell was just beautiful. Standing on a sweaty platform with a swirling vortex of emotions around us, his hair already a bit fluffy from the heat, he was perfect.

And I knew, looking at him, that he had not been taking drugs. As with last night I could see – with amazing clarity – what was coming out of him. It was not cocaine and it was not booze. It was fear and it was concern and it was kindness.

'I wasn't taking coke,' he confirmed. 'I was just hanging out with Fiona because she was in a funk.'

'Nobody uses words like "funk",' I said. 'Not even half-Americans.' Then I smiled sadly. This was how last night had started. Arguing linguistics.

'Well, I do.' Julian watched me warily. 'And she was in a funk. The Royal Ballet's website had a new picture of her or something, and she thought she looked really fat in it. She went totally mad – it was intense. Then the coke came out. I was quite stunned by the whole thing, to be honest. But she needed a friend. So I hung about.'

'I'm her friend!' I said defensively.

He nodded. 'I can see that.'

I slumped, immobilized by heavy sadness and indecision.

'I was worried about you,' he said quietly. 'You've got quite a sprint on you, girl.'

'Muh.' I didn't know what else to say. But I did quite appreciate the idea of him sprinting down Bedford Avenue after me. That had to count for something.

There was a long pause. There was so much I wanted to say to him, and I knew there was so much he wanted to say to me. Yet unseen obstacles hung down between us, stifling spontaneity.

'Come with me,' Julian said, offering me his hand. I took it but didn't move. I believed that he wasn't on drugs but everything else in my world felt impossible. 'Come with me,' he repeated. 'Let me take you on a second date.'

I watched him guardedly.

'Sally, the party'll be fine. Fiona'll be fine. For today. I'm mad about you. I want to hang out. Just you and me.'

Still I hesitated. Julian got closer and looked me in the eye. 'I was not taking coke,' he said quietly. 'I don't take drugs. Not now, not ever. Jesus, I can't even remember where I keep my socks. How do you think I'd conceal a drug habit?'

I smiled briefly.

'Do you believe me?'

I nodded, because I did.

He smiled again, that lovely, mad, cheeky smile, and I allowed myself to be led up the stairs towards the A train.

Scene Ten

Changing at Columbus Circle, we took the 1 Train up into Harlem, which was like walking straight into *Sesame Street*. Beautiful old brownstone houses trailed steps down into streets from 1930s films, and Sugar Hill towered above us like a stately cruise liner. I was disappointed not to see Oscar sticking his head out of a trash can, really, but forgot all about him when Julian walked me into a tiny soul-food restaurant next to a neon-lit church and ordered me fried chicken with macaroni cheese and green stuff with bacon in it. Or 'mac-n-cheese and collards'. It was bloody amazing. 'My GOD,' I kept exclaiming.

'Mah GOAD,' Julian imitated, until I pelted him square in the face with a piece of chicken.

We didn't talk about Fiona or the party. We were back in last night's bubble. In fact, I don't know what we actually *did* talk about, but I didn't once find myself scrabbling for something to say. I believed that he was not taking drugs. I believed that he hadn't been sitting too close to Fi and all the other things my head was telling me. I knew he was really into me.

It would be impossible to feel all of this chemistry with a human being if it wasn't mutual.

Wouldn't it?

Somewhere around midnight we walked into the sort of bar I'd always dreamed of but would never have had the nerve to go to. Paris Blues was a total dive, a sweaty, beautiful, wild, noisy place, crammed with people and literally shaking to the sounds of thumping jazz. Not Jamie Cullum, or plinky-plonky piano, but proper, driving, infectious blues, rock 'n' roll sort of jazz. An old man with a saxophone was in the middle of a rip-roaring solo, a real pork pie hat on his head. The notes fell over themselves to get out of his sax into the hot, packed bar. A large woman with a creamy blonde Afro – dazzling against her rich dark skin – stood behind a microphone watching and clapping. 'Don't tease me, baby,' she roared, as he pulled back. 'Don't tease me!'

A double bass, piano and drum set completed the act, although there was an anyone's-welcome air about the place. It was mental and it was wonderful. Had I had any lingering thoughts about Fiona, they were wiped out.

Julian was laughing at my goggling face. He pointed to a beam on my left that I was to lean on, then went to the bar and came back with two terrible-looking bright blue drinks soon after. 'Sorry,' he shouted, grinning. 'It's someone's birthday. He insisted. And I'm shit at saying no.'

'Me too!' I shouted back. 'Awful!' A big man wearing a suit waved at me, and I toasted him a happy birthday. His wife, a short woman with a huge Hollywood smile and a foxy black crop, yelled that she was going to fetch us some cake right now.

As we settled into our tiny spot by the beam she thrust two enormous slices of multicoloured birthday cake into our hands, on napkins, and shouted that we were most welcome. She was wearing a sequined blue dress. The cake tasted of strawberry-flavoured chemicals. The saxophone freestyle finished and the crowd went wild; the music roared on. I was in heaven.

'This place is really crap,' I yelled in Julian's ear.

He smiled down at me. 'I know. If I'd had more warning I'd have got us some tickets for Céline Dion. You'd have liked that, wouldn't you? I certainly would.'

'Oh, dear God, yes. That would have been so much better.'

I started singing the dreadful, whingeing 'Think Twice' in Julian's ear. 'Do you like that?' I shouted. 'Did you enjoy Céline's melodies there?' For a second I stood back and watched myself doing this free, easy banter thing and marvelled. It didn't feel forced or silly. I was basically a bit brilliant with Julian. *Perhaps I'm just a bit brilliant anyway*, I wondered briefly.

I laughed at myself, coming back to Julian. 'Well? Did you like my tunes, Julian? My Dion flavas?'

Julian scratched his nose. 'To be honest, I thought you were quite average. I can sing that lady much better than you, Sally Howlett. Listen up, kiddo.' He cleared his throat and sang the chorus into my ear – a fairly remarkable impression, in fact – until I pummelled him with my fists to stop.

'You have no understanding of music,' he said gravely. Then he wailed about how this was getting SHEREEOUSH, and was I thinking about you or us?

I laughed harder and Julian enjoyed it. 'I sing Céline Dion to Fat Pam,' he told me. 'She's crazy – she sort of sing-howls back. I *LOVE* THAT DOG.'

I am completely in love with you, I thought dizzily. *I love that you sing Céline Dion to a dog called Pam.* I smiled at him, and couldn't stop smiling.

'Shut up and let me listen to the jazz,' I ordered. The bar shimmered happily around me.

'Shut up yourself.' He shoved some hair out of his eyes and it fell straight back. 'I really do need to get a haircut.' He sighed. 'My hair is like a natural disaster.'

I giggled. 'No! It's . . . *special*, your hair. I like it.'

'But if I sorted it out I could look at you properly.' He gazed straight at me. 'You are just . . . just lovely.'

After a while he turned back to watch the music and, in a most un-Sally Howlett move, I kissed the side of his neck, which was next to my face, and said, 'Thank you,' in his ear. He smiled and put his arm round me, turning his attention back to the music, and it seemed as if we'd been like that for ever, fitting perfectly into each other's sides in rowdy bars crammed with mad bric-a-brac and peeling posters in Harlem.

Scene Eleven

Much later, the crowd thinned a little and the jazz became more reflective. Bill, whose birthday it was, had offered us a table next to a giant vat of goat curry that he'd brought for his guests. 'Eat that. Talk about love.' He grinned, shaking Julian's hand.

We sat opposite each other and suddenly it felt like a date again. My stomach knotted happily, and when Julian reached over and pulled my hand into his, drumming the rhythm of the band softly into my palm, I felt explosions of zigzagging warmth right across my body.

'Are you OK?' he asked me.

I beamed and nodded. I was truly OK.

'Just to be clear,' he said softly. 'I was talking to her. She was all cut up about that photo and she needed a friend.'

I sighed. I didn't really want to talk about Fiona while we sat in a secret place somewhere in *Sesame Street*, but there were some questions I probably still had to ask. 'I believe you. But, um, I just wanted to know . . . Were the drugs Fiona's?'

Julian looked uncomfortable. 'I think so.'

'I see. And where did she get them from?'

'I honestly have no idea.' He looked down at the table, then up at me. 'Although it won't have been Raúl, if that's what you're thinking. He doesn't go anywhere near anyone who takes that shit.'

'Then who?' I drummed my fingers on the table. 'I need to get whoever it is to stop supplying her.'

'Good luck with that.' Julian stroked my hand with his thumb. 'Drug dealers don't care, Sally. The only person who's going to stop Fiona is Fiona. And I'm not sure she can.'

'But she did, Julian. She hasn't taken anything in *months*. Well, at least three months.' Julian held my hand as I told him about the transformation in Fiona since she'd met Raúl on the plane in June. I told him about all the times when I'd expected her to get drunk, or starve herself to the point of exhaustion, or cause a scene or treat me like rubbish, and how she hadn't done any of those things. Well, not much.

'She sorted herself out somehow,' I said uncertainly. A young guy was playing a trumpet now, a rich, high line of sound drifting out over the bar like delicately unfurling smoke.

Julian frowned. 'Are you sure?' he asked eventually. 'Because it seems to me that she's got a pretty regular coke habit. She needs to take it a *lot*, Sally. Have you not noticed anything?'

'No!' I snapped defensively. Then: 'Sorry. But I don't think . . . Although actually . . .'

Julian waited for me to go on.

'She has been a bit, I don't know. Odd. Highly strung,

although in a slightly different way from normal. Talking a lot of shit.'

Julian nodded. 'Has she been worse at getting started in the morning?'

My heart began to feel heavy. 'I suppose so. Yes. And . . . she disappears quite a lot, often when she's being mental. And comes back OK.'

'And how is she generally? Quite manageable? Turning up for work and stuff?'

'Well, she's not due back for a little while,' I stammered. 'But she's . . . Well, as unreliable as ever. Forgets to do the shopping, leaves her clothes at the laundrette, gets into arguments with strangers, keeps needing to borrow money . . . But that's Freckle! She's always been rubbish!'

Julian smiled sympathetically.

'Oh, God,' I muttered fearfully. 'Do you think she's really . . . ?'

'I don't know. Possibly.'

The fear tightened. 'Oh, God,' I repeated. 'And you're sure this has nothing to do with Raúl? Because she wasn't doing drugs before. I mean I caught her once, but –'

'Trust me,' Julian cut across me. 'This has *nothing* to do with Raúl. His only involvement in it is that he's worried. He's begun to notice it too. He said she'd been getting difficult and paranoid about him over the last few weeks. He was shocked by what a nightmare she was last night, back on the booze.'

I stared at Julian's face for further clues. 'And?'

He sat back, scratching his head. 'I'm not sure he'll

stick around if she's out of control,' he said gently. 'He – well, he has his reasons.'

Shit.

'But they've been so happy!' I pleaded. 'They've been great together! He can't just stop liking her!'

Julian leaned sideways to dig something out of his pocket and produced a buzzing phone. 'Oh!' I said, momentarily forgetting our conversation. 'You got a new one!'

'No.' He frowned at it and then put it back in his pocket. 'Turns out I'd left it in Raúl's apartment last night. It never even made it out to the poetry slam.'

I smiled wanly.

'As I said, I'm a moron who loses and forgets everything. Now, where were we?'

'Raúl. You were implying that he might be about to dump Fi.'

'I don't know, I'm only guessing, so please try not to worry. The fact is, Raúl's mad about her. But she's changed quite quickly and . . . he has a lot to lose. You'll have to trust me on that. He's not a user himself, and he's not a bad man, but he can't be around that shit.'

I felt stirrings of panic. Julian, sensing this, leaned over and tucked my hair behind my ear, which I found calming. 'Let go, Sally,' he said. 'You aren't responsible for her.'

'I am, though. She's my cousin, practically my sister.'

'I know. But that still doesn't make you responsible for her.'

'No, you don't understand. She –' I stopped myself, uncertain as to whether to continue.

One of the bar staff came and cleared away a vast pile of glasses that had built up. 'Here, let me help you,' Julian said. He picked up a few and walked them over to the bar, talking to the girl. She thanked him, and he came back.

'You're so nice,' I told him. 'To everyone. You notice everyone who holds a door open for you, everyone who serves you a drink.'

He smiled, as if surprised, then thought about what I'd said. Watching his eyes my stomach shifted and swayed; a cornfield in a summer breeze. Julian was like the sun.

Oh, will you get a bloody grip! I told myself.

I ignored myself. He *was* like the sun.

'I grew up on a farm,' he said eventually. 'There were two guys who worked there when it was really busy and Dad sort of . . . It was as if he saw them as machines. He wasn't *rude* to them but he sure as hell wasn't interested in their lives.' He shrugged. 'It was odd to me. They were as human and real as he was. They had as many difficulties as he did, more, probably, but he never saw it.' He thought for a bit. 'I've never really gotten over that. You sit in a restaurant and it's like the staff aren't meant to be humans. Having a shit day. Having an amazing day. They're just smiley food-bringing machines. Everybody's somebody, aren't they?'

I nodded. It was a fair point.

Julian rested his chin on his hands. 'And don't be mad at me, but I wonder if maybe you're so busy being Fiona's mom that you forget you're somebody too?'

He had caught me off guard. 'Oh! Um, I . . . Well, I don't know about that . . .'

'Sorry. I didn't mean to be inappropriate.'

'You're not. It's just . . . As I said, I don't think you really understand.'

239

He poked the back of my hand gently with his and then traced along one of my veins. 'I could try?'

'I – No. It's family stuff. It's horrible.'

I felt myself freeze as he watched me expectantly. I couldn't tell him my family history. He'd run a mile!

As if listening to my thoughts, Julian cocked his head to one side, and as he did so, his unironed shirt collar stuck up in an adorable mongrel-dog's-ear sort of way. I looked at his face, which was the same lovely twinkly face I'd been drunk on for a little over twenty-four hours, and thought, *He is the nicest man I've ever met.*

I wanted to explain this to him.

So I did. I certainly hadn't planned to, but I told him everything. About how Aunty Mandy, my mum's sister, had always been a problem for the family because she drank too much and entertained notions of being an actress, even though my grandparents had always been ferociously conservative and private. About how she'd quite literally run away with the circus when she was thirteen, having fallen in love with one of the acrobats, but had come back a week later when his wife had turned up. Flunking school, she'd got work with a temping company that hired catering staff to work across the Midlands. Not long after her eighteenth birthday she'd got a short gig at the Birmingham Hippodrome, fallen in love with a man in the panto chorus and run off with him. Only this time she came back pregnant. In our small, somewhat nosy community where everyone knew everyone else's business, the news had spread like wildfire.

Mum's father had been a fearsome man. I'd been healthily afraid of him. Apparently he gave Mandy a stiff beating and threw her out of the family home, telling her she could find somewhere else to whore herself out. Mum had to sneak around behind Grandpa's back to maintain any sort of relationship with her sister. She also gave a generous amount of her wages to Mandy so that Mandy could rent a room in a house on our council estate belonging to some second cousin or something.

As a young girl I heard Mum bring this up repeatedly with Mandy when they fought. 'You have no idea what I risk for you,' she hissed. 'And what you cost me. Can't you even *try* to sort your life out? Stand on your own two feet?'

It seemed that she could not, and Mum must have known this because she never abandoned her sister. Quiet, reliable Mum loved her noisy, unreliable sister as if she were her own child.

Mandy had loved little Fiona desperately but had struggled to be a parent. She was erratic and whimsical, often drunk, and now suffering severe depression. Several times she had forgotten to collect Fiona from school and was visited by social services when a five-year-old Fiona told one of the teachers that she always cooked for herself.

But none of us had expected the police to arrive at our door that day. None of us had expected that they would tell Mum the body in the canal near Wolverhampton was Mandy's. None of us had expected to find out that little Fiona had been alone in the house for five days, waiting for her mum to come home.

Mandy left Mum a tear-stained note saying she couldn't do the mothering thing and if Mum couldn't find Fiona's father, the actor, then please could Mum bring up Fiona herself. She instructed Mum to keep sending Fiona to ballet classes, and then ballet school, if money permitted. Fiona was already showing exceptional promise at the local dance school and Mandy liked the idea of her following in her father's theatrical footsteps.

She signed off, *Please tell her I did love her, so very much. My beautiful Freckle.*

I would never forget Mum's face the day she told us what had happened. She was lost. Stunned, devastated, disbelieving, yet frozen in all of these emotions; almost wordless.

Fiona had moved in with us that night and a search for her father had begun. It was very half-hearted: Mum and Dad had no intention of handing over their little niece to some promiscuous stranger, but I suspected Mum had to try for Mandy's sake. Of course, the media got wind of the search, which caught the nation's imagination quickly. Soon it was all over the news that the 'canal orphan' needed to 'find her daddy!'

No daddy came forward, and she stayed with us. Already close, we lived in each other's pockets from that moment on. But although I got to live with my bestest friend, there was nothing golden about those years.

Fiona, already naughty and noisy, got worse. After years of Grandpa banging on about Aunty Mandy having brought shame on the family it must have caused Mum real agony to be hauled in to Far Hill Primary (at least once a month) to defend the conduct of her niece. She punished Fiona vigorously but it made little difference; Fiona just became more defiant. With hindsight, it was obvious to me that this was her response to her devastating loss, but Mum seemed empty of compassion. She told Fiona that she had had no trouble with Dennis and me, so why must Fiona insist on being so different?

Apart from the ballet lessons Mandy had asked for, Mum didn't let Fiona join any clubs or let her go out to play with the other kids. She would cause too much trouble, apparently. Fiona was trapped in our house a lot of the time, an imprisonment that caused an already nervy child to gain dangerous momentum. She was an unexploded bomb. A pale, lonely little meteor.

Telling Julian the story, I felt the old hurt stirring. What was *wrong* with Mum? Why couldn't she have loved her? And why was Dad so spineless? He just did what Mum did.

'Well, I see why you're so protective of her,' Julian said, subdued. We were drinking beer and I'd lost track of time. 'Sounds pretty rough.'

I was picking angrily at the label on my bottle. 'I find it hard not to hate Mum when I think about how she was. I mean, I was Fiona's only friend. In the *world*.'

'Grief makes us do crazy things,' Julian muttered. 'I should know.'

'That's not the way to express grief! Keeping your sister's baby under house arrest when she should be out playing!'

Julian leaned over and forced me to look at him. 'Hey. *I* know that,' he said. 'I wasn't trying to excuse your mom. All I meant was, maybe she went a bit mad for a while. A bit controlling. Who knows what she was thinking?'

'I'll tell you what she was thinking,' I replied hotly. 'She was thinking, *When can I get rid of Fiona?* Julian, she sent Fi off to the Royal Ballet when she was *eleven*. She said it would be best for both of us. How? How was it good for Fi to be sent away from the only family she had? How was it good for me to lose my best friend?'

Hot tears sawed at my vision. Julian passed me one of the cake napkins. 'I'm so sorry,' he said. 'I didn't mean to sound like I'm on her side. I can hear how awful it was for you. I just meant, maybe your mom didn't know what else to do with Fiona. And I suggested it because I know from first-hand experience that nobody has any idea how to deal with bereaved people.'

I watched him warily.

'My mom forced me to move in with her when I lost my wife,' he explained. 'She wouldn't let me out of her sight. For weeks I couldn't go anywhere without her following, making sure I wasn't going to end up somewhere I could get into trouble, get upset, you know.' He smiled sadly; a bittersweet memory. 'Oh, Mom.'

The trumpet was still playing, a slow, sad ribbon of sound. The man at the piano appeared almost asleep but I knew he was just lost in the music. 'Your mum sounds lovely, Julian.' I tried not to be jealous.

He grinned. 'She is. The very, very best.'

'Well, mine isn't. And I'm not being a brat. I'd love to think, *Oooh, Mum didn't know what to do with Fiona so she sent her to ballet school* . . . But that's not what happened. Apart from anything else, Mum hated Fiona dancing. She hated anything that drew attention to us. It makes no sense that she'd choose to let Fi train as a performer. I mean, it would have felt like Mandy all over again, wanting to be an actress!'

Deep anger started to pulse up again, ringed with

bitterness and helplessness. It crossed my mind that Julian might think I was mad but I was too worked up to care. I'd never had this conversation with anyone and it felt strangely cleansing. It had been inside me for years, spinning round and round at a low whine.

'Go on,' he said. 'And remember, I'm on your side, OK?'

I smiled briefly.

'Well, on top of that, Mum had spent years trying to stop me and Fi getting too close. Telling me I should make "some better friends". Julian, there's no two ways about it. She basically didn't want me being influenced by Fiona. Turning out like her. So when she realized she couldn't keep us apart, she sent Fi away.'

A single tear squeezed out of my eye and I brushed at it furiously with my sleeve. *Damn my family. Damn their cruel, conservative little lives. Never hugging Fiona. Never popping her on their knees and checking how she was doing. Getting rid of her at the first opportunity they had, acting like martyrs when Fiona had got a full grant and they hadn't had to pay a penny.*

Fury ebbed and flowed, more tears tracked down my cheeks, and I didn't try to stop them.

'It's OK,' Julian murmured, when I eventually gestured apologetically at my face, the tears and general air of madness. 'It's completely OK. Here.' He passed me some more cake napkins and I felt gratitude that he hadn't begged me not to cry, tried to stop me feeling it all. He'd just watched the whole thing with a sympathy that seeped right through to my bones. A deep, understanding kindness that was new to me.

The strangest thing, I thought – as I discharged tears and snot into a napkin – was that I hadn't known quite how angry I was with Mum and Dad. How thick and intractable the rage would feel if I ever let it out in the open. *Julian is unique*, my head told me dazedly. *I'm* me *with him. The real me.*

I'd never known there was a real me.

Julian stuck out a finger and mopped up a final mascara trail from near my mouth. 'Here lieth anger,' he remarked, looking at the black mess on his finger. 'Anger well spent.'

The trumpet wound down and lazy applause spattered around the bar. I looked at Julian's smooth, brown hand with my tears on it and smiled. His hands, I saw, were covered with reminders. And also 'Sally' with a big cheesy heart round it.

'Finally, you noticed.' He grinned. 'I was thinking of getting a tattoo. Maybe with my name too, and a small Cupid hanging around.'

I laughed, and realized how tired I was.

'I didn't mean to interfere, and I'm sorry if I did,' he said. 'Families are difficult. Really difficult. I'm honoured you told me all that stuff and I'm not surprised you feel so responsible for Fiona. Reset?'

He wiped my mascara off his index finger and held it out towards me.

I pressed mine against it. 'Reset.'

Later still, there was just a piano, a bass and a gentle drum playing. An ancient couple danced, lost in a world I'd never see. I felt lighter for having told Julian everything and I really wanted to stay there with him, in that softly lit, lovely place, but I was drunk with exhaustion. We were a long way from Brooklyn.

Sensing I was dropping, Julian stood up. 'We have to dance before we go home.' He smiled, holding out his hand. 'Then you can tell everyone you're proper ace cos you danced in Paris Blues.'

'"Proper ace".' I grinned, as he pulled me into his shirt. Julian Bell was the strangest and best mixture of people I'd ever met. A farm boy, a dignified widower, a forgetful, scruffy moron, a sparky New York wit, and the warmest, kindest Anglo-American *hottie* on earth. And he wanted to dance with me. He'd insisted on dancing with me.

I didn't really know how to dance to slow music, like some smudged, sexy woman in an American film. But, as with so many other things, I found myself able to do it with Julian Bell.

'There's something about you that I love,' he muttered, into the side of my head. 'And I think that thing is you. Can I see you tomorrow? And the next day? And the day after that?'

I grinned ecstatically into his shoulder. 'Say that again,' I whispered.

'Oh, I just sort of mentioned this strange suspicion that I've fallen in love with you,' he said. 'Not so conventional, if you look at our twenty-four-hour history, but . . . well, there it is.'

I started to reply but he put a finger on my lips and shook his head, smiling.

He already knew.

Scene Twelve

Perhaps unrealistically, I had rather hoped for an apology from Fiona the day after her party. She knew I'd spent hours organizing it and – more to the point – she must have known how devastating it would be for me to catch her taking cocaine while chatting merrily away with Julian.

I received no apology. The next day I didn't need to be at the Met until four o'clock, but by the time I left the apartment she was still asleep. I saw Raúl in the stairwell as I left the building, so I knew she was in there on her own.

'I'm sorry I left so abruptly last night,' I said.

He shrugged. 'Hey, no worries, man. You were upset.'

'I heard she never actually came to her own party.'

Raúl shook his head. 'Nope. But it was a blinder. We went on until seven a.m.'

'How come? Were there drugs?' I spoke far too quickly.

'Um – I dunno. If there were, I wasn't on them,' he said defensively.

'No, no, sorry, Raúl. That's not what I was thinking. I was actually worried about –' I stopped.

'Fiona,' he finished for me. Her name hung heavily in the air between us.

'Yes. Are you two OK?' I sounded desperate.

Raúl's face clouded. 'I hope so,' he said sadly.

It was a terrible blow – yet deadeningly predictable – when I got a call from Barry later on to say that Raúl had finished with Fiona. Barry didn't know the precise circumstances but he reported that there had been a lot of screaming and crying, and that after Raúl had gone, Fiona had thrown an ashtray through the window so we now had the challenging task of trying to find a warehouse window pane.

I thought of what Julian had said last night, about how mad Raúl was about Fiona but that he couldn't be any-where near people who took drugs. And I felt a chill.

When I got back from work that night, close to midnight, the apartment reeked of bad humour. Fiona barely acknowledged me but sat hunched on the sofa with a huge measure of Scotch, a bag of ice melting slowly beside her. Her pupils were massive, she was talking complete shit to Barry and her hands were shaking. I felt sick. When I tried to talk to her she stalked off to her bedroom with the Scotch, slamming the door behind her.

Julian arrived shortly after with a box of Yorkshire Tea. And a sachet of Bird's custard. 'I'm too old to crack open the booze after midnight,' he explained cheerfully. 'And I *miss* this shit! I get it imported! Let's make some custard and drink tea!'

I was so relieved to see things like custard and tea, rather than Scotch – and Julian's smiley face, rather than Fiona's black scowl – that I burst into spontaneous honking. It was something between laughter and tears and it made Julian hug me and honk a bit himself, although his honking was pure laughter. 'You sound like Pam the dog when she's having a bad dream,' he said. 'Are you OK?' He pulled back. 'No,' he answered. 'You're not. Well, I'm going to make you some custard. We'll sink a couple of bowls of that and then, if you want to, we can talk about Fiona, and if you don't, we'll just eat some more custard.'

Julian held me all night and didn't make even a cursory attempt to have sex with me. It was our first night together and it was very confusing. I felt madly, glowingly happy but being madly, glowingly happy felt a bit wrong, given the hole in our warehouse window that said, *She is completely out of control.*

But he was so warm. He told me what he loved about England, and it was all the same stuff that I loved about England but had never noticed before. He didn't snore. He felt strong, not in a pumped-up gym sort of way but in a gentle, dormant-strength-that-could-lift-a-car-off-you-if-you-got-run-over sort of way. And he smelt of soap and skin and good things. When he stripped down to his boxers I noticed that he'd attempted to darn a hole in them and that he had a Muppets plaster on his toe from where he 'walked into a trash can' (trash can! He said 'trash can'!) and as I stared at him, that stunning, warm, forgetful man, who needed a haircut and darned holes in his pants and walked into things, I felt positively intoxicated.

He is an actual miracle, I thought, as I drifted off to sleep. *He even likes my bottom!* I hated my bottom with a crabby little passion but tonight Julian had told me it was 'unparalleled'. He hadn't stopped cupping it wondrously and exclaiming things like 'I have been waiting for this bottom all my life!'

Maybe I've been wrong about my bum, I thought drowsily. *Maybe I've been wrong about a lot of things to do with me.*

Scene Thirteen

Over the following days I fell even more head-over-heels in love with Julian Bell, while things with Fiona went from bad to worse. She and Barry were due to start rehearsals for *Swan Lake* that week but had said they'd secured another week off so that they could stay in New York.

Three days after Fiona and Raúl's break-up we discovered that Fiona had been lying. Unlike Barry, she had failed even to email the Royal Ballet, let alone call them. They phoned her repeatedly but she ignored her mobile and, when they finally called me, they told me they had no choice but to suspend her immediately. She would face disciplinary action on her return to London.

When I relayed this to Fiona she went on a twenty-four-hour bender.

'OMG! I shagged a guy *waaaay* better looking than Raúl,' she bragged, when she got back the following night. She made a noise that sounded like a distant cousin of a laugh, and clacked around the apartment on her stilettos.

'*Favoloso,*' Bea purred. 'Get back on that horse, darling.'

I didn't even bother to try to silence Bea, whose approach to sex and relationships was beyond my comprehension. I just watched my precious little cousin marching around in last night's clothes, tossing out sordid details of her sordid night like peanut shells. She'd texted me to say she was staying out but, of course, I hadn't slept. Julian had stayed up with me, telling me funny stories about his Devon childhood that I'd barely been able to hear.

Dancers shouldn't wear stilettos, I thought numbly. *Dancers shouldn't wear stilettos. Dancers . . .*

Fiona looked thinner than ever, and was a sniffy, flushed mess. She carried on bragging, ignoring the man I'd paid to come and fix the window, and between anecdotes she gulped hungrily at a large bottle of Diet Coke.

I felt ill.

What should I do? What should I say? She cut through my panicked thoughts. 'Yeah, Sal, you know what? Fuck my job. They're never going to promote me, they don't respect me, they think I'm shit so, yeah, fuck them. I'm thinking of staying in New York. There's loads of really cool shit going on here and Julian was telling me about some guys he knows who run an experimental dance company and he said his flatmate might be moving out soon so I could rent her room maybe and, yeah, I might do that because I really think that the Royal Ballet was holding me back. I mean, they're great and everything but they deliberately put up a fat picture of me on their website –'

'Of course they didn't!' I interrupted uselessly. 'They'd never do something like that! It's *you* who thinks you're fat!'

Fiona shook her head dismissively. 'Er, whatever, Sal.' She raised her eyebrows at Bea, muttering, 'Fuck's sake!'

I hated myself for not knowing how to handle Fiona. What had happened to me? All I could think was how hurtful it was that Julian had almost offered her a spare room and not told me. I was pathetic.

I cleared my throat and spoke, my voice small and tremulous: 'Fiona, can we talk?'

She stopped clacking around and stared at me warily. 'Yes?'

'Alone?'

She crossed her arms. 'What have you possibly got to say to me that you can't say to Bea? We're all friends.'

I stared at my lap, all searing cheeks and racing pulse. I loathed myself for being so weak when she needed me to be strong.

'Freckle, I'm worried about you. I'm worried you're taking drugs . . .' I trailed off, frozen.

She threw her hands into the air and clicked off to the kitchen. '*Jeeee*sus!' she muttered, as if I were a meddling old lady.

Bea turned in her chair. 'Sally?' she said. 'You think she is on drugs? What drugs?'

'Cocaine,' I whispered.

'FUCKING BULLSHIT!' Fiona yelled from the kitchen. 'You just caught me having a cheeky line at the party! What do you think I am, some sort of *druggy*? Oh, my God! You've lost it!'

Bea was watching me curiously. 'Why do you think she is on drugs, darling?' she asked.

'Because I saw her taking coke at the party. And . . .' I dropped my voice even lower '. . . Julian's convinced of it.'

Bea stared at me thoughtfully, then smiled. 'Fiona is a

party girl, we all know this,' she said decisively. 'She is not on drugs, Sally. Of course she is not. She would have gone mad!'

I gestured frantically in the direction of the kitchen. 'Oh, *preziosa*,' Bea smiled, 'Fiona has always been like this. She is probably just sad that you have met this gorgeous man who might take you away from her.'

I sat back, slightly shocked. That hadn't occurred to me.

'Why is Julian so sure?' Bea asked gently. 'Where is he getting his information from?'

The question hung in the air, like stale smoke.

Fiona stormed back in from the kitchen with several large packs of Oreos. 'I'm going to eat all of them,' she announced, and stomped off to her room.

I remained frozen. Useless. Failing her yet again.

'I hear nothing,' said the window-repair man timidly. 'Ees OK. I hear nothing.'

The next day Fiona stopped eating but started a campaign to feed and fatten us, which was what happened when she was at her worst. Whenever she wasn't in black fury in her room she would cook huge lunches and dinners for us all, which she would watch us eat, claiming to be 'full'.

As I picked miserably at her giant home-made burritos one afternoon, Barry remarked – somewhat unhelpfully, I thought – 'Fiona, you're bein' a soddin' lunatic, my petal. Any chance you could stop force-feedin' us? If we're not careful I'm going to end up getting overly comfy like Chicken here.' He patted my stomach, then moved away in case I punched him.

Fiona usually allowed Barry to mock her. But not today.

She stormed off to the kitchen, muttering about us being ungrateful twats and, of course, I followed her because I didn't know what else to do.

She was pacing back and forth, looking wild and slightly feral. 'I ate loads of burritos while I was preparing them,' she said, her eyes darting around fearfully. 'And now I can't get it all up. I've got to get it out of me, Sally. You have to help me.'

I stared at her, aghast. 'You've made yourself sick?'

'Yes,' she snapped. 'And save me the lecture. I'll go and see the doctor and tell him I'm insane, if you want, but for now *this is an emergency*. I've got to get it out of me. Do you understand? Sally?'

Her hands, wringing together, looked disproportion- ately huge at the end of her tiny, sparrow-like arms. I wanted to cry but was paralysed with shock. I'd never known her to make herself sick.

I *had* to do something. But what? I tried to plead with her but she just stormed into the bathroom, cursing me under her breath. Barry, unaware, sat back and belched. 'I swear I'll properly die if I keep on overeating like this,' he said. He had had a quarter of a burrito. I threw a spare tortilla at him, and it landed square on his head, but nobody laughed. 'You've eaten nothing, Chicken,' Barry said, clearly confused. 'Are you well?'

Julian, who was taking me out after the burrito-fest, had watched the whole thing. After dinner he ordered me calmly into a taxi where he handed me a Jammie Dodger from his pocket. 'You need this,' he said.

The biscuit had seen better times, but it made my day. I

smiled at the lovely man with a blue jumper and blue eyes and blue biro reminders on his hand. We'd been going out (could you call it going out?) for just over a week. He leaned over and kissed my cheek, swollen and lumpy from the mouthful of sugary carbs I'd just shoved in it. 'Do you want to talk about it?' He tucked my hair behind my ear.

I munched my Jammie Dodger, staring out of the window as Driggs Avenue swept us out of McCarren Park and into Williamsburg. Simple little eateries were lighting candles; the evening was beginning. 'No, I don't think so,' I said wearily. 'I think I'd probably prefer to have a nice time with you. Where are we going?'

Julian scrumpled up his face, as he did when he was thinking hard about something. He'd refused to tell me so far where we were off to, but could probably see I'd appreciate some good news. Ok ok, I'll tell you. We're –' suddenly he clapped his hand over his pocket. 'BOLLOCKS!' he shouted. 'Why am I such a bollock? I left my phone in your bollocking bedroom! And I'll need it when we get there. Bollocks!'

I sat back and laughed as he asked the driver to turn round. Julian was a disaster. The best disaster of all time. 'It was meant to be a big thumping surprise,' he grumbled. '*And* I'd planned to bring you a Mr Kipling apple pie, but I forgot that too. I reckon Pam'll be eating it by now.'

'I'd like to meet Pam. Can I come and stay at yours soon?'

Julian looked thrilled. 'Yes! That'd be amazing! I'll take Pam to the dog parlour cos she stinks of farts, and I'll get my roommate to clean the toilet for once, and I'll make us lots of tea, and – and it'll be brilliant!' He leaned over and kissed me again. 'Sally Howlett doing a sleepover in my flat! Apartment! Whatever!'

My spirits lifted. Maybe I could have an evening off worry.

But when we ran in to get Julian's phone, Fiona was back in the toilet. *You are* never *going to have a night off worry*, my head told me tiredly. *Forget it.* I returned to the taxi somewhat deflated.

'Oh, Sal,' Julian said sadly. His eyes were so full of kindness I could hardly stand it.

'What can I do?' I asked. 'What should I say? I don't know what to do.'

Julian stroked my cheek. 'My poor little Sally Howlett,' he said softly. 'I know how awful this is. But, I promise you, there's nothing you can do.'

'But I *have* to do something! I have to make her stop!'

Our taxi was heading up the ramp to the Brooklyn-Queens Expressway, buildings falling away underneath us. 'I know you want to. But you can't,' Julian insisted. 'Does she look like a girl who has any control over what she's doing?'

'She's a free-willed human! Of course she can control herself!'

'Addiction doesn't work like that,' Julian said. 'Free will goes out of the window.'

'But she'll die!' I cried. 'I can't just sit here and say, "Yeah, she has no choice. I guess I'll just watch her die." I can't!' Tears stood in my eyes. 'She's being so selfish,' I whispered. 'So selfish. Doesn't she care what this is doing to us all?'

We were bearing round towards Williamsburg Bridge,

Manhattan sparkling at the end of a jungle of steel trusses. My heart was breaking. New York was meant to be my happy place.

'You're only being selfish if you have a choice,' Julian said, after a pause. 'And I think Fiona lost the power of choice a long time ago.'

I tried to counter his argument but couldn't because, deep down, I'd always known she had no choice. I slumped back into the taxi seat.

'She'll get help when she's ready,' Julian continued. 'I've seen this sort of shit go down before. And I'm telling you, you shouldn't exhaust yourself trying to force an intervention.'

I sighed, resigning myself to agree with him for now. A subway train chuntered past us and I tried not to feel so hopeless. Julian was reassuring but his attitude towards Fiona rankled slightly. Why was he always telling me to back off? Why was he always defending her?

Scene Fourteen

I was so lost in my thoughts that I didn't realize we'd been driving across Manhattan for nearly half an hour. Julian had been tapping away on his phone for ages, an endearing scowl of concentration on his face. From time to time he muttered things like, 'I hate smartphones.' Or 'Cocking technology.' Or just 'Grrrrrr.'

'Where are we going?' I asked. I felt dazed, as if someone had held my head under water for ages. I had to sort this out. Fiona's life had completely taken over my own.

Julian grinned. 'Aha. Nearly there.' We were crawling along Central Park South, a fact I was rather proud of knowing.

'We're heading towards Columbus Circle,' I said matter-of-factly.

Julian just laughed at me. 'Oh, you're ridiculous,' he said. He leaned over and kissed my nose. 'Wait a few more minutes and you'll see where we're going.'

I'd never seen myself as ridiculous. I was normally called things like 'a rock' and 'nice' and 'steadfast'. 'Ridiculous' was a bit odd. A bit out there. *But why not?* I asked myself, with what I thought was probably an impish grin. *Who says I have to be sensible?*

A few minutes later, we pulled up outside the Lincoln Center. The plaza's beautiful fountains leaped up in huge columns of twinkly light and behind them the Met stood proud, its immense arches blazing. Hundreds of feet swarmed towards the entrance and, behind the towering glass windows, hundreds more moved and climbed. I fell out of the taxi, wobbling like Julian's badly made Angel Delight. I'd never been out here at this time of night when the audience was arriving. A deep thrill crackled up and down my spine. I imagined the singers warming up for . . . What was on tonight? Ah, yes. *L'elisir d'amore*. Dannika Welter would have finished her vocal warm-up now and would be pacing the corridors, loosening her shoulders.

'Are we . . . Are we going to the opera?' I breathed. I sounded like a mad toddler.

Julian spoke in a bad, pseudo-Black Country accent. 'We most certainly are, bab!'

I didn't even care that he was taking the piss out of me. 'Oh, my God!' I breathed. 'Oh, my GOD! You got us tickets for the *MET*?'

Julian laughed. 'I was a bit worried you'd be disappointed. What with working here and all. But you look like you've been sniffing glue.'

'I feel like it!' I squeaked. 'ARGGGGH! The Met! The Met! The Met!' I pumped the air with my fist and Julian called me a mad hamster and I half glided, half flew across the paved circles of the plaza. 'Arggggh,' I repeated ecstatically. 'Arggh, the Met, the Met . . . Thank you thank you thank you thank you thank —'

But Julian had put a hand over my mouth. 'Sally,' he said firmly. 'Shut up. It's my pleasure. I know how much opera means to you.'

I looked at him sharply, suddenly afraid that Fiona might have said something about my wardrobe singing, but he looked perfectly innocent. So I skipped on, trying to imagine what Dannika Welter would be doing right now. And promptly decided to forget about her. I wanted the pure pleasure of being an audience member. I wanted to drink in the red carpets and spiky chandeliers and mingle with the posh people in the Grand Tier restaurant. I wanted to stare excitedly at the lush velvet curtains as I waited impatiently for the orchestra to strike up.

I stood in the vast, soaring foyer and wanted to cry. Ringing with a thousand voices, the Met ploughed on around me. 'I'll go and pick up our tickets,' Julian smiled, 'and you can carry on standing here, looking like a wide-eyed baby.'

He wove off into the crowd, then came straight back and kissed me. 'I can't help it. I'm completely in love with you.' He left me again.

I texted Julian to say I'd be at the bar and wandered off up the stairs, drinking in every detail. I stared at the audience members, the champagne, the posh crisps, the uncomfortable high heels for those who'd made the effort. I stared at handbags, up at the vast ceilings and out at the plaza below.

Giddiness quieting my usual inhibitions, I watched a fabulous-looking woman – a sort of American Helen

Mirren — with a sexy silvery crop and some very cool black-rimmed glasses. I admired her elegant neck and diamond drop earrings. Her rough but probably very expensive poncho wrap and her air of total composure. *What a brilliant woman*, I thought. *I bet she has some lovely sprawling house in Park Slope full of books and paintings. A confident, cultured, clever American woman, who knows about wines and stuff. I wish I knew her.*

Sadness overtook me. This woman, eating canapés at a little table, reading the programme and sitting with complete ease in a theatre bar, was the polar opposite of my mum. I imagined Mum, in her best outfit, hunched and angry, judging everyone around her and complaining (at a whisper) to Dad about how much a packet of crisps had cost. Mum would never go to the opera. She would never go to New York. When I'd called home yesterday she'd torn strips off me because she had also been contacted by the Royal Ballet and was furious with Fiona.

Poor Mum, I thought, rather to my surprise. *Poor Mum, never letting herself do anything. Never allowing herself to try anything new.*

'Sorry,' Julian said, appearing at my elbow. 'The tickets weren't there. I just need to call the person who actually booked them for me . . .'

'Sure.' I smiled gratefully at him and carried on watching the woman. She took out a mobile and broke into a wide smile when she saw who was calling. 'Darling!' I heard her say.

'Hi, Mom,' Julian said, next to me.

'Are you here?' asked the woman at the table.

'I'm at the Met. Um . . . are you?'

I looked slowly round at Julian. He was standing facing slightly away from me, impossibly handsome in his old soft shirt and jumper. I looked back at the woman, who'd stood up and started scanning around her. *His eyes. She had his eyes. And that delicate freckled nose.* My senses slowed down. *She was Julian's mum.* 'I'm at the bar on the second level,' she said. 'Where are you?'

I stared in amazement at her face. And back at Julian, who was saying that he was also at that bar, and what was going on? Why was she there? I saw them spot each other, saw Julian's mum break into a naughty little giggle. Julian registering shock and surprise, then shaking his head as if to say, *I might have known!* And before I even had time to be nervous, I was being swept towards her by her beaming, clearly very amused son.

'You're very naughty, Mom.' He grinned, allowing himself to be pulled in for a big hug.

'I am,' she agreed, standing back to appraise him. 'You look lovely, darling. So handsome. In spite of the unironed sweater,' she added affectionately, picking off a bit of fluff.

Julian pretended to ignore her but was patently delighted. 'Mom!' he said, shaking his head again. 'You're so bad!'

'Stevie Bell,' she said to me, pinning her steely blue eyes on me. 'And you're Sally. What a great pleasure!'

I shook her hand, saying how funny that she'd turned out to be Julian's mother because I'd just been watching her and was thinking how elegant and fabulous she looked. Stevie was delighted. 'See?' she said to Julian. 'I told you she'd be fine. He said it was too soon for us to meet,' she explained to me. 'And I told him, "OK, son, I'll leave the tickets at the box office." But then I changed my mind. A woman's prerogative, so butt out,' she said firmly, in Julian's direction.

'She very kindly got us the tickets,' Julian said, sliding his hand into mine. 'Cos they'd sold out and Mom's brilliant at knowing people. But I told her she wasn't allowed to come.'

'Well, you're a meanie,' I told him, at which Stevie cackled delightedly.

'Quite right, darling,' she said. 'And I've got a seat right next to you kids, so no making out, please. Shall we get a drink?'

'Yes!' I said. 'And we can compare notes.'

'Oh, God.' Julian sighed. 'This is worse than I thought.' But he was pleased. 'Can I leave you two alone while I go to the bathroom?'

'Of course,' we said in unison.

'Shit,' he muttered, sloping off.

Stevie cackled again, a glorious, velvety sound, and linked my arm. 'May I buy you a drink, Sally?'

'No, Mrs Bell, you may not. I'm buying you one. It was very kind of you to get the tickets. I really love this opera!'

'Darling. If you call me Mrs Bell, I'll have to throw my purse at you and I'd really rather not. I'm Stevie, OK?'

I giggled. 'Roger.'

'No, darling. It's Stevie.' Her eyes twinkled. She'd known what I meant.

'Well, Stevie, what are you drinking?' I was rather impressed with myself, remaining calm and ungabbly. But

I'd been the same when I'd met Julian. Perhaps it was just a Bell thing.

Stevie had a scan of the drinks list. 'Will we have cocktails, Sally?'

'We will.'

She smiled, a rather radiant-starlet smile. 'Julian hasn't stopped talking about you,' she said. 'My poor boy has been through a lot, and it really is so wonderful to see him happy.'

I froze momentarily, waiting for the inevitable follow-up. *So if you hurt him, I will tear you apart and feed you to my dog.* But it didn't come. 'No vulgarities,' she added, as if reading my mind. 'I'm not here as a henchman. I'm here because I trust Julian's instincts and wanted to meet you. That's all.'

I floated to the bar. Stevie was *fabulous.* I had worried, vaguely, that if I ever met the *mom* that Julian was always on about she'd look at me, with my dumpy little figure and shire-horse-tail hair and think, *Oh, God, my boy's lost it.*

I still didn't know anything about Julian's deceased wife but he'd tell me about her when he was ready. But that hadn't stopped me worrying that she had been everything I was not: tall, thin, beautiful and talented; an Ivy-Leaguer who knew about wine and could make puff pastry rather than buying it from Iceland. *But Stevie doesn't look remotely disappointed,* I thought happily. *She likes me. Already!*

I felt dizzy as I approached her with two glasses and a confident smile. I barely recognized my life, these days. I didn't have much money and my family was still a big mess. I had never owned a serious handbag or eaten caviar (Barry had told me it was fish poo) but right at this moment I was truly happy. I was *me*. I was out in the world, not drawing attention to myself but not hiding either.

And as Julian arrived back from the loo, giving his mother another big hug and giggling with her about something, I realized I was madly in love with possibly the best man on earth.

Scene Fifteen

I cried during the curtain call, of course. I always did when I went to see an opera, even if it was an absurd, happy nonsense of a show like tonight's. I cried because I loved the music so much, and because every opera felt so incredible to hear. I cried because opera reminded me of who I was and made everything in the world dance.

Julian, on one side of me, handed me a tissue. 'You do totally love opera, my little douche,' he said. 'Don't you?' I nodded, snorting into the tissue, and tried to wave an apology to Stevie, who was on my other side.

'Not at all.' She smiled, putting her glasses back on. 'I never believe anyone who says they don't like opera. They just don't understand it, that's all. To love opera is to really know it. And you really know it, don't you?'

Bell senior and junior were watching me with interest. 'A lifelong passion,' I said vaguely, as an undignified thread of snot escaped from the tissue. 'Oh, God! Sorry!'

Julian sloped off to get some toilet roll, telling us he'd wait at the main entrance.

'I like you,' Stevie said, as we descended the final staircase. 'And I don't mean that in a regal sense. God knows

I'd support anyone who made my boy happy. But I do, Sally. I like you. I think you're good news and you seem pleasingly straightforward.'

'Don't be fooled. I've got my stuff.'

'Oh, darling, come on. Haven't we all?'

Slightly amazed, I challenged her, telling her she was surely the sort of woman who had everything under control, always.

Stevie smiled, somewhat sadly, I thought, and watched her son come down the stairs. 'Don't *you* be fooled, my dear,' she said softly. 'I've made mistakes. I've made some colossal mistakes. As does any mother who loves her baby.'

'He seems to have turned out pretty well,' I said.

Stevie sniffed – a split-second weakening – then straightened. 'He's completely himself with you,' she told me. 'And you have no idea what a relief that is.'

Julian – relaxed, mildly fluffy – was nearly with us. I didn't ask Stevie what she meant.

ACT FOUR

Scene Fourteen

October 2012, Islington, London

'*YOU NEVER DID.*'

Barry stopped stretching and stared at me. I shifted from one foot to the other.

'I kind of did, actually.'

'*YOU MADE THE SEX WITH THE HUNGARIAN?*'

'Well, yes.'

'How many times?' Barry's face was cracked in two with amazement.

'Quite a few, to be honest. We've been on three dates and I've . . . we've . . . Er, I can't stop, Barry. It turns out I like wild sex a lot more than I'd thought.'

Barry shook his head dazedly. 'Oh, my days,' he said. 'Oh, my *days*. Chicken is getting regular sexings with a Hungarian dwarf.'

'He's not a dwarf! He's just shorter than me.'

Barry looked pointedly at the top of my head. 'Shorter than you, Chicken, is pretty fuckin' short.' I frowned. 'You're like a little Shetland pony, my girl. Without all the fur. Although you do have that little Shetland pot-belly thing going on –'

'SHUT IT!'

'Sorry, Chicken!' Barry was giggling. I was not.

'Barry, seriously. Enough about my weight.'

We both paused, surprised.

He peered at me. 'Chicken, are you well?'

'I'm fine. I'm just a bit over the comments about my weight. Can you put a sock in it, please?'

I hadn't known it would be so simple to stand up for myself.

'I most certainly can put a sock in it, Chicken,' he said, getting up off the floor where he'd been stretching. 'And I offer my deepest apologies, I didn't realize I was upsettin' you.'

'Imagine how you'd feel if I told you you were fat,' I said, going back over to the cooker where things were bubbling.

Barry paled. 'I think I'd die,' he admitted.

'Exactly. Just because I'm not a ballet dancer it doesn't mean I don't care about my weight. I do. I'm just not very good at keeping it under control.'

Barry helped himself to a carrot from the fridge. 'I'm only ever joshin' you anyway,' he said. 'Sorry.'

I smiled forgiveness and Barry topped up my wine glass. He held it out to me. 'Chicken, I want to propose a toast to you. You've been at that college for just three and a half weeks but you're turning into a right little firecracker.'

I batted him away. 'Oh, don't be silly!'

'No, you listen up, my girl. First, you're having all the

272

sex with the Hungarian. And now you're all like *telling me off*. And cooking proper dinners rather than eating that shite from cheap supermarkets. You're like a grown-up!'

I added some wine to the bolognese in the pan and stirred it in. I liked what Barry was saying and, actually, he had a point. Not only was I doing all of the things he'd said but I'd also recorded the stupid sanitary-towel advert without dying or passing out. *And* I'd applied to audition for the British Youth Opera in January, which would mean singing for a panel of real-life people.

But the biggest achievement of all was that today I had sung outside my wardrobe. Finally, after a year of deep, stagnant awfulness, the confidence I'd found in New York was straggling back in. Slowly, painfully, but it was coming. And it didn't rely on Julian Bell.

'Well, blow me DOWN!' Barry yelled, when I told him I'd sung outside the wardrobe. 'BLOW ME DOWN!'

We toasted and drank until he wandered off to take a call. Rather to my annoyance, I found myself thinking about Julian.

Julian, like me, seemed to have found his stride at college and just about everyone was in love with him. It infuriated me to see him chatty and quippy and sharp. As if he were a decent sort of a man, rather than a selfish, dishonest shit and probable drug dealer.

I made myself think instead about Jan Borsos.

Jan Borsos was completely crazy and I was enjoying our fling very much. So much, in fact, that I seemed to be spending most nights having bizarre and magnificent sex with him. Last night he had taken me to the Gay Hussar where he made me eat *kacsasült* and other dishes whose names were even less pronounceable. His scholarship money had finally come through so he not only paid the bill but then snuck me sideways into the Dean Street Townhouse where he had booked a surprise room for the night. It contained a bed the size of a stable. Jan insisted that we had sex on every inch of it and yodelled several times.

He was the best thing that could have been happening to me right then.

I sat down and called Fiona while my bolognese bubbled. I suspected she would be very pleased to hear about me and Jan Borsos.

She was. She shrieked with mirth when I told her about last night in the hotel. 'It's all down to you, Fi,' I told her. 'I wouldn't be doing any of this if it wasn't for you. You and your sodding *seize the day*! It's made me very brave, you know.'

Fiona was telling me that I could think again if I thought I was going to blame her for my filthy exploits with a young Hungarian, but we were interrupted by Barry. I'd had my eyes closed and hadn't heard him come in.

'Chicken?'

I sprang up guiltily, ending the call. Fiona had had to get used to me abruptly terminating our conversations.

'Who are you talking to?'

'No one.'

Barry looked sad. 'Oh, Chicken. You have to stop calling her.'

I went over to my bolognese, avoiding his eye, saying nothing. It made me sad that everyone else had abandoned Fiona. What had happened in New York was

274

dreadful, of course it was, but it angered me that nobody, not even Barry, was willing to keep lines of communication open. God knew Fiona had had a lonely enough life, especially now that she was out there in New York, miles away from her friends. Didn't he care that she had nobody else?

Before I knew it I was crying into the bolognese, and Barry was holding a tissue in front of me.

'It needed a bit of salt anyway,' he reassured me, stirring the contents of the pan. 'Sorry, Chicken, I don't mean to upset you. If you want to stay in touch with Fiona, that's your business.'

'I miss the stoic old me.' I sniffed. 'I hate being so bloody emotional, Baz.'

We stood at the stove for a while in companionable silence, Barry stirring and me dabbing bits of damp tissue under my eyes.

'Have you heard anything from your parents?' Barry asked eventually.

I shook my head. 'Course not. They hate me.'

'What about Dennis and his wife?'

'Meh. They're still talking to me, but only when they absolutely have to. Mum and Dad are still acting like I don't exist.'

Barry sighed. 'Oh, Chicken,' he said. 'This Fiona business is going to tear your family apart if you're not careful.'

I stirred the contents of the pan determinedly.

'Perhaps you could try to take a little break from Fiona – just to patch things up with them,' he added. His delicate features were colouring nervously.

'Barry,' I said sharply, 'I shouldn't have to patch things up with *anyone*. I didn't do anything wrong.'

Barry got some plates out and put them next to the stove, ready for serving. 'I know,' he said quietly. 'It was all that fuckin' Julian's fault. But your folks don't see it that way.'

'Indeed. They think it was all my doing.' Anger glowed hotly in me. *Nobody* in my family was remotely interested in how I felt, or how hard this last year had been for me.

'They don't even care about Fi,' I said angrily. 'She's out there, all on her own, and none of them give a rat's. It's as if she was just struck from the record. What's *wrong* with them?'

Barry whistled bravely. 'Bit of anger there, Chicken. That's a turn-up, eh?'

I blinked, surprised. Barry was right: I was angry. Furious, in fact. Perhaps I'd grown tired of appeasement. Perhaps I'd had enough of taking the blame for everything. 'Fuck them, Barry. They treated Fiona like rubbish. And now they're treating me like rubbish. All they care about is who to blame!'

Barry was agog. 'Did you just use the word "fuck"?'

'Yes. And I'm not afraid to use it again.'

'Steady on, Chicken,' Barry said soothingly. 'Here, let me plate up. You go and sit down an' pour yourself a nice glass of wine. I don't want you causin' no damage.

'Oh, my days,' he muttered, as I took my seat on the sofa. 'Chicken is fighting back.'

Scene Fifteen

The next morning, I arrived in the canteen, ready for my morning coffee and my chat with Norah at the tills, only to find Julian engaged in a jovial chat with her himself. He'd forgotten his hair product. His hair was still long and horrible but there was a distinct fluffiness to it. A distinctly *familiar* fluffiness that created an explosion of confusing thoughts as I watched him.

It was as if I was in the presence of Julian Bell for the first time since New York. There was still an air of Savile Row about him that I found absurd, but the Julian I knew felt somehow closer. The Julian I'd loved.

He bade Norah farewell, then wandered off to the hot drinks area, where I knew he would make a cup of Yorkshire Tea. I knew also that he'd smile as he made it, delighted by the abundance of proper tea in the UK.

He made a cup of Yorkshire Tea. A smile broke out across his face. I swallowed hard and glanced away. He looked about ten years old. He looked lovable.

Memories like this could not be indulged. Julian Bell was as good as dead to me. Clearly he wasn't about to quit his job to make life easier for me; my best hope was to think of and call this person Julian Jefferson and disassociate him from my past.

'For someone who's meant to be enjoying shagging Hungarian tenors, you spend an awful lot of time staring at your ex,' Helen observed, sliding through the canteen door. Me and my bottom had almost blocked the entrance.

'Yeah,' I said awkwardly. I felt I should defend myself but wasn't sure how.

'You don't still fancy him?'

'No.'

I really didn't. At least I was certain of that.

'Right.'

'Right.'

Helen raised an eyebrow. 'Well, Sally, I've really enjoyed our chat but I think I'm going to get some toast, if it's all the same to you . . .'

I stopped staring at Julian. 'Sorry, Helen. I really truly don't like him any more but it's still weird. Oh! You've had your hair done!'

Helen had had a fringe cut and it looked blinding. Her deep blue, slightly slanted eyes were now visible in all their delicate, feline glory. 'See? You were so busy staring at him you didn't even notice my hair,' she crowed, triumphant.

'Oh, go away.'

Helen made off for the breakfast counter. I hung back, wishing to avoid Julian's eye and maybe shrink out of the door. But it was too late. He looked sideways at Helen as she appeared next to him, exclaimed, 'Nice bangs!' then spotted me lurking. He waved, in an awkwardly jovial way.

I nodded politely in his direction and was drowned by

a tidal wave of Violet Elphinstone, all cute baker-boy hat and cosy unstructured cashmere jumper. As usual, she gave me an insincere sideways hug. 'Morning, lovely,' she said warmly.

'Oh, hi, Violet. How are you?'

'Fab!' she replied, squeezing my shoulder and sliding over to Julian. 'Hey,' she said in a special lower, huskier voice. A voice that distinguished her from the other students.

I winced. As if any English person said 'hey'.

'Hey,' he replied easily, failing to spot the flaw. He'd always seen the best in people, Julian.

Violet paused as he started loading a full English on to his plate, working out how to play him. If I'd learned anything over the last few weeks it was that Violet fancied Julian even more than the other girls did.

'Oh, I love a good fry-up,' she enthused, commencing the shovelling of sausages and beans on to a plate of her own. I nodded, impressed. Violet clearly *didn't* enjoy a good fry-up at all, but she knew a good opportunity when she saw one.

'Go, girl!' Julian said, predictably impressed.

'I'll probably get really fat soon!' She added two hash browns to show just how cool she was about that. No silly weight control here!

Julian tutted and fussed without using any actual words. He obviously wanted to say, 'You will clearly never get fat because you are a total goddess,' but of course couldn't say that because he was her vocal coach. Violet looked totally unaffected but I could feel pleasure radiating from her like a noxious gas.

She threw on a pile of fried potatoes to seal the deal, then turned back to Julian, who was helping himself to toast. 'Thanks *so* much for offering some one-on-one rehearsals, Julian. I'd love to take you up on that offer. At the moment I'm just barking that part like a dog!' She was talking about her lead role in *Manon*, and reports were that she was sounding fantastic.

I sighed as Julian began his inevitable rebuttal. 'Oh, come *on*! Barking it like a dog? You're doing great!'

'Oh, I'm really not . . . Perhaps we could do a one-on-one at the end of the day after rehearsals. I'll buy you a drink after to say thank you. I need to hear more of that lovely little accent of yours, ha-ha!'

Julian spooned a hash brown on to his plate but missed and it splatted on the floor. He picked it up, laughing amiably, but I could tell he was embarrassed. And anguished. He knew I'd heard Violet's invitation.

'Well?' Violet asked, serving Julian a hash brown.

Julian baulked, his eyes flickering to me. I could almost hear his brain at work. 'That'd be great,' he said weakly, and I hated him.

I hated myself, too. It shouldn't matter. He and Violet deserved each other.

Scene Sixteen

At lunchtime we had been called in for a special recital in the theatre. Nobody was entirely sure what it was about, but we had all been strongly encouraged to attend, in a life-or-death sort of a way.

As we queued outside the Britten Theatre clutching our sandwiches I found myself, rather unfortunately, next to Julian. But before my body started to tense I reminded myself I was in the presence of Julian Jefferson, a famous and very talented opera singer from whom I could learn a great deal. Not some turd from the past.

'Hello,' he said. He was smiling down at me.

'Hi.'

'I hear you're making great progress with Brian.'

I squirmed. 'Yeah. I suppose so.'

Julian watched me with those twinkly, mischievous eyes I'd encountered the night I'd met him. I wished he could turn them off and use normal, crappy eyes on me.

'So, how are things with your parents?' he asked. Just like that.

My heart missed a beat and my eyes swivelled down to my feet. I was stunned.

'Oh, um, bad question?' he faltered. 'Erm . . .'

'Bad question,' I mumbled. *How do you* think *things are with my parents, you twat?*

Violet, who was in front of us, swung round. 'You two know each other?'

'No,' I said.

'Yes,' Julian said.

I stared at him. Why? Why was he doing this? 'Sally worked wardrobe at the Met last year,' Julian said. 'I met her then.'

Violet looked almost as angry as I felt.

'Oh, fabbo,' she said, with an icy smile. 'Julian and I have had a few sessions in the pub recently and he's never once mentioned you! Funny!'

A few seconds later she swung round again. 'So how did you actually *meet*?' she asked, unable to help herself. 'I mean, surely you're too important to hang out in the wardrobe department, Julian? And I thought you'd had a long break from singing?'

'We met because Sally was trying to steal a candle from me,' Julian explained comfortably. In spite of the situation, he dared to smile. 'I decided to give her the benefit of the doubt. I offered her a Scotch and she said yes. Then she said she was lying and she actually wanted a glass of wine.' He started chuckling. 'It was very funny. Although you had to be there, I guess.'

The man had no shame! None! How dare he go all affectionate and start reminiscing?

'Well,' Violet was looking even more fed-up, 'that sounds a bit weird!'

'No, it was cool.' Julian grinned. 'Until Sally made me

282

go to a poetry café. Ha-ha! She looks like a normal girl, Violet, but underneath she's a really smelly old hippie.' He laughed so much that he did a pig snort, then laughed even harder. He was helpless with laughter. For another terrible moment I felt as if I was looking right at Julian Bell again, love of my life. *Stop it*, I begged. *Be a poncy coach. A singer. Anything. Just not Julian Bell.*

'HA-HA-HA!' Violet roared unconvincingly. 'God, that sounds *dreadful*!' she added. 'A poetry café!'

Before I knew it, I spoke: 'It was awesome, actually,' I told her. 'We had an incredible time. One of the best nights of my life, in fact.'

I could have slapped myself. Why? Why did I have to compete with her? And using Julian as a weapon too.

Violet's face, frozen temporarily with shock, was coming back to life. I didn't like the look of it. 'Talking of good times,' she began, 'I've heard a little rumour about you!'

Julian folded his arms across his chest. 'Oh, yes?' He grinned. 'Has Sally set up shop offering spiritual poetry readings and massage oils?'

Violet tinkled with laughter. 'No,' she said sweetly. 'What I heard is that our mutual friend here' – I shuddered – 'is having a bit of a thing with Jan Borsos!'

There was a terrible silence. Violet was triumphant, I was aghast and Julian was patently amused.

'Really?' he asked. His smile was cheeky and mischievous, and I hated myself for noticing that he was non-jealous.

As I worked out what to say I heard a jolly-sounding tenor singing arpeggios somewhere behind me.

It was Jan Borsos, fighting his way through the queue for the theatre. 'Ah-ah-ah-AH-ah-ah-aaaaah, ah-ah ah, SALLY! *BUON GIORNO!* I am HERE!'

I turned as he got down on one knee to take my hand, which he kissed extravagantly.

'I'll take that as a yes, then.' Julian sniggered. I shot him an icy glare, but my head was exploding. What should I do? What should I say? I didn't *want* the whole college to know! (Why?)

'Yes,' I said, after a pause. I drew myself up to my full stunted height. 'Jan and I are dating.'

'FANTASTIC!' Violet bellowed. It was the first thing she'd actually meant.

Julian watched me for a few seconds longer than was necessary, then shook Jan's hand. 'You're a lucky man,' he said, to a slightly confused Jan.

'I know.' Jan swelled to twice his size. 'Sally is like a delicious sponge cake.'

Julian cried with laughter. 'I'm sure she is, Jan. I'm sure she is . . .'

Violet butted in: 'So does anyone know what this lunchtime thing is about?'

Jan was holding my hand proudly.

Everyone said, 'No,' apart from Julian, whose eyes were still watching me.

'It's just some fat old singer doing a recital,' he said dismissively. 'Nothing worth writing home about.'

At that moment the doors opened and we filed in. The Britten Theatre filled quickly; it seemed that not just the opera school but the entire vocal faculty had come. The theatre was buzzing with anticipation. I concentrated on eating my sandwich and quelling the nervous rumblings in my stomach. *It was fine, it was fine.* Of course I was shy about making Jan and me public. It had only been a few weeks! And of course it was weird to tell someone I'd once been in love with!

But it was out there now, and it would hopefully encourage Julian to back off and let me get on with my singing. Helen was on my right-hand side. 'Any idea what this is about?' she asked, scanning the theatre. 'It's rammed!'

'Julian said it's a "fat old singer",' I reported. 'Nothing worth writing home about, according to him.'

Two seconds later, Hugo, the head of the opera school, walked on stage. 'I had to keep the details of this event secret,' he grinned, 'because if word got out that this was happening we'd have been mobbed! I've been begging this man to sing for us for weeks and he has consistently refused, but I wore him down in the end. Ladies and gentlemen, it is my great honour and pleasure to welcome to the stage one of the best tenors in the world for his first recital in several years. Julian Jefferson!'

By the time the thunderous applause had subsided, and Julian, looking infuriatingly relaxed, had thanked us all for coming, my heart had begun to slow down. I concentrated on his chest because I knew that his hair was fluffy and I couldn't look at that.

But then he started singing and everything went wrong. Because the sound coming out of Julian's mouth was heart-stopping.

'Oh, my God,' Helen said weakly, when it was over. 'Are you sure you don't want him? Because, if not, I do. I'm prepared to call off my wedding, I'm sure Phil'd understand.'

I was still speechless. I shook my head. Only to hear Violet, over my shoulder, telling Ismene that *enough was enough*. 'He's been flirting with me for weeks,' she said, in a stage whisper. 'I'm going to bloody well *get* him tonight.'

Scene Seventeen

As the weeks passed, I did my best to forget about Julian's extraordinary singing. I allowed myself to think of him only as Julian Jefferson, an exceptional opera singer we were all very lucky to have. Julian Bell was finally, thankfully, becoming an unpleasant memory. Which was lucky, because rumours started circulating not long after Julian's recital that he and Violet had been seen arriving at college together in the morning.

It was hardly a surprise, yet it troubled me. I was having a very nice time with my mad boyfriend but the knowledge that they were seeing each other did, at times, seem to diminish what I had with Jan Borsos. (In my head, anyway.) Suddenly our wild (and very regular) sex, involving yodelling (from Jan) and sexual positions I'd never even heard of (possibly no one had ever heard of), felt juvenile and inferior. I imagined Julian Jefferson and Violet Elphinstone to have very grown-up, sleek, shiny sex. They'd dine in dimly lit Kensington restaurants rather than my kitchen where Barry would often interrupt our badly prepared meals by storming through in a thong doing split leaps.

I imagined them to have highbrow conversations about opera and music, whereas it was hard to get Jan Borsos to talk about *anything* for longer than a few minutes. One of the things I both loved and despaired of in him was his non-existent attention span: it was entertaining being around someone who wanted to discuss the British postal service one minute and his mad-sounding ex-wife the next – but sometimes, when I saw Violet and Julian walking down a corridor rapt in conversation I felt anxious about what I had. Was it enough?

I didn't entertain these thoughts for long. Jan made me laugh until I cried and that, quite frankly, was an indispensable quality. He never made me feel anything less than good, while Julian had comprehensively ruined my life. Julian, however attractive and appealing he might seem, was dangerous and dishonest. Jan was mad and lovely. The End.

Shortly before *Manon* opened, Jan Borsos and I were booked in on our first outreach session for Lord Peter Ingle at Stourbridge Grange. Our workshop was to last two days, and if it went well, a further two would be offered. 'And then we can look at rolling this out to other schools in the area,' he said.

I wouldn't get too excited, I thought, remembering what my school had been like.

'But what *is* outreach?' Jan kept asking, when we tried to plan it. 'We do not have this thing in my town.'

'I can assure you we didn't have it in Stourbridge either. I think we just have to accept that it'll be a disaster, Jan.'

After brainstorming several ideas we decided to use *Les*

Misérables as a starting point. Lord Peter Ingle was not so keen. 'Very good,' he said unenthusiastically. There was a pause. Then: 'No. Very un-good. *Les Misérables* isn't an opera!'

He said '*Les Misérables*' in a proper French accent, which left me feeling like a bit of a tool. But I stood firm. 'Trust me, to get them to sing at all will be a triumph,' I told him. '*Les Mis* is as close as a musical's ever going to get to being an opera. *And* it's becoming cool again because of the *Les Mis* film coming out in January.'

Peter was unconvinced but when I explained that in my day it had been a thumpable offence even to join in the morning hymn at that school, he capitulated. 'This may be more ambitious than I thought,' he said ruefully.

Once we were agreed on *Les Mis*, Jan and I were able to put together a plan quite quickly. We were going to keep it very simple and had agreed not to put anyone in the spotlight unless they wanted to be there (that was my contribution). We submitted our plans to our college development centre and started to study the score of *Les Mis*.

In most respects, we were ready to go. But one thing remained outstanding, and it was keeping me awake at night. That thing was my family. Brenda and Patrick Howlett. Ramrod Hissing Woman and Pipe-smoking Doormat Man, as Barry called them.

Mum and Dad had all but cut off contact since I'd returned from New York a year ago. There had been a dreadful reunion in Stourbridge during which nobody had spoken: Dad had stayed behind his newspaper almost all night, clouds of uncomfortable smoke foaming out over the top of the *Mail*, while Mum had been mute and, as far as I could tell, furious. It was as if she didn't trust herself to open her mouth in case she spewed out abuse and blame, like molten lava. When I'd tried to talk about Fiona they had both been completely silent and I'd effectively conducted the conversation with the gas fire.

The next day, when I'd got out of the car at the station, more devastated even than I'd been when I'd arrived, I made one last attempt. 'Come down to see me next time you visit Dennis and Lisa at CrateWorld,' I offered.

'We'll see,' Mum muttered. Her eyes were darting from side to side, as if she were afraid. Afraid of what? Of people seeing us? Of the town gossiping about what had happened to me and Fiona? Then, with a strange nod, she'd got back into the car and instructed Dad to drive off. I'd been stunned, standing by the station entrance with my wheelie case, face wan and waxy from days of crying. The truth could no longer be ignored: they blamed me completely. *They hated me.*

Mum didn't call me again after that. She posted me some Tesco vouchers she'd saved from her Clubcard, and wrote to me when I got into music college saying, 'Well done,' but that she and Dad were very worried about the direction I was taking. That was it. If it hadn't been for Dennis and Lisa grudgingly taking me in for the Christmas after New York, I wouldn't have seen anyone from my immediate family in more than a year.

It would be easiest if Jan and I simply turned up at Stourbridge Grange, slept at the hotel Lord Ingle had put us in and never told Mum and Dad I was there. But that was a dangerous game. As far as I knew, Mum's friend

Carol still worked as the school secretary and it would be only a matter of time before Mum found out we were there. And, anyway, I was sick of sneaking around. If they wanted to blame me, that was their business. No more hiding.

'But your mum's been a witch,' Barry said, when I shared my decision. 'She never calls you, just sends you supermarket vouchers, and there's you dealin' with all this shit about Fiona for a *year*. Why would you call her?'

'Because I'm not going to be Mum's scapegoat any more,' I said, with more conviction than I felt. 'I hate myself enough for New York. I don't need them making it worse. If I'm in Stourbridge I should just bloody well be able to see them. They're my parents, Barry!'

Barry nodded. 'Onward, Chicken Soldier,' he said proudly. 'You're damn right. Don't you take no abusin'!'

'I won't.'

I wasn't sure I believed myself. But I was willing to try. And as soon as I knew I was game, the quiet sense of courage – still so new to me – warmed my heart.

Unfortunately, the decision as to how and when to contact my parents had been taken out of my hands.

It was the day before our trip to Stourbridge and I was sitting underneath Jan in his narrow bed in Shepherd's Bush while he held forth about the mid-section of his childhood. Jan loved telling me about his childhood and – perhaps luckily for us both – I was fascinated by the Hans Christian Andersen-ness of it all.

He was telling me about how his mother who, by all accounts, was a beautiful yet formidable woman, used to sing English folk songs to him so that when he came to learn English he would have a head start. And then, quite casually, he broke off the story, peered into my face and announced, 'And soon I meet the mother of Sally Howlett. I tell her her daughter is very beautiful and has great bottom.'

'You won't necessarily meet her,' I told him. 'Even if I do call her, she won't be inviting us round for a cosy dinner. Trust me.'

I had told Jan that my relationship with my parents was non-existent but had not really explained why. Uncharacteristically for him, perhaps, he had never pressed me on this, but there was a lot about me that Jan still didn't know. Even though I had been hearing his life story in daily instalments since we'd met.

But something in Jan's furiously smiling, ever-so-slightly-guilty face was worrying me.

He swept his hair from his forehead. 'Aha! Jan Borsos knows different things about your parents!'

My heart quickened. 'Jan?'

His eyes gleamed. 'I call your parents.'

'NO! YOU MUSTN'T!'

'Sorry, this is my English. I *called* your parents. It is done already.'

Anxiety howled through me.

'I like you, Sally Howlett, and I want to meet your family. So I call them and I say, "Hello, it is Jan Borsos here. I come to Stourbridge with your child Sally Howlett and we help children at the school. Please we come for dinner at your house."'

I gaped.

Jan's eyes narrowed. 'She is battle-hammer, your mother.'

I was too shocked to say 'axe'. All I could do was try to carry on breathing.

'At first she was saying nothing, but then she says, "Yes, you come for dinner at our house. If you are with our Sally we want to meet you."'

I couldn't believe it. Tears of panic pricked my eyes. Why couldn't he have just kept a lid on it? Why did he always have to be so bloody *impetuous*? 'Jan, I don't think this is a good idea. You don't understand the situation with my fa—'

'No words! I will sing for them! They will love me!'

'NO! You mustn't sing! That's the worst thing you could do. Oh, God, Jan!'

Why had he had to do this? Could he not have minded his own business? Just for once?

'No, Sally, it is good. We arrive into the Stourbridge on Monday, we do workshop, then later at the six thirty hours we have dinner with your parents. Then we do more out-reach workshop Tuesday and we go home to London. It is all perfect!'

I started to cry in earnest.

Jan dismounted and lay down next to me, staring at my face in dismay. He thumbed away a tear from my cheek. 'What is the problem?' he whispered.

'I wouldn't know where to start.'

'You can talk to Jan.'

'No, I can't.'

Jan nodded thoughtfully. 'Then I think it is best we have some sexing for now.'

*

Much, much later, as Jan slept with his hand flung across the pillow, Byron-like hair falling about his face, I snuck outside to the hallway to call Fiona. I'd not spoken to her for days and I missed her. As ever, I closed my eyes, as if to fool myself that she was there, next to me.

We'd had a few bad connections recently but tonight I could hear her as clearly as if she was crouched in the corridor at Jan's halls of residence. And as soon as she started to speak I knew I'd be OK.

Fiona told me I absolutely had to go and have this dinner with Mum and Dad. 'It's time, Sally,' she said. 'Time for reconciliation. And selfishly I'm glad, because this mess is all my fault. I love you, Sal, and I want you to be friends with your parents. I've done you enough harm as it is.'

She ended the conversation by reminding me that Stourbridge Grange was a tough nut to crack, but if anyone could do it, it was me. 'You and that bloody Black Country accent.' She laughed. 'They'll love you.' Then she disappeared, as she always did. She was impossible to pin down for long, even in New York.

It was only then, as I sat on the scratchy corridor carpet, leaning back against the cold wall, that I knew I'd be all right.

'Thanks, Fi,' I said to the empty corridor. 'I love you.'

And so, even when the College Development Centre called us in to say that Lord Ingle had asked if a tutor could come up with us, and that the college had asked Julian Jefferson to go, I remained calm. Fiona wanted me to do this and it didn't matter who was there to complicate things. In fact, it would be an advantage to have such an incredible singer with us.

ACT THREE

Scene Sixteen

September 2011, New York

I had a boyfriend. A proper one I was mad about. Who made me laugh, who looked after me and whom I wanted to look after. A man I was proud to be out and about with, or in with, or frankly anywhere with. A man I·was *in love with*!

Julian Bell. Julian Bell. Sometimes when I wasn't with him I just whispered his name, like a stalker from a horror film, then squeaked things like 'RAH!' and 'BEEP!' because there was no stalking and no horror film going on here. Just a gorgeous, sparkly New York Romance.

With him, I felt like the funniest woman on earth, which I really was not, and in him I felt like I'd met the funniest man on earth, which probably wasn't true either. But we spent hours – days – laughing. We didn't sit talking about philosophy until the early hours, which is how I thought proper relationships began. In fact, we often talked a load of bollocks and laughed until we hurt.

I knew it was love because it was easy to talk about a load of bollocks and laugh until we hurt.

I thought Julian Bell was the most perfect-looking man I'd ever seen and he told me I was beautiful. I'd often catch him watching me with a lovely half-smile and I'd think, *Everything about your face is AMAZING.* When I asked him what he was thinking, he replied, simply, 'That I love you.'

I knew it was love because I believed him.

The first time I saw him in his own apartment – in the middle of his books, his non-matching wine glasses, his worn jumpers and his rolled-down packets of biscuits with elastic bands round them – I fell even more in love with him. I adored all the little details of this man. We ate imported Somerset Cheddar and had some bonks and sang and danced to 'Eye of the Tiger'.

I knew it was love because here was a man who imported English cheese and owned 'Eye of the Tiger'.

I had been enjoying my life until this point. Really enjoying it, at times. But Fiona had been right: I'd never really pushed my boundaries, which had been fine until now. Pre-New York, the size of my life had been just right for me. But I was in Act Three now and things were expanding. I felt as if the Sally I'd left behind in London had been on an empty stage with a few dim spotlights here and there, but now this steady, beautiful Julian Bell character was illuminating every corner. He saw every part of me and seemed to love the complex mess that was Sally Howlett. He helped me see a bigger life for myself, not in terms of wealth or success but in terms of bravery. Being visible. Being me.

In fact, he saw things that even I'd failed to notice.

'Right. I've been polite and waited a bit,' he announced

one day. We were eating tacos at La Superior. 'But enough. Sally, what the HELL is going on with you and opera?'

I hastily shoved down a prawn taco in case I lost my appetite, and Julian laughed. He had remembered to wear his glasses tonight and he looked clever and gorgeous and a bit mad because they were still held together with gaffer tape. 'What do you mean, what's going on with me and opera?'

'I mean, you cry like a child whenever you see an opera, you work in opera and, most importantly . . .' there was an unsettlingly dramatic pause '. . . most importantly, Sally, you're clearly an opera singer.'

I choked.

'Don't deny it! I heard you sing Mimi the night we met! And don't choke. You're not allowed to choke.'

I stopped choking and shoved down another mouthful, waiting for my appetite to evaporate and my body to freeze.

They didn't.

Slowly, stunningly, I realized that I wasn't actually that bothered. *Dear God*, my head said dazedly. *You're going to tell him! Aren't you?* Dear God! I replied. Yes! I bloody well am!

'Um, well. I'm not an opera singer. That's the truth. I'm a wardrobe mistress. But I've been singing since I was seven. In private.'

'What exactly does that mean?'

'It means I sang in my wardrobe. And I still do.'

Julian sat back, folding his arms. Wonder and something I hoped was affection worked its way across his face. 'You sing in your wardrobe?' He spoke slowly. With complete amazement.

'Correct.'

'Because you didn't want your parents to hear you,' he said, almost to himself. I nodded. I didn't need to explain any more because he'd got it already. My family. The crazy fear of being noticed. The shame when we were.

'Dear God,' he murmured. 'You learned to sing like that in a wardrobe?'

'I'm not that good!' I took another taco, a pork one. This was great. Julian had stopped eating, I hadn't died of a heart attack and I was getting all the tacos.

'You're *seriously* good. On a technical level you're really quite excellent,' he said. (It didn't occur to me to ask him how he knew. A year later I would remember this moment and smack myself around the head, wondering how I could have missed it.)

'Ah, not really,' I replied. 'I've been buying master-classes for years so I've learned some stuff through them.'

Julian came to his senses again, sequestering three tacos in case I ate them all. 'Back off,' he ordered. 'So can I just be certain. You have never had a lesson? Never sung for anyone? *In your life?*'

I began to flush. 'I was supposed to sing at the school concert when I was in primary school,' I said, 'and I was so terrified that I wet myself. And then I never tried in public again until the poetry slam. And I blame it on you because you put some sort of a spell on me and I ended up singing in front of *everyone*. And while we're at it, how come YOU were so good?'

Julian batted me off. 'Oh, I had singing lessons when I was younger. Did a few things.' He sipped his Modelo, then reached over the table for my hand. 'I'm so sorry you weed yourself,' he said gravely. 'It must have been awful.'

'I'm sorry too,' I said cheerfully. 'It was.' And, out of nowhere, I was laughing. I laughed and laughed and laughed. I laughed so hard that a bit of shredded lettuce flew out of my mouth and splatted on the side of Julian's beer bottle and I didn't even care. I laughed about that awful, deadening experience because suddenly I could, and eventually Julian laughed too and trendy Williamsburg people looked at us as if we were dicks, which we were. Julian didn't push me any further. It had only been a few weeks but he knew my limits.

Had I mentioned that he was amazing?

But, for all the love and laughter, these were not halcyon days. My cousin – my sister, my best friend – was going completely off the rails. That she was on drugs was now indisputable. She had stopped drinking, because of the calories, but was distressingly wired most of the time. Mostly she was argumentative and overbearing, paranoid and noisily present, but other times she seemed almost comatose. Her appearance was going to pot and so was the flimsy thread of dependability she'd once possessed.

She would not eat, whatever I tried. Her diet was no longer something she had any control over: the only deviation she could take from her morning egg white, her lunchtime peas and her dinnertime salad was to eat nothing at all. Her eyes had begun to look bug-like and her body more obviously hairy. The disintegration, so sudden and brutal, caused me physical pain. Julian's warm arm would curl around me, as I lay watching the shadows shift across the ceiling, and I'd wonder how it would end.

I spent as much time with her as I could. I was frantic with worry.

What surprised me was that Julian seemed to want to spend so much time with her too. It was as if she had become a project, although he appeared to have no interest in trying to stop her taking drugs. He just seemed to want to hang out with her. A lot.

More than once I got back from the Met to find them sitting on the sofa, Bea or Barry watching warily from the other side of the room. Fiona was a lot more animated around Julian than she was with the rest of us. The second time I found them together on the sofa she was laughing uncontrollably at some video clip he was showing her on his phone. She grabbed his arm as gales of laughter rent her tiny, frail body.

'Hello!' I said, grateful for the sound of happiness.

'Hi, baby,' Julian said, reaching for my hand. Momentarily, it irked me that he didn't get up to kiss me. Fiona took the phone off him without acknowledging me, so she could carry on watching the clip. Her eyes were slightly bloodshot.

'Hello.' I leaned down and kissed Julian, telling my head to be quiet. He didn't need to get off the sofa to show me that he was in love with me. He'd told me last night, about a hundred times, as we'd lain around my bedroom counting each other's moles and discussing types of fart.

'Hi, Freckle,' I said.

Fiona looked up for a second. 'Oh, hi, Sally. Sorry, I'm watching this . . .'

Julian, seeing my face, winked kindly at me. As if to say, *Leave her be.*

I wandered off to the kitchen where Bea and her Brazilian masseur were making something complicated involving kale and flageolet beans. 'How long has Julian been here?' I asked Bea.

She raised her eyes to heaven. 'Hours. He must be determined to sort Fiona out,' she whispered.

'I keep thinking that. But do you ever hear him telling her to stop taking drugs? To eat some food? To start behaving like a reasonable human being? Because I don't.'

'Well, no, but he must be saying these things when we are not here.'

'I'm not sure he is, you know. He'd tell me if he had any important conversations. They just seem to be . . . *hanging out.*'

Bea looked up from the kale she was chopping. 'Darling, are you jealous?'

'No.'

I wasn't, actually. It was more just . . . confusion. Those two had separated off in recent days, forming a little club, which, while it didn't threaten me, didn't make sense. What was their connection? Why was Julian so happy to spend all this time with her? And why was Fiona happy to talk to him when she'd all but stopped talking to the rest of us?

If I could somehow understand what the bond was between them, I'd feel a lot more comfortable. I knew Julian wasn't on drugs. And I didn't think for a second he was after Fiona, or even she him.

Then why? What were they doing?

Bea ordered me to get some wine out of the fridge. 'It is time for a drink,' she announced. 'Maybe you are upset because Fiona is going to move in with Julian for a few months.'

I stopped in my tracks. 'She is?'

Bea tutted. 'Ah. Well, yes, *preziosa*, but you already knew this, no? I am sure it is nothing bad.'

'I knew it was a possibility,' I said glumly. 'But I didn't know it had been decided on.'

I stared off into the distance as Bea filled my glass with pale cold wine. I couldn't imagine not seeing Fiona for as much as a day. How would she cope with nobody to look after her?

'Hi there,' Julian said, coming into the kitchen behind me. 'I came to find you so I could snog you hard and then feel you up a bit. Bea, please leave,' he ordered, which she did amid much hooting. Julian had written *I luv Sally & Céline Dion* on his hand. He kissed me all over my face and told me I was a chipmunk. Then he gave me a long, lovely hug. 'She's not been too bad today,' he said into my hair. 'So you can relax tonight. Enjoy this kale extravaganza of Bea's and kill me with flageolet-bean trumps later on.'

I relaxed. If Fiona really did want to stay here, she was in good hands. Julian Bell lit up every room he walked into.

'I don't think I want to leave New York,' I announced. 'What shall we do?' It was the day after Bea's kale supper (ruined by Fiona and Bea having a loud screaming argument in Fiona's bedroom) and I'd realized I had only five days left.

'Mm? Hang on . . .'

Julian was sitting on his bedroom floor with his laptop on his legs, editing someone's article for his magazine. He had pushed his sleeves up to his elbows but one had slid back down again, a limp concertina of dark blue hanging from his wrist. I smiled at him, absorbing every detail of his face, his hair, his long, surprisingly elegant fingers. I wanted to slide my hand up inside his sleeve.

He doesn't touch-type, I realized to my surprise. I knew he'd started the *Brooklyn Beaver* three years ago, but because I'd not wanted to pry about his wife I was a bit hazy on the chronology of his life before that.

But that was the nice thing about what had grown between us. I was in no hurry to know everything: I trusted that it would all unfold as and when it was meant to.

'Sorry, Sally, I won't be a minute.' Julian looked up briefly, smiling over his glasses, and I felt something warm glow in my chest. I went over to the window while I waited for him.

Julian lived in a relatively modern apartment in East Williamsburg, just off Graham Avenue, and had the back of a brownstone terrace and a tangle of overhead electrical cables for a view. It lacked the scale and magnificence of Raúl's but I found it just as fascinating: here, after all, was real life, packed into small apartments, framed by peeling windows and lit by tattered lampshades and fairy lights. A small Hispanic woman sat for hours in the window of the house directly behind Julian's; she made – with ceaseless momentum – bead necklaces, which she hung on a hook coming out of the window frame. Above her there was a young couple who spent more time on their phones than talking to each other, and to their right a tired, faded room through which an old man occasionally shuffled.

Julian's apartment was on the ground floor – or the first floor, as Americans called it – and it had a small garden, which his bedroom opened on to. His room was the corridor through which Pam, his housemate's dog, travelled to her favourite spot under a mulberry tree: she burst in whenever she fancied. Which had been a bit embarrassing on more than one occasion.

'Hello, Pam,' I said, going outside to sit with her. Julian's bedroom door had one of those proper American screens that snapped shut to keep the insects out.

'Sorry,' he called, hearing it close behind me. 'I'm on the last paragraph.'

'Don't worry. Me and Pam are hanging out.'

I sat on the bench by Pam. She thumped her tail enthusiastically in the dust, then went back to sleep. I thought how cool Julian's housemate was, calling her dog Pam. Her name was Carmen and she worked nights in a homeless shelter. Because Julian almost always stayed at mine, I'd only met Carmen twice but she'd struck me as being extraordinarily chilled. I struggled to imagine Fiona taking her place.

I leaned back against Julian's building, breathing in my beloved Brooklyn, and pondered what Julian and I should do about the future.

Immediately I grinned, pinching myself. It had happened! The love thing! Something that *had* a future worth pondering! A solitary flag, left over from a row of party bunting, flapped in the warm breeze above my head. A flying insect landed on the leg of my jeans and I realized I'd not looked at myself in the mirror and thought, *You look fat in those jeans*, for weeks. Not for the first time, I sensed how deeply happy I was.

'You look extremely cute, sitting there with Pam.' Julian came outside with two bottles of cold beer. 'Please can you sit in my yard for ever?'

'Even when it's cold? And snowy?'

'Yes. I'll build you an igloo. You'll be like this funny little mad snowman in my garden and we can have naughty igloo sex.'

'Sign me up.'

'Soin meeyoop,' Julian giggled. His Black Country accent was getting worse.

He sat down on the bench and kissed me. I loved kissing Julian. I loved the feeling of his lips and the scratch of stubble and the way his eyes always opened at the same time as mine. He hooked up my legs and pulled them over his, wrapping his arms round me. 'Don't go,' he whispered. 'I might die without you. My heart might stop. Then how would you feel?'

I smiled happily. 'That's what I was trying to talk to you about just now, you knob.'

'Really?'

'Yes. I asked what we were going to do.'

Julian burst out laughing. 'Oh, my God, you must've thought I was a total fucker! You ask about the future and I carry on working!'

'It's fine. You were wrapped up in what you were doing. I like you caring so much about your job.'

'Well, I'm still sorry.'

'No, I mean it. You're passionate about journalism, aren't you?'

For a split second, Julian disappeared somewhere I couldn't follow. It was a minor thing but it caused a ripple of low-level surprise: I'd grown used to reading him effortlessly. As soon as it had begun, it was over.

'I guess I *am*,' he said, as if it were the first time he'd thought about it. 'Yeah, I guess I am. I didn't expect that to happen . . .'

You're not meant to know everything about him yet, I reminded myself.

He pulled me in again, kissing my head. 'I don't know what we should do about the future,' he said slowly. 'But I know we'll make it work. I could come over in, say, October?'

My heart leaped. 'To London?'

'Actually, I was thinking perhaps Iran.'

I pulled back and kissed him all over his face. 'Yes! Yes, please come to London! I would love that so much!'

Julian laughed. 'And maybe you could get Christmas off and come here . . . It's magical at Christmas. You don't know shit about overindulging until you have your first American Christmas. I can teach you some lessons.'

'Yes! Bingey American Christmas!'

There was a happy pause, during which Julian took my hand. 'And then we can make a more long-term plan,' he said, looking straight at me. 'Because in the same way that I know I'll always have fluffy hair to contend with, I know I'll always want you in my life.'

Deep happiness dropped anchor in my stomach. I felt like I'd burst. 'Good,' I whispered. Good didn't cover it! 'That works for me too.'

My phone rang, and I ignored it. 'Hadn't you better answer it?' Julian asked. 'It might be Fiona.'

306

Mildly irritated, I answered. It was Fiona, and she was locked out.

'Oh, well. Let's go over there and get her,' Julian said agreeably. A slight condensation formed on the shiny curve of my happiness.

'What is it, Sal?'

'Oh . . . Just Fiona. Is she really going to stay here?'

'Oh, that . . . I'm not sure.'

Julian seemed flustered; his glasses slid off his nose. 'It came up as a possibility,' he added uncertainly. 'You'll have to ask her . . .'

'Why does she talk to you? And not me?' I blurted. *Stop it*, I told myself. *Don't ruin this lovely moment.*

'She doesn't,' Julian replied. 'Well, not really,' he added. 'I guess it's cos I'm Raúl's best friend.'

'Do you think so?' I wasn't convinced. But if it wasn't that, what was it?

Julian kissed me again, his hands on either side of my face. 'I do think so, yes. Anyway, it's settled. I'll visit in October, you'll visit at Christmas, and then we'll do something more radical. Deal?'

'Deal.'

'I'd do anything to make you happy,' he told me simply. 'You are my favourite thing in the whole world ever.'

Four days later I finished at the Met and began my final hours in New York. Bea was organizing farewell drinks on the roof of the Wythe Hotel, where Julian had fed me English tea and cheese toasties on our first night.

Everyone we had met during our time in New York was coming and Julian had bought me the most beautiful dress from a boutique near his house. I'd never imagined a man could choose a dress for a woman but it was perfect: simple, silky and yearning for my chunky silver necklace. 'Unstructured,' Julian said wisely, then rolled around giggling like a boy. 'UNSTRUCTURED? I couldn't believe it when the shop assistant said that! You women are mental! It's a dress!'

There was a sad end-of-term feeling to our final day. The sky was torpid and swollen; change was in the air. I had packed, cleared out my locker at the Met and taken a final walk through the East River State Park on my own, remembering happier times there with Fiona a few weeks before.

Fiona had now officially told me that she would remain in New York for the time being, but she was refusing to tell me anything about her plans. I was doing my best at trying to be understanding but it was hard. I wasn't used to being the enemy: Fiona had always told me everything. Always. If it weren't for the promise of Julian looking after her, I would have had to resign from my job and stay.

By three o'clock I was packed and done, needing only to buy some shoes for tonight. I set out to get them in a final pilgrimage to SoHo.

The sky was heavy but my heart was light as I came up out of the subway at Spring Street. SoHo exploded around me: tourists with large cardboard shopping bags spilled in and out of the large chain shops while sleek, groomed rich girls tried on priceless jewellery and examined handbags behind the locked doors of posh boutiques. The traffic moved sluggishly along Broadway and a woman in a long skirt shouted about the love of Christ to an accompaniment of honking horns and human indifference. I stood watching her, curious, when suddenly I heard another female voice, which I knew very well.

I looked round sharply. Fiona was literally feet away from me, walking along Spring Street towards Mercer, her arm linked companionably through Julian's. I stared at them, inexplicably paralysed. Julian looked down at Fi and chuckled at what she was saying. Then he glanced at his watch and said something. They picked up their pace and walked off into the crowd.

I watched until they were out of sight and wondered why I felt so afraid.

Surely they weren't . . .

No. That was absurd. Julian had not been some sleazy flirt with Fiona, he'd been a good friend to her. How could I be anything other than grateful for that? If she hadn't latched on to him she'd have isolated herself completely.

Without realizing what I was doing, I dialled Julian's number.

'Sal!' He answered almost immediately. A fire engine was forcing its way down Broadway and I could hear its sirens relayed through his phone.

'Hi!' I sounded falsely bright.

'What's up, little ferret?'

'Nothing! I'm just shoe shopping and I thought I'd say hello.' My heart pounded sickly in my chest. I didn't want to lie to him.

'Oh, well, hi there, baby. I came round to yours earlier to do some groping but you weren't there.'

'Right.'

There was a noisy silence as the sirens made their way out of our call.

'I was joking,' he said, less confidently.

'I know! So, what are you up to?' I hated myself. Hated that my stomach was bracing in fear of what he might say. Terrified that he might lie. *Please tell me you're with Fiona in SoHo. Please.*

'I'm off to interview someone,' Julian said, after a split-second pause. 'Just walking to the Village to meet them now. But I'll be back in plenty of time for the drinks.'

I said nothing.

'I want to watch you getting ready in your new dress,' he added. 'Paint a moustache on your face, that kind of thing.'

Before I had a chance to think I ended the call and turned the phone off so he'd think I'd run out of battery. Everything had gone baggy and limp. I was not well.

A raindrop fell on my forehead, followed by another. In my state of petrification they felt like bullets on my skin.

Rain began to fall harder, yet the sun was still out. It blazed in the upper windows of the tall buildings lining Broadway, casting a strange, hyper-real glow.

It must be OK, I thought wildly. *Julian loves me! He's probably just indulging one of Fi's whims!*

But why? my head countered. *Why did he lie?*

I drifted sideways into a shoe shop and stared blankly at a pair of men's trainers for ten minutes before an assistant came to ask me what I was looking for.

ACT FOUR

Scene Eighteen

October 2012, London

From: Sally Howlett
To: Fiona Lane
Sent: 15/10/12 23.01 GMT
Message: New York

Fiona,

I feel very weird emailing you about this. I nearly didn't, because the last thing I want to do is upset you when you're out there alone in New York . . . But I kind of have to.

The day of our leaving party, just over a year ago, I went shoe shopping in SoHo and I saw you and Julian walking along Spring Street together. You were going in the direction of the Village. You had linked his arm. You were laughing.

I don't know why but I couldn't bring myself to stop you. I panicked. It's not that I don't trust you, my darling, I just . . . I dunno. Something felt weird.

I rang Julian and he lied. He told me he was off to interview someone for the magazine. And later, when he came round to our apartment before the leaving party, he lied again.

311

I don't want to talk to him about this or anything to do with New York. I'm finally beginning to relax at college and I'm trying to have a relationship with Jan. Which, God knows, isn't easy with Julian around.

So I'm asking you instead. I hate myself for doing this but I have to know. Will you tell me, Fi? Will you tell me, because I love you and I loved him once and I need to know what was going on?

All my love

Me xxxx

From: Mail Delivery subsystem
To: Sally Howlett
Sent: 15/10/12 23.02 GMT
Message: Mail Delivery Failure

Your message has not been delivered to the address below.
Error: account has been deleted. This is a permanent error.

I stared at the message on the screen and let it take me: the terrible, bottomless despair that I had tried so hard, for so long, to avoid. Barry was in the bedroom next door, laughing on the phone to a friend. As I listened to him chatter away, a muffled voice from another world, I found myself strangled by a truth too terrible to bear.

I cried slow, quiet tears of anguish at my computer. I cried until my body began to fold in on itself.

And then, as abruptly as I'd started, I stopped.

I wouldn't do this. I wouldn't go back there. Couldn't. If Fiona was determined to cut herself off from me, that was how it would have to be.

ACT THREE

Scene Seventeen

September 2011, New York

The farewell drinks were bittersweet. Infectious party spirit mingled with deep sadness as we drank cocktails and said silly things, like *Let's all set up a commune in France! Let's meet up next year and climb Mount Kilimanjaro!*

The afternoon rain had cleared, leaving a sky that seemed to have been swept clean with a giant brush. It bled pink as the sun dipped behind New Jersey, while Manhattan's buildings lost their lines and became light-dotted silhouettes.

I had something bitter and appley in my hand and was talking to Barry, who was standing with a man we'd seen quite a lot of lately but who Barry claimed was 'Just a friend, Chicken.'

'It's a sad moment all right,' Barry said, gazing at Manhattan. 'It's been a time of glory, has it not, Chicken?'

I nodded. 'Glory is a good word.' Barry's 'friend' wandered off to get more drinks.

'What's going to happen with you and Julian?' he asked

slyly. 'Do you reckon he's going to, like, *propose* tonight? I wouldn't put it past him and I'll tell you that for nothin'.'

Worry tried to ambush me but I squashed it down. Julian had been sweet and lovely and silly this evening – dancing around my room with a coffee sock on his willy, telling me I was absolutely beautiful in the dress. 'You *cannot* leave me,' he shouted, laughing. The coffee sock slid off and he jumped around the room naked. 'Look! Look at what you're abandoning! Are you INSANE?'

There had to be an explanation for him lying to me about being with Fiona. And I had to wait patiently for it.

'I don't think he's going to propose,' I said firmly. 'But he is coming over to London in three weeks . . .'

'Oh, my days! He never is!'

'He is.'

'He loves you,' Barry stated. He looked very pleased.

'He does, actually.' I blushed. 'God knows why!'

'Don't you encourage me to smack you, Chicken,' he said calmly. 'By the way, did you see that Raúl's here?'

'Yeah. I hope it's OK.'

Barry grimaced. 'Nothin' about Fiona is OK right now,' he muttered. 'I think we need to do something when we get home. Go up and see your parents or somethin'.'

'Are you out of your mind? Tell my parents she's on drugs?'

Barry nodded. 'Hmm, you might be right, Chicken. Well, we'll have a pow-wow on our return, OK? You, me and Bea? We'll sort her out. Somehow.'

'Do you think?' I asked weakly. For the first time ever I'd begun to lose hope.

'Deffo,' he replied firmly. 'She's a fuckin' mess but she's

not that bad. Not stealin' or nothin'! I promise,' he added quietly, 'we will sort this out. I want you to enjoy your night with Mr Fancy Pants, do you hear me?'

'Yes.' For the first time in weeks, I felt a chink of positivity about Fiona. Of course I couldn't sort her out alone. I'd have Barry and Bea to help me, and I'd have my lovely boyfriend on Skype. Maybe, just maybe, we could do it.

'Now, Chicken,' Barry said briskly. 'What did you bring for your present? Anything good? If so, can you describe your wrapping paper so I make sure I choose yours?'

I clapped my hand to my forehead, cursing. Of course! The presents! Bea, who had organized tonight, had come up with the idea that everyone at the party should bring a present. We would put the presents on a table and, once we were all there, we would all take one without knowing who it was from. 'It prevents us buying two hundred goodbye presents,' she had explained. We'd all gone along with it, even though probably none of us except Bea would have bought goodbye presents in the first place.

I had meant to get mine in SoHo this afternoon, but after I'd seen Julian and Fiona I'd struggled even to buy a pair of shoes.

'Oh dear.' Barry sighed. 'Don't let Bea know you haven't brought a present. She'll eat you for dinner, Chicken. Find something quickly, I urge you.' The sunset was bleaching his face and he suddenly looked incredibly distinguished in his expensive shirt and jeans.

'I love you, Barry,' I told him, haring off to find my handbag. 'I really, really love you.'

'Massive lesbian, that one . . .' I heard him say to his handsome friend.

My handbag was round the corner, on the part of the terrace that faced east across Brooklyn towards Queens and, somewhere, the Atlantic. It was mostly empty, save for two people in the far corner. *Julian and Fiona*, I thought childishly.

Then I saw that it was, in fact, Julian and Fiona.

'Um, hello,' I called, rummaging through my handbag for my wallet. I'd run off and get something from one of those little shops around Sixth and Bedford.

'Hello, my little garden gnome,' Julian said, walking over. Fiona watched him go, with a face of vague resentment. Just for a moment, I hated her. He was *mine*. My boy. She didn't get to be cross.

Julian came over and folded himself around me, hugging me hard. 'I feel sad,' he said.

'Me too,' I muttered.

'I know I'm going to see you in three weeks but it's just . . . wrong. I'll miss you so much.' He pulled back slightly and kissed my forehead, thumb stroking the back of my neck. 'I love you, Sally, you moron. You do know that, don't you?'

'Oi, stop that!' Fiona called. She was on her way over. To my surprise, she was drunk. Fiona's current method of getting off her head was calorie-free but now she had what looked like neat vodka in a glass of melting ice. My stomach spasmed nervously. I'd have to look after her tonight if she was drinking on top of everything else.

But I felt furious too. Could I not have one night enjoying myself? Would it ever end, this terrible, guilty, maternal pull?

'Hey, turnip,' Julian said quietly. He was looking down at me. 'What's going on in there?'

Fiona was only a few metres away now. I shook my head, saying I'd talk to him later.

Suddenly she was on us, throwing her bony arms round both of our backs. 'GROUP HUG,' she shouted. We all made group-hug noises and I wondered if Julian and Fiona felt as uncomfortable as I did. When I couldn't bear it any longer, I pulled away.

'Are you OK, Sally?' Fiona was peering at me, breathing – yes, vodka fumes – into my face. Her skin had got so dry that her foundation had begun to flake and her lipstick clung to her chapped lips. Up close she looked like an extra in a medical drama. Scrawny, unkempt, potentially dangerous. But so vulnerable too. Her eyes searched mine, desperate that she wasn't the cause of my mood.

'I'm fine,' I said, after a pause. 'I just forgot to buy a present.'

Fiona crossed her arms and swayed slightly. 'What's really wrong? Well, if it helps, I'm having a *nightmare*. Fucking *Raúl's* turned up. I mean, what the fuck?'

I sighed. There was no point. 'I'm just sad that it's our last day. I love New York. And I love . . .' I trailed off, embarrassed.

'Me?' Julian suggested, not embarrassed at all.

I couldn't help but smile. 'Maybe.'

Fiona shouted, 'YEAH! Even if I got dumped, at least you two are going strong!' and downed the rest of her vodka. She slammed the glass down on the table next to us but missed and it smashed on the floor. 'Ah, fuck,' she said conversationally, vaguely kicking some glass out of the way with her high heel. Her leg looked like a golf club.

'I'm going to get some water,' I said pointedly. 'Do you want some?'

'I'll have a double vodka, please.' She held my eye, daring me nervously to challenge her; beseeching me not to hate her.

I turned and left, expecting Julian to fall in next to me.

But he didn't. I looked at them as I went back inside to get the drinks, and he was standing very close to her, saying something that was making her smile grudgingly.

'Chicken?'

It was Barry.

'Chicken, you're not . . . worried, are you?'

He too was watching them.

'No,' I said automatically. Then, feeling slightly sick: 'Well, more just annoyed. They spend a lot of time together. There's obviously *something*, even if it isn't dodgy. Do you have any idea?'

Barry gazed at them. 'Nope.'

I shivered. 'I'm going out to buy a present for the table,' I told him. 'Go for a little walk.'

To my horror, Barry took my hand and said something very, very scary. 'Don't go, Chicken. Stay and fight for your man!'

I swallowed painfully. 'Um, really? You think I should be worried?'

Julian reached forward and squeezed Fiona's freckly nose and she batted him off, laughing.

'I need a drink,' I said. My voice was not steady.

'Probs a good idea, Chicken,' Barry said kindly. 'Now,

about that present. Do you have anything in that there handbag you could use?'

'No.' I sounded dead.

'Nonsense. You must have something.' He was rooting around. 'Here we go. A block of Post-it notes. Perfect.'

'I can't leave a block of Post-its,' I said distractedly. 'How about I . . . I dunno, how about I write down a pledge on one of them? Like, the person who wins this gets brunch at Schiller's or something?'

Barry thought about it, then had a better idea. 'How's about you offer them a night on the town in London?' he suggested. 'I mean, you'd be happy to take out anyone at this party, Chicken! Save for maybe Fiona,' he joked bravely.

I smiled a thin, mirthless smile. 'I'm not giving up on her just yet,' I said. 'We just agreed we'd sort her out.'

'I know,' Barry said. 'And we will. I'm not properly worried, Chicken, cos I know Julian loves you, but she's drinking as well as getting high and we don't want her lunging at your man, do we now? That's all I'm sayin'.'

I wasn't sure that was all he was saying, but I left it.

The recipient of this Post-it note gets a night out in London on me, I wrote. *You'll find me at* 36 *The Old Wharf,* 89 *Bevan Street, London* NI 2ZM. *Sally.*

Scene Eighteen

An hour later I felt really quite drunk but my anxiety had not diminished in the slightest. I talked to people but couldn't hear what they were saying. When the presents had been exchanged I'd opened one containing a massive tacky yellow ring and I'd not even been able to laugh as I'd slid it on to my finger.

Julian and Fiona were still in a club of two that nobody else was invited to. Only now the club was convening in full view of everyone: they stood on the side terrace overlooking Manhattan, huddled in a corner, exchanging jokes and stories that apparently were relevant only to them. People tried to talk to them and soon left. Fiona was visibly wasted, draped against Julian, uncoordinated, either shrieking noisily or whingeing about Raúl.

Barry was being extra nice to me and even told me at one stage that I looked 'slim'. It was a bad sign.

After struggling on for an hour or so he gave in. 'Look, Chicken,' he began nervously. I tensed. 'You don't think he –'

I looked at him sharply. 'What?'

'Well, Chicken, it's just the old drugs business, you

know. I'm just wondering if you think he . . . might be, you know . . .'

'Supplying drugs to Fiona? Of course not!'

Barry nodded soothingly. 'Yeah, of course not. Anyway, good turn-out, is it not, Chicken?'

'Why do you think he's giving her drugs?'

'Well,' Barry began, 'just, you know . . .'

'I don't know. Tell me.'

'Well, just that he was involved in some drugs thing. Around the time his wife died.'

The world stopped turning for a moment.

'What?' I stared at Barry. 'WHAT DO YOU MEAN?'

Barry dragged me away from the others to the back terrace. Out of nowhere, Bea appeared. 'You told her?' she demanded of Barry. He nodded. Bea tutted and handed me some wine, which I didn't take. Instead she patted my arm as if that would soothe me.

'STOP HIDING THINGS FROM ME,' I hissed. It was almost beyond comprehension that they could have been carrying knowledge that would alter my life yet were only telling me now.

Bea affected an expansive Italian shrug. 'Julian was involved in a *grande* scandal, I heard,' she said. 'People say his wife died in it. It involved drugs.'

I held on to the table. 'What do you mean, a scandal involving drugs?'

'I do not know the details, darling. I know only what I tell you.'

'But *how do you know*?'

'Please try to be calm, Sally. I know because Fiona told me. Raúl told her. Maybe it is all a big mistake!'

321

I swayed, sick and dizzy.

'But, my darling, I confess I have my doubts about Julian. It is obvious that he does not *take* the drugs, no?'

I agreed, with a distracted nod. Julian was clearly not taking drugs. Bea was right on that point.

'My problem is this,' Bea continued. 'Julian owns a paper that only a few people buy. Think about this paper. He does not receive many advertisements. Is it not strange that he has enough money to own a big apartment on Mulberry Street? That he takes you out for dinner? That he wears these expensive clothes?'

'What do you mean, an apartment on Mulberry? He lives in Brooklyn! He rents a room from a woman with a dog called Pam!'

'Ah,' Bea said. 'You did not know about the apartment.'

'Because there isn't one! *Is there?*'

Bea patted my arm again. 'Perhaps he wanted to surprise you with it one day,' she said reassuringly.

'No!' I cried shrilly. 'You've got it wrong! His clothes aren't expensive . . . they're *a mess*!' They were. He wore T-shirts. Sometimes shirts with jumpers over them. He looked classic, reasonably fashionable, sometimes scruffy. He didn't look expensive. And he most definitely didn't look like a drug dealer, if that was what she meant.

Bea shook her head. 'They *are* expensive clothes,' she told me. 'Trust Bea. She knows her designers. It is not all cufflinks and tapered trousers, Sally. His jeans that he wears tonight. Where are they from?'

I was bewildered. 'I have no idea. Gap?'

Bea laughed, but it was hollow. 'No, my *tesoro*. They are from Gucci. They cost five hundred dollars.'

'But that's not *that* much, I mean –'

'Sally, he has four different pairs of these jeans alone. I see these things. Tonight he wears a shirt from Armani. His jumper is Phillip Lim. Julian does not iron his clothes and he does not mend them when they get holes. But they are beautiful items of great value.'

'*This is just bullshit!*' I cried desperately. 'Why are you trying to make me suspicious?'

Bea smiled sadly. 'Oh, darling, you already are suspicious. Bea is just telling you what she knows. She wants you to have all of the facts.'

'No. No no no.'

'I do not know anything for sure, darling,' Bea said softly. 'Maybe Bea is wrong.'

My heart was hammering and I sat down quickly on a chair before I fell. Julian was not a drug dealer. He was *not* a drug dealer. I twiddled the manky ring round my finger.

Was he?

'No,' I said, decisively. 'Thank you, Bea, I know you're looking out for me but I'm just not having it. There's no way on earth Julian's a drug dealer. His wife must have left him money.'

'She had nothing when she died.' Bea had begun to speak rather quickly.

'No! I don't believe it! Thank you, but –' I stopped. 'Why didn't you say any of this before?' I asked her.

Bea held my gaze. 'I find out today,' she said, her calm ever so slightly ruffled. 'I talked to Fiona. She told me about Julian's wife. She did not know more than I have told you. And then afterwards I began to think about Julian and his lifestyle. Something is not right.'

A dull block of pain opened in my chest, pressing on my lungs. *Everything* about Julian Bell was right. It had been the easiest, most beautiful month of my life, being here with him. He was my perfect man. He couldn't be a lie! He was warm, he was generous. He kissed the tips of my ears and scrunched my bottom and smiled right into the centre of me when he woke up in the mornings.

No. I wasn't listening to Bea's paranoid bullshit any more. She was probably just bored because she wasn't shagging anyone.

I pulled myself up on Bambi legs to go and find my man. I would disprove Bea's theory and reclaim Julian. I would enjoy being his girlfriend. I would enjoy our last few hours together.

As I rounded the corner, I saw Julian take something from Fiona. A small piece of cardboard, folded up into a miniature envelope. I stopped breathing. Fiona was thrusting it at him with gay abandon, but Julian looked extremely nervous. He snatched it and shoved it into his pocket. I felt as if someone had turned off my oxygen.

Julian suddenly caught sight of me. 'Hey!' he said, his face stretching into an uncomfortable smile. His finger brushed along the ridge in his pocket created by the miniature envelope. 'Let me go and get you a drink, my favourite Sallyface.' He kissed my frozen cheek and strode inside, leaving me with my cousin.

'All righ', Sal,' Fiona said vaguely. She was seriously wasted but more friendly than earlier. I moved over and stood next to her at the railing.

'Hi.'

'You OK, babe?' she asked.

I could feel her watching me. 'What were you and Julian just doing? With that . . . that thing?'

Fiona looked anxious. 'It's not what you think, Sally,' she slurred. She grabbed my hand and pulled me closer to explain. I smelt the sharp, ugly vodka fumes and something chemical coming from her. '*Pleeeeease* don't get all serious on me. Everyone's having fun, OK? I'll explain . . .'

She sounded like a cartoon drunk.

I pulled my arm free and looked her in the eye. 'I don't want to hear your explanation. I don't believe *anything* you say any more.' My voice was heavy with anger. 'You just shared drugs with my boyfriend. I saw you with my own eyes. I . . . How *could you*?'

She shook her head manically. 'No no no! You've got it wrong. Come for a little walk and let me explain.' She dragged me into a corner of the terrace, tripping over a chair leg and smacking into the wall.

'For Christ's sake, will you be careful,' I said tightly. It was a very long way to the ground from there.

'Sally, I've decided to sort myself out,' she began. A waitress handed her another vodka. It must have been at least a double, but she knocked it back in three agonizing gulps, watching Raúl as she did so.

'Yeah, I've decided to sort myself out,' she repeated laboriously. 'And Julian . . .' She scrunched up her face nervously, trying to work out what to say. 'Hmm, how to put this. Well, he . . .' I'd already heard enough. I turned to go, but once again she pulled me back. '*No*, Sally, let's talk. I miss you – you've been so busy with Julian and work.'

'Don't. Don't put it all on me,' I cried. 'I've tried to be

there for you. My God, I've tried, Fiona. Every day for almost your whole life.'

Fiona's face crumpled with drunken remorse. 'You've been so lovely,' she murmured. 'I love you so much.' She tried to hug me but I pushed her away. She started crying. 'Sally, I'm trying,' she cried. 'I want to be better – I don't want to be like this. I don't want to be such a burden on you. I detest myself for –' she swept an arm out '– for all this. For everything I am.'

I felt exhausted. I had heard this time after time.

The truth was that Fiona couldn't sort herself out. She was a hopeless case. In England I was going to gather Bea and Barry for an emergency meeting and we were going to Call Frank, or whatever you did these days and find out about rehab. I couldn't take care of her any more and she couldn't take care of herself.

'Please,' Fiona pleaded. 'Talk to me.'

'OK. I want you to change your mind about staying in New York. I want you to fly back to London with us, and get proper help. Rehab,' I said flatly.

'What? Oh, Sally, it's not *that* bad! I just need to stop buying silly drugs! And stop drinking for a while!'

'I don't agree. You need proper help, and I can't give it to you.'

Fiona looked appalled. 'Please, Sally!' she whispered. A fleck of spit landed on my eyebrow. 'I know I need to stop but . . . You can't send me away to some shithole full of drug addicts!'

'I've run out of other options,' I said dully. '*You*'ve run out of other options, more to the point.' All I could think about was the packet in Julian's pocket. What it meant for

326

me, and the rest of my life. A life that could no longer include him.

Fiona, cornered, started to fight. 'Well, you're a fine one to talk,' she said shakily. 'Your life isn't exactly *perfect*.'

Another time, I might have been surprised.

'I mean, you've spent your whole life avoiding anything that scares you,' she told me. 'You've *wasted* your singing voice, hiding in that costume job. And you sing in a fucking wardrobe! I mean, hello? It's not just me that's fucked up, babe!'

Julian had come back and was standing uneasily behind me. I couldn't even look at him. *He had drugs in his pocket.* After all I'd shared with him about my fears for Fiona and . . . I stopped, shut down. Couldn't take the pain. It was over.

But Fiona hadn't finished with me. She was red in the face, frightened, but fighting on. 'You let your parents treat you like shit and you let every single opportunity pass you by in case it'll take you out of your comfort zone. Where are your balls?'

'I have a life,' I said dully. 'And I have an amazing job.'

'Who CARES?' Fiona was half shouting, half crying. I saw Raúl slide out of the door and off towards the lifts. 'Yeah, fuck off,' Fiona shouted in his direction. 'Scuttle off, you weak fuckwit.'

'Fiona . . .' Julian said. People around us had stopped talking and were listening quite openly.

'You can fuck off too,' I hissed, swinging round to him. 'Leave us alone.'

He didn't try to defy me: he knew he was done for.

'OK, guys, let's give them some privacy,' he said to the crowd.

'Sally just told a man to fuck off,' Bea reported proudly, before being shooed away.

Fiona turned back to me, her face softer. 'Who cares about working at the opera house when you've got a voice that brings traffic to a standstill? Who cares when you sound so beautiful when you sing that I sit outside your bedroom door and cry? You're wasting your precious gift,' Fiona sobbed. 'You're all locked up in your safe little world, trying to control everything so you never have to face your fears. Look at yourself, Sal!'

'Hey, Fi,' Julian said, stepping back in. 'Come on. I know you care about Sally but that's not really the point right now.'

Fiona's face went purple. 'Oh, so you're defending her now, are you?'

Before he had a chance to reply, Fiona marched over and shoved her hand into Julian's lovely worn jeans pocket. 'Fuck you,' she told him furiously. 'Fuck you, you traitor. I thought we were in this together! You said we were doing this as a team!'

'A team?' I repeated weakly. 'A coke team?'

The terrace was now silent, save for a repetitive beat popping synthetically from the outdoor speaker, and some insincere attempts at conversation from the crowd over at the other end of the terrace.

'Yes,' Fiona said spikily, opening the wrap. She tipped some white powder into a fingernail and inhaled, staring at me with terror and defiance. 'A coke team,' she repeated furiously, a tear sliding down her face.

'Did he sell you the drugs?' I heard myself ask. My heart was broken anyway.

Fiona looked at Julian and laughed rabidly. 'Yes! He's been giving me drugs! How do you feel now? Not so smug any more, eh?'

'*Oh, Fiona!* Jesus! Look, let me explain,' Julian said, seeing me crumple. 'Sally, I . . . the thing is . . .' He couldn't continue. He couldn't lie when the evidence was between us, in Fiona's hand.

'Drug peddler!' Bea said shrilly, from behind me.

Julian put his face into his hands. That precious, lovely, handsome face. Belonging to my beloved warm furry bear. I couldn't stand it. I literally couldn't stand it. 'I think we should go home,' I said to Fiona, after a long, desperate pause. There was nothing more to be said now. We needed to go back to London to try to sort this out. To salvage what was still salvageable of my little cousin's life, even if mine was wrecked. 'Come on.'

Fiona was perking up again, although in a nasty, chemical sort of a way. 'Fine, fine! But only if you promise to sort your own shit out. And become, like, an opera singer!'

'OK,' I agreed wearily. 'I'll try some singing, if you get some help. Please, let's just go.'

Fiona folded her arms across her chest, suddenly righteous. 'No, Sally, I'm not just talking singing lessons. You've got to train to be a professional. A proper singer!'

'Come on, Freckle,' Barry murmured, moving in quietly. 'You heard Sally, she'll do it.'

Fiona started crying, her face screwed up in an ugly, painful knot. 'No, you have to PROMISE ME, Sal. I've wasted my life and I can't let you waste yours too. You

329

have to go to college and stuff, you have to become famous . . .'

I was bewildered. Why did this matter so much?

'It's important,' she said, reading my mind for once. 'It's important to me. It's *my* fault you've always been so scared of singing. My fucking stupid fault. If it wasn't for me and my stupid mum, *your* mum wouldn't have spent her whole life trying to make us all invisible. You could've enjoyed your life.'

'But I have!'

'No! You've been hiding! All because of me and my fucking useless slag of a mother.'

She was howling now. Great wrenching sobs that tore through me.

'You've spent your whole life looking after me, trying to do what your parents wouldn't do, and you've never once thought about you and what you might want to do . . . Please, Sally, just seize the fucking day,' Fiona wept. 'Be brave. Seize the day for me. My life is fucked but you've still got a chance. I love you so much . . .'

I hugged her and we both cried, gulping for air. Of course I'd do this for her, if it meant that much. I'd do anything.

Scene Nineteen

I left the hotel and walked. My arms were folded tightly across my chest as if to protect me from pain and my head was buried deep in the scarf Barry had handed me as I left. I looked only at the uneven pavement below my feet.

'Are you going to top yourself?' Barry had asked suspiciously.

'No.'

'Certain?'

'Yes. I just need some air. Fiona needs to sober up a bit. I'll put her into a taxi when I get back and we can all go home.'

'OK, Chicken.' Barry looked grey. 'Don't go too far, now.'

I couldn't hear anything beyond my own shallow breathing. Cars passed occasionally, picking their way across the uneven cobblestones; strange other worlds on wheels. I skirted central Williamsburg and found myself passing La Superior, where I'd talked so openly with Julian about my secret love affair with singing.

I walked on.

Julian was no longer a factor in my life. Julian had sold drugs to Fiona. The agony of this was not something I could go anywhere near yet. Instead I concentrated on Fiona. Fiona was willing to go to rehab. And in return I would be willing to train as a singer.

Would I?

I'd have to be. What *I* wanted didn't matter if it could save my beloved Freckle. And, anyway, she'd probably have forgotten about it when she sobered up.

I walked on.

I remembered what Fiona had said about my life. How it was her fault that I'd learned to avoid attention at all costs. Was it true?

I walked on.

After an hour, I started heading north towards our apartment. I texted Barry, asking him to bring Fiona home. The party could survive without me and I didn't want to be anywhere near Julian.

Except I did. And that was the problem. Julian, liar, drug dealer, scumbag, had helped wreck my Freckle, yet I longed with every cell in my body to find him and curl up with him in a warm bed somewhere far away from all of this.

How? How was I supposed to stop loving him at a moment's notice? Love was a densely woven cloth. It couldn't be unpicked just like that.

I trudged on north. I would leave New York tomorrow. I had to get away from him.

A tear passed slowly down my face as I imagined a

London that Julian would not visit. A future in which he was not present, as bright as a filament, as precious as gold.

Perhaps I should go and say goodbye. Try to leave things on a civil note.

The thought of one last hug, one last kiss, however wrong, forced me sharp left into 10th Street and back across to the hotel. I had to say goodbye. I had to see him one last time. And then I would take my beautiful, emaciated little Freckle home and get her well.

The street flickered with blue light coming from near the back of the Brooklyn Brewery. As I neared the hotel my heart quickened in my throat and I imagined the feeling of a last hug. A last kiss. A last goodbye.

I looked up from the pavement, dimly aware that something was not quite right. Why was there a flashing light? Why did the air feel so charged?

Instinctively, I speeded up. A sickness was building in my stomach. The blue lights were emergency lights. I couldn't see the cars but I knew.

As I turned right into Wythe Avenue the world shimmered before me, narrowing into a tunnel. There were maybe a dozen emergency vehicles outside the hotel. One was an ambulance. Maybe two. Somewhere, police tape strained against the brisk wind that was coming in off the river. Walkie-talkies crackled and the air carried sickness and horror.

I was running. Strange noises came from my throat as I sprinted towards the hotel; adrenalin gave me a speed I'd never had.

'What's happening? What's happened?' I was screaming. Someone in a uniform had taken hold of me, and was joined quickly by another. They held me fast and I screamed. 'WHAT'S HAPPENING LET GO WHERE'S FIONA WHAT'S HAPPENED?'

'Ma'am, please step back,' one of them was saying. I clawed at his arm like an animal. *I have to find Fiona. Where is she? Where is Fiona?*

'Sally.' It was Barry, lurching towards me from the crowd of cars. 'Sally . . .' He was crying, sobbing, creased with pain. He hurled himself at me and I knew the worst.

'Fiona,' I screamed desperately. Barry shook his head in my shoulder. 'I'm so sorry, Chicken, I'm so, so sorry. I'm sorry. I'm sorry. A stupid accident. She wasn't even that drunk. She'd calmed down, she . . .'

I heard myself cry. I heard myself scream. I started to black out. And then I saw it. A stretcher on wheels with a body bag. *A stretcher on wheels with a body bag.*

Bea was being restrained by a police officer. She was howling. A man pushing the trolley looked wretched. And in my ear Barry was trying to tell me something but he could barely speak.

'She was showing off,' he cried. 'She was up there being all silly on the wall and she just disappeared, Chicken, she just went, she just went . . .'

'No. No, please, no, Barry, please, no, not my Freckle, not my Freckle, not my Freckle. Oh, God, no, not my Freckle. JULIAN! I want Julian! Where is he, Barry, where is he?'

Barry cried even harder. 'Did a fucking runner.' He wept. 'Oh, God, Chicken, oh, God . . .'

He clung to me and I clung to him until the noise and lights stopped and in their place came nothing.

ACT FOUR

Scene Nineteen

Bed, Islington
October 2012

My beautiful Freckle
East River State Park
Brooklyn, New York

Hello my darling.

I tried to email you but your account's been closed down.

I'm afraid, Fi. Your voice has got quieter and quieter when we speak. It's like you're taking yourself away from me. Please don't, my little one. I'm not ready to say goodbye. I did what you said, Freckle. I'm at college, and I'm staying at college, and I will be a singer. But, my darling, you have to stay with me! I can't do it on my own. I love you, Fiona, I love you so very, very much.

I can't just let you wander off into Heaven or whatever's there. We're a team, Freckle. Carry on talking to me. Please, my love.

It's just over a year since you went. I've been thinking about it constantly. About how dead I felt, and how strong and alive Bea was, getting us on to the plane. I miss her. I know we're all dealing with it differently but I feel so lost and sad that she's moved to

337

Glyndebourne and just shut us all out. One minute there were four of us and then there were two.

I've been thinking about the inquest and how awful it is that Julian got away with it. He shouldn't be allowed to just rock up to England and teach singing and have all these people act like he's God. Can you imagine what the college would do if they found out? I keep wondering if I should say something – you know, tip them off. But I feel paralysed. Like I hate him but a part of me still feels some sort of . . . I dunno, loyalty, I guess.

I wrote that your address is the East River State Park. It feels right. I see us there sometimes, sitting on that log in the sun. I think about your pale skin breaking out in freckles and you telling me how hopeful you felt about the future.

I'm going back up to Stourbridge today and I can hardly bear the thought of being there, knowing you're not in the world any more. All of our games in that dead end on the estate. Cola bottles from the Happy Shopper. Dancing with rotters at Millennium's. Saturday-night takeaways. You and me, always giggling.

If only I'd known. If only I'd seen what was coming. I'd never have let you out of my sight. I still feel like someone's ripped me in two. I've been jammed back together and I walk round as if I'm whole but it's still there. A split all the way through my life.

Barry says I have to stop talking to you but he doesn't understand. He's still a whole person. I'm not.

I miss you so very much, Freckle.
Xxxxxxxx

I'd been getting better and better at pretending Julian Jefferson was just another vocal coach at college, rather than a drug-peddling liar. It helped that he had moronic clothes and that people practically fainted when they walked past him in the corridor, because none of those things bore any relation to my ex-lover Julian Bell, who looked after a dog called Pam and had fluffy hair and broken glasses.

But this self-deception became harder when Julian turned up at Euston station ready to accompany Jan and me to the school workshop in Stourbridge, with his newly cut-off hair in disarray and now his horrible posh clothes gone. He was wandering around looking for us with a bacon roll and an air of warm absent-mindedness; indistinguishable from the Julian Bell I'd loved so much. He made my heart stop.

I ducked behind Paperchase and stared at him.

It was all there again. That slow, shambolic gentleness. That air of disarray and warmth. That lovely –

What is he doing? Why has he changed his clothes? And why the flaming KNOBS is he wearing my favourite of all his jumpers? With that lovely old dog-eared shirt collar poking out over it? Does he smell like he used to? Does he –

'Be quiet,' I told my head furiously. 'Be quiet and leave me alone. It doesn't matter. He's a turd.' It was only seven fifty-five a.m. but I was already full of anxiety.

And as the day passed it would get much, much worse.

Five minutes later I was cramped around a narrow table with Julian and Jan, heading north out of Euston. I was feeling fairly dreadful anyway, returning to the town where I'd grown up with Freckle. Where resided my parents, who blamed me for her death. Julian's presence – Julian's low-key, familiar *Julian Bell*-like presence – in this mix was not dissimilar to a firebomb for my fragile state of mind.

'Why are you here?' Jan asked Julian, in the way that only Jan could. We were speeding through the tangled mess of train tracks at Hendon, sipping weak tea.

Julian, who'd been picking at the cuff of his shirt, grinned at Jan's bluntness. 'All new outreach projects need to be supervised by someone from the college. Apparently. So here I am.'

'But you are vocal coach! You are not in the staff,' Jan persisted. He'd had three espressos that morning and was already quite mad. His eyes darted excitably from Julian to me. He was blithely unaware of the hornets' nest he was in.

'I know I'm not staff,' Julian said amusedly. 'And, my friend, I wish I could let you just get on with it but nobody else was free today. So, brother, you're stuck with my ass, yo.'

Bugger off, I thought. *Stop trying to make me laugh.*

'Well, I am happy they send you,' Jan said. He reached forward and helped himself to one of Julian's shortbread fingers. 'I think we have fun, these three . . . we three . . .'

'The three of us,' I muttered, avoiding Julian's eye. I could do without Jan and Julian becoming friends.

'Yes! The three of us.' Jan popped a whole shortbread finger into his mouth. 'And, Julian, you look very different. Why are you dressing like peasant today?' he asked cordially.

Julian laughed out loud. 'My mom often asks me the same.'

'Well?' Jan wasn't going to let this go, which was fortunate because I very much wanted to know the answer.

'This is how I dress.' Julian looked down apologetically at his clothes. 'I'm not really very smart at all.'

'So why you wear smart clothes at college?' Jan persisted. 'Why did you have long hair with grease added to it?'

'PURGGGH!'

'Excuse me?' Julian was looking at me, his eyes twinkling.

'Sorry. I was just choking on my tea,' I said. Jan was amazing. Completely amazing.

'Why do I wear smart clothes and add grease to my hair,' Julian mused delightedly. 'Ha-ha! Well, it's just what I've always done as an opera singer, I guess. When I graduated from college and got an agent he had this vision of me as quite a smart, shiny sort of a bloke whom middle-aged women would fall in love with. His idea, not mine,' he added hastily. 'On our first photo-shoot he had someone style me like that and it just stuck. That's what people want Julian Jefferson to look like.'

'But . . .' Jan was at a loss. Conforming was not something he understood. 'But why? If it is not representing your trueness, then why are you dressing like businessman who has naked ladies in his swimming-pool?'

This time I couldn't help myself, and neither could Julian. We both roared with laughter and Jan, pleased, joined in. 'HA-HA-HA!' he shouted delightedly. 'HA-HA-HA!'

Just as abruptly I stopped laughing because it didn't feel right to be laughing with Julian and the churning anxiety returned. This whole trip was wrong. Wrong, wrong, wrong. Maybe I should abscond at Hemel Hempstead.

Julian took a slug of tea. 'This is so minging,' he said sadly. He turned back to Jan. 'I asked myself the same question recently. "Why are you *still* wearing all this smart shit? The college doesn't require you to look like a smarmy twat." And I didn't have a good answer so I just thought, *Fuck it,* and I went to the Turkish man round the corner who did me a nine-quid haircut, and I got all my old clothes out. Boom.'

'BOOM!' Jan repeated, offering Julian a palm to high-five. Julian took it, chuckling.

Then Jan started to smile in an evil manner. 'And what does Violet say about your new style?' he asked.

'Sorry?' I sensed Julian's jaw tightening minutely. I felt mine do the same.

'Oh, Mr Julian Jefferson!' Jan giggled. 'You are not fooling us! All of the people in the *world* they are saying that you are making sexual intercourses with Violet Elphinstone,' he crowed. 'Ha-ha!'

The train hummed on. I cultivated a look of supreme disinterest, although my heart was pumping in my mouth or possibly even my forehead.

Julian, on the other hand, seemed somewhat paralysed. 'Everyone's talking about us?' he said nervously.

'Aha! You confirm it, HA-HA!'

'Oh. Er . . .'

My heart plummeted into my chest, then down into my feet. I cursed it. *Get a grip. He's the enemy! He and Violet deserve each other!*

'If you were proper staff it would be very bad, no?' Jan asked Julian happily. 'But you are not staff so it is OK, yes? We men of the college, of the world, we bow down to you. VIOLET ELPHINSTONE!'

'No, it *is* bad,' Julian said weakly. 'Seriously unprofessional. Um . . .' He downed his tea and yelped as it burned his throat.

I got out my notebook and pen, feigning nonchalance. My hands were shaking. I had absolutely no idea how to get through the next thirty-six hours. I felt sick, distressed and trapped. *Help*, I prayed, to a God I'd never believed in. *Help?*

The workshop got off to a better start than we'd imagined in that the thirty year-elevens assigned to us actually turned up. They stood in the gym, a depressing space with dreadful acoustics and high, unreachable windows, either ignoring us silently or ignoring us loudly. Most, with a few exceptions, were either centrally or peripherally involved in a flirtatious conversation conducted in a scream.

Things have changed, I marvelled, taking in an assortment of veils, turbans and caps. When I'd been growing up Stourbridge had still been a very traditional white working-class town but today it was a sea of different-coloured faces.

'WOZNIT? WOZNIT, OH MA GOD!' one of the girls screamed, just as Jan Borsos bellowed a piercing G sharp.

The gym was suddenly silent. Thirty pairs of eyes swivelled towards us, some surprised, most disgusted. I flushed, horribly uncomfortable and afraid.

I remembered being in that hall when I was a teenager, feeling fat and anguished in my gym knickers, hoping nobody would notice me. What had got me through it? What had carried me through the putrid stink of adolescence? Fiona, of course. She had written to me from ballet school three times a week; week in, week out. She was relentlessly upbeat, egging me on, encouraging me to

343

get up to no good, writing foul-mouthed (and hilarious) stories about our imaginary escapades.

Being Fiona she'd needed a lot of help from me: advice on bullies; reassurance that Mum and Dad wanted her home at Christmas; motivation to keep on polishing her craft. But even though I'd had to act as a parent, our letters had, over the years, helped scaffold my own modest confidence. In our never-ending stream of envelopes and scraps of paper was evidence that I was part of a team. A reminder that to one person, at least, I was important and worthwhile.

My little Freckle. Of course I hadn't been able to cut off our conversations. Barry should have understood that. She might have been mad but she was my teammate. My mainstay. My foundation.

Stop it, I warned myself. *Not here.*

I looked back at the kids. Jan and I were practically dwarfs in front of them. Jan with his miniature portly figure and little me, with my large bum and 'comfortable' body, stood before this tribe of noisy Amazons and for a moment said nothing.

Then Jan, who was apparently afraid of nothing and no one, began. 'ORANGES AND LEMONS, SAY THE BELLS OF ST CLEMENT'S. I OWE YOU FIVE FARTHINGS, SAY THE BELLS OF ST MARTIN'S.'

The gym was silent, save for a kid with a comb in his Afro muttering about this man being sick but-not-in-a-good-way-know-what-I'm-sayin'-like.

Jan stopped and looked at the kids. 'You do not know this song?'

One or two of the stragglers at the back raised tentative hands but put them quickly down. The rest stared at Jan with a mixture of disinterest and hostility.

'I see,' Jan continued. 'Perhaps not all of you are English. Perhaps we have many foreigners here.' I cringed right down to my core. Why did Jan never think before he spoke?

'I am also not English,' he continued cheerfully. 'But my mother teach me this song when I was child. She tell me every child in England knows this song!'

'Well, she don't know shit about England, then,' offered one boy. He was pale, skinny and badly dressed. His tie was absent and he wore scuffed trainers rather than the uniform black flats. Worst of all, he had what looked like the remains of a black eye.

I baulked, angry for Jan, who should not have had to hear his mother insulted within the first five minutes. Of course, this being my school, I felt wholly responsible. I sensed him next to me, small, stout and clearly taken aback. In Jan's world all people loved him. He was laughed at, frequently (and rightly so), but nobody ever insulted him. He was too adorable. *I CAN'T DO THIS!* my head screamed. *I can't be here in Stourbridge with Julian while Jan gets insulted, no Fiona and no parents worth having and – I CAN'T DO IT.*

'You are right,' Jan said, cutting through my mental hysteria. 'My mother did not "know shit" about England. But she did know shit about singing. And that is why I am here today. I am here to show you what my mother was showing me: how to love music.'

The scruffy kid held Jan's gaze for a few seconds, then

dropped it, picking at his fingernails, which were bitten and grubby.

In spite of my fragile and fevered mental state, the afternoon got off to a good start. After we'd talked about ourselves and our lives, to prove to the kids that opera wasn't all about posh fat people, Jan sang 'La donna è mobile' which quite a few of them, reassuringly, showed signs of recognizing. We had agreed I would not sing.

There were a few uncomfortable questions and almost all of them refused to get involved with the 'fun' vocal warm-up we'd devised (which, we realized only too late, was excruciating) but Jan strode through every hitch with his endearing wit and wild charm. At my suggestion we took them outside into the windy afternoon and encouraged them to sing anything they liked, walking around the AstroTurf courts. Their voices would be lost in the fast-moving air and they would have to look nobody in the eye.

In these easier circumstances, several of them sang. Many whipped out mobile phones and whined along to rubbish R&B or 2-step Turkish, the girls shrieking with laughter to hide their embarrassment. But by the time we moved inside to start on *Les Mis*, the prospect of full participation had become a real possibility.

Sixteen isn't too old, I thought. There was still a child in there somewhere, sufficiently uninhibited to enjoy something as primal as music. *I wish someone had swooped in when I was sixteen. Taken advantage of that lingering courage.*

'Sally Howlett, you're doing an amazing job,' Julian said, at one point. He'd appeared out of nowhere. 'I don't think half these kids'd be able to relax and sing without your help. I'm very impressed.' He smiled right at me, looking nothing like Julian Jefferson and everything like Julian Bell. I tried not to think about the familiar body underneath the familiar clothes. Tried not to think about how much I'd loved him and how desperately he had let me down.

I looked at my watch. Still another thirty-one hours to go in Stourbridge. My stomach crunched and billowed. I couldn't stand it.

An hour later, Jan and I were weaving through a crowd of kids, who were singing with quite plausible anger about life in a Parisian slum. '*Look down and see the sweepings of the street. Look down, look down, upon your fellow man,*' they chanted. Some were still messing around, a few others were stolidly refusing to sing but, for the most part, the rest were going for it.

Julian fell into step beside me. We wove through the crowd of beggars and I felt my body tense defensively. 'They're doing great!' he remarked. 'Just goes to show what happens when you let go, right?'

I blushed. 'Your point being?'

'My point being that you can do it too. Let go. Sing without reserve.'

I was speechless. What right did Julian have to talk to me about my fear of singing? What right did Julian have to talk to me about *anything*? I walked on, giving a thumbs-up to a girl who had begun to sing her first few words. 'Thank you for your comments,' I replied. I wanted to cry. 'Now, if you'll excuse me . . .'

The boy who'd insulted Jan's mother was in a corner of the room, ignoring everyone. He was playing a game on his phone and drinking something disgusting and bright blue out of a plastic bottle. He scared me a bit but I felt instinctively drawn to him.

'Don't you like *Les Mis*?' I asked him, sitting on the floor next to him.

He ignored me.

'What sort of music do you like, then?' I tried.

Nothing. Something was brutally murdered on the screen of his phone.

'We won't be doing *Les Mis* all afternoon, we'll –'

'I like *Les Mis*,' he muttered.

I smiled. I felt so at home hearing that accent. It was like talking to Dennis as a teenager.

Then I realized what he'd said. '*Really?* You like *Les Mis*?'

He shrugged, continuing with his game.

'Have you seen the show?'

'No. It's on in London.'

'I just wondered if you'd been down to see it perhaps.'

He frowned witheringly, shaking his head into his phone. 'We can't afford to take a horse and carriage to fucking London to see a stupid fucking show.'

I nodded. 'Right. Of course.'

The game ended; the boy had won. He smiled victoriously, then looked up at me. 'Me mam had it on tape. She listened to it all the time. I was brought up on that silly shit.'

I smiled encouragingly.

'It's quite good,' he said, scratching his head. He looked over at Julian, who was writing something in his notebook. 'Who's he?'

'One of the coaches at my opera school. He's also an opera singer. Quite a famous one.'

348

The boy seemed impressed. He turned back to me. 'He doesn't look like one.'

'No,' I admitted sadly. 'He doesn't. He did, but then he . . . Well, never mind.'

'Are you an opera singer?' the boy asked.

'Yes! Well, I'm training to be one.'

'I couldn't do that shit.' He shuddered.

'I understand. I feel like I'm going to be sick every time I prepare to sing. Once I open my mouth it's OK, though.'

The boy looked at me as if I was mad, which was probably a reasonable response.

'Do you sing at all?'

The boy jammed his phone into his fraying pocket. 'Sometimes.'

He stopped talking. The other kids sang on in the background, accompanied by a tinny CD player that Jan had up on his shoulder like a beat box.

'I like singing *Les Mis* actually. Only in the bathroom. My brothers'd rip the shit out of me if they heard.'

I beamed. 'You don't like people hearing you?'

'Fuck, no. Singing's for twats. Proper twats. Sorry, Miss.'

'Oh, swear away,' I told him. 'Do you have a favourite song, then?'

He shifted awkwardly and I wondered how far I could push him before he clamped down. '"Stars"? "Empty Chairs"? "Bring Him Home"?'

'"Empty Chairs",' he muttered, cheeks glowing red. 'Fucking wicked song.'

Scene Twenty

Twenty minutes later, the workshop was over and, for the first time that day, I felt calm. It had been an unprecedented success and several of the kids had asked if we could fiddle it for them to come back tomorrow, when a different class was scheduled. In spite of the tangled mess in my head of grief about being in Stourbridge without Fiona, fear about seeing my parents that night and some other messy feelings about Julian and Violet that I didn't want to look at just yet, I was rather exhilarated.

But the best was yet to come. Jan had removed everyone from the hall at my instruction – even our chaperone, who had agreed to wait just outside the door – and I stood now in the empty, echoing gym with the boy. His name was Dean and he lived on the same estate as my parents. The afternoon was growing darker and his face was bleached a deathly white by the huge strip-lights hanging from the ceiling.

'How's about you give it a go in the locker room, if the gym's too big,' I was suggesting. 'I spent years singing in a wardrobe, where everything sounds awful. The first time I sang into an actual room it was a revelation. It sounded amazing!'

'Mm.'

'The problem was, someone came in and heard me. But I can make sure nobody comes and interrupts you. Go on, you've got nothing to lose. This could be your only chance to sing that song in a proper room!'

Dean snorted. 'You're weird, Miss. You want to be a singer and you don't like singing?'

'Well, yes.'

'Don't believe you, Miss.'

'Ask the receptionist at the Hagley Premier Inn.' I grinned. 'He knows we're singers, and begged us to sing . . . Jan sang about four songs and I was just like a silent weirdo in the corner!'

Dean laughed. 'You're *proper* weird.'

'Yes. Although no more weird than you. Go on, give it a go. Even if it's the only time in your life you hear yourself sing properly! Trust me, it'll be worth it!'

Dean was fidgeting. He wanted to sing, I could tell. Jan had performed 'Empty Chairs' for the group earlier and the kids had been spellbound, save for the worst of the troublemakers. Dean in particular had been rapt. Watching him was like watching a ghost of myself.

Without further ado I started 'Empty Chairs' and put the CD player on the bench inside the locker room. 'Go on,' I said, gesturing towards the room. He went in, swearing a bit, and I closed the door behind him.

He let the accompaniment play and he didn't sing. Even though I'd hardly dared believe he would, my heart sank a little. It had been a stupid idea anyway, I supposed. It had taken weeks of intensive help to get me out of a wardrobe and I was a lot older than that boy.

'Can't do it, Miss.' He opened the door a crack. 'Feel like a twat.'

I looked at Dean, at the delicate greeny-yellow skin around his left eye, and imagined what his home life must be like. *I was just like you*, I thought. Paralysed by fear and awkwardness.

Before I knew it, I'd started the track again and begun singing it myself. I walked back out into the gym, which – now empty – carried my voice beautifully. The song was below my bottom range, but even in those conditions I could feel that warm, rushing freedom opening up in my chest again. I walked slowly around the gym, sensing Dean watching me by the locker-room door. I didn't look at him, partly out of embarrassment, and partly in the hope that he'd sing too.

And then he did. *He began to sing.* Quietly at first, but building quickly until his voice – a surprisingly powerful wall of sound – filled the hall. I quietened, then stopped singing altogether, watching Dean, terrified he would stop, too, but rooted to the spot. As he approached the highest, most emotive notes, he began to lose himself.

> *'Oh my friends, my friends forgive me,*
> *That I live and you are gone.*
> *There's a grief that can't be spoken.*
> *There's a pain, goes on and on.'*

I watched Dean with his scuffed trainers and black eye, and I cried. For me, for him and most of all for Fiona. When the song finished and he became paralysed with awkwardness once again, I clapped, slowly, and dried my eyes. 'That was perfect,' I told him. 'That was bloody perfect, Dean.'

'Hear hear,' said a half-American half-Devon voice behind me. I spun round. 'That was *totally* brilliant, mate.' Julian grinned. He was leaning against the doorframe with the chaperone, arms folded over his chest. I was temporarily slammed by a memory of him standing in another doorway the night we met, looking every bit as handsome as he did now, smiling in that same irresistible way. My calm was shattered; the churning anxiety returned.

Dean slid out of a fire-escape door without a word. 'I promised him I wouldn't let anyone in,' I told Julian tightly. 'Could you not have stayed out?' *And bogged off back to bogging Violet Elphinstone*, I nearly added.

'The teacher said they can't be left on their own with visitors,' Julian told me. Then he walked right up to me, until he was centimetres from my face. He bent down slightly towards my ear and I could feel the warmth of his breath on my neck. 'And could you stop being so rude to me, Sally?'

Scene Twenty-one

'I like this man!' Jan Borsos exclaimed furiously. He was flushed with good humour and what looked like Scotch, having been in the hotel bar with Julian since we got back from school. I'd been upstairs showering and trying to manage my panicking, fractured mind. I was simply not up to the challenge of seeing my parents tonight and I didn't know what to do.

Briefly, I pondered whether it would be OK to kiss Jan in front of Julian, and then felt angry with myself for even wondering. 'Hello,' I said, kissing Jan firmly on the mouth.

'I like him so much I invite him to dinner!' Jan cried. 'We all go to see your parents!

'Sally?' he added, plucking at my sleeve when I whited out. 'Sally, are you OK? Are you happy that I invite Julian?'

Julian, I noted, was studiously avoiding my eye.

'I'm delighted,' I said woodenly. 'Really very happy indeed.'

'Let's PARTY!' Jan shouted excitedly. 'I must go empty bowels!' And with that he sprinted off towards the toilets, bellowing 'Do You Hear the People Sing?'.

'He's quite a character.' Julian smiled, after a long, tense pause.

'Yes.' I drew an uneasy circle on the patterned carpet with my toe. 'There's nobody else quite like Jan. And that's pretty cool.'

Julian nodded. 'Pretty cool.'

He toyed with the key card. 'Are you happy, then?' he asked casually.

'Er, yes! Yes, actually, I am.'

'Good.'

'Good,' I concurred.

Julian was watching me, slightly accusingly. His collar was still poking up like the ear of a naughty dog. 'I just want you to be happy, Sal.'

Let it go, I begged myself. *Just let it go*. But I was powerless. 'And what's that supposed to mean?'

Julian had a brief inner battle, which was as clear to me as if he had tickertape running across his forehead. Then he spoke: 'I *mean*, I can't help but wonder if this relationship you're in with him is a bit disingenuous, and I'm not sure I understand what your connection is, and I guess most of all I mean he's not really your thing, in my opinion.'

'Oh, really?' I said angrily. 'He's not my thing, isn't he? And why is that?'

But Julian was also angry. His face had flushed and he looked at me in the same determined way he'd looked at me the first time he'd told me he loved me. 'He's . . . Well, he's a bit mad,' he said. 'And he's about sixteen years old. And I think you're making a mistake.'

I gaped at him. 'You think I'm making a mistake? Because you think Jan is *mad*?' I glanced at the toilets, but Jan was still inside. I could hear him singing gaily over the hand dryer.

'OK, OK, not mad. Just . . . not *you*. Do you two really connect? Deeply? Spiritually?'

How *dare* he wank on about spiritual connections after what he'd done to me? I tried to reply but couldn't.

Julian folded an arm tightly across himself, like he always had when he was uncomfortable. 'I know I'm being out of order,' he said mulishly. 'But come on. Look at what you did today. Jan was great, he made them laugh and stuff, but *look what you did*, Sally. Look how many kids you got singing! Look how well you understood them, got their trust, made them let go. That kid Dean, you could just have changed his life for all you know!'

I went to sit down but realized I wasn't near a chair so just shifted around on the spot, staring at the carpet. It spiralled colourfully, like my mind.

'I like Jan a lot,' Julian persisted. 'But I have to wonder what you're up to, Sal.'

'Well, I have to wonder what you're up to with Violet Elphinstone. But unlike you I had the manners not to say it.' It shot out of my mouth before I had time to think.

Julian went silent. 'OK. I'll take that.' He took his glasses off and put them back on again in rapid succession, just like he had on our first night when he'd got all shy and confused about his hair fluff. 'But, um, is everyone really talking about it?' he asked. 'Because it – I mean, we . . .'

'Oh, spare me.'

'It's stupid of me,' he said tiredly. 'I keep wondering if I should resign. It's such bad practice, a coach and a student . . .' Then, astonishingly, the defiance returned. 'But that's not the point,' he said, eyes narrowing. 'You can carry on pretending, if you want, but we both know you're making a mistake. Jan is not right for you. Period.'

'Well, thanks for your analysis of my boyfriend,' I hissed furiously. He had no right. *No bloody right!* Jan was emerging from the toilets at the other end of the bar. 'But you know what, Julian? At least he's got *passion.* At least he cares about singing. At least he got off his *backside* and got himself into college. He practises for hours every day, Julian. Is that a bit distasteful for someone who can't be arsed singing any more? Who just wasted their training, jacked it in because they couldn't be bothered – and started some *newspaper* instead?'

I wondered how it had come to this. How I could be saying horrible, venomous things to Julian Bell in a Premier Inn near Birmingham, when last year I'd stood with him on a roof in Brooklyn and fallen head over heels in love with him.

Julian swallowed painfully and I knew I'd gone too far. 'I didn't just jack it in,' he whispered. His eyes flashed with sudden tears and a pain I'd never seen before. 'You have no idea. No idea at all.'

'And you have no idea about my relationship with Jan,' I stammered. 'So kindly back off.'

We stared at each other and the air crackled with dissipating anger and growing sadness. And something else, some echo of the past. I had never felt so insane in my life. I had to escape – but where to? Mum and Dad were expecting us. And I was cornered.

Jan burst in. 'Let us go to have laughter and love with your family,' he said expansively.

I gripped his hand like a vice all the way to Mum and Dad's. I adored Jan Borsos and I would not, *would not*, let Julian patronize him or harm him in any way. It was horrible of him to wander in, so selfishly and forcefully, and pull apart the life I'd forged for myself since Fiona's death. He was cruel. Shameless. And wrong.

Help me, I implored Fiona in a silent scream, but she refused to comment. *I can't do this! I feel totally mad! I can't go and see Mum and Dad – they'll just blame me for losing you and I'll go bonkers, Fi, I'll implode, I'll just die!*

By the time we turned into my estate I was like a boiling kettle.

Dad answered the door. He looked older, more stooped than when I'd last seen him, and his jumper was cheap and bobbly. He shook Jan's hand warily, and Julian's, then turned to me, awkward and hesitant. Should he hug me, kiss me, smile? Dad didn't hate me; I'd always known that. He just had no idea what to do with me. (Or with anyone, really.) Tonight, though, I needed him to show he cared.

Eventually he held out his hand. *For me to shake.* 'All right, our Sal,' he said, as if nothing had happened. As if we'd all been the best of friends since Fiona died.

'Hi, Dad,' I said sadly. 'How are you?'

Dad's eyes looked watery for a moment. He didn't just seem stooped but actually shorter; a little old man with shadows on his face. 'Getting by,' he said. 'Go on through. Let's get you a drink. Bren's got some wine in.'

'Are you OK?' Julian asked, as we shuffled through.

An image of him kissing Violet sprang into my hot, cauldron-like mind and I ignored him.

Mum couldn't make eye contact with me. She was louder and fractionally more welcoming than usual, and I noticed makeup and a new top. She bustled around, topping up the boys' glasses with wine I'd never imagined her buying, and gave me a glass too, telling me to take a seat on the couch. But she couldn't look me straight in the eye. She asked how I was, then ran off to the kitchen before I could answer.

Julian, who knew everything about my family, was watching. Jan, who knew almost nothing about my family, was not. Jan Borsos was unfortunately quite drunk. His hair was wilder than usual and his cheeks bright red and dramatic. I watched him, feeling both tender and uneasy. I liked him very, very much, I thought – his energy, his optimism and his humour. And, my God, I admired him. Nobody at college had worked as hard as Jan had to become a singer.

But tonight I hoped – prayed, even – that Jan would magically transform himself into a measured, thoughtful man who intuitively knew how to handle my parents.

No chance.

'Mrs Howlett, you look VERY BEAUTIFUL tonight,' he said grandly, grabbing Mum's hand.

Mum tried at first to shake his but when she realized Jan was going to kiss it she froze with horror. 'Let me get some snacks down you,' she muttered, scuttling off to the sideboard.

Jan shoved his hands happily into his pockets. He moved around the room, smiling furiously, admiring Mum's massive TV and odd collection of ornaments. 'I am liking these plates!' he said excitedly, pointing at the three mounted willow patterns above the fireplace. 'And this! This is my Sally! LOOK!' Before I knew it he had grabbed my hand and yanked me over to the picture of Dennis and me, sitting on the front doorstep with Fiona in 1986.

'Look at you! You little angel of fatness!' He kissed the side of my face enthusiastically and I felt the room draw breath. Public Displays of Affection were unheard of in our house. I ducked out of his grasp to see Dad searching urgently for his pipe.

Jan started singing 'I Feel Pretty', ensuring with absolute finality that the night was ruined. He shouted about me being pretty and witty and gay and then broke off laughing. 'Except you are not gay, no? You love Jan Borsos!' I wondered if I would pass out soon. Surely no human body could survive panic and anguish on this level.

Half an hour later we were starting on the leathery steaks that Mum had served. They were cooked badly but everyone in the room was grateful for the diversion. Cutlery chinked jarringly on our worn plates while *The Million Pound Drop* wittered on in the background.

Mum still hadn't properly looked at me. And Dad had barely talked to me. I couldn't stand it.

'Sally told me you both worked in textiles,' Julian said, breaking the silence. 'Is that a big industry around here?'

Profoundly grateful for the intervention, Dad sat taller in his chair. 'Well, son, there's always been a bit of it round here, although not as much as in areas like Nuneaton – do you know Nuneaton?'

'I know *of* it,' Julian replied politely.

Dad continued, undeterred: 'This area was more about mining, but Hall's was a great employer. They're shutting down soon, though. We're having terrible trouble with all those blinking Chinese making clothes on the cheap.'

'Dreadful quality,' Mum said. 'And then the Indians, and the bloody Eastern Europeans are getting involved. They're killing us off,' she finished spiritedly.

Bloody Eastern Europeans? Where did Mum think Jan was from? Bognor fucking Regis? Mum and Dad's faces were red and indignant. They obviously didn't care where their guest was from. It was the third time today I'd heard my lovely Jan Borsos insulted and my blood was boiling.

Jan's face, however, remained the same. 'Many of my people have been poor for a very long time,' he said calmly. 'We need the business.'

Four sets of eyes swivelled towards him. 'I am from Hungary,' he explained. 'I am a bloody Eastern European! But, Mrs Howlett, you must understand that we need the industry, and that we take great pride in it. Our neighbours in the Balkans are much poorer than us. They need it even more. We are certainly not trying to kill off the people of Stourbridge.'

Dad knew he was cornered and so, as usual, he shut down. Mum did no such thing. 'Well, I can understand that, but those *Chinese*.' She grimaced. Mum always needed someone to blame. 'Blinking nightmare!'

'*Mum!*' I whispered. I could not let anyone else insult Jan today! I could not! My temples were pounding and my pulse was going through the roof. *MAKE IT STOP!* my head screamed. *MAKE ALL THIS GO AWAY!*

Mum kept her eyes on her oven chips. 'You don't know the half of it, Sally,' she muttered. 'I know you like to be all multicultural, but it's different for us. Us locals don't get work any more what with all those foreigners.'

That's Mum, I thought. *Attacks Jan, then attacks me*. I had to get out. I couldn't do this. I dropped my fork because my hands were shaking so much, then felt Jan's foot touch mine, momentarily balancing me. I looked at him, grateful, then realized it couldn't be his foot. It was Julian's.

'It *is* hard,' Julian said to my parents. 'My dad's a farmer and he's worked like stink all his life, but now he's being undercut by cheap imported meat sellers and he's really fighting for survival.'

Mum and Dad nodded vigorously.

'Exactly,' Mum said triumphantly. 'You understand the situation perfectly.'

'He's just being polite,' I exploded tearfully. Everyone stopped eating. 'And he's blaming *capitalism*, not foreigners. He's not being racist!' My voice dissolved into sobs.

'Neither am I —' Mum began, but I interrupted.

'Yes, you are! Yes, you are! You were rude to Jan! I expect you to be horrible to me, but not my guest! Say sorry!' I buried my face in my hands and sobbed silently, while the deepest, purest silence spread across our dining room. Even the steaks were terrified.

'I wasn't being a racist,' Mum responded querulously. 'I'm great friends with Mrs Yu from the takeaway.' She looked uncertainly at Dad, who was there in body but most definitely not in spirit.

Just for a second, among all my rage and despair, I had a flash of insight, recognition of how hard it must have been for my mum never to be backed up, married to a man who spoke only when completely necessary. But I was devastated; the compassion was short-lived.

'What you said was awful,' I wept. 'Please apologize to Jan.'

'I'm sorry, Jan,' Mum said dazedly. She suddenly seemed tiny. 'I really didn't mean no offence or nothing . . .'

Jan waved her off. He was far more interested in me. 'Are you very drunk, Sally?' he asked curiously. 'Or are you ill? Your mother is not offending me at all!'

'I'm not drunk,' I cried. Julian was staring at his plate. His hair was fluffy and his face anguished; he looked like my Julian. I looked back up at Mum and Dad. 'You can't just sit there slagging off Eastern Europe or China or whoever. You can't just sit there blaming everyone else all the time! I'm sick of it!'

I was an out-of-control freight train, hurtling along into God only knew where, all sparks and alarms but no brakes. 'Here's a thing,' I sobbed. 'Here's a thing about blame. My cousin died more than a year ago because she fell off a roof and since then I've spoken to Mum and Dad once. And you know why? You know why, Jan Borsos? It's because they *blame* me! They think I didn't look after her properly! They just wrote me off! Stopped calling! Stopped inviting me home! Stopped everything! I don't have a family any more!'

'Sally . . .' Julian said quietly.

'Shut up!' I wept. 'You don't get to comment on Fiona. You, of all people . . .'

Jan poured some more wine. 'This is like an evening at the cinema,' he said.

I looked back at Mum and Dad. Mum was crying and Dad looked like he wasn't far off.

Startled, I stared at them through my own tears.

'We don't blame you,' Mum whispered eventually. 'Of course we don't blame you. What are you *talking* about, Sal?'

She got up and shuffled off to the kitchen with the plates and, for the first time ever, Dad got up to help her. They left Jan, Julian and me at the table in a stunned, terrible silence.

Twenty minutes later, we were in the car. Mum and Dad had come outside to wave us off, much to my surprise. Although it was Julian they were waving off, not Jan Borsos and certainly not me. Julian had miraculously turned the conversation around after I'd gone mad, while Jan had passed out. Somehow he'd smoothed things over and even made Dad smile with tales of his father's legendary bad temper.

They look like frail pensioners, I thought, as we pulled away.

I felt, if possible, even crazier than I had done before. Nothing made sense any more. I didn't know what to think or who to believe. I didn't even know who I was.

I need my wardrobe, I thought. *I need to get into my wardrobe and possibly not come out. Ever.*

Scene Twenty-two

On my return to London I climbed into my wardrobe and tried to speak to Fiona because I didn't know what else to do.

She said nothing.

'Freckle?' I whispered. A tear slid down my face. 'Freckle, won't you talk to me?'

Silence. The green glow of my alarm clock flared in coldly through a crack in the door. I heard a noise in my room and wondered, briefly, if Fiona was sending some sort of a signal.

'Please, Fiona,' I whispered helplessly. 'Please come back and talk to me.'

Then there was a soft knock on my wardrobe door. Barry? I balled up in a corner and nearly screamed when I realized it was Julian.

'*What are you doing here?*'

Julian's face was shadowed. 'Sssh,' he said. 'I haven't come to make any trouble. Barry threatened to beat me to death if I did.'

I hugged my knees as Julian crouched in front of the wardrobe. 'Come out,' he said gently. 'Come out of there,

Sally.' He was wearing one of my favourite of his T-shirts, an old worn thing with three monkeys on the front. I wanted to bury my face in it and hide. In spite of everything he had done. What was wrong with me?

Nothing made sense any more.

'I . . . can't.'

'You can't?'

'This is the only place I feel safe,' I mumbled. Even though he already knew. Because, of course, however great the distance that had sprung up between us, Julian still knew everything about me.

He sat back on his heels. 'You were talking to her, weren't you?'

I blushed painfully. 'Yes. It helps me.'

Julian leaned over to turn on my bedside lamp.

He opened the other wardrobe door and got in, leaving the doors open so that the lamp lit our faces, and sat cross-legged opposite me. His face was full of such incredible kindness that I felt quite weak. It didn't fit. He was a drug-using liar, a . . . I stopped there because I didn't know what he was any more.

'Who are you?' I heard myself say. 'And why are you here?'

'I'm me,' he said simply. 'You can give me whatever surname you want, whatever job you want. But I'm still me. Julian. The man you . . . Well, him.'

I picked up Carrot and held him close. I was back in my pig pyjamas.

'And I think I've done a pretty good job of respecting your feelings,' Julian continued gently, 'but I'd like to ask if you'd listen to me now.'

I didn't like the sound of this. But after he'd smoothed things over at Mum and Dad's I owed him one. And even though I detested myself for it, I loved the sound of Julian's voice. I wanted to listen to him.

'Um, OK.'

'Thanks.'

We sat in my wardrobe in silence for a few moments. I could feel him pulling himself together.

'None of this is going to be easy,' Julian said quietly. 'I need to talk to you about what happened that night. When Fiona . . . went.'

I stiffened, suddenly fearful. I wasn't sure I could take it after such a horrible few days. 'Um, do we really need to go over it again?'

'Yes. We do. Because –' Julian sighed. 'Look. I have to ask you. Do you really, *truly* think I gave Fiona drugs? Do you *really* think I'm a liar and a scumbag? Do you believe that in your heart, Sally?'

I went to respond and couldn't.

Because even though I *knew* he had given the drugs to my Freckle – even though Fi and Bea and pretty much Julian himself had admitted it on the night – I couldn't fully believe it. It was almost too implausible that a man this gentle, this respectful, this nice could have done it.

But he did! my head cried. *You saw the whole thing! You know what happened!*

'Um, hello? Sal?'

Eventually I had to pinch my own arm. 'I don't know,' I said unsteadily. 'I don't know. Everyone said you did. Fiona said. Bea said. And you didn't deny it. How could it not have been you?'

I heard myself say the words yet I had already begun to doubt them. The whole universe around me was realigning. I knew that Julian was about to tell me a different version of events, and the most shocking thing about this was that I wanted him to. I wanted to hear an alternative narrative to the horror story that had spooled round and round in my head for the last year. Would I believe the alternative? I didn't know. But I was at least ready to hear it.

'There were reasons why I went along with Bea and Fiona's story,' he began. 'And I'll get to that in a bit. But before that I have to tell you that I *never* took drugs with Fiona, or gave her drugs, or sold her drugs. I never encouraged her and I never enabled her. Never, never, never.'

I couldn't take my eyes off him. I wanted desperately to believe him. It made *sense* to believe him: he was the best man I'd ever known. And yet . . . ?

Julian expelled air from his mouth. 'What really happened was . . .' He rubbed his face tiredly. 'No, I have to go back to the beginning.'

Thank God Julian had had the decency to conduct this conversation in my wardrobe. I hugged Carrot hard and tried to ignore Julian's lovely clean laundry smell. And the small hole in his sock through which a bit of toe was visible.

He looked me in the eye. 'My wife was an opera singer and she died because of a heroin overdose.' I felt the air tighten around me. 'She passed out and choked on her own vomit. She was found in a hotel room in Vienna by a chambermaid.'

A gaping silence opened out between us.

I stared at Julian, almost disbelieving. 'Oh, God.' My voice caught. 'I didn't know. I'm so sorry.'

'Of course you didn't know. That's why I'm telling you now.'

'I wanted you to tell me about her when you were ready,' I said sadly. 'I didn't want to push you.'

'And I appreciated that. It was respectful.'

I nestled Carrot closer to my belly.

'But then Fiona dismantled our relationship and our lives,' he continued sadly. 'And we didn't get a chance to talk about my past. Or, indeed, about anything.'

I nodded. The wardrobe was stuffed with grief and loss, yet it felt like the safest place on earth. Julian felt like the safest person on earth. Which was potentially quite dangerous.

'My name *is* Julian Bell. Jefferson is my dad's name. Mom changed our surname back to Bell after their divorce cos I was thirteen. But my agent decided that Julian Jefferson was a better name for an opera singer, so it became my stage name.'

'It's more boy band than opera singer,' I heard myself remark, then cringed. 'Oh, God, sorry, this isn't time for jokes. I'm just nervous.'

Julian grinned. 'Pipe down,' he ordered. 'So, my ex-wife. Catherine.'

'Really, I don't know what to say. How totally, utterly awful.' My eyes filled with tears. Poor, poor Julian.

He interrupted my thoughts. 'It was terrible. But it was more than six years ago, Sally, and I'm all right.'

I wanted so much to hug him, to tell him I knew the

vicious pain he must have gone through, but he was watching me keenly, needing to know that I believed him.

'Got it. You're OK. Well, carry on.'

Julian smiled gratefully. 'Catherine was a fantastic opera singer. A contralto, not like you at all – in any way, really. Fiona reminded me a lot of her.' He paused reflectively. 'Catherine hated herself, just like Fiona. She had so much pain.' His eyes shone in the semi-dark with sudden tears. 'After a long struggle we got her into a recovery programme but it was too late. There was so much pain by then that she couldn't stay clean. She went off to Vienna to do an audition and never came back.'

'Sounds familiar,' I whispered. A ghostly smile of acknowledgement passed between us.

'I was having a long run of contracts at the Met but in the end I left because I was too fucked to sing. I just cried all the time and my throat and sinuses were a mess. And then when I'd got myself together again I just . . . couldn't bring myself to go back. I rented the first room I found in Brooklyn and just sort of fled Manhattan.'

I nodded thoughtfully. I'd have fled somewhere if I could, back in those dreadful days after Fiona's death. Only I had been immobile, the living dead. It was my flat or nothing. 'So you did own an apartment on Mulberry?'

'I do.'

'Wow.' It must be worth a fortune. Bea had been right there.

He shrugged. 'The opera world was still calling me and emailing me but it just wasn't . . . feasible to go back to work. Even though I never planned it, I just found myself starting a new life. The magazine, the move to Brooklyn.

It did me a lot of good. Reconnected me with who I really am.' He gestured apologetically at his holey T-shirt and rumpled jeans.

I smiled guardedly, wondering if I would have fallen so madly in love with him in smart Jefferson mode. 'So, um, what made you go back to opera, if the magazine was working so well for you?'

'You. You made me go back to opera.'

I froze.

'For a long time, Sally, there was nothing. And then there was you. You rolled back the clouds.'

There was a long silence. 'I was at peace about Catherine by the time I met you, of course, but being with you cleared up any remaining shit I might have been carrying round. I was so, so happy . . . You reminded me of who I was, which was a total dick. We were both a pair of dicks, really. We laughed so much and it was such a happy fucking time and –' He broke off, taking a deep breath.

'You and I were great. We got together and I came out of hibernation and I remembered what I had inside me. Nobody can keep the music inside them for ever.' He smiled. 'Not even you.' I couldn't look at him. *Mustn't* look at him. Frightening things were happening in my chest.

'But . . .' My mouth was dry. 'But you're coaching. Not singing.' Pedantry seemed like the only option right now.

'Towards the end of your stay I made my decision. I was going to go back to singing. I was going to tell you on your final day. But then everything fucked up badly. And it set me back a long way. Pretty much back to square one, in fact.'

I felt ashamed. When had it become all about me? It

371

must have been horrific for him to witness Fiona's death after what he'd been through.

Julian continued, 'After you left I dragged myself back to lessons and did a small role in *Médée*. The critics came to gawp at me, and although they said I was back on form, I couldn't relax into it. Every time I opened my mouth I thought all of this grief would just fall out of me.'

I nodded, encouraging him to go on. He seemed so fragile all of a sudden. So small. Not a big, suited opera singer; just a man – a *boy* – sitting in a wardrobe, grappling with loss.

'So I did some coaching at a few of the opera schools and I quite enjoyed it. Then I had an email from Hugo at the RCM, who was my singing teacher when I trained there. He made this offer for me to coach and I just thought, *Fuck it*. I was happy at the RCM. Maybe if I do that for a year it'll make me brave again.'

For a frightening moment I wanted to pull him towards me and hug him hard. *Sally, you are with Jan*, I reminded myself. *You are a grown-up, having a conversation with another grown-up. Anything beyond that is pure fantasy.*

Julian gave a ghost of a smile. 'I couldn't believe my eyes when I got to London and saw you were going to be on the course. It was like the best worst news.'

I nodded again, guiltily. A little voice was pointing out that I had only ever thought about myself until now; about how bad it was for *me* to have him in London. I had never stopped to consider how difficult it must have been for Julian. Trying to gather together what little scraps of confidence he still had and put on a professional face, while his ex-girlfriend froze him out and all but accused him of manslaughter.

Although that had yet to be discussed.

Julian was watching me. 'I was so proud when I saw you were on the course, even though I knew it'd be a nightmare. I was like, wow! That brave, brave girl! She seized the day – she did it!'

I smiled gratefully. 'I still can't believe it myself! Carry on.'

Julian shifted, trying to make himself comfortable in my wardrobe. 'So. I met you on the anniversary of Catherine's death.'

I stiffened, knowing it was time to talk about Fiona. I had never felt so confused in my life. Everything he'd said so far made sense. It all confirmed that he was the man I'd originally believed him to be. *But the drugs*, my head insisted. *He had the drugs!*

'It was so weird, Sal, meeting you, because in the middle of all these crazy feelings I was having for you, there was Fiona, who reminded me so much of Catherine it was almost like she was there in the room with us. I saw where Fiona was at, and I saw how worried you were. I remembered what it was like to feel so desperately afraid, watching someone you love basically killing herself, and I couldn't stand it.'

He gazed at his hands and I stared at the top of his head. At that soft, mousy hair, so precious. I balled my fists to stop myself reaching forward and touching it. Julian still had some explaining to do.

'I wanted to help you, Sal, but I tried to do it the wrong way.'

'What do you mean?'

'I tried to help you by helping Fiona.'

I bit my thumbnail, uncertain as to what he meant.

'I tried to help her. I told her about Catherine and I took her to a couple of programme meetings that Catherine used to go to in the West Village. I introduced her to a friend of Catherine's who got clean.'

'Oh,' I whispered eventually. I was very surprised by this. 'Um, thank you, Julian. I had no idea.'

'It still wasn't enough.'

'Well, if you're telling the truth, then you gained her trust, which was a damn sight more than I managed.'

'I am telling the truth, Sal. You know I am.'

Silently, I nodded. It was getting harder to deny.

'Yes, I gained her trust, but I'm not convinced I went about it the right way.'

'There *was* no right way with Fi by then.' I was still dumbfounded by his news. Fi had gone to a drugs programme? With Julian? I simply couldn't imagine it. She had become so brittle, so closed.

'So . . .' I began, not knowing where to start. 'So how did she get on at the – what did you call it? Programme? Meetings?'

'Narcotics Anonymous.'

I sat back, even more shocked. 'Oh.'

Julian watched me taking this in.

'Fi went to Narcotics Anonymous? Seriously?'

'She did. We went to five meetings. The final one was the day of the party. I walked her there.'

I remembered seeing him and Fiona in SoHo, and cursed myself. This whole mess might have been a lot easier had I not jumped to the worst possible conclusion about everything. 'I genuinely had no idea,' I mumbled.

'Of course you didn't,' he reassured me. 'And you weren't meant to either. I deliberately didn't tell you.'

'Why?'

He sighed. 'Those programmes are anonymous. Fiona knew she could do or say literally *anything* to me and she'd still be safe.'

'But . . . but she was safe talking to me,' I said. I knew I sounded selfish but I was hurt. Why had she trusted a complete stranger and not me?

'Addicts only ever open up to other addicts,' Julian explained. 'They struggle to talk to normal people about their stuff.'

'But you're not an addict. Oh, God, are you?'

'No! But I was really connected to that world. I knew from my own shitty experience with Catherine how it all works. What you can and can't do with addicts. What might help them, what might push them over the edge. I guess she just knew she could trust me.'

'Right. Sorry. I didn't mean to sound selfish.'

'You were utterly unselfish with Fiona,' Julian said gently. 'You did everything you could for her. You put her before everyone else, for your whole life by the sound of it. There was only one thing you didn't have that might have got you closer to her, and that was an addiction.'

I watched Julian's face, took in his soft silly hair, smelt his Julian smell and knew I was beginning to believe him. It was terrifying, trying out a new version of the past, but I was ready to give it a go.

Julian sat opposite me, waiting for me to speak, and I felt a deep sense of gratitude to him. He'd done more for Fiona than I ever could have done, and for what?

For me.

I took a deep breath. 'So how did she get on at, um, Narcotics Anonymous?'

'She hated it at first,' Julian said, smiling sadly. 'Refused to acknowledge that she was in the same boat as everyone else. But the more meetings she went to, the more she identified with what everyone was saying. She –'

He paused. 'This is hard, Sal.'

I felt tears pricking at my eyes. Fiona. My Freckle. 'Go on,' I said shakily.

'That last meeting. She – she basically *got it* that day. Got the programme. Started believing she could get clean. She told me she'd join NA and she meant it, Sally. She really did.'

'Are you serious?'

He nodded.

My heart ached as I imagined how brave she'd been, smashing through all that denial and admitting she had a problem. It would have taken courage I hadn't known she had.

And at the thought of that little shred of courage I put my head into my hands and cried. Cried for that fragile little Freckle, almost but not quite beaten. Finally believing she could get better and then falling to her death a few hours later.

Julian slid his foot on to mine as I sobbed. 'It's OK,' he whispered. 'It's OK.'

'It's not! How could she go from that to – to *dying* the same day? I can't stand it . . .'

'Well, I guess the only person who can really explain that is Fiona,' he said. He rubbed my foot with his and my heart ached. 'But I think it's quite common. People decide to get clean from drugs and then the fear sets in so they have a drink instead. And *that* turns into an almighty bender, during which they get so wasted they stop caring and pick up the drugs again. I imagine that seeing Raúl at the party made things worse, although it certainly wasn't his fault.'

He looked unbearably sad. 'The awful thing is, they sometimes say, "Let them have a final bender. That's when they'll hit rock bottom. That's when they'll really become willing." But they don't mention what to do if the person in question falls off a fucking roof.' Julian's eyes swelled with tears. 'They didn't tell me that could happen.'

For a moment we sat in silence, indulging the *what-ifs* and *might-have-beens* that we both knew to be pointless. 'It wasn't your fault, Julian,' I said. 'You said it yourself. She couldn't even get through a party without those filthy bloody drugs.'

'No,' Julian agreed sadly. 'But the real tragedy in all of this is that she wasn't even that fucked. She never lost it completely. She was manageable, still just about getting on with her life. She could still have made it as a principal ballerina.'

'Really? She seemed pretty messed up to me.'

Julian nodded. 'Trust me, it can get so much worse. If she'd really lost it she'd have been stealing, off her face most of the time, lying all day long, and she'd have got into more serious stuff than coke. Make no mistake, she was in a bad way, but she wasn't a dead loss. Far from it.' Then he laughed. 'Actually, it's not at all funny, but she did steal my phone.'

'She *what*?'

'Yeah! The night we met – remember I thought I'd left it in the taxi? Turns out Fiona had nicked it. Raúl texted me and my phone went off in her handbag, and he was like, *what the fuck?*'

'Are you serious? She stole your phone?'

He laughed again. 'She did, and she had no idea what to do with it. I had to laugh when I found out. Although Raúl didn't find it funny at all.'

'Is that why he dumped her?'

Julian hugged his knees. In spite of myself I caught sight of the monkey T-shirt and smiled.

'Yeah. Raúl was right there with me throughout the whole thing with Catherine and I guess he just got super-sensitive. He cut his losses and ran before he fell for her.'

Once again I was knifed by sadness. Fiona could have found real love. She could have got clean. She could have –

I looked at my lap. I was bowled over by what Julian had told me. By his generosity, by his courage, by his understanding of Fiona's fragile state of mind. But there were still unanswered questions. Why that wrap of coke had been passing between them. Why she had said he'd been selling drugs to her. And – above all – why he'd done a runner when she fell off the roof.

'So, there's a few grey areas,' I said guardedly.

'There are. First, I'm a tosser. Bea accused me of selling the drugs. And Fiona agreed with her. And I . . . Ah, shit, it was so dumb of me. I just went along with it, because I thought it'd be the final straw for Fiona if I called her a liar in front of everyone. Catherine used to lie all the time, and when I challenged her, she'd go completely mental. I was going to tell you the truth as soon as we were alone.'

'But why did you put the coke in your pocket?'

'Because I'd finally persuaded her to hand it over. But then she picked a fight with you and wanted it back.' In spite of the agony of talking about that night, I felt a growing warmth inside. It hadn't been Julian. He hadn't dealt her drugs. He hadn't killed her. *Of course he hadn't! He was the love of my life!*

'So . . . who sold her the drugs? Where was she getting it all from?'

Julian looked at his hands. 'I'm so sorry,' he said, 'but, well, it was Bea.'

Everything swayed, including me.

'Breathe, Sally!' Julian said, half frightened. 'Are you OK?' He peered into my face. 'I'm sorry to just break it to you . . . Ah, shit, how else was I going to tell you? It was Bea.'

'*Bea?*'

'Sally? Sally?' Julian had shuffled forward and grabbed my shoulders.

Momentarily I allowed myself to loll sideways on to his arm. I felt his lovely warmth spread into me and smelt his lovely Julian smell and felt so lost I could hardly bear it. With a dizzying effort, I pulled myself upright.

'I'm OK,' I whispered. 'Just . . . Bea?'

"Fraid so. She was nothing like Fiona, obviously. She just took coke for fun. But apparently she'd been selling it to Fiona for years.'

Of course, I thought weakly. *Of course.* Bea had all but disappeared from our lives; she'd run off to Glyndebourne and neither Barry nor I had managed to get a peep out of her in months.

'The traitorous bitch,' I said. 'She didn't need to sell drugs to Fiona, she was stinking rich! Fuck! How *could* she?'

Julian laughed, slightly to my surprise. 'Ahem. Sorry. I've just never heard you say "fuck" before.'

'I – I'll *kill her*,' I whispered furiously. 'She's loaded! She knew how worried I was! She – oh, my *God*!' I gazed at him, appalled.

'From what I gather Bea just sold Fiona some grams here and there. But by the time Fiona died she would have been getting it from all over the shop, certainly not just Bea.'

'But she blamed you,' I said. 'Bea told me she was suspicious about you having nice clothes and money and – and an apartment on Mulberry.'

Julian smiled wistfully. 'Yeah. That was quite clever of her, really. I think she'd begun to realize she had a minor role in it all and was panicking.'

'Why are you defending her?' I was incredulous. 'I blamed you for Fiona's death! I treated you like absolute shit! I cut off all contact! I – oh, my God. When it was her fault!'

Julian watched me. 'No, it wasn't,' he said.

And, like he always had done, he took the wind out of my sails.

He moved back to his side of the wardrobe, putting both of his warm socked feet on top of my cold bare ones. 'It wasn't her fault,' he repeated.

There was a long silence.

'I suppose not,' I said eventually. 'Fi would've got it from somewhere. But . . . but I've spent all this time thinking you were the devil when you were actually a saint. I can't stand it. I could have . . . We could have . . .'

'Sssh. We couldn't have stayed together. You were insane with grief. And so was I. We needed to be apart.'

'But not with me hating and blaming you! Why didn't you insist on telling me?'

'Because I wanted to protect you,' he said softly. 'I didn't think you'd be able to cope with the truth. Bea was one of your best buddies, wasn't she?'

I nodded mutely as my brain turned over the events of that awful night, trying out this new information. 'You didn't do a runner, did you?' I said.

Julian shook his head. The light from my bedside lamp spilled warmly on to the side of his face and for a second I could see each little hair on his cheek; each precious little –

STOP IT.

I looked at his eyes again. 'You'd gone looking for me.'

He nodded. 'I had to find you,' he said simply. 'I couldn't let you come back and find her there in the road. I was running around Brooklyn like a psycho, crying and yelling your name. It was stupid. I was just desperate. I wanted to keep you from the pain, because I know how it feels. I wanted to protect you –' He broke off, crying.

After a while he spoke. 'Sally, I will regret for the rest of my life that you got back to the hotel and found out the way you did.'

I leaned forward and took his hand. 'Hey,' I said quietly, 'you have nothing to feel bad about. *Nothing.* Do you understand?' It felt desperately important that he got this, that he realized what a kind, good man he was. That it should have been me begging him for forgiveness.

'Bleugh.' A tear fell down his cheek on to the monkey T-shirt.

'No. Not bleugh. You've been so good to me and I've treated you like you were a monster. I'll never be able to put into words how grateful I am for what you did.' I stroked his hair for a second, then drew my hand away. It wasn't safe.

I handed him Carrot instead. 'Have a hug with Carrot. He's good for moments like these.'

Julian took him, a smile emerging. 'Hello, Carrot,' he said, balancing my ancient teddy on his knees. 'It's good to meet you at last.'

'Try a hug,' I urged. 'He's fantastic for that kind of stuff.'

'I'd rather have a hug from you,' Julian said.

Momentarily, I paused, weighing up the danger. There were a lot of feelings in me just then. I ignored them and shuffled forward to hug him.

But while the wardrobe was a good space for one, it didn't have room to accommodate hugs between two full-sized adults. Realizing I was at risk of sprawling on to him, Julian took my hand and guided me round so I had my back to him. He sat me between his legs, slid his arms round my tummy and held me tightly, his face buried in my hair.

'Did you ever really, honestly believe it was my fault?'

'No,' I admitted. 'Although I didn't know that until today.'

I felt him nod, and melt deeper into my hair.

It felt so good to be wrapped up in him that I hardly dared breathe. *What are you doing?* my head shouted. *You have a boyfriend! GET THE HELL OUT OF THERE!*

I closed my eyes and shut the voice out, enjoying Julian's size and shape. That perfect tessellation of bodies I'd missed so much.

After what felt like nowhere near enough time, Julian shifted. 'I think we should probably get out of the wardrobe,' he said softly.

I clamped my hands over his arms as they prepared to release me. 'No. I want to stay here.'

Julian laughed quietly. 'I know you do. But I've got to get home cos my mom's just about to land at Heathrow.'

'Oh! Stevie! Wow!'

I felt Julian smile behind me. A big, lazy, lovely smile. 'Yep. Mrs Bell is in da house.'

There was a silence as we both thought about Julian's brilliant mother.

'How are you feeling after Stourbridge?' Julian asked tentatively. 'Have you been thinking about your own folks?'

'Constantly.'

'And?'

I bit my lip. A thousand thoughts were dancing around in my mind. 'And I don't know. I need more time to think.'

Julian said nothing.

'It's all very well for Mum to say, "Oh, no, of course we don't blame you!" when there's guests there,' I continued. 'But they hadn't called me, Julian. Not in a year. I nearly died of grief and they . . . Nothing. Always nothing. Since I was tiny.'

'I know,' Julian said sympathetically. 'I know how hard it's been.'

I breathed out, more confused than ever. There was so much about my parents' conduct that I didn't understand.

So much anger balled up inside me, liable to explode at the slightest provocation.

But something had changed in Stourbridge. A door had been opened, just a tiny crack, but opened all the same. Whether I walked through it or not was quite another matter, but I knew it was there. And that would have to be enough for now.

'When's your mum arriving?' I asked.

I could feel Julian smiling again. 'Soon. I should get going. But, Sally – and I say this with absolute respect for all you've been through – I think it's time you got out of this wardrobe. For good.'

I listened.

'I know it's kept you safe since you were little but, Sal, you *are* safe out there in the world. And I think you're beginning to know that.'

I shrugged nervously.

'No, don't shrug. I'm serious. There's a new chapter of your life in progress. One that doesn't involve Fiona, or wardrobes, or hiding of any sort.'

'My life will *always* involve Fiona.'

'Of course. But you still have to let her go.'

'But this is all for her! This singing and college and . . . stuff . . .'

Julian shook his head. 'It *was* for her. And it's wonderful that you're going to make it as a singer, even though she couldn't make it as a dancer. But it's time you started doing it for you. Let go of Fiona. Let her rest. And start out again for Sally Howlett. Because she's still alive, she's being brave and awesome and, above all, she's really precious. She deserves to be out there in the open.'

384

I felt my lip wobble childishly. 'But I'm not ready . . .' I whispered. She's been like my coach. My friend. My advisor.'

Julian stroked my arm with his thumb. 'You're so much stronger than you realize.'

Carefully, he slid sideways out of the wardrobe. Once out he knelt down in the doorway, holding my hand. 'I know how this feels,' he said. 'But it gets easier once you let them go.'

'I'm afraid.'

Julian smiled. 'There's nothing to be afraid of out here,' he said. 'You can do it, Sal. I believe in you.'

Never taking my eyes off his, I uncurled my legs and – slowly, ever so slowly – I got out of my wardrobe, somehow knowing that this was the last time.

Scene Twenty-three

Today has to be very calm, I reflected, as I drifted into college the next morning. *The law of averages says so.* I'd had enough drama in the last forty-eight hours to last me the rest of my life; today would be a millpond.

It was not.

'Sit down,' Brian said pleasantly, when I walked into my singing lesson. 'I brought you some tea. And a Twix for us to share. It's – oh.' He pulled a warm, misshapen Twix out of his pocket and stared at it sadly. 'It's ruined.'

'It most certainly is not!' I replied spiritedly. 'Open it right now! And then tell me what's going on.'

'Hmm?'

'Come off it, Brian. Something's going on if you're feeding me rather than teaching me.'

'Ah,' he admitted. 'Ah, yes.'

How I loved Brian.

We sat by the piano, dunking our chocolate fingers into Brian's tea, and I waited for him to break his news. To my surprise, I found I wasn't actually nervous at all. Since Julian had left last night I'd been filled with hope, an emergent, fragile sort of hope; a feeling that maybe I *could* start a life free of guilt or fear. That I could do this course for me, while never forgetting my beautiful Freckle.

'Now, Sally Howlett, there are two things I want to talk to you about. First, Peter Ingle has heard fantastic things about your work in Stourbridge. I think you've really impressed him, young lady.'

'With my common touch, you mean?'

'Aye,' Brian agreed, in his best Huddersfield accent. 'He likes us rough folk. Anyway, he's invited you to sing at some big do in Mayfair.'

'Oh.'

Brian tapped his fingers together, watching me. 'And he's paying you five thousand pounds.'

I nearly threw up my chocolate. 'WHAT?'

Brian started chuckling. 'I think that's his way of giving you an extra boost. A little bit higher than the standard fee, as I'm sure you'll appreciate.'

'I can't take that sort of money!'

Brian grinned. 'You most certainly can, my girl,' he said firmly. 'I've known Peter since we were spotty youths, and if I know anything it's that he wants you to have this. He thinks you're brilliant.'

'Brian, I'm from Stourbridge! I'm not a starving peasant! He can't do that!'

'Sally, be quiet.' Brian smiled. 'Peter could fart five thousand pounds out in his sleep.'

'Shit!' I breathed. 'Are you sure?'

'Quite sure. Jan will be performing alongside you. It seems Peter's taken to the boy too . . .'

'Good. Cos Jan was brilliant.'

Brian's brow knitted. 'There is one thing, though. You'll

need to wear a performance dress. And I suspect that's something you don't own, my dear.'

He was right. Unlike my coursemates I did not possess one of those long, satiny monstrosities that opera singers insisted on wearing for concert performances. But with all of this positive energy bubbling around in me, I didn't care. I had five grand to spare!

'I'll go and buy one! I used to be a wardrobe mistress, Brian, it's about time I learned how to dress myself!'

Brian shook his head. 'Your transformation really is remarkable.' He folded his arms across his chest, watching me. 'Your musicianship lessons are coming along in leaps and bounds, I hear, you're reading music quite confidently now . . . you're singing out of the wardrobe and look at you! You're accepting offers to sing in concerts! It's really quite unbelievable!'

He cocked his head to one side. 'What do you think did it, Sally? What do you think has brought you out of yourself so beautifully?'

I wanted to say that it was Fiona, and Brian, and even Julian, to a certain extent. But I had begun to realize that someone else was involved, a lot more heavily than I'd known.

'It was me,' I said, after a long pause. 'I changed myself.'

Brian looked a bit misty in the eye area. He nodded his agreement, a proud, dad-like gesture that made me want to cry.

'The second thing I wanted to tell you was . . .' he took his glasses off and polished them on the corner of his shirt '. . . we want to cast you as Mimi in next term's production of *La Bohème*. But it was agreed that we would ask you first, because we know how hard you find it to sing in public. We don't want to give you something that feels too much, too soon.'

I gaped at him. My favourite opera in the universe. The role I had secretly dreamed of singing since I was a little girl. Not to mention the duet I'd sung in the poetry café with Julian.

'We plan to cast Jan as Rodolfo,' Brian continued, 'Hussein as Marcello and Helen as Musetta. So you'll have your gang around you.'

Still I said nothing. As much as I wanted it, was it not a bit more than I could handle?

Then I felt my heart beating slowly and steadily in my chest, my hands cool and still in my lap, and knew that – just as Julian had said last night – I was far stronger than I'd ever realized.

'Yes,' I replied. 'I'd love to play Mimi. Thank you, Brian.'

In the canteen I sat with Helen at an otherwise deserted Singers' Table. I told her we were playing the leads in *La Bohème*. We sat opposite each other, saying nothing other than 'Shit. Oh, my God. Arggh. Bollocks. Fuck! What the Jiminy Cricket? Shit.'

This went on, on a loop, for a good ten minutes before Helen had to leave for Italian coaching.

I carried on solo.

After a while, Julian and some other teacher, neither of whom I could focus on, came to sit at the table with me. 'Fuck. Jesus. Crap. Whoa. Shit. Rah! Oh, God,' I muttered, unseeing. 'And I have to buy a dress! I'm a bloody wardrobe mistress who still has no idea how to dress herself! I have to find a great big shiny shitbag dress! Crap, crap, crap . . .'

'I agree, crap,' said the woman to Julian's right. 'Jetlag and old age are not happy companions.'

Her voice was crisp and American and very familiar.

'Oh, God! Stevie!' I wailed, as she came into focus. 'I'm so sorry! I had no idea you were there!'

'I could see that, my dear,' Stevie Bell replied drily. 'I shan't ask how you are, Sally darling, because it's quite obvious. Julian just told me about your forthcoming success,' she added. 'I'm thrilled for you. Don't you give silly gowns another thought.'

Stevie Bell was the most awesome woman in America. I'd just 'cursed and profaned' in her direction and she hadn't turned a hair. Not to mention the letters that I'd sent back unopened during those early days of bone-chilling grief. Or that I'd put the phone down on her in JFK airport, so devastated by what I thought her son had done to Fiona that I couldn't even be civil. In spite of all that, here she was, her hair in a crop that was both elegant and sexy, a beautiful navy jumper and very cool spectacles framing her sharp and not remotely jetlagged eyes.

'You are completely stunning,' I told her, and didn't even feel embarrassed. 'I'm so happy to see you!' I got up and hugged her. Julian's delight was almost palpable. 'And, Stevie, I . . .' I blushed. 'Stevie, about the letters and stuff, I'm really sorry I –'

'Oh hush, darling,' she said smoothly. 'No need.'

I hugged her again. I loved Stevie almost as much as I loved –

I stopped there. Right there.

'Mom insisted on coming into college,' Julian said happily. 'She's bollocked me about my appearance, of course.'

'He was really smart before!' I told Stevie. 'Honestly, you wouldn't have recognized him!'

'Oh, I know that look,' Stevie replied crisply. 'And I strongly dislike it. That cursed agent of his. Did he tell you I fired him and became Julian's manager myself?'

'Um . . . no!'

Julian pulled a packet of Wotsits out of his coat pocket and sat back, shaking his head. 'I am here, you know,' he said, but we ignored him.

'When he told me he was going back into singing I took matters into my own hands,' Stevie announced. 'I'm sick of seeing my lovely boy all gelled and polished. He grew up in gum-boots, Sally! And wore hay in his hair as standard! Dressing to impress is such a waste of time. His fans don't care what he wears to go buy a quart of milk.'

I thought suddenly of little twenty-one-year-old me, blowing my entire salary on *natural fibres* so that I could look like a proper wardrobe assistant. Then buying loads of trendiness to fit in here at college. *Aged thirty*. 'Um, I've been guilty of that,' I admitted ruefully.

'Oh, me too, sweetie, me too. I kitted myself out in all manner of waxed cotton to attract his father. I even bought a flat cap. The shame! I was a professor of linguistics!'

If someone as clever and brilliant as Stevie had got caught up in that madness, perhaps I wasn't as weak a moron as I'd imagined.

'We're all flawed,' Stevie remarked, as if reading my mind. 'We all struggle to believe in ourselves.'

'Mm,' Julian and I said, at the same time. I wasn't quite sure who was mm-ing about what.

'But there's still a happy medium,' Stevie rounded on her son sternly. 'Such as ironing one's clothes, Julian . . .'

Julian pretended not to hear her.

'Julian's very attached to creased shirts and crumpled jumpers,' I said. 'I never really believed the smart suits.' Immediately I blushed. Far too familiar.

'Oh, Sally, it really is such a joy to see you.' Stevie grinned. 'Tell me how you're finding college.'

'Well, it's been really nice to chat,' Julian said peevishly. 'I enjoyed our catch-up. But now I've got a student to coach.' He grinned. 'Bye, Mom,' he said, ambling off.

'Tuck your shirt in!' Stevie yelled after him.

We watched Julian go. 'I do wish I could stop telling him what to do.' She smiled. 'You know, a mother tries her best but we just make mistake after mistake, doing what we think is right for our child. We're blind, Sally! And that, my dear, is because we love too much. Nothing prepares a woman for how she feels about her child,' she said. 'Nobody warns you of that fierce, wild love . . .'

I fiddled with my yellow ring, wondering if Mum had ever felt that way about me. Certainly there had been scant evidence of fierce, wild love in my childhood.

'Was your mother in your face all the time?' Stevie asked. 'Always trying to "help" you and being a pain in the butt?'

'Um, well . . . No. She kind of kept me at arm's length.'

Stevie cocked her head. 'Really?'

I didn't answer. I was still extremely confused about Mum and Dad. I gave a non-committal shrug. 'Pretty much.'

There was a long pause. I stared out of the window at a very drab autumn sky.

'I often wonder if Julian felt that I did the same to him,' Stevie said eventually.

'I doubt that very much. He raves about you!'

'Good. But, still, I worry . . .'

'Honestly! I don't think you have anything to worry about!'

Stevie traced a finger round one of her chunky silver bangles. Something sad had come over her. 'When he was eight I realized I couldn't stay with his father any more. He's a good man, in his own closed way, Sally, but he couldn't communicate. With me or anyone. And, well, you may have noticed that I'm quite fond of talking.'

We both giggled.

'I'd fallen in love with the idea of living on an English farm. In Devonshire! All those cream teas and wild moors and cows! Even educated Americans are susceptible to all that,' she said drily. 'But although I could have coped with the disappointment of the greyness and the solitude of that farm, the ceaseless mud, vets and broken fences, I couldn't live with a man who couldn't talk to me. I'm a Brooklynite. I missed my home. I missed my life. I missed *talking*. I felt like I was dying of loneliness. I delayed and procrastinated because I couldn't bear to disrupt my little boy's life. But in the end I had to go.'

Julian had told me about the move to America; how confused and lost but thrilled he'd been. And how, after a year, his mother had sent him back to Devon because he was falling in with a bad crowd at high school and had stopped singing. 'I did what I thought was best for him,' she said helplessly. 'I cried every night for two years, wondering if he thought I'd abandoned him. Or that I didn't love him.'

There was a long silence. 'Did I do the right thing?' she asked, eyes bright. 'I don't know, Sally. But I did the best I could do as his mother. The very best I could do at the time.'

I nodded thoughtfully.

'Ignore me,' she said, smiling. 'As I said, a mother never stops worrying!'

'I have to go,' I said. 'It's so lovely to see you, but I've got some . . . things to do.'

Jan Borsos bowled into the canteen and swooped over, kissing me on my cheek, nose and chin. 'My big furry Chinese panda,' he exclaimed loudly. 'Good day!'

He turned to Stevie. 'I am Sally's boyfriend,' he announced. 'How do you do?'

'I am Julian Jefferson's mom.' Stevie twinkled. 'And I'm very well, thank you.'

'I was just heading off,' I told Jan. 'Shall I come round tonight?'

'YES! We will have fun times, Sally!'

'I'm so glad I saw you,' I told Stevie. 'So glad. Have a good trip.'

'And I'm glad you're happy,' Stevie said. There was a slight crack in her smile as she watched Jan and me heading off. 'You take care, Sally.'

Scene Twenty-four

I drifted into Kensington Gardens, deep in thought. It had been a beautiful morning, sunny and sharp, but now London was compressed under the weight of a thick, cold fog. It fitted quite well with the state of my head.

I sat on a damp bench, not particularly caring if I got a wet bum. I needed to think.

Since Mum and Dad's house I'd found myself in an impossible quandary. Nothing had changed about my childhood, or even my adult relationship with them: the facts were immutable. Yet it had dismayed me to see them so stunted and old. They'd seemed fragile, somehow, rather than cold and indifferent. Why? Had they actually changed? Or had I just seen them through a different lens, having come to the house with company for the first time since I was tiny?

Whatever it was, it had blunted my sharp defences. I was worried about them. I seemed somehow to have harmed them by telling them what I thought to be the truth.

I watched a squirrel ferreting around in a dustbin. 'What's going on?' I asked him. He stared defensively at me, a crisp in his paws. 'It's OK,' I told him. 'I really, really don't want your crisp. I just want some clarity.'

The squirrel gave me a look as if to say, *You are a moron of epic proportions. Piss off.* He plunged back into the dustbin.

I smiled. And, before I knew it, I'd dialled home.

I jammed my bottom into the back of the cold, slimy bench, my chest and abdomen engaging in a complex dance routine. I didn't know what I was calling to say. The squirrel was right. I was a moron of epic proportions. *Abort! Abort!*

But before I could Mum answered. 'Hello?' she said. A tiny voice shot through fibre-optic cables and blasted into the sky, only to be funnelled down into my phone. My mother. Creator of Sally Howlett.

Nemesis? Friend?

'BARP.'

'Hello?' She sounded worried now, which was understandable.

I cleared my throat. 'Sorry, Mum, it's me. Got a bit of a frog in my throat there . . .'

A shocked silence whizzed down the fibre-optics. Then, '*Sally?*'

'Yes.' My voice was almost lost in the dank air. *I* was almost lost in the dank air. It was just me and the squirrel, the only two people in the world.

'Oh,' Mum said unwelcomingly. My hackles rose, and then – to my surprise – flattened down again. *That's just how she is,* said a rather unexpected voice in my head. *It's the best she can do.*

'Um, I was calling to . . . to apologize,' I said.

Was I? Apparently so.

A tremulous silence. 'I shouldn't have said that you blame me for Fi,' I mumbled.

Still more silence.

'Hello?'

'Oh, sorry, Sally, I was just . . .' She trailed off uselessly. Then she cleared her throat. 'You shouldn't have *thought* that we blame you for Fiona,' she said, all of a sudden. I could tell she'd surprised herself. 'Of course we don't. Where did you get that idea?'

'Oh, you know. Just you warning me in quite a threatening way that I *had* to look after her out there, then not talking to me since I got back.'

It was as if someone else was talking. The squirrel, beady eyes fixed on me, was munching a piece of chocolate now. He was probably wondering, quite reasonably, if I'd lost it. Was I calling to apologize or to start a fight? I wasn't really sure.

'I see,' Mum said. There was some rustling, and then she came back. 'I think you should talk to your father,' she said.

I sighed. This was a waste of time. She still didn't want to talk to me. Or couldn't talk to me. Or whatever. I wasn't sure I cared.

I could tell Dad was appalled at having the phone shoved at him.

'All right, our Sal,' he said uncertainly.

'All right, Dad.' I sounded weary. 'I was calling to say sorry for making a scene. I don't want to disturb you both. I'll go.'

'Oh,' Dad said. 'Oh.'

I sighed.

Then Dad said something extraordinary. 'I'm glad you called, Sal. We both are. Thank you.'

And that was pretty much that. After some disjointed farewells, the call was ended.

The squirrel watched me keenly. 'I haven't got a bloody clue,' I said. 'No idea what just happened.'

He cocked his head to one side, and I smiled. Something in me was lighter. 'But I'm glad I did it, Squirrel.'

Scene Twenty-five

Just before we broke for Christmas, I found myself staring at my reflection in the mirror in deep horror. I had no idea whether to laugh or cry. Some MA students were practising carols for a charity concert down the corridor, and our dressing room had been decked out in illegal fairy lights and holly stolen from Hyde Park. I had every reason to be jolly.

I was not jolly. I looked absolutely preposterous. Like a big shiny golden banana, but with extra wide squashy bits that bananas didn't have, and a whole lot of wrinkling where my generous hips pulled tight this humdinger of a satin dress.

'Lovely,' Violet said, wrapping a long cashmere scarf around her neck. She was still wearing the leather jacket she'd been wearing in September. What was it about posh skinny girls that meant they never felt the cold?

For once, Violet's smile was sincere, albeit for all the wrong reasons. I looked like a fat blob shoved into a

399

horrible dress and she knew it. 'You look a million dollars, darling. You'll knock their socks off at this concert!'

She slid out of the door, waggling her fingers at me. 'Night!'

'Night,' I said to the empty room. I looked in the mirror again and despaired. Why was it that I could now sing in a room full of people, navigate my way through a new friendship with my half-American ex-lover while maintaining a dizzyingly sexual relationship with my current Hungarian lover – all with commendable aplomb – and yet found myself incapable of saying no to a shopping trip with Violet Elphinstone? A trip that I had *known* would turn out like this.

I sighed, trying to squash down the stretched bits across my hips but succeeded only in creating a camel toe.

Lord Peter Ingle's concert was tomorrow. Jan and I had been rehearsing for the last few days and – save for the dress – we were ready to go. My first proper public performance. Ever. For more than an hour I would have to stand on a stage, like a proper opera singer, hair in billowing waves, makeup fit for a cruise liner and a dress that could stand up on its own without me in it.

And this was it. This fat golden banana dress. Violet, overhearing me telling Helen that I was going to buy a dress today, had dragged me off to Knightsbridge at lunch. She was still high from her tremendous success in *Manon* last week, and from being the girlfriend of world-famous tenor Julian Jefferson, and could not sit still. We walked along the Old Brompton Road, Violet's arm linked through mine, while she chatted non-stop about Julian.

Strangely – even though we were talking about her relationship with my ex-lover – I found myself hating her less: the more time I spent with Violet the more I realized that she was quite possibly more insecure even than I was.

'He's so mysterious,' she babbled, as she selected various awful dresses for the shop assistant to prepare. We were in a small boutique on Beauchamp Place. A boutique where you actually had to ring a doorbell to enter. If I was to nurture the tiny seed of a relationship with my family that had grown over the last few weeks (Mum had sent me Tesco vouchers, Dad had sent me a newspaper article about a Birmingham opera company, and I had made myself call them for another awkward chat), it would be important to make sure they never found out that I'd shopped in an entry-by-doorbell shop.

'I just love working out what's going on behind those lovely big blue eyes of his. I think he's actually quite sensitive, like on Tuesday he came round to mine after college and he just said, "Actually, can you just hold me? I need a hug."'

Something sharp poked at my heart.

Things between Julian and me had been a lot more cordial over the past few weeks. We now smiled and talked when we passed each other in the corridor, and once or twice – like the time I'd found him choking on a Cadbury Creme Egg and performed an emergency Heimlich on him – we'd even found our old banter. But the whole thing was beset with weirdness and sadness.

Helen, whom I'd since told everything, had not been

helpful. 'If you wrote down the perfect romantic lead for a film script, it would be Julian,' she had stated forcefully. 'If you aren't still in love with him then you're completely mental.'

I had reassured her spiritedly that I was not still in love with him.

But that didn't stop me feeling as if someone was applying a cheese grater to my heart as I listened to Violet talking about him.

'I mean, when do you ever hear men saying things like that? "Can you hold me?" God, Sally, I just *totally* melted.'

It's fine, I told myself. *I used to love him. It was never going to be easy when he met someone else.*

I started trying dresses on, Violet sipping a dry cappuccino – 'Just coffee and some skimmed milk foam,' she instructed. 'Fewer calories!' – and continuing to yabber on about their relationship. Thankfully, I was too absorbed in the horror of the dresses to focus on what she was saying.

After trying on a few I settled – reluctantly – on a royal-blue affair with cap sleeves and less sparkly than the others.

'No,' Violet said, screwing up her face. 'It makes your arms look fat. How come you can't see that for yourself, sweetie? I thought you were a wardrobe mistress?'

Violet was not the first to flag this up, and she would probably not be the last. The answer was as pathetic as it was true: I simply did not like looking at my reflection and went a bit barmy and useless when I had to buy clothes. Everything I knew went out of the window, and if I bought anything at all it was generally the wrong thing. That was part of the reason I'd so loved my swishy bohemian linens from my opera house days. God, I missed them.

I tried to unzip the blue dress, too embarrassed to ask for help, but the shop assistant almost rugby-tackled me to stop me doing it myself. 'No no,' she cried shrilly. 'Clients do NOT unzip themselves!' Pink spots had appeared on her cheeks.

Between her and Violet they decided that I should buy the gold dress, which I'd tried on first, and I gave in because I couldn't take another second of listening to Violet talk about Julian.

'YAY!' Violet squealed, as we left the shop with a huge cardboard bag. 'Happy days!'

'Happy days,' I echoed weakly.

'Enough about me and Jules,' she said brightly. 'How are things with Jan?'

'Um, good, I think.'

They were good. Jan still seemed to want to have sex at least three times a day, and he was still noisy, chaotic and at times insane, but he was funny, charming and sparky, and when my head wasn't running off on worrying tangents, I was pretty sure we were actually very happy indeed.

'Are you sure?' Violet was watching me with forced concern.

'Yes, sorry. I was miles away.'

'If you and Jan are having problems you can always tell me.' She simpered. 'It's important to talk about these things. I mean, if anything went wrong with Jules I'd be totally devastated. I'm falling for him big-time.'

She smiled, embarrassed, and blushed into her Hermès scarf. I realized she was serious.

'Violet, you're beautiful,' I said sincerely. 'Julian would be totally insane to leave you.'

'I hope you're right.' She bit her lip, and I felt a wave of genuine sympathy for her.

I resolved to respect her and her relationship. She had not treated me very well but that didn't mean I shouldn't keep my side of the street clean.

Nonetheless, I thought now, standing in the girls' dressing room at college, Violet was a total fucker who deserved to be stabbed with a sharp stiletto. The fat golden banana dress was appalling.

The door opened and someone's head popped round. 'Oh,' said Julian.

'Oh,' I said, relieved I'd not yet unzipped myself.

Julian gaped at me. 'What the fuck is that?'

'What the fuck is what?'

'Sal! What is that dress? Who did this to you?' He was dangerously close to laughing.

I found myself struggling to keep a straight face. It *was* funny, really. 'Your girlfriend did this to me, as it goes.'

Julian's eyes widened. '*Violet* lent you this dress?'

'No. Violet made me *buy* this dress.'

Julian's hand went to his mouth but not in time. Laughter spilled through his fingers like water. 'It's *dreadful*!' he howled.

I shrugged, grinning ruefully. 'She doesn't like me much, Violet.'

'I think you may be right. Is this for Lord Ingle's concert?'

'Sure is.'

'Here, let me help,' Julian said, moving forward to unzip me.

I caught my breath as his hand touched my neck. 'No, I can do it, thanks, Julian.'

'Sorry, yes.' Julian moved away from me. He was still laughing. 'Oh, Sally.'

'Hmm,' I said, wriggling my top over my head so I could slide the dress off without exposing myself.

'Right,' Julian said decisively. 'Let's go shopping. I am going to sort this mess out.'

I looked at him in the mirror, weighing up his proposition, which felt both appealing and dangerous. Julian had a great eye for clothes – I still owned the lovely blue dress he'd bought for our final-night party in New York – so I *knew* I'd find something nice with him in charge.

I also knew that my heart was hammering at the thought of going shopping with him. Which meant that it was a bad idea. Briefly, I hated myself. What was wrong with me?

'Thanks, but I'll be OK,' I said firmly. It took every ounce of strength I had.

'Oh, Sal, come on.' His face softened and I saw a flash of need. 'There was something I wanted to talk to you about.'

'LET HIM HELP YOU,' Helen shouted, bursting suddenly from the toilet.

'Er, Helen?'

'Sorry. I was stuck in there with constipation,' she explained. Julian laughed. 'He's right, Sally. That dress is disgusting beyond words. Let him take you shopping.'

Julian's eyes sparkled with amusement.

405

'Well?' Helen was looking ominously at me.

'Let me help you,' Julian repeated.

I had no more fight in me. 'OK.'

He left while I got changed.

'What are you doing?' I hissed at Helen, who was unzipping me with a triumphant grin.

'I'm looking after your best interests.'

'You're doing nothing of the sort. And you just told Julian you're constipated.'

'I took one for the team. *Do this*,' Helen ordered. 'Just do it. Jan will probably be grateful. He won't want to sing next to you tomorrow night if you're looking like a twat.'

Scene Twenty-six

There are some people with whom your body *works*. With whom you fall into stride without trying; with whom you're warm when it's cold; with whom you always feel the right size even if you feel the wrong size everywhere else.

As I walked along Old Brompton Road with Julian, the bitter wind biting at my face, I remembered that my body worked perfectly with his. We talked as we walked – mostly about safe topics like next term's *La Bohème* – and it was only when I heard a woman with a rock-hard bouffant complain that the streets were too packed that I realized we'd been manoeuvring expertly through dense crowds of people without even knowing it.

Light bled on to the pavements from Knightsbridge's shops and restaurants, accentuating the laughter lines around Julian's face. I felt an alarming urge to touch the soft, delicate skin by his eyes. My stomach twisted itself in knots just thinking about it.

He can't make you happy, I reminded myself desperately. *Too much has happened now.* But it wouldn't go away.

This could not be repeated, I thought. Ever. We'd go

shopping, I'd take myself home for a serious word. Even if I didn't care enough about myself I owed Jan some bloody respect. Not to mention Violet. Julian's laughter lines belonged to her.

A few minutes later, we were standing outside Harrods. *'Harrods?'*

Julian smiled, holding a door open for me. 'Harrods.'

'But I can't afford a dress from Harrods! I've already spent a fortune on the banana!'

'Trust me, Sal.'

'But –'

'I said, trust me.'

I followed him in.

Some of the sparkle of this secret mission faded, which was probably a good thing. What was I going to find in Harrods, other than another round of expensive, middle-aged dresses? Perhaps Julian was not the clever sartorial expert I'd imagined.

We arrived on the third floor and Julian started weaving expertly through the concessions, chatting easily about nothing in particular. He clearly knew where he was going. I clearly did not. I did feel certain, though, that we were on the wrong floor. This stuff looked wildly expensive.

'Aha! Here we go.'

I looked up at the sign above us. *Hannah Coffin.*

'I read about her in a magazine Mom had,' he explained. 'I thought she was an amazing designer and I thought you'd look lovely in one of her dresses. You're not meant to wear a stupid ballgown, Sally, but you have every right to wear something fit for a red carpet. Such as, I dunno, *this.'*

He pointed at a total knockout of a dress: floor length, chalk-coloured and embellished from head to toe with the most exquisite delicate beading. I drank it in, every tiny little detail, and felt slightly delirious. It *was* beautiful – stunning, in fact – and, to my astonishment, I could actually see myself wearing it. 'Oh my God! That's a *fantasy* dress! I could never afford it!'

'At least try it on. And, Sally, you of all people should know that this sort of thing is called a gown. This goes way beyond dresses.'

I stared longingly at the 'gown'. Maybe I *could* look fabulous on stage tomorrow night. Maybe I didn't have to look like a fat banana. 'But hang on.' I dragged myself back to reality. 'Surely I should wear a satin shocker? Isn't that what you're supposed to do?'

Julian stopped browsing. 'Sally. You're *supposed* to start singing lessons when you're six and get Mom to drive you to all the singing competitions. You're *supposed* to march into opera school and tell everyone how great you are, and who you've sung with, and what you're in next. Did you do any of that?'

I shrugged.

'No, you didn't. You sidled in looking terrified, not even knowing what a semiquaver was. You had no names to drop, no dresses to wear and you fell apart if anyone so much as looked at you. Why would you want to start doing the same thing as everyone else now?'

I chewed my little finger anxiously. Wasn't the whole point of opera school just that, though – to learn how to fit in? From day one they'd hammered into us that we were being trained not just to be the best singers in the world but to know our highly competitive industry inside out. We were meant to be developing the most impeccable CVs, the most professional audition techniques, the most rounded repertoires. Surely we were meant to get our wardrobes in line, too.

'Stop eating your pinkie,' Julian said gently. 'There's no rulebook. You can only do what feels comfortable. Otherwise, what's the point? Your singing might be great, but you'll just be a dick.'

And so, for the second time that day, I gave in. It was seven thirty p.m., we really didn't have a great deal of time left, and I wanted to hear whatever Julian had to say to me. 'OK. Find me a dress in which I won't be a dick.'

Julian picked three gowns before sending me to the changing rooms. I hardly dared look at them, they were so beautiful. They were so heavily beaded that they weighed almost as much as I did, but I knew that if I was wearing something this stunning I'd have no trouble singing. I felt like royalty already.

And then the assistant brought me Louboutin heels to try them on with, and a scarf to protect the dresses from my crappy makeup, and pooled the dresses on the floor for me to step into, and talked about getting them hemmed by the Harrods tailor overnight and I began to lose the plot. This was like something that happened in bloody Hollywood.

'I used to be a wardrobe mistress,' I said dazedly, as she moved round me, shifting and tucking and smoothing. 'I should know how to do this. But I . . .'

I was kind of lost for words.

The first dress, a vivid pink *trompe l'œil* gown (which

410

Julian said he'd seen Emilia Fox wearing on a red carpet) was incredible. As the assistant fitted me into it I gasped, remembering that I was not fat and ugly, like the banana had suggested, just curvy and maybe even a bit pretty. 'Stunning,' grinned the sales assistant.

The second, a floor-length black version of the chalk gown, was a knockout but I wasn't quite sure about wearing black onstage. Julian agreed. Just to wear it, though, with those beautiful expensive heels, and my own dedicated assistant sliding around doing clever things to make it look even more extraordinary, was like nothing I'd ever experienced.

'What's going on in there?' Julian called.

The sales assistant fitted me into the third dress – the chalk-coloured gown – and when I looked at myself in the mirror I thought I'd cry. 'Julian . . .' I called, awed. The sales assistant let him in, then disappeared. He stood behind me, taking in my reflection. He smiled – a lovely, shy sort of a smile – knowing as I did that it was perfect. His eyes came slowly back up again and I knew I had to look away, but couldn't. Time passed, memories fluttered and I forgot the present. Just for now the only two people breathing were him, lovely, handsome Julian Bell, and me, Sally Howlett, the beautiful woman he'd helped me realize I was.

'You are perfect,' he said. His eyes were bright with a pain I couldn't quite understand.

'Julian . . .'

'You are perfect,' he repeated. 'And I want you to know that, whatever happens, I will never forget you. I will never forget us.'

'Julian?' I turned round, confused. 'Why are you saying that? What do you mean?'

He looked at me for a few seconds, some sort of conflict playing out in his mind, then shook his head, smiling slightly. As if to say, *Ignore me.*

I couldn't. Neither could I pretend any longer: we'd crossed a line in my wardrobe that night. A line that could not be erased or forgotten.

'Julian . . .' I began softly.

'No.' He backed away. 'Sally. Remember what we said. Let go of the past.'

My breath caught in my throat. 'I did. I let go of Fiona. But I don't think I can let go of . . . of . . .'

Tears shone in his eyes. 'No,' he whispered. 'Don't do this to yourself, Sally. We both had to move on.'

Before I knew it he had pulled me into him. He hugged me so hard I thought I'd stop breathing, but before I had time to enjoy it he'd pulled away. 'I'll wait outside,' he muttered. 'You look sensational.'

When I emerged five minutes later, Julian was nowhere to be seen.

'He asked me to tell you he had to go,' said the sales assistant. 'But the good news is, he bought you the gown!' She pushed a big, beautiful bag across the counter towards me with a folded note on the top.

This is from Mom, not me. After seeing you at the Royal College she gave me some money and instructed me to get you a proper dress. She also asked me to say, 'Don't mess with me, Princess – it's yours. With love, Stevie.' Julian xx

'Your boyfriend is rather amazing.' The sales assistant smiled. 'So handsome! And so generous! You must be madly in love with him!'

I took the bag and smiled bravely. 'Yes,' I said. 'I am. That's the problem.'

Scene Twenty-seven

The next day

Another envelope. Another letter addressed to me in Julian's handwriting. Only this, I knew before even opening it, was the very worst sort of a letter. I slumped against the wall by the college noticeboards, looking out at the flat, grey sky, and wondered how I could have let this happen.

Dearest Sally

By the time you read this I will be on a plane back to New York.

I handed in my notice almost as soon as I started working here, because I could see that my presence was causing you too much trouble. I wanted you to be able to learn and grow without being reminded of your past every five minutes.

I promised Hugo I'd see out a term but after last night I've realized that even by seeing out my notice period I'm making it worse for you. I looked at you, standing there in that dress, and I loved you more than I ever had. But I could see that you were wondering if you felt the same and that's when I knew I had to go, even if it meant missing the last day of term.

I can't cause you any more confusion. I don't want to ruin your relationship with Jan Borsos. And I don't want to get in the way of what is without doubt going to be a wonderful singing career. I just want you to be happy and to get on with your new life. I am part of a past that you have to leave behind.

I know that because, like you, I've lost someone I love. I know what it takes to move on.

Over the last twelve weeks I have watched you blossom, and become the person you were always meant to be. You have overcome so much, Sal, and have done it with such dignity and courage — you absolutely blow me away. Tonight I will think of you singing in that dress, and I'll smile as I hear all of the applause and cheering. I will feel even more proud than I do now.

I hope that you will be brave enough to agree that it's for the best that we don't remain friends. I think contact would be too confusing.

You and I could have been awesome together, but life had other ideas. So let's get on with our new lives. Let's celebrate who we are and what we taught each other.

Let's start a new chapter. A new act!

With all my love,

Julian X

'Sally.'

It was Helen.

'Hello?'

I looked back out of the window and wondered blankly where Julian had bought such nice writing paper.

'Oi!' Helen was beginning to look concerned. 'Is anyone in there?'

415

I handed her the letter. Helen looked down at it. 'Oh, shit,' she said quietly. She took my hand and began to read Julian's note. When she'd finished she hugged me for a very long time. 'You do understand what's going on here, don't you?' she said.

I did not. I had no idea about anything any more.

'*La Bohème*,' Helen said, clarifying nothing.

'Eh?'

'*La Bohème*,' she repeated. 'You two are bloody Rodolfo and Mimi. You meet in some ridiculous rooftop apartment. You fall in love on the spot. You go off to some wanky art café and fall even more in love. You start a relationship and then he leaves you because he thinks he's bad for your health. I mean, hello?!'

I gave the matter some thought and saw that – as usual – Helen Quinn was bang on. 'Wow. That's insane.'

Helen nodded.

'But what happens next, eh?' I asked her weakly. 'Mimi tracks down Rodolfo to give it one last try and then she dies?'

'Well, yes.'

'So I guess he really does mean it,' I said sadly. 'He really is trying to set me free.'

'I suppose so. But, oh, God, Sally, that *sucks*. You and he were meant to be.'

'Apparently not.' I placed the letter carefully in my satchel.

Jan came barrelling along the corridor, singing scales. 'HELLO, hello,' he sang, patting my bottom and giving Helen a big smile. He barrelled off towards the canteen, full of energy and good humour.

416

I watched him go and tried to pull myself together. I'd done enough crying in this corridor over the last three months. 'Well, then,' I said, taking a long, shaky breath. 'I suppose I'd better get on with my new life.'

'With Jan?'

'With Jan. I have to give him a chance, Helen. I really like him, in spite of everything. He made me laugh when no one else could.'

Helen nodded thoughtfully.

'And Julian seems to think that that's what I should be doing too. Staying with Jan. Laughing.'

'Well, I'm not sure he was saying *that*, exactly.'

'I'm going to try to make it work with Jan,' I said determinedly. 'And I'm going to go and sing my arse off at Lord Ingle's concert tonight. And then in January I'm going to concentrate on being the best Mimi I can possibly be, and audition for the British Youth Opera. That's what my new life is going to look like.'

'Right you are,' Helen said, after a long pause. She linked my arm and we walked off down the corridor. This time Julian and I really were over.

Scene Twenty-eight

'Happy Christmas, you morons!' Helen pulled a party-popper and whooped. Her fiancé, Phil, handed glasses of champagne to Jan and me.

'Happy Christmas, yourself,' I said, hugging her.

'You're spilling champagne down my back, you clumsy oaf! Do you think we're made of money, Sally?'

I was very grateful for Helen Quinn and her hospitality that day. Even though Mum and I had actually had a couple of phone calls in the last couple of weeks – tense, awkward ones, but phone calls all the same – there had been no invitation to join them for Christmas. Jan and I were festive refugees.

'Thank you so much for having us over,' I said, taking in her lovely warm kitchen. There were fairy lights all over the place, not trendy white blobs but multicoloured chaotic strings draped from haphazard nails banged into the walls. Half-chopped vegetables were all over the surfaces, fighting with packets of stuffing, half-drunk bottles of wine and big overgrown pots of herbs. 'Have some mulled wine!' Helen said merrily, dunking a mug into a pan. 'And do you want a brandy or something?'

'Calm down, H,' Phil said mildly. 'The poor girl's trying to drink her champagne.'

'Ah, yes.' Helen poured the mug's contents back into the pan, then filled it straight back up when Jan announced that he had no problem taking champagne and mulled wine together. 'I suppose I'm probably just trying to get you drunk, Sally,' she admitted, as the boys wandered off to look at Phil's enormous new Canon camera. 'Are you OK?'

'What do you mean, *are you OK* in that tone?' I grinned.

'I mean, your family are still being dickheads and the love of your life has gone back to America.'

'Helen, shut up.'

'Very well. But only because it's Christmas and we're meant to be BFFs.' She handed me a turkey baster. 'Any idea what I'm supposed to do with this?'

I giggled. 'Yes. You just use it like a giant pipette, getting the fat out from under the turkey, then pouring it over the top so it goes all crispy.'

I caught a fleeting memory of Mum teaching me to do the very same thing on Christmas Day when I was ten. Fiona had been sulking in her tiny bedroom under the stairs because of something to do with presents and I'd ached with guilt at being in the kitchen with everyone else. 'Ignore her,' Mum had advised.

'*Stop it*,' I said to myself, as the same old resentment came thundering in. '*Let it go*.' And suddenly I was OK again. Who knew?

'Oh dear,' Helen said, peering at me. 'Are you mad, sad or drunk?'

'Sad, I suppose. I'm so happy to be here but I just . . . I dunno. Why didn't they invite me home?'

'Families are fucked up,' Helen said, handing me some parsnips to peel. 'And yours sound like they're special contenders. But, here's a question – did *you* mention Christmas to them?'

'What do you mean?'

'I mean, did *you* ask if you could come? Or were you just waiting for them not to invite you, thereby proving they don't care about you?'

I stared at her. 'What?'

Helen looked worried. 'Twat,' she said, slapping her head. 'Sorry, I shouldn't have asked. Just that I have a habit of doing things like that. You know, testing people. Waiting for them to prove they don't love me. I discovered it in therapy. Along with a whole load of other shit I wish I'd never dug up. Ignore me.'

I got on with the parsnips, but I didn't really hear anything else she said. All I could think about was her question because it was a very, very good one.

After a stupendous Christmas lunch we piled on coats and went for a walk in Brockwell Park before the light faded. If we ignored the tower blocks behind us, we could have been in frosty fields deep in the heart of the country. Across the park's small valley a little church poked up out of the trees, like a pastoral village scene – Tulse Hill, Helen informed me, whose connection with villages was only the presence of several Chicken Cottages – and the silver-tipped grass beneath our feet crunched like cornflakes.

Phil and Jan were walking ahead, Phil chuckling at whatever Jan was saying. I smiled, feeling big swathes of warmth for my little pocket-rocket Borsos. There was not a day when he didn't make me smile, or laugh, or do something silly that a year ago would have been inconceivable.

Helen was watching me. 'Smiling at Jan?'

We were walking slowly down the hill towards Brixton City Farm and the dying rays of the afternoon sun had painted Helen a beautiful sepia.

'Yes. He's good news, you know.'

'He is?'

'Stop it.'

'Stop what?'

I stopped walking. 'Stop acting like Jan's just a rehearsal for the main event. He's my boyfriend. Not a practice.'

'Hmm.'

'Helen!'

'Look, Sally, I adore your boyfriend too. Jan Borsos is one of the most awesome people I've ever met. But I don't need to have sex with him ten times a day – or however often he makes you do it – to prove that I love him. He's twenty-three, for God's sake!'

'And Phil's forty-one. Age gaps are fine.'

'Not your way round they're not,' Helen said firmly. 'You should give him up so someone his own age can enjoy him.'

'Gah, you're annoying. Can't I just have fun?'

'Are you going to marry him one day?' she asked.

'*What?* Jesus, Helen, I don't know. Who cares?'

'If someone had asked you if you'd marry Julian when you were with him, what would you have said?'

I sighed. I wished she wouldn't do this. 'I don't know.'

'Bollocks. You'd have said, "YES OF COURSE I'D

MARRY JULIAN. HE IS THE MOST AMAZING MAN ON EARTH."'

'Stop it.' I jammed my hands into my pockets. 'Julian's in New York and I'm here. And we've started new lives.'

'Meh.'

'Don't do that, Helen. It's working for me, this new life. I'm actually happy.'

Helen squeezed my arm. 'Sorry. I can see that, really I can. And I promised myself I wouldn't do this. I just . . . I just wish everything was different. Julian's so amazing it's beyond a joke. And yet he's still humble and nice and bumbly. Oh, God, maybe *I*'m in love with him. Phil? Phil, sweetheart, could you come and snog my face off?'

'No,' Phil shouted back. 'Jan and I are looking for moles.'

Helen sighed. 'No, I do love Phil, not Julian. But I wish you could just get back together with him.'

'Well, I can't. Poor old Violet would probably kill me, apart from anything else!'

Helen smiled briefly. 'Yes. Poor old Violet. She didn't take it too well, did she?'

'No. And I feel really, really guilty about that. She hasn't the faintest idea.' Violet had not come to college on the final day, and her bum chums, Sophie and Summer, had reported in the canteen that she was devastated. Not knowing what to do I'd sent her a lame text message, to which I'd received a feature-length reply about how TOTALLY FINE she was about it.

'Stop blaming yourself,' Helen instructed. 'Your behaviour was exemplary and her broken heart is not your problem. Plus she's Violet Elphinstone. She'll probably be engaged to David Cameron by the time the spring term starts. Well, maybe not him. But someone influential.'

Eventually Helen sidled off to persuade Phil to give her that kiss and Jan threw me over his shoulder and made me kiss him upside down. I laughed until I cried, especially when he dropped me on my head, then wondered how it was that I could be so happy with one man while being unable to completely forget about another.

I hung back as the group made their way down the hill towards the Lido and Helen's flat. It was four o'clock, and in the twilight hundreds of windows were illuminated. I imagined the board games, post-binge slumbers, fractious children and drunken Wham! singing, and, in spite of my resolve not to think about them, pictured the scene at my parents' house. Dad would be asleep, quietly and tidily, with his pipe lying along the arm of his chair, and Mum would be in the kitchen tidying up because she never really sat down. Lisa and Dennis would be smoking and eating chocolate, sorting out punch-ups and tantrums among their children, and Mum's ancient aunt, Gloria, would be watching *EastEnders* with her dog that looked like a rat. The picture was so clear, the smells so vivid, the over-heated fug so familiar that I felt a pain in my chest. *I should be there*, I thought sadly. *I should be part of that.*

I had no idea what the truth was any more. Whether my family blamed me, disliked me or indeed had any feelings towards me at all. Very little had been said in the conversations we'd had since my visit to Stourbridge, and the telling silence at the end of the last call, when Mum didn't ask what my Christmas plans were, spoke volumes.

But a small seed of doubt had been niggling away at me since that conversation with Helen earlier: *could I be wrong?*

I'd been confused ever since I'd seen Mum telling me, in genuine shock and distress, that she didn't blame me for Fiona's death, then her hand manically waving us off that night, such a contrast with her stooped, sad body that I'd had to wonder if it was a code – an unspoken communication; a sign that she cared but had no idea how to say so.

Could I be wrong? Did Mum actually care? And Dad, too, behind all those pipes and copies of the *Sun*?

Then there was my conversation with Stevie in the canteen recently when she'd told me she'd sent Julian away because she was frightened for him and didn't know what else to do. Did it mean she didn't care about him? Of course not. She had cried every day and was clearly still blaming herself two decades later.

Could that have been what Mum was doing for Fiona in sending her to ballet school? Could she have made the decision because she was scared witless about how her little niece was turning out – and had no idea what to do with her?

The likelihood that she'd just wanted to get rid of her seemed far greater, given that she'd repeatedly tried to stop me getting too close to Fiona, but maybe that was part of it too. Maybe she was trying to protect me. Maybe she felt history repeating itself and didn't want me to experience what she'd gone through with Aunty Mandy.

I called Barry. 'Christmas fuckin' GREETIN'S to you, Chicken,' he shouted. 'Are you havin' a crisis?'

'Ha! Happy Christmas to you too. Not a crisis, just wondering if I should call my family to say hi . . . And I

424

can't make up my mind ... And I'd ask Helen but she's busy trying to stop Jan breaking into the Lido cos he wants to take a skinny dip.'

'Oh, my days.' He sighed. 'Of course you should call them, Chicken. I know they're crazy ogres but you love them, don't you?'

'Yes,' I said, surprised.

And so it was settled. Helen bundled Jan inside and I sat at a frosty table outside the Prince Regent and called home. And although all we said was 'Merry Christmas' and 'What did you eat?' and 'It's really cold, isn't it?' I finished the call with a new glow. 'You take care,' Dad mumbled. 'All the best.' Rather than hearing 'all the best' and feeling angry and upset that Dad was speaking to me as if I were a distant colleague, I instead heard the 'You take care.'

There was still a lot to wade through, and a lot that I didn't think I could ever forgive. But I was willing to try.

Scene Twenty-nine

'Why not? Sally, this is an act of love!'

Jan Borsos was trying to persuade me to let him throw doughnuts at my breasts, like erotic hoopla.

'I'm too cold to get my boobs out!'

Jan grumbled, putting the doughnuts away. 'But you will have nipples enough big for hoops in this cold weather,' he protested.

I pulled Jan's frilly duvet over me, giggling. We were in his single bed in halls after a long and lovely day sledging in the Surrey hills. The south-east was six inches deep in snow and, of course, Jan had chosen that day to demand a trip into the English countryside. Tomorrow was our first day back at college and I'd come to Jan's in the hope of a longer sleep and a shorter journey to South Kensington.

He went off to the loo, muttering darkly that he'd had enough of this stupid British winter: it meant that I spent most of my time covered up in fleecy pyjamas and one-sies, which meant reduced access to my body.

I fiddled idly with my diamante ring, wondering what the term would bring.

What would it be like at college without Julian? *It'll be*

good. I can really knuckle down with my training and La Bohème. *Julian's definitely done me a favour!*

The ring got stuck on my knuckle and, for the thousandth time, I thought about taking the bloody thing off and throwing it away. It really was a monstrosity and it was always catching on my clothes. But I couldn't. Not yet. It was right, not talking to Fiona any more, but I couldn't quite bring myself to throw it away. It was like the last piece of her that I had, the last scrap of our time in New York together.

The ring stayed.

Jan appeared in the bathroom doorway. With a snaking hip movement he threw off his towel and leapfrogged into the bed. 'Will we have sexual intercourses?' he asked me sweetly.

I could wallow around in the past or I could enjoy the present. What was it to be?

'Yes,' I said firmly. 'Yes, we will.'

Term started, bringing with it a tranche of rehearsal schedules, instrument-wielding music students and icy gusts of wind.

Rehearsals began in the second week of term, a short but nonetheless agonizing wait. But I stayed afloat. I didn't give in to the terror. I'd sung rather brilliantly at Peter Ingle's Christmas concert and was determined to stay on an upward trajectory.

It wasn't so much that my fear of singing had vanished but that I now found myself with the tools to fight it. Every time I felt myself panic at the thought of singing Mimi I remembered one of the things Brian had taught me or I simply relived the night Julian had helped me out of my wardrobe for good. And that same sense of quiet strength filled me once more.

Most days I listened to *La Bohème*, barely able to believe that I would sing those lines in front of an audience of several hundred people. It was almost laughable. I had been out of my wardrobe a mere three months!

But sing them I would, Brian told me, in our first singing lesson of the New Year. 'I'll be with you every step of the way,' he promised.

'A big *poufff* breath,' he cried, from the piano, a few minutes later. 'I want you to fully engage!' And I'd smiled, because now I knew exactly what he was talking about. I knew what to do when he told me to inhabit my body, or to open up my folds. I sang a top C sharp without great difficulty and could sustain decent volume on a low E. I could make jokes using Italian music terms.

'It was all there already,' Brian said merrily, handing me Tatyana's aria from *Eugene Onegin*. 'You had done such fantastic work with your video tapes, Sally, you just needed to learn the nuts and bolts. But now we're really under the bonnet, fine-tuning.'

'I love it,' I admitted. 'I really love it.'

'And so you should, my girl! You sound sensational. And you should know that we singing teachers never say things like that. We're tough.'

I smiled. 'It's your brilliant teaching.'

Brian shook his head. 'No, my dear. It's all you. I'm so proud of you. Prouder than I can say.'

And then, of course, I started crying, and even Brian got a little misty-eyed, and we had to stop for a glass of water and a little hug. 'I'm a battleaxe with all of my other students,' he claimed. 'This won't do!'

In the canteen I found myself to have become more sociable, and marvelled as I watched myself as if in the third person, an integral member of a family of singers drifting in and out of the Singers' Table.

I needn't have worried about Violet. She was a lot more subdued than normal in the first few weeks, but she was still Violet Elphinstone, still pretending to be my friend while hating me, and still the most attractive woman in England. Rumours were already circulating (at her instigation) about her friendship with a silver-medal-winning Olympic rower.

The second week brought the start of our music calls for *La Bohème* with Colin, the opera's conductor.

I walked into the rehearsal room on our first day, desperately proud of myself for doing so without dying, and found Jan standing in the middle of the room, his eyes like saucers. He was staring at the *répétiteur*, a rather passionate-looking girl with long raven hair and blood-red lips. She was smiling at him coquettishly. 'Hello, baby,' she said, in a Russian accent.

Jan seemed to be at risk of a seizure so I pulled out a chair for him. 'Jan?'

He continued to stare at the girl sitting by the piano.

I looked at her, then at Jan, and sensed a great bolt of energy passing between them.

'Dima?' Jan croaked. 'It is you?'

I took Jan's chair and sat on it myself. Jan's ex-wife was our *répétiteur*.

Excellent.

Helen, who walked in a minute or two later, worked it out in less than five seconds. I knew this because she looked at me sharply and mouthed, 'ARE YOU OK?' in full view of Dima and Jan. Which was fine because they were still staring at each other.

'Hi,' Helen said minxily, walking over to the piano. 'I'm Helen. I'm playing Musetta.'

'I know,' Dima said, breaking eye contact with Jan for a few seconds. Her accent told of exotic train journeys and vodka, which was just about all I knew of Russia. 'It is pleasant to meet you and to be working on *La Bohème*. I have loved it since I was ten,' she purred. *Which must have been only a few weeks ago*, I thought, taking her in. She was tall, much taller than Jan, and had slender limbs and cold, creamy skin with an elasticity and firmness I'd long forgotten.

Jan Borsos came briefly to his senses, realizing that it was perhaps not optimal to conduct an unexpected reunion with his ex-wife in full view of Helen and me. 'May we . . .' he faltered. 'Can we . . . have some minutes together, my friends? We were previously married.'

Helen smiled and nodded. 'Take all the time you need.'

Jan became aware of me again. 'Sally,' he said apologetically, grasping my hand. 'I want you to meet my past wife. I was not knowing she is going to be here. I am surprised. I am also happy,' he added, catching a dangerous flash in Dima's eye. I didn't much rate Jan Borsos's chances in a fight with her.

'Oh, this is your girlfriend,' Dima said serenely. 'It is nice to meet you.' She held out her hand and, just like Helen, I walked to the piano to shake it. 'Do not worry.' She smiled. 'I do not try to take Jan back!'

I swiped the air, muttering things like 'not at all', even though it was very plain that she was here to do just that. I smiled almost politely at Jan Borsos as I left, knowing that I'd lost him. He was mesmerized.

And the saddest thing was that I didn't mind. Looking at his little face, ablaze with fear and excitement, I knew that that woman was his true match.

I stepped outside into the corridor with Helen and she closed the door behind us.

'Wow,' I said.

'*Wow*,' Helen agreed. 'So, that's quite an issue for your relationship, eh?'

'Oh, Helen, stop it!'

'I'm just saying!'

'I know what you're saying.'

'I mean,' Helen countered, 'she looks like she's still keen on Jan, doesn't she?'

'Of course she is. This is Jan Borsos we're talking about! Married, divorced, orphaned, all by the age of twenty-three. And then he walked across Europe with only one shoe. What's not to love?' I was speaking brightly, as if it were hilarious that we'd both witnessed Jan falling head over heels back in love with Dima in less than a minute.

To my embarrassment and fury, I felt a tear come out of my eye, then another. Helen rubbed my arm. 'Oh, Sally, they might not –'

'No, it's OK!' I gasped, blotting my face with my sleeve. Helen handed me a tissue from her pocket but it did little to stem the flow. 'I'm fine, I'm fine,' I told her.

And that was the problem. I *was* fine. It was OK. I'd

woken up this morning with Jan in my bed, had lovely, slightly bonkers sex with him, eaten toast with him in my kitchen and giggled all the way to South Kensington on the Piccadilly Line. I'd walked into the college holding his hand. Then I'd walked into a rehearsal room and lost him.

And while it was sad, it was completely OK.

'He's been there for me at a very difficult time of my life.' I sniffled. 'But I don't want to sound like I was using him. I wasn't, I adore him . . . He means a lot to me.'

Helen handed me another tissue and put her arms round me. 'I know, Sal. I'm glad he was there. And I'm sorry to wind you up. Jan Borsos is a gem and this is definitely a sad moment.'

But as I began to pull myself together, she added, 'Perhaps you could just send a quick email to Julian, though. No?'

Scene Thirty

'Ahem. A-huh. Arggh. We need to talk,' Jan said. He was sitting on my living-room floor, poring over one of Barry's ballet shoes. Barry had given Jan Borsos a ballet lesson earlier, much to my amusement. I had watched them both, the two most ridiculous men I'd ever known – both so very precious to me – and welled up a little, knowing that these silly evenings would soon come to an end.

The last week since Dima had arrived had been odd, to say the least. Jan kept cornering me to tell me that everything was OK between us. That Dima's appearance had been nothing more than a huge coincidence, rather than the carefully planned and expertly staged campaign that everyone else at college knew it to have been. Dima, it had been revealed, had split up with her wealthy Belarussian husband because she had realized she was still in love with her ex, one Jan Borsos. She had gone to Budapest to find him – rather than simply sending him a message on Facebook – and had been told he'd come to London. She had flown to the UK, wangled a visa, somewhat surprisingly, and had been applying for *répétiteur* jobs at the Royal College of Music since September.

'SALLY!' Jan hissed. He was kneeling in front of the sofa. 'We must talk!'

'Oh, Jan,' I said sadly. 'There's nothing to say.'

'What are you meaning? I love you!' he said furiously. 'It is true! I am loving you!' He knelt in front of me and I realized this poor man – this poor *boy*, because that was what he looked like at that moment – was utterly shattered. His face was grey and his skin almost translucent.

'Sssh,' I said, interrupting him.

Jan blinked, confused. 'Do not stop me in anger,' he whispered. 'I am telling you things between us are OK, Sally.'

I put my finger on his lips. 'Jan.' I smiled. 'My lovely, funny, gorgeous Jan. I have loved every minute of our time together.'

Jan sat back on his heels, listening for once in silence.

'But, my darling Jan Borsos, you love Dima, and while I know how fond you are of me, it's nothing compared to what you have with her.'

'No!'

'Yes. Jan, look at yourself in the mirror. You look terrible. I know a lovesick puppy when I see one.'

Jan tried to fight me for a few seconds, then hung his head, defeated. 'Maybe this is true.'

'Definitely, Jan. I've been there in the room too. I can see the feelings between the two of you.'

'I think you are right, Sally. I am sorry,' he muttered. 'I am so sorry.'

'Don't be! Seeing you and Dima reminds me of what love is,' I said.

'You have felt strong love before? Love that could melt a mountain?'

I tried not to giggle at the metaphor. 'Yes. I've had love that could melt a mountain.'

Jan looked at me shrewdly, sitting back on his heels. 'I am thinking you have had this love with Julian Jefferson,' he said.

'*What?*'

Jan smiled, and took both of my hands. 'Do you think I am stupid?' he asked gently. 'You see the love with Dima and Jan. I see the love with Sally and Julian.'

I stared at him.

'Our time in Stourbridge was ... how do you say? ... very *fruity*,' Jan said, with a twinkle in his eye. 'But I was having fun with my sexy Sally, I did not mind.' He put his head to one side. 'Why did you not tell me about Julian?' he asked.

I shut my eyes. 'He was part of a chapter in my life I was trying to forget. He – he was there the night Fiona died. In fact, for a long time I thought it was his fault.'

Jan nodded. 'This has sense,' he said.

I opened my eyes to find him smiling. 'I *am* mad,' he said. 'But, as I tell you, I am not stupid. You must go and find Julian Jefferson!'

'I can't.' I looked down at my hands, trying not to sound too sad. 'He said we need to call it a day. Too much water under the bridge and all that.'

'No!'

'Yes. His wife died, my cousin died, we both somehow ended up at the Royal College of Music and it was a disaster. He wants me to be happy here. He's going to get on with being a singer again. It makes sense. But it's shit.'

Jan looked sad. 'I want you to have a big great love,' he said childishly. 'I do not like that it is finished.'

I shrugged. 'I guess my big love affair is going to be with *La Bohème* instead.'

Jan sighed, deflated. 'Pah.'

I leaned forward and cupped his cheeks. 'You are the most precious man I know,' I told him. He smiled, a lovely, furious, silly Jan smile. I kissed him on the lips and he stroked my hair and then we hugged each other for what felt like hours. It was the loveliest goodbye I could have imagined.

'Grow some testicles,' he whispered, as we hugged. 'Fight for him. Or send him an electronic message. I know you have enough testicles to be doing this.'

After he'd gone, I had another cry, then sat down at my desk. I thought about writing to Julian, of course. I'd thought about writing to him often, but I knew I wouldn't. Julian was no longer a part of my life.

I wrote instead to my family. I knew the chances of them coming to London to watch an opera were slim, but I was game to try.

Scene Thirty-one

April 2013, three months later

'Baby, *baaaaby*.' Dima panted like a beautifully naff pop star. She had Jan rammed up against a wall and was kissing him vigorously, as she had been doing every day since he had given in.

'Yes, yes,' Jan muttered hungrily. He was her slave and very happy about it too.

I walked on. Bloody everyone was in wild love. Helen and Phil had got married at Easter, Jan and Dima were performing live sex shows – or close approximations of live sex shows – in the corridors with gay abandon, and Barry had gone completely batty over a Canadian photographer called Teddy. He was literally manic all day long, and during the few moments when they weren't together, he would sit in my room with a fake Elizabethan lute that he'd bought in Camden Passage, screaming Tudor love songs. He was in a ballet about the Tudors, although that did not excuse anything.

I was not in love with anyone. No one I could have, anyway. And that was lucky because I was flat out rehearsing for *La Bohème* while trying to keep up with college work, plus handling my suddenly crazed housemate and trying grimly to build my relationship with my family.

We'd continued our stunted weekly phone calls but our progress, if any, was slow, and they didn't mention my forthcoming performance in *La Bohème*.

I was doing my best with them, but it hurt. Maybe I had been wrong, again.

'It's probably for the best,' Helen said, on our opening night. It was an hour before the beginners' call and we were in the middle of warming up. 'I mean, you're so nervous you're actually see-through, Sally. You don't want your folks to have to watch you weeing yourself again. Oh. Sorry. Too close to the bone?'

'HA-HA-HA-HA-HA-HA,' I shouted hysterically. 'HILARIOUS! YOU'VE MADE ME LAUGH. I FEEL LESS NERVOUS NOW. THANKS, MY LOVE!'

Helen stared at me, nodding thoughtfully. She obviously hadn't noticed until now quite how petrified I was.

'Sally,' she said slowly, 'should we get you some drugs? Legal ones, I mean. I think you might be on the verge of a psychotic outburst.'

'YesNoYesNoYesNo – ARGGGGH!'

'Right.'

She had a think and realized she had no idea what to do. 'Um, we need to sort you out, Sally, my darling. Any thoughts?'

I froze, trying to think. She was right: there was no way I could sing in this state. Everything I'd learned about courage had evaporated and I was left with insides like white-water rapids. 'Jesus,' Helen cried, catching the end of a terrified trump. 'SALLY! We have to do something! You'll kill Jan if you do one of those onstage!'

Come on, think! I implored my pounding head.

'I'll be back,' I muttered, after a short pause.

Three minutes later, I started to breathe again. It was pitch black and I had four wooden walls close by. Everything was still.

Once my pulse had slowed down, I closed my eyes. 'Fiona?' I asked into the darkness. 'Freckle? Can you help me, darling? I've gone mad and I'm shaking and guffing and mostly frozen to the spot.'

I didn't talk to Fiona any more, not since Julian had helped me let her go. But right now, sweat turning cold on my back, I needed a sense of her presence and, what's more, I felt it. Stronger than ever. It was as if her pale little hand was holding mine, down here in a wardrobe of umbrellas in the prop store.

'Freckle?' I said, into the small oblong of air. (How had I ever sung in a wardrobe?) 'Freckle? You're here, aren't you?'

Silence. A warm silence; something gentle and soothing.

'Well, any advice welcome.' I laughed nervously. 'Feeling slightly alone at the moment. What with you mincing around in Heaven or somewhere, and our family as usual ignoring me.'

I held on to my ankles as if they might run away. 'Yeah, and there's the matter of Julian,' I admitted. 'That's all a bit shit too. The whole new-life thing.'

I imagined Fiona frowning.

'But I'm trying, Freckle, my God, I'm trying! Look

how bloody brave I've been, rehearsing this thing! And trying not to care about Mum and Dad. I'm doing all right, aren't I?'

The silence swayed as if in agreement.

'I did it, Fi, I became a singer!'

I smiled into the silence.

'I'm quite good,' I added proudly.

I could feel Fiona nodding agreement. Punching the air, maybe, with some customary swearing.

'Um, but I'm still asking for your help,' I said. 'I wonder if you could make me brave again. I've kind of lost it today.'

For a short while, there was nothing. And then there was a feeling so strong it seemed almost to have a voice.

You are brave.

You are so very, very brave.

Look at you. Look where you came from and what you've been through. Look what you did! Look who you touched, who you helped. Look how humble you stayed through it all. You are remarkable, Sally Howlett. You are truly, wonderfully precious.

It doesn't matter who loves you. You love yourself now, and that's enough.

You can do it!

For a moment I stayed absolutely still, absorbing her words. An image of Julian sprang to mind, helping me step out of my wardrobe. His insistence that I could do it on my own, that I didn't need to carry on hiding, talking to Fiona.

What came next was one of the most extraordinary thoughts I'd had in my life.

That hadn't been Fiona talking. It had been me.

And it had always been me.

That small voice of courage, of self-belief: *it was mine!*

I leaned back against the wardrobe wall, giddy with astonishment.

My voice! My strength! I'd just made it sound like Fiona's voice because I'd never believed I was big or strong enough!

But I was strong enough. Somewhere, deep within me, there was a little pocket of trust. Of courage, dignity and determination. It didn't come from Fiona or Julian or Carrot or my wardrobe. *It came from me!*

You can sing Mimi bloody brilliantly, the voice said. *Get out there and do it!*

I climbed out of the wardrobe. I was going to bloody well nail this performance.

And nail it I did. My voice wobbled fearfully on my very first line, which didn't matter anyway because I was pretending to be freezing cold and candle-less in a pitch-black building. But I dipped back into that pocket of strength and my voice came back stronger than ever. Jan, transformed as Rodolfo, smiled with absolute pride as he opened his front door to me, the Mimi who might never have happened.

The performance was a blur. Before I knew it, I was bowing and people were cheering and my heart was in my throat and I could barely breathe for joy and relief and pride and exhilaration. 'You fucking did it! WE fucking did it!' Helen screamed, in my ear. 'RAAAAAH!'

Just as we stepped back for the curtains to close for a final time, Hugo, the head of the faculty, walked onstage.

Amid the euphoria I registered a mild sense of irritation: I was looking forward to the curtains closing properly so we could all jump up and down and scream and hug and hump each other.

Hugo had been rambling on for a couple of minutes when I realized that the audience had started cheering again and the cast had started gasping and hugging each other. 'SHIIIIIIT!' Helen was crying. 'SHIIIIIIT!'

'Eh?'

'For God's sake!' she said, as the curtains closed for the final time. 'Didn't you hear any of that?'

'No.'

'We're going to do a summer exchange with the Juilliard!' she hissed. I looked blank but Jan's face was exploding. 'We perform in NEW YORK!' he yelled.

'AT THE FUCKING METROPOLITAN OPERA!' Helen screamed. 'OH, MY GOD! WE'RE DOING A PERFORMANCE AT THE MET! THE METROPOLITAN FRIGGING OPERA!'

I stared at them. Out of the corner of my eye I could see Hector the ginger bouffant having some sort of a faint, then Noon grabbing Summer and snogging her hard.

'WHAT?'

'The Juilliard is one of the world's most prestigious performing arts schools, Sally, you IDIOT, and they're based at the Lincoln Center WHERE THE FUCKING MET IS. WE ARE DOING AN EXCHANGE WITH THEM. THEY PERFORM THEIR OPERA AT THE ALBERT HALL AND WE PERFORM OURS AT THE MET. AT THE FUCKING MET.'

442

She paused, wild-eyed, staring at me.

I stared, wild-eyed, right back at her.

'You mean, I –'

'YES! I MEAN YOU ARE GOING TO PLAY MIMI IN *LA BOHÈME* AT THE FUCKING METROPOLITAN OPERA HOUSE!'

'Oh, my God,' I croaked.

Helen laughed, then started to cry. 'We are performing at the Met. We are performing at the Met. We are – oh, my God . . .'

After a lot of screaming and more champagne than was advisable in the middle of a run of performances, I slid out of college, strangely deflated. It had probably been the best day of my life, yet there was still something missing. Specifically, my family. I hadn't expected them to come, or even to acknowledge my letter, but the certainty that everyone was now off to the pub to meet their proud families stung just a little too much.

Barry and Teddy were coming to watch the next performance in a couple of days; I'd go out then.

I smiled politely at a family huddled by the doorway, waiting for their clever offspring to appear. The father was wearing an Aston Villa scarf, which made me feel even sadder. Dad. Why wasn't my dad here?

'There she is!' said the father. He was pointing at me.

'All right, sis!' yelled an overweight man, who also had a Villa scarf on. 'Surprise!'

I stared at them, uncertain as to what was happening here. Who were these weirdos? Noon's family, probably. You couldn't trust a family who called their son Noon.

'Surprise, Sally, ha-ha!' echoed the woman. Then she

clapped her hand over her mouth in case she'd been too loud.

I stared at them, goggle-eyed, and they stared at me. My family. My family were here, for the first time in my life. Mum was clutching Dad as if she were a sapling and he an oak. Dad was trying to go along with the oak role but he was far too excited. 'You were FANTASTIC, you were!' he cried. 'Great!'

Tears filled my eyes. 'Bet you didn't expect us, eh?' crowed Dennis's wife, Lisa. In all the years I'd known Lisa she'd only ever worn jeans and fake Ugg boots. Tonight she was wearing some sort of a dress. With a heel! A medium heel!

'Great legs,' I said, staring at them in wonder. My family were here!

'You were great,' Mum said nervously. She moved over and patted my arm self-consciously. 'We were ever so proud, and the story was actually quite easy to follow . . . Although I was gutted that you didn't sing that "Nessun dorma" song. Do you remember when Paul Potts sang it on *Britain's Got Talent*? It was still great, though, and now you're off to New York to do it!'

It was the most Mum had said to me in one go for as long as I could remember. I smiled tearfully at her, feeling no compulsion whatsoever to explain that 'Nessun dorma' was from a different opera and written for a male tenor. Mum and Dad had got into a car and driven to London. Not for Dennis and Lisa, but for me. For me!

I didn't hug them, because I knew it would be a bit too much. But I touched Mum's hand as it rested on my arm and I half punched Dad on his anorak and I saw it in their eyes: love. *Real love.* Love way out of its comfort zone, but indisputable love all the same, suffused with pride and respect.

'I can't believe you're here.' I snuffled. 'Thank you so much!'

'Weren't going to miss this, were we?' Dad said shyly. 'Our Sal up there with the big knobs! Next stop, New York!'

'Do you . . . Do you fancy getting a bite to eat? Or a drink?' I asked tentatively. 'I'm starving?' I trailed off, allowing them ample opportunity to say no.

'What do you think, Pat?' Mum turned to Dad. She looked keen, albeit anxious.

Lisa spoke: 'We've got to get back for the babysitter,' she said. 'But the trains run till midnight. You'll be fine. You know where you're going, right?'

'Right,' Dad said.

'Right,' Mum echoed dazedly. 'I reckon we could have a quick bite,' she said. 'But, Sally, it's after ten – won't everywhere be shut?'

I smiled. 'London never shuts.'

'We surprised her good and proper.' Dennis chuckled as he and Lisa walked off towards the tube. I still couldn't believe it.

We went to Byron Burger and Mum asked if they did ham, egg and chips. Every now and then she stared at the young, rich Kensingtonites around her in their quilted jackets and ruby trousers, bewildered beyond any imagining. 'These girls look like they should be in a TV advert,' she muttered at one point. 'Why are they so dressed up, Sally? It's a Tuesday night.'

I said I had yet to understand the people in these parts and we all laughed. It didn't last long, the communal Howlett laugh, but that it had happened at all was a miracle.

'So, how's it going with Jan?' Dad asked bravely. 'He was an energetic young thing!'

I smiled. 'We split up. He got back together with his ex-wife. Which is fine,' I added hastily, when they looked panicky. 'I think we were just very good friends, really.' Mum and Dad nodded. While they both had exceptionally conservative values, they watched enough soaps and TV dramas to accept that young people *did* do mad things, like getting divorced and changing their minds in the space of four years.

'And what about the other one? The one with the funny accent?' Mum asked. She blushed slightly. 'He was ever so nice, he was.'

'They are both very nice,' I said firmly. I still wasn't OK about how they'd behaved towards Jan that night.

'Oh, yes, yes! Jan was nice too. I hope he didn't think badly of . . . I hope he didn't . . .' Mum looked anxiously at Dad, asking him to take over. For once he did. The trip to London had evidently emboldened him.

'What your mum's trying to say is that we hope he didn't take offence when we were talking about the Chinese. Or, um, the Eastern Europeans,' he mumbled. 'We didn't mean anything bad, Sal, honest, it was just one of those things.'

I took a deep breath. Here was another fork in the path. I could turn left, accept what they were saying and move on, or I could turn right and continue to wallow in resentment. 'It's OK,' I said, choosing the left-hand path and feeling rather proud of myself for it. 'Jan wasn't offended. It was me who was, on his behalf. And I clearly didn't need to be.'

I paused as the waitress put my burger in front of me. 'Sometimes I get upset about things I've decided other people are thinking,' I added quietly.

There was a long silence. Was I going to go there?

Yes, I was. I needed to. And for all their fear of confrontation – of any sort of conversation, really – I sensed that my parents wanted to talk now.

'For example. Deciding that you two blamed me for Fiona,' I began. 'I don't believe that any more. In fact, I think the only person who blamed me for Fi's death was me.' Mum's eyes glazed over with distress but, like me, she seemed determined to stick with the conversation. Perhaps we all knew that the gap between us had grown too wide; that this was our last chance to bridge it.

'I'm beginning to wonder if some of the other things I've thought about you aren't true either.' I coughed nervously; Dad followed suit. We sat and did some rubbish coughs for a bit.

'I'm sure it's all OK,' Mum began, in what she probably thought was a soothing voice. (It was not.) 'We can put it behind us.'

'No, I, um, I've not finished.'

Dad did some more coughing.

To everyone's dismay I started crying. And continued

to cry. In the end I gave up even trying to stop. Years and years of sadness and frustration and disappointment leaked out of me like a thick, sad soup. I knew Mum and Dad loved me and yet – and yet –

'Why didn't you call me?' I wept. 'Why didn't you call me after New York? Why didn't you do anything after Fi died?' Great sobs racked me. 'I felt like *I* was dying, I could hardly breathe at times. Mum, Dad, why didn't you call me?'

Mum and Dad stared alternately at their plates and at me. Both were anguished but neither really knew what to do.

My sobs eventually lost momentum.

Then: 'I'm so sorry,' Mum whispered. 'I'm so sorry, our Sal.' A tear fell out of her eye into the lap of her new trousers. 'I . . . we . . .' She wrung her hands. 'I didn't know what to say. I'm not very good with words, me. And you know what your dad's like.'

Dad nodded in guilty agreement. 'We never meant no harm,' he muttered. 'We were worried about you, Sal, but you never called us and we . . .' He scratched his temple tiredly. 'You seem to like this life of yours down here.' He was almost whispering. I had to lean forward to hear him amid the horsy shouts of posh people. 'You didn't seem to want to come home or speak to us either, so we thought we'd . . .' He trailed off. 'We're sorry, Sally.'

I wanted to get angry, to shout that it didn't matter how they *thought* I was, that it didn't matter that they were 'not very good with words'. I was their daughter! I'd practically lost my sister!

'That's why we decided to come down,' Mum faltered. 'Thought, you know, try and patch things up . . .'

'I feel like you've always disapproved of me,' I persisted miserably. 'My job, my decision to live here, going to New York, going to college. You've questioned it all, everything. You've never sounded happy for me.'

'That's not true,' Mum objected. 'We just worry about you, bab. We don't want no harm coming to you like it did to – other people.' Her lip trembled. It was the second time in my life that I'd seen Mum in tears and it was strangely moving.

I sighed, accepting that, however mad it sounded, she was telling the truth.

'OK.' I took a deep breath. 'But . . . what about Fiona? Did you care about her?' Just saying her name, here in front of my parents, started me crying again.

'Like she was our own,' Mum said immediately. 'She was more like Mandy than Mandy herself. Of course we cared about her.'

'Then why? Why couldn't I be friends with her? Why did you send her to London? Why were you *always* telling her off?'

Mum started crying properly. She cried into her hand, pulling a worn hankie out of her sleeve, and Dad put his arm round her, which made me cry even harder because I'd never seen him do that.

And as we cried I felt myself somehow let go. I stopped fighting. Because it was all there in front of me: the truth of my family. The reasons why they were as they were. I didn't need to keep on poking around.

At this moment I knew – had perhaps always known – that they simply hadn't known what to do with Fiona, that they were terrified of her losing control, and that they'd kept on punishing her in the desperate hope that she'd change. That they'd sent her to London because they were out of ideas, and that they'd tried to stop me getting too close because they feared the worst. And, of course, the worst had happened anyway and I'd experienced all the desperate agony from which they'd tried so fruitlessly to protect me.

It made everything no less painful, but it at least made sense.

Mum cried, Dad comforted her, and I cried. Dad even reached out and took my hand too. Neither of them seemed to care that they were being emotional in public.

'It's OK. You don't need to explain,' I said eventually. I sounded calmer; kinder now. 'I think I get it.'

Mum eventually stopped crying and Dad, probably quite relieved, removed his arm from her shoulders. There was an awkward transition as we all came back to the busy restaurant. I wondered if Mum might one day want to talk about her own dreadful loss, but small steps. This was not the time.

'Well, that was very dramatic,' Mum said shakily. Dad got to work with his burger. *Please don't make us talk about this any longer*, their body language begged.

I smiled wearily. I was done. I was also exhausted. The adrenalin had stopped and I was left with my parents, who loved me probably quite a lot but would never really know how to show it. And that was OK. I'd learn, somehow, to accept it. In fact, I was already halfway there. Enough of anger and sadness. Enough.

I took them up to Baker Street to get the Metropolitan Line and Dad fell asleep twice en route. Mum alternated between reading adverts out loud and talking about tonight's opera and Paul Potts off *Britain's Got Talent*.

Just as we went to say goodbye, she put her hand on my arm. 'That Julian,' she began awkwardly.

'Yes?' I asked innocently.

'Is he the one you were, um, dating in New York?'

'Er – yes. How did you know?'

Mum smiled sheepishly. 'Fiona sent us a postcard. Said you were seeing a man called Julian who had a half-Devon half-American accent.'

I was taken aback. I didn't remember Fiona being capable of buying stamps and posting an airmail postcard. It was rather touching, especially that she'd told them about me. 'Um, well, yes. That was him.'

Mum looked pleased. 'How funny that he ended up being one of your teachers!' Her eyes narrowed. 'He was gorgeous, he was,' she said. 'I wondered if you and him . . . you know, now that you're single again . . .'

'He's in New York,' I said brightly. 'Went back at Christmas. He went back to being a singer.'

Mum nodded. 'Oh.'

There was an awkward moment when they got on the Metropolitan Line train – to hug or not to hug? – we settled on a half hand-claspy thing and then Mum turned back to me. 'You still like him, don't you?' she said shyly.

'And we thought he was great, we did. Don't let him go, Sal! Send him an email!'

It might have been that I got carried away in the excitement of seeing my family, or perhaps it was just that I couldn't take it any more. Another moment without contact. But whatever it was, against all my better instincts, against everything Julian had asked of me, I went home and wrote to him.

Scene Thirty-two

From: Sally Howlett [mailto howler_78@gmail.com)
To: Julian Bell [mailto JulianBellSmells@hotmail.com)
Sent: Tuesday, 16 April 2013, 23.59.55 GMT

Hello you.

I hope it's OK to contact you and I hope you're well.

Tonight I played Mimi and it went brilliantly and I didn't die. Mum and Dad came. And Dennis and Lisa. We sorted some stuff out and I think we're going to be OK. I can still hardly believe it.

I know it was never your intention but you really helped me arrive at this point with my family and I wanted to say thank you.

You told me once that you sent your wife off to do that audition in Vienna because you thought it would help get her well. Did it work? No. But it was the best solution you could come up with at the time. You told me that when Catherine died, your mum forced you to move in with her because she didn't know how else to look after you. You said it probably helped your mum more than it helped you.

It really got me thinking about the things we do to protect those we love. We all try to do what we think is best but really

453

we have no idea! As often as not we can make things worse. Look at how I spent years being Fiona's mother because I thought I could save her from herself. Did it work? No! But I was doing what I thought was best because I loved her.

I am realizing, finally, that my family aren't monsters. They're just a bit useless and emotionally constipated, but most of the stuff I couldn't forgive them for happened because they loved me. And Fiona.

So, again, thank you so much for helping me see that. It took a while but I'm there now and I think we can start again as a family, which is amazing.

I miss you. I wish you were part of all of this. I understand that for us to move on and lead our new lives we can't be in touch but . . . I dunno. I miss you.

If I don't hear from you I promise I won't contact you again.

Love, Sally X

I didn't hear from him. And although I was sad, I knew it was right. I'd lost Julian but I'd gained a family and my life was truly beginning again.

Act Four was over. I was ready for Act Five to begin.

ACT FIVE

Scene One

May 2013, one month later

Act Five started well.

Then disaster struck. It was a disaster with a Hungarian accent.

Spring had come slowly but when it did arrive it was beautiful. 'I reckon it's going to be boiling in New York,' Helen remarked, shovelling a vast spoonful of syrupy porridge into her mouth. Her new wedding ring sparkled in the sunlight streaming in from the plate-glass window beside us and I basked in the oddly summery feel of Terminal Five, even though it was only May.

We were sitting in a café near the check-in desks, having got there five hours too early because of wild excitement. Jan was so crazed he'd had to go to the toilet and had been there for quite a long time.

'I'm not sure it'll be boiling just yet, Helen . . .'

'Rubbish. New York's always boiling, isn't it?' I thought about my own boiling hot summer there, nearly two years ago, and felt a twinge of sadness. Helen cocked her head to one side. 'Do you still love him?' she asked conversationally.

I chose to ignore her.

'Oi,' she said, poking me in the ribs.

'Bog off.'

'No. Answer my question.'

I sighed. I did still love Julian. It was now five months since I'd seen or heard from him, yet nothing had changed. Every part of me loved him. Tibia. Lungs. Kidneys. Bladder. *Even my bladder still loved Julian Bell.*

I snorted, wondering if I was going insane.

'What?'

'I was just thinking something odd about my bladder.'

'Well, stop it. Answer my question.'

I stopped eating and looked at her. 'Yes,' I said. 'Yes, I do. I think it'll take a long time for me to stop loving him.' Her face lit up. 'And no. I'm not going to try and find him in New York.'

Helen's feline eyes narrowed. 'You're mental,' she announced.

'No.' I laughed. 'I'm just respecting him. He asked me not to contact him, and I disobeyed him. He didn't reply to my stupid email and nor should he have done. It. Is. Totally. Over.'

'Meh. OK.' Helen helped herself to the rest of my sultanas. 'But I think you're a dick,' she added sulkily. 'By the way, where's Jan? He can't still be having a dump, can he?'

Jan was in a bad mood at the moment, which was an odd thing to witness. When our piano rehearsals for *La Bohème* had finished and Dima had found herself without further work (the college staff were fed up with the live sex shows) she had demanded that Jan go back to Minsk with her, and when he had refused, there had been some fairly dramatic scenes. She had gone and Jan had howled with agony for days on end, uncertain as to whether to finish his diploma or follow his love.

When I'd asked him about her yesterday his face had reddened. 'Ah, Dima. We are writing many letters.'

'And?'

Jan's face had reddened further and he'd grinned furiously. 'I think there is maybe a reconissance.'

'"Reconciliation", Jan.'

'Yes, yes. She is writing me a letter now. I think she is ready to decide what we do!'

I had touched his cheek briefly. 'That's great. You deserve to be happy.'

He had nodded enthusiastically. 'I am very afraid of Dima,' he'd admitted cheerfully. 'But if she tells me she will have me back in her life, I will be MUCH JOY.'

I scanned the check-in hall. No sign. 'He'll be around somewhere,' I said. 'Probably making a long-distance call. I just hope Dima doesn't upset him. We need him to be at his absolute best this week!'

But Jan didn't check in, and he didn't board the plane. By the time they closed the cabin door Helen, the rest of the cast and I were green and vomity. We all knew what Jan was capable of.

Surely he hadn't gone and . . .

He had. On arrival at JFK we sprinted to the Delta desk, desperate with hope. But he was not on the next flight or the one after that. Delta confirmed that he'd never checked in, and when we called his mobile phone, it was switched off.

Jan had done a runner. And there were no prizes for guessing where he'd gone. Neither was there any hope he'd come back. We were fucked. *La Bohème* would be a disaster.

It was there when we checked into our hotel in Murray Hill. A mad, scrawled fax, which I would one day come to laugh about. Not any time soon, though.

> *Sally and everyone, I am very sorry but I have business in Minsk. I have a wedding to go to and it is my own wedding. I am marriage Dima my love. I do know that this is not very brilliant. I am very sorry. I am being given no choices by my bride. She is Bridezilla! Hector is my understudy and we know he is very excellent. I do know he is going to be very happy, and Sally is going to be probably happy also, because she is thinking that I do not perform a very perfect Rodolfo at the moment. I love you all! I am sorry! I know you do all understand! Best wishes and love!! JAN BORSOS!!!!!!*

Scene Two

It was meant to be day one of our rehearsals but everyone had been summoned to an emergency meeting in the stalls. Once upon a time I might have felt pleasure to be sitting inside that vast jewellery box of an auditorium but today I alternated between fury and despair. Jetlag and disappointment threatened to suffocate me. Just for once, I hated Jan.

We should have started rehearsing Hector straight away that morning but Hector, to his utter devastation, had caught a cold on the plane and was no more able to sing Rodolfo's part than Helen was.

He sat alone in the auditorium, trying not to cry. 'My one chance,' he croaked. 'My one bloody chance.' Everyone sent him sympathetic glances but kept well away from him.

The second understudy, Noon, had not come to New York because he had a huge audition and, besides, second covers never got the chance to go on. Zachary, the director, and Colin, the conductor, looking quite ill themselves, had called in the Met's bigwigs.

'So who do we get in?' Carol was a creative executive at

the Met, a woman whose face (and large, powerful backside) inspired respect and awe. She stared at her group of minions.

'Luigi Donato's in town,' one offered. 'And so's Claude-Pierre Pascale. Does anyone know what their schedule is?'

I gaped. They were two of the finest opera singers in the world. Literally, the *world*.

'No,' Carol snapped. 'Claude's on as Faust on Friday. He can't sing *La Bohème* on top of that. And Luigi's a dramatic tenor.'

A short argument ensued, during which it was argued that Luigi Donato was a perfectly viable lyric tenor and not a dramatic tenor at all.

I let it all fly over my head; I was still only getting to grips with these terms. And, really, I didn't care. I could feel my chance slipping away from me and I couldn't stand it.

'Julian Jefferson's singing again,' someone was saying. 'He brought the house down singing Lensky at the Civic Chicago last month.'

I felt Helen's eyes burning a hole in my side.

Carol sat back, folding her arms. 'Now there's an idea,' she said thoughtfully. 'We've been talking to him about next season . . . It'd be a great little teaser for his fans . . .'

'I agree. He'd be perfect if we could get him,' Zachary chipped in. 'Plus he trained at the Royal College of Music back in the nineties. Having him as Rodolfo would make a nice little story. Star alumnus comes back to save the day.'

No, I mouthed weakly at Helen, who had gone puce with excitement. *No no no.*

Yes yes yes! she mouthed back.

'Sally?' Zachary was looking at me. 'Did you get on with Julian Jefferson when he was coaching at the Royal College? Do you think you could sing opposite him?'

'Mergh,' I said weakly.

'*Excuse me?*' Carol was not in the mood for indecision.

'I suppose so,' I tried. My voice was barely a whisper.

Carol whipped out her phone and stood up to leave the room. 'I'm getting on to him right away,' she barked.

Scene Three

Although it was pointless, I prayed that Julian would suddenly have flown to the Antarctic to live in a penguin colony. Or that he'd just say no. After all, it was he who'd been so emphatic that we should move on.

He did neither. Two hours later I found myself rolled up into a terrified ball in my plush, red-carpeted dressing room trying to ignore the tannoy, over which was being transmitted something both awful and wonderful: 'Mr Jefferson to the stage, please, for warm-up, that's Mr Jefferson to the stage, please, for warm-up. Thank you.'

Terror tore through me. What would I say to him?

'Miss Howlett to the stage for warm-up, please. That's Miss Howlett for warm-up, please.'

When I walked on to the stage, as if in a strange dream, Julian was stretching, lost in thought.

He was *there*. Metres away. All six foot of him, wearing his monkey T-shirt and jeans, looking much younger than the tired, anxious man I'd last seen in London. His face was lined with concentration but there was a lightness to him that I hadn't seen in two years. I couldn't put my finger on what it was, exactly, just . . . a freedom. A happiness that I'd long forgotten.

He's met someone! I decided immediately. Apart from anything else, there was product in his hair. An absence of fluff. And his glasses were new. *Telltale signs*, I muttered madly to myself. *Telltale bloody signs.*

I tried to stay in the wings but Helen grabbed my hand and marched me on to the stage. 'HI, JULIAN!' she shouted. He straightened up.

When he saw me his face broke into that beautiful smile and I knew I was done for.

I began to understand what people meant when they talked about being weak at the knees. He walked over to us, grinning and saying things like 'Hey, lovely girls!' and 'Isn't this funny?' and I had to hold so hard on to Helen's hand that I nearly pulled it off.

I loved him more than ever. A huge ball in my chest, pressing on everything.

Julian hugged Helen first. 'Great to see you, Helen,' he said easily. 'And onstage at the Met too! I'm so happy you guys got a chance like this.'

Helen gazed up at him. 'God, you're so fit I can't stand it,' she said. 'Do you mind if I go and warm up over there?'

Julian roared with laughter, then turned back to me. There were no butterflies in my stomach but there were at least twenty giant birds.

'Hello,' I bleated.

'Hello,' Julian said. He renewed his huge, dazzling megastar of a smile, then gave me a brief, perfunctory hug. 'Great to see you, my old buddy,' he said cheerfully.

My old buddy? *MY OLD **BUDDY**?*

Worried that I might start howling – or that I might just slide to the floor – I stepped back from him. It was all too much. The feel of him around me, the smell of his laundry powder, the smell of his *skin*. 'You smell the same,' some goon mumbled.

I did a double-take. Had I said that?

Oh, hellfire and damnation. I had said that.

'I hate myself. Ignore me,' I told him.

Julian grinned. 'We should all go for a drink later,' he said comfortably. *We should all*, I noted.

He must have met someone. I mean, they said he was back singing again. Which had to mean he'd nailed the whole 'sorting my life out' thing. And if he'd sorted his life out, he must, of course, be *dating*. Bloody Americans. Why did they have to DATE? Why couldn't they just spend their time ignoring each other, like the English? If he'd stayed in London he would never have met anyone. He'd be alone and unhappy, like me, but at least he wouldn't be DATING.

His new girlfriend was lean of bum, I knew instantly. And as relaxed and lovely and amazing as him. She probably wore vintage clothes and had a pretty little pixie face and a –

'Hello?' Julian was watching me with that bloody smile. 'Are you OK? You look fucking mental, Sal.'

'Ah, just nerves,' I stammered. 'Bit of a shocker, this Jan business.'

Julian laughed, leaning over to stretch his hamstrings. 'Jan Borsos? Hightailing it off to Belarus without warning?

464

Come on!' he said, from somewhere down by his knees. 'Glad he's found true love again.'

I shifted nervously from one foot to the other. 'Yeah. Good to find true love,' I said.

Then I walked away. It was clear that I should not be talking to Julian. I was being a moron and he had probably met someone else. And *EVEN IF HE HASN'T*, my head pointed out hysterically, *HE TOLD YOU IT WAS OVER AND HE IS TRYING TO MOVE ON WITH HIS LIFE AND SO SHOULD YOU AND – ARGGGGH!*

I tried to focus on the emergency rehearsal ahead. We had our tech at six this evening, a mere three hours away, and by then Julian and I needed to know *exactly* where on the stage we were meant to be.

As each minute passed my conviction grew that Julian was probably the best man on earth. Quite apart from being appallingly handsome and kind and funny, he just got *La Bohème*. It had taken Jan and me weeks to get it right, yet Julian had it seemingly before he'd even begun.

'Shit, he's good,' Helen whispered, as we sipped from water bottles in the wings. Julian was onstage, laughing with Hussein as if they were best friends. The banter between them as Marcello and Rodolfo was like watching *Friends* for the first time in the 1990s. You laughed and laughed and laughed and felt happy.

I stared morosely at a patch of Julian's hair that had broken free of product and was looking soft and yummy.

'You have to jump on him,' Helen told me. 'He's like

God. If you won't, Sally, I will. I'm sure Phil would allow me a one-off.'

'I'd like you to stop talking,' I said weakly. 'Do you think you could manage that?'

Helen cackled. 'No bloody chance! Roll on the snogging practice!'

Scene Four

Three days later I was pacing a corridor deep below the stage, warming up my voice for my first – and, no doubt, last – performance at the Metropolitan Opera House.

There were few indications that tonight was going to be the stunning success that the music press – tipped off that Julian Jefferson was back at the Met – predicted it would be.

Everyone's singing, even mine, was faultless, but the acting was diabolical. Mimi and Rodolfo had about as much chemistry as a limp condom and the fault was all mine. Zachary, our exasperated and now desperate director, had given me hours of notes that afternoon but in the end had just clasped my arm and begged me not to be so shit.

Astonishingly, it wasn't the pressure of performing in such an iconic building. Nor was it the fact that my parents had FLOWN TO NEW YORK TO WATCH ME.

It was a broken heart. It was a girl who felt like her chest had been cloven open, who could hardly bear to be near Julian and his rich, golden voice and lovely Julian smell and silly hair and infectious laugh and notes written on his hand and delightful silliness and quiet intelligence and wonderful humour and . . .

And everything. I couldn't stand it.

It had not helped that Julian was being lavishly amorous onstage and militantly neutral off. As Rodolfo he stared into my eyes with deep, French bohemian love . . . and when the scene was over he wandered off to play shithead in the wings with one of the assistant stage managers, barely giving me a second glance.

Last night had been the final straw. We'd all gone to the Film Center café across from the Met where for some reason I had ordered chilli octopus, even though I didn't like chilli or octopus, and Julian had been on fire. He and Hussein had called Hector to wish him better and had ended up singing 'Eye Of The Tiger' into his voicemail. That was our bloody song. He didn't even look at me.

Later on, he'd come and sat next to me. 'It's really nice to see you,' he said, in a friendly manner. I tried to unknot myself and go with the flow.

'You too. I've missed you.' I cringed. *What?*

'Ah, I've missed you too,' he said cheerfully. 'But it was the right thing to do, wasn't it?'

'Yes, of course,' I lied. *No breaking hearts here! Everything's JUST FINE!*

'Good,' he said. He ruffled my hair, as if I were his teenage daughter. 'And I hear your parents have come!'

'Yeah.' I calmed down a little. 'Mum's not coping very well with the cheerfulness over here. And Dad's just like this wide-eyed alien.'

'How's Barry?' he asked pleasantly. 'Still having trouble with those dance belts?'

'Barry's met someone! Teddy. Barry and Teddy. You couldn't make it up. They're like two puppies, except they mate all the time.'

Julian was delighted. 'Excellent! I loved Barry. And he did need a good mating. And college, how's it all going?'

Why did he find this so easy? 'Good, I think,' I said tentatively. 'We're doing *Rusalka* this summer, although I've not got a big role. Oh, my God, and I've been offered Tatyana in *Eugene Onegin* for the British Youth Opera this summer! Me in the main bloody part! Can you believe it?!'

'Yes,' Julian said. 'Of course. You're the best lyric soprano of your age that I've ever heard.'

'Stop it.' I could feel the blush spreading up from underneath my dress.

'Oh, for God's sake.' Julian smiled. 'When are you going to learn to say thank you?'

'When I start to believe compliments like that,' I mumbled.

'Believe it, you fool,' he said.

I went even redder. 'Hmm.'

'You're the best,' he said. 'The very best. And that's why you got this part. Shit, I've got to be somewhere. See you!'

And he was gone, leaving some banknotes on the table, before I had time even to say goodbye. Helen, never having stopped watching us all night, came over immediately to console me.

I was inconsolable.

'You just need a good sleep,' she tried.

'What I need, Helen, is to believe that Julian loves me. Even the tiniest bit. Because with all of our history I'm

469

not sure I can play Mimi alongside his Rodolfo otherwise.'

Helen squeezed my arm. 'I'm *sure* he still does a little bit.'

'No, you're not.'

'Well . . . It's not looking amazingly promising, but . . . maybe he's playing a game.'

'Julian? He wears his heart on his sleeve! He kissed me forty-five minutes after meeting me! It's OVER! Oh, God, I want to cut my head off.'

Helen searched for inspiration. 'Ballbags,' she muttered eventually, defeated. 'I wish I could get you drunk.'

Now, in the below-stage corridor, I tried to sing. 'Babababababa,' I croaked. My voice sounded like a wilted salad.

I checked my watch. Eighty minutes until curtain up. It was all hopeless.

'You have lovely deep eye sockets,' murmured the makeup artist, Kendra.

'Er, thanks.'

I concentrated on breathing deeply.

'So, are your family here?' she asked. 'Look down, please.'

'Yes,' I said. 'Which is more surprising than it sounds.'

Kendra straightened up to check her work. 'Uh-huh? What about your boyfriend? Friends?'

'No boyfriend,' I said weakly. 'And it'd be a bit much to ask my friends to come over here to watch me, I think!'

'I guess! But maybe your *best* friend . . .'

'My best friend died nearly two years ago.'

Kendra stopped applying eye makeup and stood back, anguished. 'Oh, I am so sorry to hear that,' she whispered.

'And my other best friend is here, but it's a bit cack because I'm in love with him and he's not in love with me.'

'I'm sorry, what was that word? "Cack", did you say?'

Kendra sounded like she'd just been plucked from a Texan ranch and parachuted into the Met.

'Cack, yes. Meaning, um, a bummer.'

'Sweetie, that there is the biggest bummer I ever heard! Well, save for your friend dying,' she added, blushing. 'Oh, I sure am sorry, Sally.'

'Thanks. They're both bummers. And I feel so guilty saying this but right at this moment the fact that I'm in love with Julian and he's not in love with me is probably the worst of the two. Oh, God, Kendra, am I going to Hell?'

Kendra, who looked like the kind of lady to whom you didn't say either 'God' or 'Hell' (especially in the same sentence), gasped.

'Sorry,' I muttered uselessly. 'Bad language.'

'You're never in love with Julian Jefferson?' she cried.

I cringed. 'Oh, erm, no, another Julian . . .'

Kendra, who was obviously sassier than I'd realized, arched one of her very precise eyebrows. 'Honey, *everyone* loves Julian Jefferson!'

'Really?'

'Bless my *soul*, yes! I swear I'd leave my Joe tomorrow if Julian came a-knocking!'

I grinned at Kendra. She was like an oasis of rural charm in this mad city.

Then I stopped grinning because she'd reminded me that I was no better off than any other woman in this building.

The world felt hopeless again.

A few minutes after Kendra had finished with me ('I'll be back!' she tinkled), my phone beeped with an incoming message. From . . . *Dad*! This was a turn-up.

Toi toi our Sal! was all he had written. Dad, who had never sent a text message in his life, had somehow found out how to say 'good luck' to an opera singer and had managed to send it to me. *Toi toi our Sal.* I imagined him saying it in his Stourbridge accent. *Toi toi.* Suddenly tearful, I stared at my phone, at the message and all it symbolized.

In spite of how painful and hopeless it felt to go onstage and be Mimi to Julian's Rodolfo, there was absolutely no denying it: *my life had changed beyond all recognition.* Here was I, a trained opera singer, about to perform in front of more than a thousand people. In New York! With my family watching!

I thought about all that had happened since the day that Bea had marched into the laundry room at the opera house, telling me that I was going on tour with the Royal Ballet and that she was buying me proper luggage because mine was made of nylon. All that I'd made it through: so much love and loss; growth and pain. I was a truly strong woman, it had turned out. A talented, strong, brave woman. Who knew?

You're amazing, you are, I acknowledged silently, to the girl in the mirror. *You are ruddy amazing, Sally Howlett!*

And that was it. Without pausing to explain or

472

apologize to Kendra, I was off and running. Down the hallway, past a pacing, nervous Hussein and a tearful Hector, past Helen, who, of course, being Helen was somehow outside her dressing room just at the moment that I should sprint past, directly towards a room marked 'Julian Jefferson'.

'Get in, my son!' she yelled, like a football fan. 'GET IN!'

Scene Five

Julian's room was empty. His wig was on its block, waiting to be pinned on to his lovely fluffy hair, and his costume hanging calmly on a rail by the door. There was makeup everywhere, a TV playing a documentary about polar bears and a large bottle of water. And no sign of Julian.

I smiled briefly at the sight of a very English packet of Jaffa Cakes on Julian's desk and decided to nick one while I waited for him. I wasn't leaving this room until I'd told him.

'Oi! Who's nicking my Jaffa Cakes?' came a voice from within the dressing-room wardrobe. I froze.

'I know you're there,' he shouted. 'Identify yourself!'

'Erm . . .' I mumbled, opening the door. 'Erm, it was me.'

Julian was sitting inside the wardrobe in his pants. Even for a major performance at the Met he was wearing the same pair of faded old boxers he'd had on the first time we'd taken our clothes off. I started to laugh but then stopped: there was serious business at hand here.

'What are you doing in there?' I asked. I sounded very severe, which hadn't really been my intention.

'I stole the idea off you,' he said easily. 'I don't get stage fright like yours but I find it useful to collect myself.'

'You're not nervous?'

'Not really.'

'You feel sane? Sound of mind? Calm?'

'Um, well, yes.'

Well, that bloody well proves it, I thought angrily. *There's me all mad and crumpled and anguished, and here's Julian all calm and smooth and chilled. HE IS SO OVER ME IT HURTS.*

I shook my head, as if to dislodge the thoughts. It didn't matter that Julian didn't feel the same. I'd come here solely to tell him how I felt because that was just the way I rolled, these days. I was damned if I was going to shrivel and die onstage because I was too chicken to tell this man I loved him.

I took a deep breath. 'I came here to inform you that I still love you. I know you don't feel the same . . .' I paused, just in case he jumped in to argue to the contrary. He didn't, he just looked guilty.

'I know you don't feel the same,' I continued, my heart bleeding all over the floor. *Focus.* 'But I couldn't go onstage and not tell you. Not on a night like this. It means too much. And, besides, it's my policy to say what I think, these days.'

Julian nodded politely.

'I didn't realize it was my policy until just now, but it is.'

He stared at his feet, a pulse beating in his temple. He clearly wanted me out of there as soon as possible. 'I hope you have a good show tonight,' I continued formally. 'And I bid you a pleasant evening. Good night. Toi toi.'

I turned on my heel and made to leave the room. But as I did, he spoke. 'I love you too,' he said quietly.

I stopped.

'I love you too,' he repeated.

'No, you don't.'

'I don't?'

I turned round and faced him. 'No. If you loved me you wouldn't have gone back to New York at Christmas. You wouldn't have told me not to contact you. And you would have replied to my email. I'm afraid, Julian, that you don't love me.'

I marvelled at the confidence of my voice. It bore no relation to the storm inside me. I leaned against the wall of his dressing room, suddenly wobbly.

'But I do,' he said stubbornly. 'I'm telling you right now. I do.'

'No, you don't!'

'Yes, I do!'

I sat down next to him by the wardrobe. The world was moving with exaggerated slowness. Did he love me? Of course not. *Why not?* I asked myself angrily. *You are worth being loved! Stop being a twat!*

I turned to look at him, hardly daring imagine what might happen. Julian gazed at me, his eyes warm and unguarded. Deep, dark pools of honour, kindness and humour. I loved his eyes. I loved all of him.

'Sally,' he said eventually, in that dear, crazy accent. 'I do love you. And I'm sorry I went back to America. It was a mistake.'

I wanted to say a million things but found myself

saying none of them. I just stared at his face; so familiar, so precious.

Julian ran his fingers through his hair, which, in preparation for his wig, had no product in it at all. It was as fluffy as a long-haired cat's. He smiled gently. 'Sally, you seem to think I'm this really sorted, mature sort of a person, who's like really poised and never gets things wrong. But I'm a penis, Sal. It's not just the glasses and the hair and the holes in my clothes, it's everything. I make mistakes. Violet, for starters! I mean, she was hot but – come *on*!'

'Oh.'

'I've made mistakes all the way through my life,' he said. 'I made the mistake of letting you go back to England after Fiona died, sick with grief, and I didn't tell you the truth about that night because – I dunno, I thought it would hurt you even more.'

I traced my hands along my shin bones. I felt strangely detached, as if I were watching this conversation unfold between two strangers.

'I made the mistake of arriving at your house with that Post-it note rather than calling or emailing or doing fucking anything, really, other than arriving at your door with a Post-it. I made the mistake of letting you get on with your relationship with Jan rather than fighting for you, like I wanted to.' He laughed hollowly. 'I thought I'd lose.'

I exhaled. Even the most amazing men on earth struggled to believe in themselves.

'And finally I made the mistake of running back to America, being all *Oh, this is for the best, I must let you go, I must set you free, rah rah rah* . . . Bollocks! Total bollocks! You were growing and changing with or without me! You didn't need me to disappear out of your life for you to heal. You *had* healed! Because you're amazing!'

I wondered why I wasn't crying. I had dreamed every day of a conversation like this, yet I felt strangely calm.

'I got it wrong yet again. Because I'm as rubbish and imperfect and malfunctioning as the next person. But thank fuck you've become this amazing strong woman who can just march in, help herself to a Jaffa Cake and tell me she loves me. You've changed so much, without actually changing at all, Sally, and I love you even more than I did five minutes ago. I don't care about anything else, and I'm sorry I was such a moron. I'm sorry we were *both* such morons. I just want to be with you.'

He took a deep breath and stopped talking. His hands were trembling. His hair was trembling because his hands were trembling.

'Thirty minutes to beginners',' murmured the tannoy. 'Ladies and gentlemen of the orchestra and the cast, that's thirty minutes to your beginners' call. Thank you.'

After a strange, empty pause, during which my brain caught up with what was going on here, a smile began somewhere in my middle. It spread outwards, calm and magnificent, until every part of me was in glorious sunlight. Of course I was calm. Of course! There *was* no drama now. We'd got through all of that, the pyrotechnics, the furies, the despair. All that was left was the two of us. And all of that love.

'Hello,' I said, touching the side of his face. 'Hello, you silly thing.'

Julian turned and kissed my fingers, then slid his arms

round me. He buried his face in my hair and I didn't care what Kendra from Makeup or Julie from Hair might have to say. I let my whole body go, wading out into a warm, safe place. 'I love you,' I said happily. 'You are my best person in the whole world.'

Julian melded even closer to me, even his legs pressed against mine. 'Snap,' he said. 'You're my best person. Ever.'

The tannoy was saying something about us but I ignored it.

He leaned forward and rubbed his nose against mine. I was so happy I could hardly breathe. 'I'm going to kiss you.' He grinned.

'Let's wait,' I said. 'Let's wait till we're onstage! How magical would that be?'

Julian pulled back, thinking about it. Then: 'No way!' he said. 'No fucking way! I'm not waiting a moment longer. Kiss me right now, you moron.'

He kissed me and everything in the world was good. We kissed and kissed, cuddled and kissed, and only stopped kissing when Terrance the security guard physically pulled us apart and told us he'd been mandated by Kendra to apprehend me and return me immediately to my dressing room.

'Let's go sing some stuff,' Julian said, kissing me one last time. 'For Fiona. And for us.'

I grinned. 'Mr Jefferson. I'll see you onstage.'

Julian bowed. 'Miss Howlett.'

Scene Six

When I was a teenager watching *Dirty Dancing* and *Bridget Jones* on repeat, I believed that the actors were truly in love with each other and that they would be having it off constantly when the cameras stopped rolling.

It had come as a terrible shock to learn that they were not frotting and shagging and singing love ballads to each other in their dressing rooms. How could they possibly be so convincing? Surely you *had* to love your co-star for it to be truly magical.

My first major performance as an opera singer vindicated all that I had believed as a teenager. Rodolfo and Mimi gave '... *an ebullient display of quite magical chemistry that sets a new standard for* La Bohème.' (*New York Post*) They were '*touchingly in love. Jefferson and Howlett were spellbinding together.*' (*Metro New York*)

The *Brooklyn Beaver* gave the performance five stars and declared that while they as a magazine might have lost an invaluable editor the city had regained a world-class singer and discovered a '*truly exciting young talent in the magnificent Sally Howlett. It is hard to imagine a Rodolfo and Mimi more happily, devastatingly in love.*'

Everything I'd believed about actors had happened. After our first duet together we left the stage and kissed until my dresser forcibly wrenched me off Julian to get me changed. And by the time I was meant to have died tragically in my bed in Act Four, I was so happy that my corpse found itself in real danger of snogging Rodolfo when he flung himself on Mimi's lifeless form.

The applause was thunderous. I held tightly on to Julian's hand and laughed and cried. I kissed him on the mouth, not caring what anyone thought.

'We were the best!' Julian shouted. His face was pink with excitement. He hugged the life out of me and the audience loved it. 'I love you,' he told me, again.

'YESSSSSSSSSS!' Helen screamed. 'MEGA!'

Scene Seven

Three days later

'We really shouldn't be doing this,' Mum said nervously. She checked over her shoulder for the millionth time, and dug further into the ground with her little trowel. She looked like a demented mole.

'Mum, we're in Williamsburg.' I laughed. 'Nobody here cares. They're all too busy trimming their beards and making artisan beer.'

Mum smiled. 'I've never understood trendy people, me,' she said, digging away.

'Me neither, Mrs Howlett,' said Julian.

'You scrub up nice enough,' Dad said, smiling bemusedly at Julian's (admittedly odd) T-shirt. I watched my man, tendrils of love and pride sprouting out of me, as he passed the little tree to Mum, who, for all her fear of being caught digging a totally illegal hole in the East River State Park, had now dug deep enough to bury a treasure chest.

Clouds scudded briskly overhead as she eased the tree out of its pot. 'Let's all put it in,' she said, quieter now. Julian nodded, moving away to a respectable distance as

Mum, Dad and I knelt down in the bright green grass. 'She'd love this,' I said. 'Us planting an illegal tree. The Howletts, of all people! And in Brooklyn too!'

Mum smiled bravely. She was smiling a lot more, these days. 'Naughty little bugger, our Fiona.' She grinned. I knew now that this was the closest Mum could get to saying, 'I loved that girl.' I put a hand on her back and she didn't even look uncomfortable.

We lowered the lively little tree into its hole, patting the earth down around it. Nobody spoke.

Dad sat back on his heels, admiring our handiwork. 'Should we say a few words?' he asked.

Mum immediately looked anxious. 'Oh, I'm not sure about that,' she began.

I sat back. 'Let's all just have a quiet moment. To say goodbye.'

Fiona's tree swayed shyly in the breeze as we sat around it, each of us suspended in a bittersweet memory. I could feel it, the intense, wrenching sadness, yet I knew it wasn't as strong as it might have been. Borne alone, the pain had been too much for us all; borne together, it was softer.

To my amazement, Mum broke the silence. 'Actually, I think I would like to say something,' she announced. Her face was taut and nervous but full of determination. She took Dad's hand and he took mine. For a few moments we sat, hand in hand, as a family. For perhaps the first time ever.

There was a band playing somewhere nearby, and the chug of the Williamsburg ferry coming into the port. And yet a wonderful peacefulness had sprung up between us.

'Fiona,' Mum began. Her voice wobbled, and I sensed

Dad squeezing her hand. 'Fiona, I want to say sorry. I don't think I ever told you I loved you. But I did, you mad little thing. I loved you, all right?'

'Me too,' Dad muttered. 'Me too, our Fi. Rest in peace, pet.'

He sniffed, wiping his eyes. Mum breathed out, as if letting go, and a sad smile crossed her face.

'Me three, Freckle,' I whispered. 'I hope you're up to no good wherever you are.'

I stared at the tree until it blurred through the stinging procession of tears coursing down my cheeks. For a few sad, lovely moments, the Howlett family held hands and cried. Nobody got embarrassed.

Cloud shadows sped over the grass and the river lapped lazily behind us. Fiona's tree swayed more confidently in the gathering breeze, and a ladybird began to climb it.

Later on, when my parents had gone off to have lunch in 'one of those poky little places' that Mum had taken a shine to, Julian and I sat on a log by the water. He had promised to take my dad to Coney Island later (Dad had, rather worryingly, bought a New York guidebook and discovered an adventurous spirit that had lain dormant for most of his sixty-three years), but for now he was mine. As every second passed I loved Julian Bell more.

I smiled up at him, pulling him closer to me. 'Yo.'

'Yo yourself. You OK?'

I nodded, staring out across the river. 'I don't think I'll ever be completely OK, but I'm all right.' Julian nodded.

'Really, I'm just grateful,' I said. 'Without the singing and the ... well, everything, I'd be stuck in the grief.

Nothing would have changed. I'd be mad and frightened and hopeless.'

Julian chuckled. A low, cheeky rumble through his T-shirt. 'You were never hopeless. Deffo a bit mad, though.'

He slid his arm around me and we sat, side by side, looking beyond the river to the giant theatrical spectacle of the New York skyline.

'You'll have to start rehearsing for the British Youth Opera soon,' he said. 'That's so exciting!'

'I know! I can't believe it! And that agent calling me too! What the hell is going on?'

He squeezed me. 'The world has just caught up with me, that's all. Discovering how amazing you are.'

I craned round to look up at him. Julian was smiling down at me, those lovely laughter lines around his eyes creasing proudly. 'Although I'm still the only one who knows that you're a total dick.'

'True. But . . . I don't get it,' I said quietly. 'I'm just a girl from a depressed council estate. The whole thing just seems . . . insane.'

Julian pulled me in and kissed me, a long, happy kiss that made me forget everything else. Eventually we stopped and looked at each other, our eyes so close they almost touched. 'Doesn't matter how small you started,' he told me. 'You still get to have big dreams. And a rich, happy life.'

A seagull landed near to us, just like the one that had been there on the day of Fiona's birthday party. He looked at us irritably, then took straight off again, dropping a big disdainful turd.

'I mean, look at him.' Julian grinned. 'He's an eighth of my size but he still sees no reason why he shouldn't be king of the world.'

I smiled. 'I don't want to start crapping on everyone just yet. But I see what you mean!'

'I couldn't give a crap where you were born, Sally Howlett. I just know that I want to be on your team.'

I grinned madly. 'And I want to be on yours,' I said.

Julian looked thoughtful for a minute, then took my right hand. He fiddled with the big ugly rock that I still wore on my finger. Tiny warm needles of yellow light reflected from its surface on our faces and I remembered sitting on the swings in the park, holding a buttercup under Fi's chin to see if she liked butter. 'I bought this for you,' he said, sliding the ring around.

'Eh? No, you didn't, I got it . . .' I dug around in my memory. 'I got it at the party. *The* Party. Which you kind of ruined,' I added, in the direction of Fiona's tree.

'I know.' Julian was grinning mischievously. 'We all had to bring presents, remember? You forgot. You wrote something ridiculous on a Post-it note.'

'Hmm. Yes.'

Julian removed the ring from my finger.

'We all had to buy presents,' he continued. 'And I bought this one. For you.'

I was confused. 'But how did you know? That I'd choose it?'

'Because I told everyone else that I'd kill them if they took it.'

Something began to dawn on me.

Julian watched me for a moment, letting me stew in

uncertainty, then kissed me again. Gently, barely touching my lips. 'I was going to ask you to marry me,' he said, quite casually. 'But Fi fucked that plan up good and proper.' We smiled shyly, knowing she would have allowed the joke.

'So unfortunately all you got was a hideous comedy ring. I was going to take you to a jeweller's,' he added. 'If you'd said yes.'

He tried to shove the ring on his own finger and got it as far as his first knuckle.

'I love you for keeping it on all this time.' Julian smiled. He turned the ring over in his palm, flecking our faces with little spots of light. 'Maybe a little part of you still wanted us to work.'

I stared at him, marvelling at this unforeseen twist in our story. 'Wow!'

Julian stared out at Manhattan. 'You've made me happier than anyone has ever made me,' he said. 'Our team is the most important thing in my life.'

'Mine too!' I was radiantly happy. Even with the seagull poo by my foot. I was so happy it almost hurt.

'So . . . Yes. So I think I'll just ask you to marry me,' he decided. 'I'm not getting down on one knee. It'd be a bit knobbish. And there's too much seagull shit around here.'

I nodded vehemently. 'Knobbish. Seagull shit.'

'Oh, hang on.' He glanced at the sapling swaying in the breeze. 'No, Fiona says I do have to get down on one knee.' Sighing comically, he poked around in the sand to find a safe spot. Once installed, he grinned up at me, brandishing the ring. 'You're everything that's good and funny and brilliant in my life, Sally Howlett. Can we make that official?'

I turned to the tree. 'Do you approve?' I asked it. I heard Fiona's response, clear as day, and started laughing. I laughed and laughed, then found I was crying, warm fat tears of absolute joy. I plopped tears all over Julian's smiling face.

'She said, "Oh, for fuck's *sake*, Sally!"'

He sniggered. 'That sounds about right.'

I looked him, square in the eye, and smiled and cried and laughed and made strange happy noises a bit like a cow mooing. 'Yes, Julian Bell! I would like to join the team.'

Julian put the ring on my finger and pulled me down into the sand with him. We kissed and hugged until a dog came and did a wee on Julian's trainer, and then we lay on our backs and watched the clouds slide by, each one lined sharply with brilliant sun.

Acknowledgements

Without the great army of people who helped me research and write this book, I would have written maybe ten pages and then run off and hidden on a remote island until Penguin forgot I owed them a book. So many brilliant people opened up their wonderful musical and theatrical worlds, luckily, and in so doing they saved my skin. Heartfelt thanks to all! But especially . . .

Elizabeth Gottschalk and Adam Music for getting me started with opera.

Garsington Young Artists Programme for allowing me to come and watch *Magic Flute* rehearsals.

The wonderful British Youth Opera for allowing me to be present all through rehearsals of their fantastic production of *The Bartered Bride.* Everyone made me feel welcome, nobody threw me out of their dressing room and when I saw the finished production I finally understood why opera is such a magical, wonderful thing.

Special thanks to the very talented and inspiring soprano Katy Crompton.

To Frazer Scott for becoming my singing teacher (!).

Thank you to my great grandparents for their own contribution to the opera world, and for sparking my curiosity.

To Rachael Wright and Lindsey Kelk for New York education and also Julian Ingle for sheltering me and The Man during Hurricane Sandy. That was crazy.

Thanks to Bridget Foster at the Royal Opera House for letting me poke around the wonderful wig and makeup department.

To Lynette Mauro for inviting me into the National Theatre's magical wardrobe department.

Thanks to my amazing agent, Lizzy Kremer ('Agent of the Year, every year'), who is so brilliant I still can't quite believe she is mine. Or I am hers. Or something like that.

To Harriet Moore for being fantastically helpful with almost everything, Laura West for getting me Stateside, and Tine Nielssen and Stella Giatrakou – best of luck to you both.

The team at Penguin have been especially brilliant this year, which has been (I hope) a rather more unusual year in my life as a writer. Thanks to Celine Kelly for being a wonderful, clever and very diplomatic editor. To Mari Evans for her brilliant input and then Maxine Hitchcock for taking this novel by storm! Liz Smith, Francesca Russell and Joe Yule for putting me out there into the world, and Lee Motley for my beautiful book jackets. Anna Derkacz, Sophie Overment, Isabel Coburn, Roseanne Bantick and Samantha Fanaken for selling me so successfully. Nick Lowndes for pulling together my books into the beautiful things they become and Hazel Orme for rigorous copy-editing! Thank you to Lyn, Brian and Caroline Walsh for being my A team. I love you all very much. To George for looking after me and being the best thing in the world. My friends – all of you, thank you for getting me back to health. X

And to my wonderful, loyal, batty, brilliant readers who've really had my back this year. You guys and all the wonderful bloggers and reviewers are the reason I have a job and I'm so grateful to you all.

And I guess my final thank you goes to all of the composers, singers and musicians of times present and anterior who've blown my mind with their works. Sometimes, when I was meant to be writing, I'd just listen to arias and duets and bawl my eyes out.